Once Upon An Autumn Eve

By Dennis L. McKiernan

Caverns of Socrates

BOOKS IN THE FAERY SERIES

Once Upon a Winter's Night

Once Upon a Summer Day

Once Upon an Autumn Eve

BOOKS IN THE MITHGAR SERIES

The Dragonstone

Voyage of the Fox Rider

Hél's Crucible:
Book 1: *Into the Forge*
Book 2: *Into the Fire*

Dragondoom

The Iron Tower (omnibus edition)

The Silver Call (omnibus editon)

Tales of Mithgar (a story collection)

The Vulgmaster (the graphic novel)

The Eye of the Hunter

Silver Wolf, Black Falcon

Red Slippers: More Tales of Mithgar (a story collection)

DENNIS L. McKIERNAN

Once Upon An Autumn Eve

RoC

A ROC BOOK

ROC
Published by New American Library, a division of
Penguin Group (USA) Inc., 375 Hudson Street,
New York, New York 10014, USA
Penguin Group (Canada), 90 Eglinton Avenue East, Suite 700, Toronto,
Ontario M4P 2Y3, Canada (a division of Pearson Penguin Canada Inc.)
Penguin Books Ltd., 80 Strand, London WC2R 0RL, England
Penguin Ireland, 25 St. Stephen's Green, Dublin 2,
Ireland (a division of Penguin Books Ltd.)
Penguin Group (Australia), 250 Camberwell Road, Camberwell, Victoria 3124,
Australia (a division of Pearson Australia Group Pty. Ltd.)
Penguin Books India Pvt. Ltd., 11 Community Centre, Panchsheel Park,
New Delhi - 110 017, India
Penguin Group (NZ), cnr Airborne and Rosedale Roads, Albany,
Auckland 1310, New Zealand (a division of Pearson New Zealand Ltd.)
Penguin Books (South Africa) (Pty.) Ltd., 24 Sturdee Avenue,
Rosebank, Johannesburg 2196, South Africa

Penguin Books Ltd., Registered Offices:
80 Strand, London WC2R 0RL, England

First published by Roc, an imprint of New American Library,
a division of Penguin Group (USA) Inc.

First Printing, April 2006
10 9 8 7 6 5 4 3 2 1

RoC REGISTERED TRADEMARK—MARCA REGISTRADA

LIBRARY OF CONGRESS CATALOGING-IN-PUBLICATION DATA:

McKiernan, Dennis L., 1932–
  Once upon an autumn eve / Dennis L. McKiernan.
    p. cm.
  ISBN 0-451-46069-3
  I. Title.
  PS3563.C376O53 2006
  813'.54—dc22   2005029164

Set in Trump Mediaeval
Designed by Leonard Telesca

Printed in the United States of America

PUBLISHER'S NOTE
This is a work of fiction. Names, characters, places, and incidents either are the product of the
author's imagination or are used fictitiously, and any resemblance to actual persons, living or dead,
business establishments, events, or locales is entirely coincidental.
  The publisher does not have any control over and does not assume any responsibility for author
or third-party Web sites or their content.

Once again to all lovers,
As well as to lovers of fairy tales . . .
And to the Roses

Acknowledgments

My dear Martha Lee, my heart, once more I am most grateful for your enduring support, careful reading, patience, and love. I know I have said this many times before, but it most surely bears repeating, *ma chérie*.

And again I thank the members of the Tanque Wordies Writers' Group—Diane, Katherine, John—for your encouragement throughout the writing of this Faery tale.

And thank you, Christine J. McDowell, for your help with the French language. (I would add, though, that any errors in usage are entirely mine. Of course, the errors in English are mine as well.)

Contents

Foreword

If you have read the forewords of the first two tales of my Faery series—*Once Upon a Winter's Night* and *Once Upon a Summer Day*—you will know my thesis is that once upon a time many (if not most) fairy tales were epics of love and seduction and copious sex and bloody fights and knights and witches and dragons and ogres and giants and other fantastic beings all scattered throughout the scope of the tale as the hero or heroine struggled on.

Bardic sagas were these, but as the minstrels and troubadours and sonneteers and tale-spinners and bards and other such dwindled, and common folks took up the task of entertaining one another with these well-loved sagas, I believe bits were omitted—fell by the wayside—and the stories grew shorter, or fragmented into several stories, or changed to fit the current culture or religion or whatever other agendas the tale-tellers might have had.

And so, if I'm right, the grand and sweeping tales bards used to keep their royal audiences enthralled for hours on end became less and less as the tales were spread from mouth to mouth.

As the years went on, the stories continued to dwindle, until they became what the collectors of those tales—Andrew Lang, the Grimm brothers, and others—finally recorded and produced for others to read . . . or so it is I contend—

—pale reflections of what they once were—

—mere fragments—

—holding a small portion of the essence—

—and so on.

But guess what: they still hold audiences rapt.

They still charm.

They still are much admired by many, and certainly I am among those.

Even so, I would really like to hear some of these stories such as I have imagined them once to have been: long, gripping, romantic, perilous epics of love and hatred and loss and redemption and revenge and forgiveness and life and death and other such grand themes.

But told as a fairy tale.

Especially a favorite fairy tale.

Expanded to include all the above.

With *Once Upon an Autumn Eve* again I take a favorite of mine (in fact several favorites of mine woven together) to tell the tale as it once might have been told—as an epic, a saga, a story of length.

As with my other stories, since it is a romance in addition to being an adventure, once more you will find French words sprinkled throughout, for French is well suited to tales of love.

By the bye, the best-known version of the central story is but a few pages long. Once again, I thought that much too brief, and, as is apparent, I did lengthen it a bit. But then again,

I claim that I am telling the "real" story, and who is to say I am not?

I hope it holds you enthralled.

Dennis L. McKiernan
Tucson, Arizona, 2004

Nothin be certain, m'lady

Autumnwood

Separated from the mortal world by looming walls of twilight is a wondrous place called Faery. It is now quite difficult to find, though once upon a time it wasn't. Faery is a place of marvel and adventure and magic and peril, populated by mythical and mystical creatures and uncommon beings . . . along with ordinary folks—if anyone who lives in Faery can be said to be ordinary. Yet the creatures and beings of Faery aren't the only things of enchantment, for there are items of magic within—grimoires, amulets, swords, rings, cloaks, helms, and the like, most of them quite rare. Even the lands of Faery are numinous, for Faery itself is composed of many mystical realms, rather like an enormous and strange jigsaw puzzle, the individual domains all separated from one another by great tenebrous walls of twilight. And like a mystifying riddle, some of the realms touch upon many others, while some touch upon but few. Caution must be taken when stepping through these dusky walls in going from one place to another, else one might end up somewhere altogether different from where one intended. Too, directions in Faery do not seem to be constant; there may be no true east, south, west, and north, though occasionally those compass points are ascribed by some therein, for when one goes from realm to realm, bearings seem to shift. Instead it may be more accurate to say that east, south, west, and north respectively align with sunup or dawnwise, sunwise, sundown or duskwise, and starwise. Whether or not this jigsaw puzzle makes an overall coherent picture is questionable, for each of the pieces, each of the domains, seems unique; after all, 'tis Faery, an endless place, with uncounted realms all separated from one another by looming walls of shadowlight, and with Faery itself separated from the common world by twilight as well.

Among the many remarkable domains within this mystical place are the Forests of the Seasons. In one of these four woodlands eternal autumn lies upon the land; here it is that crops afield remain ever for the reaping, and vines are overburdened with their largesse, and trees bear an abundance ripe for the plucking, and the ground holds rootstock and tubers for the taking. Yet no matter how often a harvest is gathered, when one isn't looking the bounty somehow replaces itself. How such a place can be—endless autumn—is quite mysterious; nevertheless it is so.

On one side of this magical realm and separated from it by a great wall of twilight is another equally enigmatic province, a domain graced by eternal summer, and it is a region of forests and fields, of vales and clearings, of streams and rivers and other such 'scapes, where soft summer breezes flow across the weald, though occasionally towering thunderstorms fill the afternoon skies and rain sweeps o'er all.

Likewise, on a different side of the autumnal realm, beyond another great wall of half-light, there stands a land of eternal winter, where snow ever lies on the ground, and ice clads the sleeping trees and covers the still meres or, in thin sheets, encroaches upon the edges of swift-running streams, and the stars at night glimmer in crystalline skies.

And farther on and past yet another twilight border lies a place of eternal springtime, where everlasting meltwater trickles across the soil, and trees are abud and blossoms abloom, where birds call for mates and beetles crawl through decaying leaves and mushrooms push up through soft loam, and where other such signs of a world coming awake manifest themselves in the gentle, cool breezes and delicate rains.

These four provinces are the Autumnwood and Summerwood and Winterwood and Springwood, four of the many magical domains in the twilit world of Faery.

And as to these four regions, a prince or a princess rules each—Liaze, Alain, Borel, and Celeste—siblings all: the sisters Liaze and Celeste, respectively having reign o'er the Autumn- and Springwoods; their brothers Alain and Borel respectively the Summer- and Winterwoods.

They loved one another, these siblings, and seldom did trouble come their way. Oh, there was that strangeness with Borel and his dagger-filled dreams, yet he had managed to successfully deal with that perilous episode. And earlier, there was that difficulty with the disappearance of King Valeray and Queen Saissa, and the two curses leveled upon Prince Alain, but Camille had come along to resolve those trials.

After Borel's harrowing ordeal, everything seemed quite well, though the Fates would have it that there yet loomed a portent of darker days to come. But at that time joy lay upon the land, for Camille and Alain were newlyweds, and Borel and his truelove Michelle had gone off immediately after those nuptials to see Chelle's sire and dam, after which the banns would be posted and preparations for another wedding would get underway.

Yes, at that time all was well in these Forests of the Seasons, or so it seemed.

But then . . .

. . . Once upon an autumn eve . . .

Sss . . . the arrow sped true to—*thock!*—strike the silhouette, fair spitting the heart of the Goblin. Again and again Liaze winged shafts into the ebon shape, while off to one side Handmaiden Zoé marveled at the skill of her tall and lithe auburn-haired mistress. And even though the sun was nigh gone, still in the long shadows lying across the sward the princess did not miss.

Finally all the arrows were spent, and as Liaze stepped to the standing haycock and retrieved her shafts, Zoé glanced at the disappearing limb of the setting sun and then at Autumnwood Manor and said, "My lady, the dinner mark approaches. Would you have me draw a bath and lay out a gown?"

Liaze sighed and stood a moment, then peered up at the waxing half-moon and said, "I think this eve I will bathe in the pool."

"The pool?"

"*Oui.* I feel the need for solitude."

"Oh, my lady, that place is"—her brown eyes filled with trepidation, Zoé looked toward the cluster of great willows among which the pool lay, hidden by the drooping branches reaching all the way down to the ground, their autumn gold leaves ablaze in the last rays of sunlight—"is, well, I don't know, dark in some manner, I would say."

"Dark?" said Liaze. "But Zoé, how can you think of it being dark among all those bright leaves?"

"I don't know," said Zoé. "Perhaps instead of 'dark' I mean it feels, umm, 'closed in,' as if . . . as if— Oh, it's just that you can't see out or in, and things can come creeping through the branches unseen. Regardless, my lady, instead of seeking solitude, I think you need cheerful company about."

"Company?" Liaze frowned, puzzlement in her amber—some would say "golden-brown"—eyes. "Why so?"

Zoé turned up a noncommittal hand. "Well, for these past three weeks, ever since the wedding—on the journey from Summerwood Manor all the way here and in the days since—you seem . . . um, how shall I say . . . morose? Oui, morose."

Liaze slipped the last of the arrows into the quiver. "Morose?"

"Saddened, somehow," said Zoé, brushing away a stray lock of her own brown hair.

Liaze shook her head. "No, Zoé. Not saddened. Reflective instead."

"Reflective?"

Liaze took a deep breath and slowly let it out. "Yes, reflective. I have been pondering the ways of love and the way I would have things be. My brothers, you see, have found their heart mates, whereas Celeste and I . . ." Her words fell to silence.

"Ah, pishposh," said Zoé. "You are so beautiful, my lady, and one day the right man will come along and—"

Liaze held up a hand to stop the flow of Zoé's words. "One day, you say? Well, Zoé, for all of my life these one days have flown by and still he hasn't appeared."

"Oh, Princess, do not be dejected. Perhaps this is the very day, or tomorrow, or the next—"

"Hush, Zoé, and leave me to my reflections. I shall bathe at the pool and treasure my solitude."

"As you wish, my lady. Shall I ready a change of clothes? One of your splendid gowns should cheer you up."

Liaze looked down at her hunting leathers and sighed and then turned to Zoé and forced a smile and said. "The pale green one. I'll come in a candlemark or so."

As Zoé walked toward Autumnwood Manor, Liaze unstrung her bow and then set out for the stand of willows, where she pushed aside the dangling branches and made her way inward, the gold of the leaves fading to bronze in the deepening twilight. As she passed through curtains of foliage and among the great boles, behind her the swaying branches of her passage swept the ground, as if to eliminate her track. Finally she came to the very center of the grove, where the trees gave way to a small open glade, and there, among great, flat white stones, lay a broad, deep pool, limpid and welling with spring-fed water, a rill flowing out from one end to dance and sing between mossy banks on its journey to a distant sea.

Liaze strode past a small stand of cattails and to one of the horizontal slabs, where she set down her bow and unslung her quiver, and then quickly doffed her boots and hunting leathers and the silken undergarments 'neath.

And in the silvery light of the half-moon above, she stepped to the edge of the pool and stood a moment, her reflection in the slow-welling water that of an athletic woman, trim and tall with auburn hair and firm, high breasts, her roseate nipples erect in the crisp autumn air, her narrow waist flaring into slim hips and down into long, sleek legs, a reddish triangle captured between.

And then she dived into the pool, her entry smooth with little splash, and she swam down and through the crystalline water and across, the moonlight from above illumining the lucid depths below, where more large, flat white stones scattered upon the bottom with white sand between brightened the whole of the basin.

To the other end she swam and up, and surfaced, blowing, the chill water bracing, invigorating. She stroked to a large rock at the verge, the pool deep at its edge, and with her arms and a kick or two, she levered herself up onto the brink of the slab, and twisted about to sit with her feet in the water.

And that's when she heard the sound of pounding hooves, and the nearby call of a silver clarion, answered by distant blares of horns less precious.

And even as she stood and turned, an ebon horse bearing a rider came pounding through the golden willow branches and up the rill, water splatting aside. And it hammered to the rim of the pool, where it skidded to a halt, the horse squatting on its haunches to stop, spray flying.

And the rider, a broken sword in hand, blood streaming down his face, fell from his horse as if slain.

And the raucous blats of following horns drew nearer.

2

Conflict

With the blare of horns drawing closer, Liaze glanced across the pool to where lay her bow, and then at the fallen rider and the dark horse at his side, the steed blowing and snorting, its eyes rolling, whites flaring in the moonlight. Making up her mind, she stepped toward the downed man, but the ears of the black flattened, and it bared its teeth.

It has been trained.

"Doucement, mon beau! Du calme!" Liaze demanded in the old tongue, trying to find a command the horse would obey. When she struck upon *"Recules!"* the black horse's ears flicked forward and then back. *"Recules-toi!"* she said, and the horse backed away, still blowing.

Swiftly, Liaze stepped to the collapsed rider where he lay on the mossy bank and knelt at his side and rolled him over. At the movement, his eyes opened, and he looked up at her, his gaze momentarily widening. *"Ange?"* he said, and then he swooned.

Liaze only had time to note that he had dark hair and his forehead bore a brutal wound, and he wore a light chain shirt—*A chevalier*—when horns blatted just outside the grove, and someone nigh at hand barked guttural commands as running feet thudded past.

Liaze again glanced at her bow lying too far away. Then she looked at the horse and back at the wounded chevalier.

She sat the man up, and in that moment a dark form—swart and some four foot tall, skinny-armed and bandy-legged—came crashing through the willow branches. And even as it yelled in triumph at the sight of easy prey—a downed man and a naked woman—it charged toward her, cudgel raised. Liaze snatched up the damaged sword, nought but a jagged half-blade, and spitted the onrushing creature through and through, the Goblin to shriek and collapse, its ruddy hat falling from its head.

Redcaps! Here in the Autumnwood! And he called out!

Once more horns blatted, and from the direction of the manor clarion cries answered.

And as nearby feet now pounded *toward* the willow grove, again she sat the man up, and, struggling, got him to his feet, and somehow she managed to lift him onto the horse's withers in spite of the black's skitting and shying.

Harsh shouts and raucous blares sounded in the willow grove, and Redcaps poured forth from the dangling branches. And among the Goblins a massive form moved. *A Troll!*

Jerking the broken sword from the dead Goblin, unclothed Liaze leapt into the saddle, and, crying out *"Yah! Yah!"* she heeled the horse in the flanks, and, blade in hand and swinging low and wide, she charged through the recoiling Goblins and past the oncoming Troll, and then galloped in among the willow branches, the limbs lashing her naked form as would whips.

Out from the grove she raced, her still-damp red hair flying, the wounded man bellydown before her across the steed. Toward Autumnwood Manor she hammered, crouching low in the saddle in case the Redcaps had bows. And toward her came running a warband from the mansion, weapons in hand, horns sounding. And from behind charged the Redcaps and the Troll.

As Liaze galloped by she called out, "Rémy, 'ware, they have a Troll among them!"

"Oui, madam," cried Rémy in return, the rangy, rawboned armsmaster grinning in relief to see his princess alive and well, no matter that she was naked, "and we have a large crossbow."

Across the sward and toward the forecourt raced Liaze, where she could see in the moonlight armed men gathered on the lawn and the walkway before the mansion door.

"Healers, healers!" cried Liaze, dropping the grume-slathered sword in the grass as she haled the horse up short among the assembly. "I have a wounded warrior."

As she sprang from the steed and began to pull the man from the withers, two of the men leapt forward to help her; "Here, Princess," said one, "we'll take care of him."

The doors flew open and a ginger-haired woman—Margaux, a healer—bearing a shielded candle rushed out. Zoé, unable to contain herself, came running out as well.

"Lay him down," Margaux barked to the men, even as Zoé wrung her hands and hovered about Liaze and asked if she were all right.

From the doorway a scandalized matron called out in the old tongue, *"Princesse, vous ne portez pas de vêtements!"*

Even as Zacharie, steward of Autumnwood Manor—a tall thin man in black—cast a cape 'round her shoulders, and she pulled it tight about, Liaze replied in kind: *"Tutrice Martine, c'est pas comme si j'avais le temps de revêtir mes vêtements quand des lutins me soufflaient sur le goulot!"*

The men lowered the chevalier to the lawn. Margaux took a moment by candlelight to examine the man, and then turned toward the door and cried "Litter!"

Several more women came rushing out, a stretcher among

them, even as the matron in the doorway called for Zoé to come back in.

"Take care," commanded Margaux, as the men placed the chevalier on the litter, and then took him up to bear into the house. As they stepped away, Margaux, leading, called out, "We'll need unguents, needle and gut, and bandages."

Horns sounded in the near distance, along with the cries of battle and death.

At the sound of combat: "A bow," said Liaze, stepping toward the circle of men. "I need a bow and full quiver. There are Goblins and a Troll out there."

"Princess," said Zacharie, wrapping an arm about her to halt her movement, "Rémy and the warband will take care of them."

Wild-eyed, Liaze started to push away, but then she looked into Zacharie's face and the fire left her gaze. She sighed and nodded and said, "The warband, yes." She glanced at the black and said, "Someone should care for the horse."

A lad—a stable boy—stepped forward to take the skittish steed, only to be met with flattened ears and bared teeth.

" 'Ware, son," called out the stable master. " 'Tis trained for war." He stepped toward the animal and frowned in thought, then commanded *"Calmes-toi!"* and the horse settled and permitted himself to be led away by the man.

"Rub him down well and feed him an extra ration of oats," called Liaze after. "He performed with merit."

Without turning about, the stable master raised a hand of acknowledgement and continued on 'round the mansion.

Zoé and the matron Martine, portly, a white streak through her black hair, came bustling out, Zoé bearing a blue dressing gown.

Liaze shook her head and clutched her wrap tighter. "This cloak will do until the men return."

Martine huffed in exasperation and shook her head and *tch-tch*ed, while Zoé sighed, and together they headed toward the mansion, taking the garment with them.

In the distance the sounds of battle faded, as if the warband pursued the encroaching Goblins and the Troll farther into the woods.

Time passed, and still there came sporadic sounds of combat.

As the distant and intermittent engagements continued, Margaux stepped back through the door and to the princess. "He looks to be quite battered, my lady, as if beaten with clubs. He was certainly struck across his forehead—knocked him clear out I would think. Right bloody it was, the skin torn, but we stitched what we could—nine altogether—and salved and bandaged it. Withal he should recover nicely."

Liaze frowned. "Margaux, he was not, as you say, 'knocked clear out,' at least not immediately, for after the blow he managed to ride his horse into the willows, and he looked straight at me when I rolled him over."

"Then he must have a very thick skull . . . or great strength of will to remain aware after that strike," said the healer.

"Did he say anything?" asked Zacharie.

Liaze shook her head, for though he had asked if she were an "ange"—in the old tongue the word meant "angel"—surely it was but the product of an addled mind.

In the distance, silver clarions—horns of the manor—sounded the recall.

"It seems the battle is over, my lady," said Zacharie. "I will send some of the guard to fetch your garments."

"My bow and quiver are there, too," said Liaze, pulling the cloak closer 'round. "Tell those who go to be alert, for there might be more foe lurking about."

A short while later, Rémy and the warband returned, along with the men who had gone to fetch Liaze's apparel, a lad among them bearing the leathers and silks, another with the boots and the bow and quiver and linens, both of them somewhat red-faced and shy at carrying Her Highness's gear, especially the intimate garments. And women rushed out to greet the men of the warband as well as those on houseguard, concern on their faces, Martine and Zoé among them.

"We skewered the Troll, my lady," called Rémy, grinning, running a hand through his red hair, "and a number of the Goblins, too. And we only took a scrape or three." Rémy nodded toward one of the men cradling his left arm, a bone obviously broken, and another man bleeding from the nose. As they were tended, Rémy said, "They ran and we pursued, but some got away. —Oh, and we found more dead out in the forest, slain by someone else's hand."

"The chevalier," said Liaze, glancing at the blood-slathered, jagged half-blade yet lying on the sward. "Surely he is the one who did so. Broke his sword in twain."

As the stable boy sprang forward and took up the damaged weapon and wiped it in the grass to clean away the grume, Rémy said, "You deem the chevalier came alone?"

Liaze shrugged. "If others were with him, where are they now?"

"Mayhap lying dead in the forest, or perhaps fled away."

"Regardless," said the princess, "as soon as he awakens and tells his tale, then we shall know."

Liaze turned to the men and called out, "Well done! Indeed, well done!" Then with a sweeping gesture she took in everyone there on the forecourt lawn. "Well done, all!

"*Huzzah!*" she cried, "and *huzzah!*"

Her shout was echoed tenfold and more, when all the gathering called out a *Huzzah!* in reply.

Liaze then turned to the pair of red-faced but smiling lads carrying her gear. "Zacharie, will you see to my bow and quiver?" And as the steward stepped forward and took the weapons from the one lad, Liaze said to Martine, "And, madam, would you please relieve these young men of their, um, embarrassing burdens, and see that my garments get to my quarters?"

Grinding her teeth at being asked to act as nought but a common maid, Martine snatched the leathers and silks and linens and boots from the two boys and stalked off toward the manor.

The other women began drifting toward the mansion, and among them there came a giggle, and someone pointed at the retreating matron and said sotto voce, "Did you hear what Martine said when Princess Liaze came agallop with the man?"

"Oui," came the reply, and the voice took on a portentous tone, somewhat like that of Martine: " 'Princess, you are not wearing clothes!' As if that were the only important thing, the princess having just saved the man from the Goblins and the Troll, and him wounded and all."

" 'Tutor Martine, it's not like I had time to don my clothing when Goblins were breathing on my neck!' That's what she said, the princess."

The two laughed, accompanied by titters from the others, and then one said, "This brave chevalier, I wonder where he is from, and how he came to be in the Autumnwood, and why was he fighting Goblins, and where did *they* come from and . . ." Their voices faded away as they moved onward, guards going at their sides.

Encircled by the warband, Liaze turned to Rémy. "Set a double ward this night, Armsmaster, and tomorrow I would have you and your men search the surround and get an accurate count of the fallen foe. See if you can tell whence they came . . . as well as what you can discover of the path of the chevalier, too."

"Yes, my lady," said Rémy, touching a finger to his forehead in salute.

"Princess," said Zacharie, glancing 'round through the moonlit night, "we best get you inside, for as you said, there might be more foe about."

Liaze nodded and then turned and padded toward the manor, an escort of armed men going ahead and aflank and aft of their barefooted lady, a lad bearing a shattered sword at her side.

3

Chevalier

Zoé stood waiting under the high portico as Liaze and her escort of men paced up the three steps to the landing.

"Where is the chevalier, Zoé?"

"The infirmary, my lady."

Through the entry they went, the brass-studded, thick doors of oak standing back against the walls of a short corridor. As members of the houseguard closed those doors behind, the princess and her escort stepped along the passage and through another oaken doorway to come to a broad landing opening into a vast front hall. Down two steps the princess went and onto a wide floor of white marble, where centered within and inset in stone lay a large depiction of a scarlet maple leaf in a broad circle, the perimeter of which showed ripened heads of grain—the leaf crafted of shades of red granite, the grain of shades of brown. Three storeys above, the alabaster ceiling held a leaded-glass skylight portraying the same leaf and grain—a reflection of the one below. To either side, a massive staircase—one left, one right—swept from landings up and 'round, curving to a high balcony encircling the floor below, and higher up still were individual balconies jutting out of the three facing walls, with recessed doors leading into chambers beyond. On the main floor itself were doors and archways ranged to left, right, and fore, both at the great-hall floor level and the balcony level just above; beyond those archways corridors receded into the interior of the manor. Sconces bearing lit candles and lanterns were ranged along on the walls around, giving the chamber a pale yellow glow, augmented by argent moonlight slanting in through high front windows and the leaded-glass skylight above.

Many members of the staff stood arrayed all 'round within the hall, and most faces held looks of anxiety.

Liaze stopped upon the red maple leaf—a symbol of her station—and gazed about. Then she said, "I know not why a Trolled band of Goblins was within the Autumnwood, yet be assured that the Troll is dead and many Goblins were slain, and the remaining few fled for their lives. Be also assured that we are well armed, and the warband and the houseguard are not only up to the task of defending this place, but also of routing the foe. So, tend to your responsibilities, and sleep well this night, for those whose duty it is will remain vigilant and watch o'er you."

A murmur of assent whispered 'round the room, and Zacharie said, "My lady, we thank you for these heartening words." Most of those in the hall nodded in agreement, though a few yet held pensive looks. And then, with a gesture, Zacharie dismissed the staff, and the members vanished into the surrounding corridors.

"Zacharie, with me," said Liaze. "Let us see what this chevalier can tell us." She glanced at her armsmaster. "You as well, Rémy."

Rightward she turned, and she and Rémy and Zacharie, with Zoé trotting after, headed toward the infirmary.

"When we heard the clarion call," said Rémy, "followed by what I knew to be the sound of Goblin horns, that's when we grabbed up our arms and came running."

"As did the houseguard," said Zacharie.

"Who sounded the call, my lady?" asked Rémy.

"The chevalier, I believe."

"It is well that he did," said Rémy. "Else, my lady, you at the pool might have been—"

"Oh, don't even think that, Rémy," said Zoé from behind, the handmaiden aghast.

"I can only say it was good that he rode a horse," said Liaze, "else we might not have escaped at all."

"Why are they here, I wonder?" said Zacharie. "—The Goblins, I mean, and the Troll."

"The chevalier, too," said Rémy.

"Oh, my," volunteered Zoé. "Do you think it had anything to do with those sisters, those witches?"

Liaze frowned. "Hradian, Iniquí, Nefasí?"

"Forget not Rhensibé," said Zacharie.

"But Rhensibé is dead," said Zoé.

"Exactly so," said Rémy. "It could be a raid of revenge."

As Zoé's mouth curved into a silent *O*, Rémy said, "But wouldn't they attack Winterwood Manor first? I mean, after all, it was Borel who—"

Liaze turned to Zacharie. "At first light send falcons. Perhaps Goblins and Trolls have already attacked there. Send falcons to the Summerwood and Springwood as well, bearing warnings and telling of what happened here."

"Perhaps they attacked here first," said Zacharie. "I mean, we have no defensive wall about the estate."

Liaze shook her head. "We haven't needed one."

"But Summerwood Manor has a wall about," said Zoé.

"It is not one for protection," said Rémy. "Even so, were we to have a true defensive wall—"

"Let us not rehash old arguments," said Liaze, waving a dismissive hand. "The manor itself is strong enough, and I would not live in a fort."

"As you will, my lady," said Rémy, the armsmaster sighing.

Zacharie shrugged. "Still, they could come at us again with another raid of revenge."

Liaze frowned and said, "I wonder."

"My lady?" said Zacharie.

"Well," said Liaze, "because they came back when the Goblin I slew called out, it seems they were after the knight, rather than coming to mount an attack on the manor."

"Why would they be after him, my lady?" asked Zoé.

"Perhaps he can tell us," said Liaze, even as they came to the door of the infirmary.

As they entered, several women standing at the side of a bed turned at the sound of their footsteps. Margaux was among them, and her face lit up and she smiled and said, "My lady." The women moved aside, making room for the princess and her party.

In the bed 'neath cotton sheets lay the now-unclothed chevalier, his forehead bandaged 'round, his black hair spread on the pillow framing his rather handsome face, a day's growth of stubble thereon. Even as the princess stepped to his side, he gave a faint moan and shifted, revealing about his neck a silver chain, leading down to a blue gemstone in a silver setting lying upon his chest. He did not waken.

"Did you give him a sleeping draught?" asked Zoé.

"Oh, *non*," said Margaux. "He received a rather severe blow to the head. Natural sleep should restore him, but we must make certain that he is not slipping into a dark realm beyond recovery, and so we'll rouse him every now and again to make certain that he responds. —In fact, we were just about to do so."

"I would question him," said Liaze.

Margaux frowned. "Oh, my lady, I think you should wait until the morrow, for he is likely to be addled, and whatever he says, we should take it with a grain of salt."

Liaze pursed her lips and said, "Very well. On the morrow, then." She canted her head toward the knight and said, "Proceed."

Margaux glanced from princess to chevalier and back and smiled and said, "Perhaps you should call to him, Princess."

"Has he given you his name?" asked Liaze.

"Non," said Margaux. "And he had nothing upon him to identify just who he is."

" 'Tis likely to be on his horse," said Liaze. "Perhaps in the saddlebags or bedroll. Still . . ."

"His clothing, however," said Josette, one of the women standing by, "is of luxurious cloth and sewn with a fine hand. I would think he comes from wealth."

"Still, that does not identify him," said Margaux, "and if there is nought borne upon his horse to say, I believe we'll need him to tell us just who he is." She stepped aside and gestured to Liaze.

The princess leaned down and softly said, "Awaken, sir knight."

The man stirred faintly.

"Awaken, sir knight," said Liaze again. "I would thank you for alerting my holt." She gently touched him on the shoulder. "Awaken."

The chevalier's eyes opened, and they were a deep blue beyond blue. Even as a thrill flooded Liaze's entire being, the knight's eyes locked with hers and he said, *"Mon ange. Mon bel ange."*

Liaze flushed, her heart leaping, while all 'round the women sighed and one whispered, "So handsome." A murmur of *beau* and *élégant* came in agreement.

Zoé laughed and twirled about and clapped her hands.

Rémy frowned and looked at Zacharie in puzzlement, and Zacharie merely shrugged.

With a faint smile on his lips, the chevalier closed his eyes and sank back into sleep.

Her face yet ablush, Liaze straightened and looked at the women standing nearby, yet they all had expressions of innocence upon their features. Liaze sighed in exasperation and turned to Zacharie. "Would you please see if there is ought in the knight's saddlebags or upon the trappings of his steed to let us know just who he might be?"

As Zacharie nodded, Liaze frowned a moment and turned back to the chevalier and said, "Perhaps on the pendant there is engraved a name."

In spite of the fact that the cloak she wore gaped open a bit, Liaze reached out toward the silver-clasped jewel, and the moment she did so the women drew a collective gasp and Margaux cried, "Oh my lady, do not touch the—"

The princess's fingers came into contact with the—

"Oh!" she cried and jerked back, cupping her fingers in her other hand, her cloak gaping wide and revealing even more, and Zacharie and Rémy looked away.

Amid a babble, "—amulet," finished Margaux, too late, then added, "It stings." She reached out to take Liaze's hand.

"I saw a spark," declared Zacharie, stepping forward, yet looking elsewhere but at the princess. "It leapt out from the gem."

Rémy, a dagger in hand, interposed himself between the knight and Liaze and glared down at the unconscious man.

Zoé cried out, "Oh, are you hurt, my lady? Are you hurt?" as the princess turned her back to the men.

With women babbling and Rémy glowering and Zacharie now glancing back and forth between Liaze and the pendant, the princess shook her hand as if to throw off the pain and said, "I'll be all right."

" 'Tis some sort of magic," said Margaux. She gestured toward one of the women. "Aurélie discovered it, much to her dismay, even as we disrobed him."

"For protection, I would say," said Zacharie.

"What?" said Liaze, turning toward the gaunt steward.

"The pendant," said Zacharie, looking away. "I believe it is some sort of protective charm."

"It did not save him from a blow to the head," said Liaze.

Zacharie shrugged and turned up his hands.

"Goblins, a Troll, a tall and handsome and mysterious knight," said Zoé, "and now a magic amulet. What is it all about?"

Liaze shook her head. "We'll just have to wait until he regains consciousness."

"On the morrow," said Margeaux. "I think I can safely say that by then he will be awake."

Liaze sighed and nodded and said, "Come, Zoé, I believe I'll have that bath after all."

Not bothering to clutch the cloak tight, with wide strides the princess headed for her chambers, Zoé running ahead. Behind, Rémy finally sheathed his dagger and then set out to canvass the various guard stations, while Zacharie went to the stables to see what the chevalier had borne upon his midnight-dark horse.

4

Reflections

As she luxuriated in the warm water, Liaze's thoughts kept spinning back to the knight and his dark, dark eyes of blue and his black hair and what he had said: *"Mon ange. Mon bel ange."*

Why did he affect me so? It's not as if I haven't had liaisons with men ere now—there was Duc Laurent, and Comte Benoît, and the Baronet Yves, but he was just a fling when I discovered the comte was after Autumnwood and not my heart—yet none of them thrilled me to the core with nought but a glance as did this wounded man in the infirmary. But why? He said only five words in all: "Mon ange. Mon bel ange."

Liaze's heart echoed and reechoed with those five words—*"Mon ange. Mon bel ange"*—and whenever she closed her own amber eyes, she saw his of indigo.

Snap out of it, Liaze! He is a stranger and you know nothing of him. He could be nought but a poor hedge knight, yet would that make any difference? Josette, though, said his clothing is of luxurious cloth and sewn with a fine hand. She thinks he comes from wealth, but he could have won them in a tourna-

ment. Ah me, he could be a terrible bore, a selfish pig. A fortune hunter, as was the comte. Still, I hope not, for I would— Liaze veered away from those thoughts.

"Mon ange. Mon bel ange."

Handsome he is and tall and slender, though but for a brief moment, I've only seen him lying down. —Oh, I do hope he is taller than my own height, for— Ah, Liaze, already you are spinning dreams. Still, he seemed tall when I saw him upon his steed, though he was falling off even as he came into sight. Yet he nigh filled the infirmary bed from headboard to foot. I wonder how he would look in my own bed— Now stop it, Liaze! You are giving to him in your daydreams that which you might not in truth. After all, what do you know of him? Nothing, that's what. Still, he must be a mighty fighter—broken sword and all. And he is sturdy, for Margaux said he had taken a terrible beating, but he managed to stay on his steed . . . for a while, at least. And he— Oh, I remember now. He had a silver horn on a baldric at his side. He was the one who sounded the alert. A noble deed, that . . . or was it a cry for aid? Ah, but—

"Here is your wine, my lady," said Zoé, stepping into the bathing chamber. "Oh, my, you've put out the lamp and lit the scented candles. How nice." She held out the goblet of dark red wine to Liaze.

Liaze sighed and reached up for the drink and took a sip and then set it on the edge of the bronze tub.

Zoé, humming to herself, went about fluffing towels and draped one over the fireguard to warm it for the princess. Then she whirled around and danced about and laughed. Of a sudden she sobered, and looked at the princess and said, "Did I not tell you that one day the right man would come along and—"

"Zoé, Zoé, we know nothing of him."

"My lady, recall: I said that this might be the day, and he is so handsome and tall and strong in spite of being slender, and—"

"Zoé, again I say, we know nothing of him."

"Ah, Princess, I saw how he made you blush. And his words were so romantic: 'My angel,' he said. 'My beautiful angel.' What could be more fitting?" Zoé sighed, and her eyes lost focus, as if she were captured in a *rêve*. But then she started and exclaimed, "Oh, my, I just had a thought. At the pool. He must have seen you naked. Did he? Did he?"

"He had already swooned," said Liaze, taking up her glass and peering into the depths.

Zoé giggled and clasped her hands together. "Oh, I think not, my lady, for you are blushing again."

Liaze swirled her wine and smiled unto herself, then said, "After he had fallen from his horse, when I went to him in the moonlight he opened his eyes long enough to look at me, but only my face. Then he swooned."

"He said nothing?"

"Just one word," said Liaze. "Ange."

"Angel!" squealed Zoé, clapping her hands. "I knew it!"

"I repeat, he only saw my face."

"Ah, but non, I think not, for men are sneaky in the way they look at us and manage to see more than they let on."

Liaze sipped her wine. *I think this one would look frankly and openly at anyone or anything that interested him.* Liaze did not say so to Zoé, for that would attribute to the knight something that she knew not. *Thrusting my own ways upon him.*

Zoé smiled, and then, all handmaiden business, she held out a washcloth and a bar of lavender-scented soap. "Cook says the meal will be ready within a candlemark."

The princess tossed down the last of her wine and traded her glass for the cloth and soap.

Just after dawn the next morn, Liaze, wearing her hunting leathers, saddled her horse, Stablemaster Eugéne standing by.

An outer door opened, and Zacharie entered. "The falcons have flown with their messages, my lady."

"Well and good," said Liaze. "Let us hope when they return they do not bear ill tidings." She glanced across at the chevalier's black horse, the stallion's attention on Liaze's mare. "Zacharie, are you certain there was nought in our mysterious knight's baggage to identify him?"

"Non, my lady," replied the steward. He looked at Eugéne. "And we searched most thoroughly."

Eugéne nodded in agreement and said, "Though his steed put up a ruckus last night, still he is a noble one, and the trappings are of worth. Perhaps the knight is highborn."

Liaze cinched the girth and said, "Unless the blow to his head has removed his memory, when he wakens we shall know." As she took up a saddle quiver filled with arrows and tied it to the forebow, Liaze frowned and glanced at the black and said, "Put up a ruckus, you say? Why so?"

Eugéne shrugged. "Something disturbed him, I would say, though I cannot say what. Got the other horses in a rumpus, too. By the time I arrived, they'd begun calming down. Whatever it was, a badger or some such, it was gone."

"When was this?" asked Liaze.

"Just before Zacharie and I went through the knight's goods; searching for his identity, we were," said the stable master.

"My lady, mayhap it was one of the Goblins," said Zacharie.

"If so, it's no longer about," said Liaze, taking up her horn bow.

"Even so, my lady," said the steward, fretting, "I would rather you let Rémy and the men make certain that the woods are clear of—"

"Non, Zacharie," said Liaze, stringing the weapon. "I would see for myself these raiders." She tested the pull and said, "Besides, it will hearten the staff to see that I go unafraid."

As she slipped the bow into the saddle scabbard Zacharie sighed and nodded in acceptance, for Liaze had always been headstrong, even as a child. Still, he had to admit, her instincts were true, and she was more than capable.

Liaze then mounted up and rode out from the stables and 'round the manor and across the lawn to where stood Rémy and the warband.

"My lady, with you on a horse," said Rémy, the rangy man's face twisted in alarm, "you are an obvious target. I suggest that you dismount and—"

"Non, Rémy. Rather would I let the staff see me astride than down among a protecting ward."

"As you will, Princess," said Rémy, though he shook his head. Then he gestured to the men, and, armed with crossbows and blades and armored in boiled-leather breastplates, they spread out to the fore and flank and aft, and toward the willows they all went, Liaze high in the saddle midst all.

And since all eyes were fixed on the Princess, none saw the crow winging away in the morn, going who knows where.

Slain Goblins—Redcaps all—lay strewn across the far reaches of the lawn, and at the edge of the grove lay a dead Troll, pierced through by a large crossbow bolt.

Within the willow grove and nigh the pool lay the Goblin Liaze had slain. On beyond, here and there they found a few more Goblins amid the forest trees. "These are the ones we slew as they fled," said Rémy.

Farther on still, they came upon a scene of slaughter—nine Goblins in all.

"As you said last night, Princess, this must be the work of our lone chevalier," said Rémy, "for there is but a single horse track."

Liaze dismounted and studied the ground. "From the tracks, it seems he was surrounded. —Ah, look, there is the other half of his sword." Liaze pointed at the fragment of blade embedded in the bark of an oak. At hand lay the beheaded corpse of a Goblin among the roots below. The head itself was not evident.

"Ah," said Rémy, looking at the hoof marks. "His horse was running, and he swung so hard that he sheared through the Redcap's neck and struck the bole, and *that's* what broke his blade."

Liaze nodded, then said, "I would follow the tracks back along his trail, perhaps to see whence he came."

"As you wish, my lady," said Rémy.

For much of the morning they followed the path of the knight's steed, twisting and turning back along the way the knight had ridden. Now and again they found the hacked remains of a Redcap.

"He was pursued a goodly distance," said Rémy, "for with all the jinks this way and that and riding up and down streams, surely he was trying to lose them."

Liaze nodded. "It does not look as if he rode in from either the Winterwood or Summerwood, for generally his trail comes from the sunward bound of the Autumnwood. Still, as you say, it appears he was trying to lose his pursuers, and so could have come from virtually anywhere."

Liaze sighed and looked about, then said, "Enough, Rémy. Let us return to the manor. Of those corpses deep in the woods leave them for the scavengers to find, though I would have a hierophant come and lay their spirits to rest, for I would not have my demesne haunted. As to the ones nigh the manor, burn them."

"As you will, my lady," said Rémy. He turned to one of the men. "Grégorie, blaze a trail for the hierophant to follow."

Grégorie nodded and took a hand axe from his belt and notched the bark of a nearby tree, and as they all headed back along the route they had come, he continued to mark the way.

Even as Liaze rode into the stables and attendants took hold of her steed, Zoé came rushing out, crying, "My lady! My lady! He's awake, and oh my!"

5

Transformation

"Oh my?" asked Liaze as she and Zoé strode toward the manor, the princess bearing her unstrung bow and the arrow-filled quiver.

"What?" asked Zoé.

"You said, 'He's awake, and oh my.' "

"Oh, that. All I meant is that he is witty and charming and more handsome than ever. Why, he even has Tutrice Martine giggling like a *jeune fille*."

"Has he a name?"

"If he said it, Princess, I was not present at the time."

"Has he said why he was in the Autumnwood, or ought about the Goblins?"

Zoé shook her head. "Non. Zacharie is waiting for you before asking."

"Where?"

"They are in the blue room, my lady."

"Then run and fetch Rémy, for I would have him present when the chevalier tells his tale."

As Zoé hied away, Liaze strode on and found herself wondering what she should wear to meet the man who had called her his angel.

Liaze took a quick bath and chose a flowing russet dress with a yellow bodice, russet laces crisscrossing, the yellow so faint as to seem nearly white. She wore a light yellow, ruffle-trimmed pettiskirt beneath. Russet silken slippers shod her yellow-stockinged feet and peeked from under the hem. Zoé combed out the princess's long auburn tresses, and upon her head she placed a circlet of gold, inset with a yellow diamond.

"Now for the earrings, my lady," said Zoé, "do you prefer the—"

"Zoé, it's not as if I am trying to impress this fellow, you know."

"Oh, aren't you?" said Zoé, feigning innocence.

"In fact, I think this circlet is too ostentatious," said Liaze, removing the golden ring.

"Oh, but my lady, you are a princess and must wear something denoting such. It's your station, you know. Besides, it will draw his eyes to your face and hair and—"

Zoé took up another circlet, this one twined 'round with small yellow ivy leaves, with russet and yellow ribbons falling down the back.

"Zoé! That's for the harvest dance."

Zoé groaned in frustration, then said, "Well, what about a ribbon or two twined through your locks?"

Liaze sighed and glanced in the mirror and said, "Oh, very well."

In moments Zoé had fixed pale yellow ribbons among Liaze's auburn tresses in such a way as to not bind the hair but let it flow gracefully—the ribbons flowing gracefully as well—with every movement of the princess.

Liaze stood and turned before the mirror, the dress belling out from her slim waist and down over slender hips to hang in elegant folds. Her breasts were high, pushed up by the bodice, though not immodestly so.

Zoé stepped back and eyed the result. "Oh, my lady, you are beautiful beyond compare."

Liaze smiled unto herself, for she, too, was pleased.

"Princess, a necklace would—"

Liaze shook her head. "No, no more jewelry, other than this." She held up her right hand, her ring finger graced by a wide gold band, with a ruby carved in the shape of a maple leaf and inset in a heavy golden collet, tiny sculpted heads of grain circling 'round.

She glanced at herself once more in the mirror, then said, "Now to the blue room to hear what this knight has to say."

Liaze stepped to the door and out, Zoé trailing after. "Am I to go with you, my lady?"

"Yes, but only to usher away any company that might be hanging about. I think the chevalier would feel more comfortable telling his tale to just Zacharie, Rémy, and me, rather than among a giggling and sighing bevy of women."

"Last I saw, my lady, only Tutrice Martine, Healer Margaux, and Aurélie were there, though several others had been with him earlier. But for Aurélie, Margaux shooed the gaggle out, yet Martine wouldn't go."

"If necessary, I'll deal with Martine," said Liaze.

Down one of the two staircases in the welcoming hall they stepped, and turned rightward at the bottom, for the blue room was in a wing opposite from the infirmary.

Past members of the staff they went, men bowing, women curtseying, all looking after Liaze as she swept by, for they were used to seeing her in leathers or work clothes, and only on special occasions did she dress as a princess should—or so many of them opined.

Whispers followed her along the corridor:

Oh, my.

Stunning.

Belle.

They came to the door of the blue room, and Liaze paused a moment and glanced at her reflection in the pane of an outer window. Then she stepped within.

Zacharie leapt to his feet, as did Rémy. Margaux, Aurélie, and Tutrice Martine stood as well. In a chair facing the doorway sat the black-haired young man, and his deep-blue eyes flew wide at the sight of her and he blurted, "I thought you but a dream."

6

Luc

Even as Liaze blushed, and behind her Zoé gave a joyful laugh, the knight got to his feet, somewhat gingerly and wincing a bit, and bowed along with Zacharie and Rémy. Martine, Aurélie, and Margaux curtseyed, Aurélie and Margaux smiling broadly, Martine with a neutral look upon her matronly features.

Liaze acknowledged them all with a nod as she came into the room, a room with pale blue walls and heavily padded blue velvet chairs trimmed in white and arranged for conversation nigh a large fireplace. Against one wall stood a black oak sideboard. On another wall a black oak escritoire sat open, with quills and parchment and an inkwell at hand, as well as a few books on the shelf above, and an armless blue velvet chair waiting for someone to sit and take pen in hand and write.

As Liaze stepped in among the gathering, Zacharie said, "Princess Liaze, may I present *Sieur* Luc, knight-errant. Chevalier Luc, Princess Liaze of the Autumnwood."

Dressed in black boots and a black silken shirt open at the

neck and black trews held by a silver-buckled black belt, Luc stepped forward and again bowed, once more wincing a bit, stray locks of his shoulder-length ebon hair falling down 'round his face, though the bandage on his forehead and wrapped about held most of it back. Liaze extended her right hand, and Luc took it in his and kissed her fingers. When he straightened up—not quite a head taller than she—he looked down into her amber eyes with his of indigo blue, and a thrill shot through Liaze and she almost did not hear him say, "Princess, I truly did think you but a wishful dream, and I am so happy to find that you are quite real. But here I must correct an assumption: I am not a knight, though someday I hope to win my spurs."

Both Rémy and Zacharie seemed taken aback, but Liaze said, "Pfah! Given what you have done for my demesne, a knight you surely are."

"But, my lady—"

"Rémy, your sword," said Liaze, holding out her hand.

Rémy placed the rapier in Liaze's hand.

"Kneel, Luc," said Liaze.

Wincing and with Zacharie's help, Luc managed to get down on one knee, and Liaze touched him on each shoulder with the tip of the blade, saying, "I, Princess Liaze of the Autumnwood, by my right of sovereignty declare you a chevalier. You may have knelt as a warrior, but now rise up, Sieur Luc, as a Knight of the Autumnwood."

As Zacharie aided the man to his feet, "Please, Sir Luc, sit," said Liaze, glancing at Margaux the healer and then again at the knight. "I would not have you stand any more on ceremony, as battered as you must be."

As Luc stepped back to his chair, Liaze gave Rémy back his rapier and then turned to the women and said, "If you will excuse us, *mesdames*."

Zoé faced the three and made an "after you" gesture toward the door, and Margaux and Aurélie bade their good-byes and stepped away. Tutrice Martine hesitated a moment, but then turned and with her nose somewhat elevated followed after. Zoé shot Liaze a grin and brought up the rear, and as she exited she closed the door after.

Liaze sat down as then did Luc, Rémy following, but Zacharie remained standing and asked, "Tea, my lady?"

"With cheese and bread and scones and jellies," said Liaze. She looked at Rémy and then at Luc. "We were backtracking your trail all morning, Sir Luc, and I am quite famished. Rémy?"

"Oui, my lady," said the leather-clad armsmaster, and he turned to Zacharie. "I'd appreciate a bit of beef as well."

"And you, Sir Luc?" asked the princess. "A tot of brandy or glass of wine to soothe your aches? I am told you took quite a battering."

"Oui, my lady . . . that I did. I believe beef and bread and a bit of fruit and a hearty wine would go a long way toward easing my hurts as well as restoring my strength."

Zacharie nodded and stepped to a bell cord. In but a moment a servant appeared, and Zacharie spoke to him.

When Zacharie took his seat, Luc turned to the princess and said, "You were backtracking my trail?"

"Oui," said Liaze. "And it seems you slew a goodly number of Goblins along the way. I would ask, whence came you? And what brought you here to the Autumnwood? And what of the Goblins and the Troll?"

"As to whence I came," said Luc. " 'Twas from a small wood-cutter's cote, sunwise through three, no, four twilight walls. The woodcutter is my *père*, or mayhap I should say my foster père, for I know not who sired and birthed me."

"You are an orphan, Sieur Luc?" asked Zacharie.

Luc shrugged. "My blood parents, alive or dead, I do not know, hence I could be an orphan, but then again not, though an orphan I might as well be. My foster father—Léon—tells me that he found me in the woods one day. And none in the nearby villages knows ought of who my père and *mère* could possibly be."

Rémy sighed and said, "Though I briefly knew my parents, I am an orphan, too. Slain by Redcaps, they were."

They sat a moment in silence, and then Liaze said, "Go on with your tale, Sir Luc."

Luc smiled and said, "As to riding into your demesne, I am simply arove, yet I am so glad that Léon and I chose this way for me to go." Again Luc's indigo eyes caught Liaze's of amber. He held her gaze for a moment, and then looked away toward Rémy.

"And as to the Goblins and Trolls I fought, I know nought of their mission, or even if they had one. However, shortly after I rode into the Autumnwood, I sensed someone trailing me, and it happened to be that band. Thrice or mayhap four times they assaulted me, but, in spite of their being Redcaps, I think they were not after blood. Instead, I believe they were out to capture me, though as a hostage I deem I would prove to be of little ransom worth, foundling that I am, and my provisional sire nought but a woodcutter."

"We thought as much," said Rémy. "—About them being out to capture you, I mean."

"And why might you think that would be the case?" asked Zacharie.

Luc shrugged. "As I said, ransom could not be the reason."

"Unless they knew who your true père might be—or your mère," said Liaze. "What do you know of them?"

Luc turned up his hands. "Nothing. —Or wait, almost nothing."

"Almost nothing?" said Liaze.

Luc fished the amulet out from under his shirt. Liaze winced, for when he had done so, she could see dark bruises where he had been beaten.

"Only this," said Luc, looping the chain over his head and holding out the pendant to Liaze.

As the princess drew back, Rémy's hand fell to the hilt of the dagger at his side, but he did not draw it.

When Liaze hesitated, Luc said, "I give it to you freely, my lady. It will do you no harm."

Tentatively, Liaze held out her hand, and Luc dropped it into her palm.

It did not sting, but instead felt chill.

She turned it 'round in her fingers and studied it closely. It seemed to be nought but a sapphire in a silver setting on a silver chain. There were no markings on it, and the chain had no clasp.

"My sire, my foster sire Léon, that is, told me it was around my neck when he found me. I was then but a wee babe, and for some reason, the chain was shorter then—it seems to have grown as have I. Regardless, when he tried to remove it for safekeeping, it nearly killed him. It seems that I must give it freely, else it will do great harm."

"A magic talisman, then?" asked Liaze, handing it back.

Luc nodded, and looped the silver chain over his head, dropping the amulet down the front of his shirt.

"My foster father says that it must have come from my real parents."

"Have you taken it to a mage, a seer, to find out what he could tell you?"

"Non, Princess. Though on my errantry I hoped to do so."

"Were you swaddled in blankets?" asked Liaze. "If so, what of them? Were they fine or coarse? That might tell you something of your origins."

Luc shrugged. "Fine or coarse, that I do not know, my lady. For by the time I knew to ask, they were no longer about."

In that moment the servant returned, followed by several more, and they brought platters of breads and meats and cheeses and grapes and an assortment of melons and fruit, along with scones and jellies and jams and clotted cream and a large urn of tea. And there were two bottles of hearty red wine, as well as one of white.

Along with utensils and napkins and various porcelain and glassware, they set it all on the sideboard and decanted the wine and then withdrew.

As Luc started to rise, Liaze said, "Stay where you are, Sir Luc, and ease your hurts. I will serve you up a trencher myself. What would you have?"

As soon as everyone had settled, 'round a mouthful of bread Rémy asked, "And, as the son of a poor woodcutter, where did you come upon your fine steed and clothes and weaponry?"

"Ah, that is a mystery, indeed," said Luc, cutting off a chunk of beef and popping it into his mouth. He chewed a moment and then said, "My foster father had trained me in weaponry. It seems in an earlier time Léon had been an armsmaster. And so I learned my lessons well: the bow, the lance, the blade. He had a small collection, you see. Épées, rapiers, foils, sabers, spears, shields and bucklers, and other such gear, two of each, it seems. Yet he only had a single steed, and so my training ahorse suffered somewhat."

"You took his only steed?" asked Rémy, taking up the decanter of red wine and offering it about, pouring a goblet for Luc and himself. Zacharie and Liaze continued drinking tea.

"Oh, no," said Luc, taking a sip of wine and setting the goblet down. "And here is the mystery to that: one day, not long past, a horse—the black—appeared at my foster père's doorstone. It was accoutered with a fine saddle and trappings, and laden with clothes and arms and armor and a silver horn and a small pouch of gold. In one of the saddlebags we found a note written in a fine hand saying that the goods and the horse— Deadly Nightshade is his name, for he is trained for combat— were for me. Whence they came, I know not, nor did my foster father, it seems.

"Léon then taught me just what a combat-ready steed can

do and the commands to give, and after a bit more training—me and the horse together—he insisted that I go and seek my fortune, faring forth on errantry. As much as I hated to leave him alone, I did so, riding with my back to the sun, as Léon did advise."

"What did you do with the note?" asked Zacharie, taking up a bit of cheese to clear his palate.

"My foster father kept it, saying that he would one day set forth on a journey to find the benefactor, but that I was to ride this direction, he said, for perils lay along the other, and I needed more seasoning ere I took them on."

"Hmm . . ." mused Liaze, spreading clotted cream upon a scone. "I suspect he knew more than he told you."

"I thought so, too, but who am I to question my sire, foster or no?"

"Regardless," said Zacharie, now pouring himself a goblet of wine, "we are glad you came, for if the Redcaps and Troll had been on their way here, and they just happened to see you as a victim of opportunity, then your fair warning no doubt saved lives." Zacharie raised his glass in salute.

"I wonder," said Luc. "Oh, Goblins are Goblins, but why would they be on their way here? Have you wronged them in some manner?"

"Not directly," said Liaze. She took a sip of tea, then said, "But we have clashed with their masters—or mistresses I should say."

"Mistresses?"

"Oui," said Liaze. "Have you ever heard of Hradian, Rhensibé, Iniquí, Nefasí, or Orbane?"

"Orbane, certainly," said Luc, "but he is a man, a dark wizard. These others, they are all women?"

At Liaze's nod, Luc said, "Regardless, I know nought of them. These clashes you spoke of . . ."

"There are, or were, four sisters, four witches, four acolytes of the wizard Orbane, all sworn to set him free from his imprisonment in the Castle of Shadows in the Great Darkness beyond the Black Wall of the World. These witches blame my sire—King Valeray, who was a cunning thief at the time—and his companion—Lord Roulan, a swordsman of considerable merit—for Orbane's eventual downfall."

Liaze paused to take a bite of scone and a sip of tea, and Luc said, "I thought it was the Firsts who entrapped Orbane."

Liaze nodded. "Oui. You are correct, but they did it through Orbane's own wizardry."

"How so?"

"Disguised as a hag, my father tricked the witch Nefasí into allowing him into one of Orbane's castles, where he stole two clay amulets imbued with the wizard's own powerful magic, and when he and Lord Roulan gave these to the Firsts, they were used to cast Orbane into his imprisonment."

"Nefasí is one of those you named, right? One of the acolytes?"

Liaze nodded. "Hradian, Rhensibé, Iniquí, and Nefasí: they are the four—or *were* the four—acolytes, but now are just three, for Rhensibé is dead."

"Slain by Prince Borel's Wolves," declared Rémy. "Tore her apart, they did, and a more deserving death no one ever had."

"Prince Borel?" asked Luc.

"My brother, eldest of Valeray and Saissa's get," said Liaze.

"Whether or no I have siblings, I cannot say," said Luc, a bit chapfallen.

"There are four of us," said Liaze. "Borel, myself, Alain, and Celeste, to name us in birth order. We rule over four principalities: respectively, the Winterwood, Autumnwood, Summerwood, and Springwood."

"This, then, is your demesne," said Luc.

"Oui."

Zacharie frowned into his wine, and then looked up. "My lady, I have a thought."

Liaze gazed at him, a query in her eyes.

"Just this: there are four witches and four of you. Hradian was indirectly responsible for the curses laid upon Alain, and Rhensibé was behind Borel's plight. That leaves Nefasí and Iniquí, as well as you and Celeste. If the acolytes are out for revenge on King Valeray, mayhap they think to accomplish such through his four children. Hence, perhaps this Goblin and Troll attack was meant to be a raid on Autumnwood Manor after all, and Sieur Luc just happened to get in the way."

7

Heart

They sat in silence for a moment, pondering Zacharie's words. Finally, Liaze said, "Perhaps you are right, but then again, that does not explain why they came back to the willows when they heard the Redcap call out."

"Mayhap they did not want a deadly foe at their back," said Rémy, "and by the count of their slain, Luc is a deadly foe indeed."

"Nightshade dealt death blows to some of them," said Luc, "for he is trained to lash out at the enemy when I command him to attack—*Night, attaques!*"

" 'Night'? I thought his name was Deadly Nightshade," said Liaze.

Luc smiled. "It is, Princess, though most of the time I simply call him Nightshade, but the note said I was to use Night for his combat commands; it is quicker than calling out the full of his name. Regardless, that's how I breached their last encirclement after my sword broke. They gave way before his flailing hooves, but only after three were slain."

"Ah, then, he truly is Deadly Nightshade," said Liaze.

Luc smiled and nodded and said, "Yes, in combat."

"We saw that on your backtrail," said Luc. " 'Tis a fine steed you have."

"Did you find my spear, my helm?"

"Non. You had a spear?"

"It's lodged in a Troll somewhere. From horseback I lanced him through and through, and couldn't free the shaft before the others came at me again."

"Formidable!" said Liaze.

Luc grinned at her, his teeth even and white, and she again felt a thrill rush through her, caught by his eyes as she was.

"We must not have backtracked far enough," said Rémy.

"W-what?" asked Liaze, breaking her gaze from Luc's.

"I said, Princess, we must not have backtracked far enough," repeated Rémy.

"Oh. Right. Send a warband first thing on the morrow. Have them look for the helm as well." She turned to Luc. "Where did you lose it, sieur?"

"It must have been when I was struck across the brow by what I believe was a flung cudgel. It was just after I sounded the warning. I saw the lights of your manse, and I knew I must needs alert whoever was within. And then the cudgel struck me.

"The next I knew, I was on the ground somewhere by running water. That's where I saw the Nymph."

"Nymph?" said Zacharie.

Luc grinned again and caught at Liaze's eyes with his own. "The beautiful princess here, though in a different state of dress."

Liaze cast her gaze down and away, and she could feel redness creeping up her neck and into her face, and she wondered if she were blushing all over, even unto the ends of her feet.

"I thought her a Water Nymph, an angel, a dream come true."

Liaze's racing heart hammered in her chest, as of a caged bird seeking escape, and she thought it might burst free in joyous flight. *Perhaps Zoé is right: perhaps this is the man I have been waiting for, and he has come at last.* Something . . . something—she knew not what—welled up from deep inside and shook her soul, and she felt her eyes glisten, as if she were preparing to shed tears.

"My life was saved several times that night," said Luc. He raised a hand and ticked off a count on his fingers, turning them down one by one: "Once by my spear; many times by my sword; once by Nightshade; once by my helm, for surely the cudgel would have done me in had I been bareheaded." He looked at the princess and smiled and turned down the last of his fingers and said, "And once by an angel true."

After a moment of silence, "Harrumph!" Zacharie cleared his throat and said, "Well, my boy, I think it's time I escorted you to another hot bath and then back to your bed. I promised Margaux we wouldn't keep you overlong, for, as she said, you need your rest, and you must recover from the battering you took." He looked at Liaze and said, "By your leave, Princess?"

Liaze glanced at Rémy and when he shrugged she nodded to Zacharie and looked at Luc and smiled, but said nought, for she was not certain she could trust her voice.

Groaning softly, Luc stood, and he stepped to the princess and bowed. She extended her hand and he kissed her fingers. Zacharie and Rémy were on their feet, and they bowed as well. Rémy said, "Shall I escort you somewhere, Princess?"

She shook her head and managed to say, "Non, Rémy. Close the door after you leave, for I would be alone to think."

"As you wish," said Rémy.

The three walked away, Luc erect and pacing slowly, a slight limp in his step, Zacharie at his side. Rémy strode ahead to the portal and held it open as they passed through. And then they were gone.

Sipping white wine, Liaze sat in the blue room for a considerable time, fanciful dreams spinning in the air.

8

Pyre

Finally, Liaze stood and stepped into the corridor, where she found late-afternoon sunlight shining in through the hallway window. *Oh, my, but the day has fled as I gathered wool, dreaming of what might be. But I still know little of this chevalier, this Luc. Charming, yes, and witty, and I thrill at even his glance, yet though I think not, still he could be nought but a fortune hunter after my demesne. Are you afraid, Liaze, because it happened once before with someone you briefly thought to be noble? Afraid? Nay. Cautious? Yes, for I cannot let my longing for true love blind me to what is real. Hence, I will have to genuinely come to know Luc ere I can see him for what he is: a flatterer, a cad, a rake, or someone just as he seems. Still, he called me his angel when he knew me not and was addled, and mayhap in that state he was speaking his heart, rather than trying to sway me.*

Liaze suddenly realized that she had been standing before the window and seeing nought outside. Movement caught her eye, and she watched as a pony-drawn flatbed cart crossed her line of vision, a man leading the little steed. On the cart were three or four corpses of Goblins. *What—? Ah, oui. Rémy and the war-band are preparing to burn them.*

Liaze turned and walked toward the welcoming hall, and there she found her head gardener waiting on one of the marble benches along the window wall. He leapt to his feet and doffed his cap from his fair locks and bowed.

"What is it, Georges?"

"My lady, when they burn the corpses on the pyre they've piled up downwind, there at the edge of the woods, it will leave a great scar on the ground, and the grass and plants thereunder, having burnt down roots and all, will not come anew. What would you have me put in their place?"

"What would you suggest, Georges?"

"Armsmaster Rémy thinks we should leave it barren as a warning to all who would do harm, but I says that such a thing won't work, for how would som'n know that *that's* what it means? Were it mine to decide, I think I'd plant one of the hollies in that place, say, black alder winterberry. I mean, Margaux says that we need such, for when the bark be boiled with other of her simples, a draught taken every morning is very effectual against the jaundice, dropsy, and evil dispositions of the body. Besides, those bright red berries among the glossy, green leaves will look nice out there."

"Then holly it is," said Liaze.

Georges grinned and bowed again, then slapped his cap back on and headed for the door.

Liaze turned and went up the stairs and to her quarters and summoned Zoé.

"Yes, my lady?"

"I would have you go to Margaux and see if Sir Luc will be fit enough to dine with me this eve."

"Oh, Princess, isn't he just perfect? I mean for you, of course. But if you don't want him, you can cast him my way."

"Zoé, Zoé, run and see what Margaux has to say."

Zoé bobbed a curtsey and then was out the door.

Now what will I wear? —Oh, speaking of wear . . .

Liaze stepped to one of the bell cords and tugged.

As the princess stood at the threshold of her extensive closet, peering at the manifold selection of gowns, there came a tapping on the outer door. *"Entrez,"* Liaze called out, and a woman, red-faced from hurrying, came into the room.

"Ah, Sabine. Good."

"My lady," said Sabine, curtseying. "You summoned."

"Oui. It occurred to me that our guest, Sieur Luc, needs a wardrobe, for all he brought with him was what he could carry upon a single horse. I would have you and your seamstresses outfit him. He will need clothes to suit formal affairs, clothes for riding, clothes for work should he take that into mind, though the riding and work garb can come last, for he will not be ready for strenuous—" Liaze's words came to a halt as the seamstress meekly held out a hand.

"What is it, Sabine?"

"Princess, Zoé already has us working on such . . . the cobbler, too. We took Sieur Luc's measure this morning. And we have some formal wear for him even now."

Liaze slowly shook her head and smiled unto herself and said, "I should have known." She looked up at Sabine and said, "Carry on."

"Yes, my lady," said Sabine, curtseying, and then the seamstress withdrew.

It was only after Sabine had gone that Liaze realized her own unspoken assumption with the making of such a variety of clothes was that Luc would stay a long while.

"Have you someone back home waiting for you, Luc?"

"Léon, Princess."

Luc sat at one end of a long black-walnut table, Liaze at the other end. He was dressed in a dark blue that matched his eyes—trews and shirt, that is—though his silver-buckled belt was black as were his silver-buckled shoes.

At the other end of the table Liaze wore pale green—gown, bodice, slippers, stockings and shoes, and pettiskirts—and once again Zoé had woven ribbons through her auburn hair, the ribbons pale green as well.

"I meant anyone other than your foster père," said Liaze.

"Non. I have not known many other people, certainly none long enough to become fast friends."

"No children of your age as you were growing up? Oh my, how sad."

"We lived a league and a mile from the nearest village, and for as long as I can remember it was only when we went to sell wood did I meet any other children. Even then, I did not form any lasting friendships, for my père and I were in town but for brief moments, long enough to off-load the wood and buy a few provisions and to borrow a book or two."

"The village had books?"

"Oui. There was a small bookseller there. How he survived, I cannot say, for many in the town could not read. Yet he was always happy to see me, even though we only borrowed and did not buy."

"Did not Père Léon pay him a fee? —In wood, if nothing else."

"Not that I ever saw," said Luc.

"A mystery, that," said Liaze, frowning. "A bookseller who doesn't sell books and earns no fee for loaning them."

"I believe that he saw how eager I was to learn," said Luc. "Perhaps it gave him joy."

They ate in silence for a while—medallions of veal in a white cream mushroom sauce, along with crisply sautéed green beans and squash, as well as croissants and goblets of a hearty red wine. And as they dined, Liaze watched her guest.

Finally, she said, "Your foster père must have been quite a teacher, not only in reading but also in etiquette, for your manners are impeccable."

"Oh, Léon did not teach me to read, nor drill me in manners of etiquette. His forte was in arms and armor, and the hewing of wood. Instead a number of teachers—itinerants, all—for years came and stayed with us throughout the winters. They treated my père with deference, and always called him Armsmaster, and often engaged him in hushed conversations." Luc barked a laugh. "I thought they were speaking of my progress, and I was determined to not let Léon down. Regardless, they are the ones who saw to my education, teaching me the lot: from reading to writing to ciphering to courtly manners and more, much more, even though most of the time all I wanted to do was learn everything I could of arms and armor and go ahunting in the woods. Yet Léon insisted I not shirk my studies, and told me that these other things I simply must learn, for I would need them one day. And so, from late autumn to early spring, I spent much of my waking time in lessons." Again Luc laughed. "Why, there was even a dance teacher who came, and he taught me the quadrille and the minuet and the reel and the other dances of the court, though I never got the chance to put them to use, except in practice."

"Oh, Luc," said Liaze, smiling broadly, "how splendid. When you are well, we shall have to put your training to use here, for I have a penchant for organizing dances."

Luc smiled and said, "I would be most happy and honored to dance with you, Princess, if I can remember how they went."

"Oh, la!" said Liaze. "It's rather like riding a horse: once you learn, you can take it up anytime thereafter."

"Then I shall give it my best," said Luc.

Again silence descended upon them as they concentrated on their food. But then Luc set down his knife and looked up at Liaze and raised his goblet in salute and said, "Here's to père

Léon, for I just realized: you are the Princess of the Autumn-wood, and this is indeed a court. And so my père was right: I *did* need to learn to dance, else I would not have the pleasure of squiring an angel upon a ballroom floor."

Liaze was glad that she had deliberately chosen to eat in this formal dining room, rather than the intimate one she had briefly considered, else she did not know what she might have done at that moment—something spontaneous, no doubt.

She raised her glass in return and said, "To père Léon." They laughed together and took a sip and then once more they concentrated on eating. And just as dessert was served—a raspberry tort with cream—Zacharie stepped within the chamber and leaned down and whispered in the princess's ear. She nodded and said, "Have them wait for Luc and me to join them. We'll be there anon."

"Yes, my lady," said the steward.

As Zacharie withdrew, Liaze lay down her spoon and said, "I suddenly have no appetite."

"My lady, are you ill?" Luc set his napkin aside and stood, wincing a bit as he did so.

"Non, Luc. Please sit and deal with the tort and cream. When you are finished, there is a place we must be."

"Princess, what is it?" asked Luc, yet standing.

"Rémy is ready to light the pyre under the bodies of the Troll and Goblins, those from the lawn and the woods nearby. The ones deeper in—the Troll speared and Goblins you slew—we leave for the scavengers. Rémy and Zacherie would have us join the others in seeing the dead of our enemies burn."

"The others?"

"The warband and houseguard and any of the staff who care to attend. In this grim task it will hearten them to see the chevalier who sounded the alert and roused the manor and thereby gave us time to prepare, as well as to see standing among them the princess to whom they owe fealty."

*   *   *

Slowly they walked across the long lawn, Liaze now in an ermine-trimmed white cloak against the autumn chill; Luc in a blue long-coat of soft wool. Luc's limp was becoming a bit more pronounced with the walk, for it was far to the site of the pyre.

"Oh, Luc, how thoughtless of me," said Liaze. "I shall have a carriage come and fetch us back."

"Non, Princess. It would not do to have the warband and houseguard see me that helpless. Fear not, I shall rally."

Finally, they came in among the men, as well as other members of the staff, and therein Luc did not limp at all.

Before them a great pile of wood was waiting to be lit, from logs to branches to sticks to shavings. In the slanting light of the waxing half-moon and the glitter from the stars above, amid the heap of combustibles, Liaze could see corpses of Goblins here and there within, and atop lay the Troll slain by Rémy, the large crossbow bolt still piercing him through. A sheen of oil lay over all, the moonlight glimmering thereon.

Rémy handed Liaze a torch, and said, "Princess."

"A torch for everyone!" Liaze called out.

Brands were lit and handed to all attendees, and they spread out to encircle the pyre.

Rémy walked 'round the great heap, and when he came back to Liaze he said, "Ready, Princess."

Liaze stepped forward, her torch held high and she cried, "Thus to all our enemies!" And she thrust the burning brand within and then stepped back.

At her side, Luc did likewise, as did Rémy and the warband and Zacharie and the houseguard and the various members of the staff.

Slowly at first and then with a *whoom!* the massive pile caught fire, and a great plume of dark oily smoke rose into the starry night sky, moonlight and firelight illumining all, red from below, silver from above. And within the roar of the blaze they could hear a popping and sizzling.

"Quite savage," murmured Luc to the princess.

"I know," she whispered back, and reached out with trembling fingers and took his steady hand in hers.

9

Contemplations

That night, in her bed, thoughts of Luc spun all 'round Liaze: *Why would anyone abandon him in the woods, and he nought but a babe? Mayhap he was stolen from someone and left in the forest to die. Mayhap his père or mère, or whoever it might be, put him at a place where it was certain the woodcutter would find him.*

And why would an armsmaster become a woodcutter? Was he simply tired of combat and took up a more peaceful occupation?

And this bookseller who never charged and perhaps couldn't make a living in a village where few could read, what of him? Is he a fugitive in hiding?

And the teachers: were they willing to work for room and board and little else, or did the armsmaster have a stash of gold or silver or copper to pay them for Luc's education?

And the training that Luc underwent: for what purpose? Did the armsmaster know that this babe that he had cared for would one day become a knight-errant? Perhaps that was the goal all along. Perhaps the armsmaster himself had been a chevalier, or mayhap he always wished to be one and is living out his dream through Luc.

And the horse and weapons: who and where did they come from? Rémy says that the sword is of the best bronze, and Eugéne tells me that the steed—Nightshade—is elegant and of great worth. He says that when he travelled in the mortal world, he saw such in Andalusia, though most were grey or white and some were bay and only a few were black, and the blacks are highly prized.

Is Luc telling the truth, or is he simply a charming rogue?

Rogue? Luc? No, I think not.

La, here I lie awake, consumed with thoughts of Luc, yet I wonder if he, too, is lying awake, mayhap thinking of me, mayhap as he first saw me.

Liaze flushed, and a surge of yearning filled her being. After a moment she rose from her bed and stepped to a basin and poured cold water from an ewer. She splashed the chill liquid on her face and neck and breasts, trying to cool down. She padded back to her bed and slid under the covers, yet she still felt the heat of a passion unquenched.

After long moments of tossing and turning, once more she rose, and this time went to the nearest window and drew wide the drapes and lowered the sash and threw open the shutters, and moonlight and air streamed in. In the brisk autumn night, she stood and looked out upon the manor grounds. Argent rays slanted across the sward below, the silver half orb low in the sky and nigh to setting. A ruddy dim light reflected against distant trees; red coals from the pyre yet lived. Below and pacing their rounds, two members of the houseguard strolled by, and Liaze drew back into the shadows, unwilling for them to see her standing nude in her window above.

Thoroughly chilled and leaving the window open, back to her bed she went, and, shivering, climbed under the covers for warmth. Yet in spite of the cold, her ardor had not diminished, and she felt the heat of it, and with thoughts of Luc—his eyes, his smile, his soft voice, his gentle and open way, and his long and lean body—it was quite a while ere she fell into a shallow and restless sleep.

"My lady, my lady, 'tis time to rise."

The voice came from a distant place.

"My lady," again came the call, this time seeming right at hand.

Liaze opened her eyes. Zoé stood at one of the windows, having just drawn back the remaining drapes and opened the shutters wide. Sunlight streamed in at a high angle.

Liaze yawned and stretched, Zoé suppressing a yawn in echo to Liaze.

"What mark is it, Zoé?"

"Midmorn, Princess," said Zoé, holding out a robe. "You've slept quite late."

"Oh, my," said Liaze, scrambling from bed and slipping into the garment. "And here I thought I would never get to sleep."

Zoé laughed and said, "Ah, visions of Luc kept you awake, eh?"

"Zoé!" exclaimed Liaze, and she headed for the bath, Zoé trailing behind and smiling unto herself, for the Princess had not denied Zoé's claim.

"I wonder if he plays *échecs?*" said Liaze as she slid into the warm water.

"Échecs?" asked Zoé.

"It is something amusing we can do and it will not tax his injuries."

"Oh, my lady, isn't there something else even more amusing that—"

"Zoé!" snapped Liaze, even as she reddened.

Zoé turned away from the princess, and grinning widely the

handmaiden began fluffing a towel ere laying it across the fire-guard.

"Why, yes, I do," said Luc. "Père Léon and I spent many an eve in the game."

"My whole family plays échecs," said Liaze. "It came to us through père and mère. Of all of us, perhaps Borel is the best, but he met his match when Camille came into our lives."

"Camille?"

"Alain's new bride."

"And Alain is your brother," said Luc. "The one who was cursed."

"Oui."

Margaux came into the infirmary. "Princess, though this is but his second morn here, and though he is badly bruised, I believe Luc is fit enough to take other quarters."

"Ah, splendid," said Liaze. "We shall install him in the guest wing."

"He will yet need treatment for his forehead and those awful knocks he took," said Margaux. "Still, he can come here for the salves and the ointment and the drink."

Luc groaned. "I will yet have to drink that evil concoction?"

"Certainement," declared Margaux, smiling.

Luc sighed and turned up a hand and, grinning, said, "If I must, I must." He turned to Liaze. "Healer's orders, you know."

"Come, Luc," said Liaze. "I shall show you to your quarters."

Standing nearby, Zoé said, "The azure suite, my lady?"

"Oui," said Liaze.

Zoé turned away and smiled to herself, for the azure suite was as close to the princess's own rooms as a guest could be and not have accommodations in the royal wing itself.

That afternoon the falcons returned, winging in one by one—first from the Summerwood, then the Winterwood, and lastly the Springwood, for it lay the farthest away—and they bore messages: no Redcaps or Trolls had attacked the other manors. When that last message had come, Liaze sighed in relief, for Alain and Celeste were safe, and Borel was away, visiting Lord Roulan, Lady Michelle's father. But Arnot, the steward of Winterwood, reported all was well therein. Only the Autumnwood had suffered an incursion; perhaps they had been after Luc, but then again it could have been a raid on Autumnwood Manor itself.

"Check."

"Ah, Princess," said Luc, "perhaps you have fallen for what my foster père calls . . . hmm, let me term it a gambit."

"So you say," said Liaze.

"Oui, so I say. Chevalier to red king's three."

They were sitting at a small cherrywood table in a chamber in the sunset wing. Other small tables and chairs of like wood sat here and there in the room, with *damier* boards for playing *dames,* or *échiquiers* for échecs. The playing sets were of varying colors, and some were carved of ivory or amber, or of onyx and jade and other semiprecious stone. In one corner sat a large round table, cherrywood as well, with chairs about, a deck of taroc cards thereon. Against one wall sat a long sideboard, and as with all the furniture, it was cherrywood, too. On the opposite wall heavy brown stones embraced a large fireplace, and logs blazed within.

The floor of the chamber was of pale brown marble, and the walls of a slightly darker hue, with the ceiling white.

On the walls themselves were sconces 'round, holding lanterns alight. Portraits of Borel and Liaze and Alain and Celeste, as well as their parents—Valeray and Saissa—looked out upon the players. As if fixing them in his mind, these Luc had studied over the past three days of gaming with the princess.

"So, you move the chevalier to block me," said Liaze. "Well

then, green hierophant takes that impudent red knight. Check.—Oh my, that was a mistake."

Luc smiled. "Tower takes hierophant. Check and mate."

Liaze stared at the board. "I could have seen that coming, had I not been too eager to capture your chevalier."

"You have captured more than one chevalier, my lady."

Liaze looked up to see Luc gazing at her, and her heart leapt.

Boldly, Liaze said, "And you, Luc, captured the queen right from the start."

Luc reached across the table and took Liaze's left hand in his right, and she did not withdraw from him. Luc whispered, "My lady, you are so beautiful. Why hasn't someone come and carried you away: a king, a prince, a duke, an earl?"

Liaze put her right hand on top of his, there among the captured pieces. "Why not a knight, Sieur Luc?"

Luc shook his head. "Princess, you are worthy of a true noble and not a common chevalier."

"You are no common chevalier, Luc."

Luc withdrew his hand and pushed both out in a gesture of denial. "Me? But I am just a poor woodcutter's son."

"Luc," said Liaze, taking his left hand—his heart hand—in both of hers. "You know not whose child you are, yet this I say: in these days you have been here, I have come to realize a nobler person I have never met. You are anything but common."

"But princesses do not companion with commoners, my lady," said Luc.

Liaze shook her head. "Then, by that rule, Camille, a so-called commoner from the mortal world, and Prince Alain should never have wed." At mention of Alain, Luc glanced at the portrait of the Summerwood prince. "Ah, non, Luc," continued Liaze, "Camille is a rare and uncommon person . . . just as are you."

Luc sat without speaking, and after long moments Liaze said, "Whatever happens between us, let it be."

Luc sighed and said, "Princess, you deserve someone much better than me, and that I truly believe. Even so, it will be difficult to keep a rein on my ardor."

Liaze's pulse quickened, still she said, "Keep a rein?"

Luc nodded. "My lady, some believe love at first sight is but a mad fancy, yet I tell you it is not, for at the first moment I saw you, you captured my heart."

Liaze's soul filled with joy, and her laugh came silvery, and she said, "Luc, you had been hit in the head and had fallen off your horse when you first saw me."

Luc laughed along with her, but he quickly sobered and said, "Nevertheless, Princess . . ." His words died, and his eyes filled with an unfathomable expression. And then he said, "That was the very moment, though I didn't know whether you were real or a dream."

"To fall in love with a dream would indeed be a mad fancy, for dreams are not real," said Liaze. "Yet heed me, Luc, I am no dream."

"Non, my princess, you are not, and for that I give my most fervent thanks to almighty Mithras above."

10

Fulfillment

Over the next two weeks, in the evenings Luc and Liaze continued to play échecs, and on rainy nights they read before the fireplace in the manor's library, oft quoting poems to one another, many of them concerning love—unrequited, consummated, lost, gained, and the like—as well as parts of sagas and bits of familiar tales. And during sunny days they flew arrows at targets, and in this Liaze proved the better. But in croquet, Luc had a keen eye and hand, and oft Liaze found her ball far from the next wicket, driven away by Luc. They dined together—breakfast, lunch, dinner—yet there were times Liaze had to attend to matters of the principality. During some of these, Luc sat high in the gallery that ran 'round three sides of the throne chamber, and he listened to judgments and arbitrations and settlements of quarrels. There were times of courtly functions, and these Luc did attend, such as when some of the Fey Folk came to pay respects: over three days Luc met five tattooed Lynx Riders, and a Gnome and three Kobolds who asked to have a mining dispute settled, and Brownies, Hobs, Pixies, Sprites, and one great shambling thing, and a Ghillie Dhu in his clothes made of leaves and moss.

During this time, Luc's bruises cleared, and the bandage came off his forehead. A small circular scar remained, but Margaux told him it would soon fade.

And then Luc and Liaze began riding in the woods, exercising Nightshade and Liaze's own horse—Pied Agile, Nimble Foot in the old tongue—a dark grey mare with a white face as well as white fetlocks on all four feet. And on these excursions Liaze carried her bow, and Luc went well armed, with his own bow and arrows, and a long-knife strapped to his thigh, and a new sword in his scabbard, the blade presented to him by Rémy and Zacharie as a token of their respect. His spear had been found, as well as his helm, but these he generally left behind.

When Rémy objected to these forest rides and said that Goblins and Trolls might yet be about, Liaze laughed and asked, "What better escort than Luc?"

"My warband," replied Rémy.

Liaze shook her head.

Rémy sighed and said, "Then, Princess, fare not deep in the woods, and I will have men standing by in case of need. —And have that knight bear his silver horn."

Now Liaze sighed and made a minor gesture of assent.

There came a cool morn, fog twisting among the trees, and as they rode Luc said, "Let us go on a hunt."

"What after?" asked Liaze.

"A stag if we can jump one up."

"Capital," said Liaze. "Would you have others come with us?"

Luc grinned and glanced in the direction of the manor well beyond seeing and said, "And share the chase?"

Liaze laughed and shook her head. "I know where deer come to graze on low-hanging apples. If there is a stag among the doe—"

"Then we jump him," said Luc, "and yield a bit of ground, for it would be most unfair to take him unawares at his breakfast."

"Splendid," said Liaze. "Follow me." And she heeled her grey in the flanks, and in spite of her halfhearted promise to Rémy, toward a distant woodland orchard they rode.

There was a stag at one of the trees, and away it flew, and laughing in the chase they pursued, Liaze's nimble mare swift through the forest, Luc's black stallion faster in the open.

They did not bring down a stag that day, yet they were well pleased when they called a halt to the chase.

Chatting and laughing, slowly they rode back toward the manor, the day growing quite warm with the mounting sun, the fog having been burned off long past.

As they came in sight of the mansion, "I know just what we need do," said Liaze, and she led Luc toward the willows.

They rode in among the drooping yellow branches, brushing them aside with their hands. "I seem to recall such," said Luc as he frowned at the dangles, "though the memory is hazy."

They came at last to a small open glade there in the center of the grove. And across the sward, among great, flat white stones, lay the broad pool. Here they dismounted and turned loose their horses—stallion and mare—among the sweet grasses of the small, tree-sheltered meadow.

They walked to one of the stones at the edge of the pool, the spring-fed water lucid and welling, and a rill flowed out from one end to dance and sing over a stony bed on its journey to a faraway sea. And Luc looked about and smiled in recognition and said, "Somewhere in this place in the moonlight is where I first saw my Water Nymph."

Liaze laughed and said, "Let me show you where," and she sat down and pulled off her boots and stockings, then unlaced her leather jacket and flung it aside, along with her silken shirt.

Luc's breath was taken away with the sight of her, yet he

stood looking at her high breasts and slim waist, his gaze frank and admiring.

And she got to her feet and stripped out of her leather breeks and the waist-to-ankle silk garment beneath.

And Luc unfastened his long-knife and sword belt and scabbard, and he sat down to pull off his own boots.

Now completely unclothed, Liaze stepped to the edge of the pool, her form belling out from her trim waist over slender hips and then down into long, sleek legs. She stood there a moment, her back to him, and then, with a joyous cry, she dived into the crystal-clear water. She stroked down and across the pellucid mere, with its white bottom of flat stones and sand, the chill water bright with sunlight. To the other end she stroked and up the vertical face of the large rock at the verge. She surfaced and shook water from her eyes, then placed her hands on the low, flat top of the monolith and, with a kick, levered herself up onto the brink of the slab, and twisted about to sit. Laughing, she called out, "Luc!" but he was nowhere to be seen. She stood and peered about the glade. *Where—?*

In that moment, blowing, Luc surfaced in the water at her feet. And he looked up at her and again his breath was taken away. And then with a lift and a turn, he was on the stone as well.

Liaze reached down and took his hand, and he rose to his feet, and she led him to the mossy bank along the edge of the dancing rill. "And here is where I first found you," she said, and she pulled him down beside her.

And embracing one another, face to face they lay, and she held him close and kissed him deeply. His manhood was hard and pressing against her, and she could feel the beat of his pulse.

"Luc," she said, her voice husky, her eyes lidded with desire.

"My lady, I have no experience whatsoever with—"

"You have never?"

"Never."

"Here, then," she said, and she rolled astraddle him and reached down and guided him in.

"Oh!" he said, and, "Oh!" just as did Liaze.

In the meadow that warm afternoon, with sunlight shining down, a stallion and a mare cropped the sweet, sweet grass.

11

Idyll

They lay side by side in Luc's bed, and by the flame of a single candle they looked upon one another. Twenty-one more days had passed, and often they had made love, and every night they slept in each other's arms. Gently, Liaze had guided him, and Luc had learned quickly, and their passion had grown with each passing day.

Liaze reached up and brushed back a stray lock of Luc's dark hair, and then tenderly cupped his cheek in her hand. "What are you thinking, *chéri?*"

Luc took her hand away from his cheek and held it in both of his and said, "I believe my errantry has ended but a few days after it began, for here I have found the only thing worthy of quests."

"And what might that be, Luc?"

"True love, my lady, true love."

"And for this you would give up errantry?"

"I ask: what is errantry, *ma chérie?* And I answer: nought but a roaming search for adventure."

"But you are a man, and men crave excitement."

"And I suppose women don't?" asked Luc.

Liaze laughed. "Oh yes, we crave excitement, but perhaps of a different sort. Women don't usually run about and bash at Dragons, as do the heroes of the old sagas."

Now Luc laughed and looked into Liaze's eyes, dark in the candlelight. "Methinks those who tell such tales have never come upon a Dragon."

Liaze sat up in surprise, the sheet falling from her breasts and down to her thighs. "And you have?"

"Mmm, what?" said Luc, his gaze now elsewhere.

Liaze laughed a throaty laugh, and she reached out and took his face in her hands and tilted his gaze up and away from her bosom, and he grinned mischievously. Liaze said, "I asked, Sieur Knight, have you seen a Dragon?"

"Um, yes, nigh a year ago."

"Tell me, then."

Luc said, "Well, it was as I was training upon Nightshade that there came a skreigh from above, and when I looked up, there it was, high in the sky, its vast wings rowing the air. A dark ruddy color were its scales, with splashes of obsidian glittering here and there, and it was enormous; that I could tell, even though it was far aloft, for—and here is the unbelievable part—I swear it had a rider, a man, astride at the base of the Drake's neck, there where the nape meets the shoulders, just ahead of its wide-spread wings. It was a Dragon, all right, yet, because it had a rider, I think I might have dreamt it, even though I thought I was awake."

Liaze laughed. "It was no dream, my love. What you saw was the Drake Raseri and the rider was the Elf Rondalo."

"Raseri? Rondalo?" said Luc. "But the tales say that they are mortal enemies."

"Once, perhaps, but no more, for Camille laid the enmity to rest."

"You must tell me how she did so," said Luc.

"I will," said Liaze, "after."

"After?" asked Luc.

Liaze smiled. "Yes, after."

"Oh," said Luc, then he grinned, too, and added, "indeed after," and he took her in his arms.

A fortnight later, "I tell you, Zacharie," said Rémy, "this Luc is a marvel, he is. I've never seen a finer hand with a rapier, and I've seen more than a few. Over these past fourteen days he's taught my warband and your houseguard a thing or three with a blade . . . cudgels, too."

"War axes and hammers as well," added the steward.

They watched the men drill under Luc's tutelage—shields and bucklers, now. After a while, Rémy said, "Be a good thing if the princess marries him."

Zacharie nodded and said, "She's heels over head in love, you know."

"How can you tell?" asked Rémy, feigning seriousness, and Zacharie looked at the armsmaster askance, and then they both broke out in laughter.

"What is so joyous?" said Liaze, smiling, as she walked up from behind, Tutrice Martine at her side.

"Er, nothing, my lady," said Rémy, giving the princess a slight bow.

Martine looked through disapproving eyes at Zacharie and said, "Is this one of your vile men's stories?"

"You could call it that," said Zacharie.

"You don't want to hear this, Princess," said the matron, and she raised her hands as if to cover Liaze's ears.

Liaze shook her head and lifted an eyebrow at her former tutrice, and Martine let her hands fall back to her sides and huffed and turned away.

They stood and watched as Luc—shirtless, his amulet swinging with his moves—demonstrated the various ways of the shield bash, as well as how the edge of the shield could become a terrible weapon true. And he showed how a small, round buckler could be thrown, to sail far and bring down a foe at range, especially one that is fleeing.

"This man of yours," said Rémy without thinking, "he's a wonder, and that's a fact."

"He is at that," said Liaze.

"Oh, my lady, forgive me," said Rémy. "It's just . . . well . . . you know. Not that I'm saying he's *your* man. Instead, what I mean—"

"I know what you mean, Armsmaster," said Liaze, smiling, "and all of it is true. Luc's asked me to marry him, and I will, as soon as my sire and dam come here on their annual rade, for a king must be notified, and I would rather it were him than any other. After that, the banns must be posted and a hierophant found, and then Autumnwood Manor will see a wedding."

Martine, who had been gazing through slitted eyes at the agile chevalier, spun around to face the princess. "But he is a common knight," objected the tutrice, "and you know nothing of him. You deserve better: a *duc* . . . or a *comte*, at least."

"Martine, he is anything but common, though I do admit there is a mystery concerning his birth and parentage."

"I say send him on his way, for he could be a bastard child," said Martine, fairly spewing in ire.

Rémy looked at Martine and said, "And he could just as well be a king."

"*Hmph!*" huffed the matron, turning to Liaze. "For all we know, he could be your half brother."

Liaze turned a cold eye toward Martine. "Are you accusing my sire, King Valeray, of infidelity? Or my mother, Queen Saissa? Take care, for their bond is strong and well known, as is the lineage of their offspring."

Martine blenched. "No, no, Princess. I'm accusing no one of

anything. It's just that we know nought of this upstart chevalier's parentage."

"And I say it matters not," said Liaze.

Unbelieving, Martine blew out air in angry puffs. "Princess, I—"

"And when might this wedding occur?" interrupted Zacharie.

Liaze glanced at the red and gold leaves gracing the nearby woods. "In autumn," she said and laughed and then sobered. "Seriously, Zacharie, within a year. Until then he is my consort, my lover."

"Your consort! Your lover!" cried Martine, throwing up her hands in exasperation. "Princess, when you were a child I thought I taught you better, in spite of your willful ways."

Before the Princess could respond, "Martine," said Zacharie, "you have said quite enough."

In that moment, with his shirt slung over a shoulder, Luc walked from the practice field toward the four, and Tutrice Martine spun on her heel and stormed away.

A slight sheen of perspiration on his face and chest and abdomen, and down the lean muscles of his arm, Luc stepped to Liaze, and she took him by his free hand and smiled up into his eyes. Then she turned and said to her steward, "Zacharie, I think it's time we had held a dance. Refreshments as well, if you please. Invite everyone to the grand ballroom, and rotate the guards in and out. Would you arrange for such?"

A great grin split Zacharie's features. "Gladly, my lady. 'Tis a grand party we'll have."

That afternoon Luc moved into the royal wing, his quarters adjoining Liaze's rooms. And the entire staff breathed a sigh of relief, for their princess was pledged to a man they all approved of—all but Martine, that is, for she yet referred to him as a low-born, upstart, common hedge knight.

Zacharie dispatched falcons to the siblings' manors, bearing the news that Liaze was betrothed. Liaze sent her own falcon winging unto her sire and dam, and the message it bore told what she knew of Luc and of the woodcutter—the former arms-master—who had taken him in, and she asked if they knew of a child abandoned in a like manner in a forest some three or four twilight borders sunwise of her own demesne.

That eve, Liaze presented Luc with a pair of silver spurs, saying, "A knight of my realm should never be without the badges of his office."

Luc looked at her with tears in his eyes. "Ah, but père Léon would be so proud. Thank you, my love."

"Put them on," urged Liaze. "I would see you in them."

Luc kicked off his shoes and slipped into his boots, and in moments and with great exaggeration, he strutted about the chamber, spurs agleam. Liaze laughed with joy and told him just how splendid he looked. Then Luc sobered and changed back into his shoes and held out his arm. "Shall we?"

After a sumptuous dinner, Liaze led Luc toward the grand ballroom, Liaze dressed in a satin gown, somewhere in that indeterminate range between a gentle yellow and a soft green, with pettiskirts and stockings and shoes to match. This night she also wore her golden circlet, the one with the yellow diamond.

Luc, on the other hand, wore a waistcoat 'neath a doublet, and shirt with belled sleeves, and tights and long stockings and black-buckled shoes. Deep violet was the prime color of his clothes, with pipings and insets of pale blue.

As they neared the vast chamber, they could hear music and laughter and gaiety, and they entered a ballroom full of people waiting their turn to dance the minuet: the women in silks and satins, their long, flowing gowns of white, lavender, yellow, peach, of pale red and of deep jade, of umber and rust and puce, and of blue. The men were arrayed in silken tights and knee hose and buckled shoes, with doublets and waist-coats and silken shirts and ruffles galore, their colors in darker shades than those of the women, but running throughout the same range. Liaze was the only woman wearing a gown of a hue between yellow and green, and Luc the only man in violet.

A door ward thumped the floor three times with a long staff, and the music stopped and everyone turned toward the grand ballroom entrance, and a great cheer rose up, led by Zacharie: *Huzzah! Huzzah! Huzzah!*

Amid the following applause, the musicians again began to play—harpsichord, and a bass viol and a cello, a viola and a violin, as well as a flute and a harp. And they sounded some notes of a minuet, then the music segued into an interlude and one by one the instruments fell to silence, until only the harp remained. The crowd grew quiet and looked at the princess and her consort in expectation.

"Sieur Luc," said Liaze, "may I have this dance?"

"Indeed, my lady," he said, and bowed and took her hand.

A great, wide circle formed, and Luc led Liaze to the center, and when they stopped and took their positions, the flute and violin, viol, cello, bass viol, and harpsichord took up the play, and slid into a minuet.

Luc bowed low, and Liaze deeply curtseyed, and then Luc held out his hand to the princess, and they moved in time to the moderate tempo, the stately court dance one of small steps and erect posture and curtseys and bows and hand holdings and pacings side by side while facing one another. And they turned and drew close and then stepped apart, and struck the requisite poses, all having an air of restrained flirtation.

"It is called the kissing dance, Luc," said Liaze, with an impish grin.

"I know, my lady," said Luc, smiling back. "My teachers taught me so."

"Fear not, Sieur Luc, I will not attack you in front of these guests."

Luc laughed but said nought in return.

They continued the dance, effecting the various steps and postures and carriage, and Liaze said, "You are doing quite splendidly. Your *tuteur* taught you well."

Gracefully, lithely, the pair glided through the dance, while those about occasionally applauded at some nimble step or turn, Liaze willowy, Luc agile, a perfectly matched pair.

As the minuet came to an end, Luc leaned as if to kiss Liaze, and she raised her face to meet him, and their lips did touch, to the delight of all, and in that moment the music slipped into the interlude, and all the spectators suddenly broke out in applause.

Liaze called above the ovation, "Now all take part," and the crowd broke up into several rings, and couples took center, and the music segued into the minuet and the kissing dance went on.

That evening Liaze and Luc stepped out the cotillion, with its varied and intricate patterns, and they danced the *countredanses*, and lively they were with much gaiety, four or eight couples in a square, crossing over, changing partners, pacing lightly in pairs 'round and 'round.

And they danced many vigorous reels—the men in a line on one side, the women in a line opposite—couples tripping out to meet one another, or romping down the center in various steps and poses, to the laughter and joy of the other dancers, while the exuberant music played on.

And Liaze taught Luc and the gathering another reel: the Dance of the Bees it was called, something that her brother Borel and his intended Michelle had taught the attendees during Alain and Camille's wedding; Borel had seen the dance of Buzzer the bee during the trials the Prince of the Winterwood had undergone, and when he could he turned Buzzer's gyrations and wriggles into a dance. And so Luc and Liaze wiggled and buzzed and raced to and fro and 'round the lines of dancers, while the violin played a frenetic air, and everyone laughed.

And between dances and during refreshments, some sang, and some recited poetry, and some told tall tales. And then several called upon Luc to perform, and grinning he took center stage. He put his fingers to his lips and shushed, and the crowd fell silent. And in a melodramatic voice and with histrionic gestures Luc began:

> *The fog upon the misty moors*
> *Came creeping in my sleep,*
> *And clung unto the eaves and doors,*
> *And made the windows weep.*
>
> *I rose within the clammy night*
> *And drifted from my bed,*
> *And looked upon the ghastly sight*
> *And thought I might be dead.*
>
> *I deeply wept to think of all*
> *That I had left undone.*
> *But then there came through Mithras' vault*
> *The first rays of the sun.*
>
> *I found I wasn't dead at all*
> *But much alive instead.*
> *I took those very same regrets*
> *And put them back to bed.*

Luc laughed and bowed, and the crowd roared, and the musicians struck up an air, and applause sounded heartily. Luc stepped from the stage, where, delighted, Liaze waited, and she kissed him on the cheek.

"That was splendid, my love," she said. "Humorous while at

the same time speaking of things unregretted until it is too late."

Smiling, Luc nodded, and then sobered and said, "And yet when more time is given, undone they continue to be."

"*Saisez le jour,* eh?" said Liaze.

"Oui," replied Luc. "Seize the day, and leave nothing to regret, nothing undone."

Liaze leaned closer to him and whispered, "Then why did you resist me so long?" She laughed a silvery laugh, and drew him onto the dance floor, and they joined another reel, and romped through the line of arched hands.

"Oh, my, what a wonderful evening," declared Liaze, falling backwards onto her bed.

"Indeed," said Luc. "That I remembered the dances amazes me."

"Did I not say it was like riding a horse: once learned, ever remembered?"

"You did, chérie," said Luc, pouring two glasses of dark wine. "Even so, I was a bit anxious. I have never been with so many people, and all of them having fun."

"The poem, Luc, the one you recited, whence?" asked Liaze, sitting up.

"It came to me all at once on a foggy morn," said Luc as he handed a glass to Liaze. "I believe it is my own creation, though mayhap it is only remembered from something I once read."

"Well, it was quite splendid," said Liaze, "and quite splendidly told."

She raised her glass in a salute, but before sipping she said, "Here's to many more nights such as this, the happiest of my life."

Luc raised his glass in response. "And in my life, too," he said, and they sipped the wine and smiled at one another, and both began shedding clothes. Nude, Liaze threw back the covers and leapt upon the bed, Luc an instant after.

They made precious and gentle love, and lay together awhile in murmured converse. But at last Luc stepped 'round the room and capped the lanterns and blew out the candles and crawled into bed. They kissed one another sweetly, and quickly fell into slumber.

12

Shadow

It was well after the mark of midnight when Liaze awakened trembling, not from the cold but from a feeling of dread. She looked at Luc lying asleep, but the darkness obscured his face, and so she slipped from the bed and went to a nearby window and drew aside the drapes. She lowered the sash and opened the shutters, and once again she shivered in the chill autumn air. This night was the dark of the moon, and only starlight shone in.

What did awaken me, and why this sense of anxiety, as if something quite ghastly is creeping upon us?

Liaze looked out upon the lawn, and she saw a small dark form scuttling across the sward and pointing up at her open window. Yet that wasn't what affrighted her so; instead it was a huge dark shadow following, the shadow slithering back and forth, like a giant serpent, or perhaps more as if it were a questing hound, seeking, seeking, flowing upon the grass like some dreadful—

Of a sudden Liaze saw what it resembled: *A shadow of a great hand, creeping this way, with clawed fingers and—*

Liaze spun and cried out, "Luc! Luc, waken!" And even as Luc started up from the bed, Liaze shouted to the unseen ward below, "A foe comes!"

Luc bolted up and into his chamber, and by the starlight shining in through his open-shuttered, open-draped windows, he snatched his sword from its scabbard lying upon a bedside table. And he grabbed his silver horn and chain shirt and silks and leathers and boots from their rack-stand.

Back into Liaze's chamber he ran and to the window, and he said to Liaze, "Step away, they might fly arrows."

He sounded his horn, and it was answered from below by the houseguard.

Luc looked out and down. "What—?"

He flung on his silks and then his leathers, saying, "I know not what that black thing is, but you need to stay back and safe."

As he slipped into his chain shirt, ignoring the warning Liaze stepped again to the window. "Oh, Luc, it's creeping up the side of the house." She hauled up the sash and slammed the window shut.

"My bow, I need to get my bow." Liaze ran through an archway to an adjoining room.

A darkness blotted out the starlight, and the house creaked and groaned, as if its timbers were shifting, as if someone or something were trying to crush it.

Luc stomped his last boot onto his foot, and grabbed up his sword and stepped to the window.

Just as Liaze came running back in, her strung bow in hand and a quiver at her side, Luc lowered—

"Luc, don't!"

—the sash.

Her cry came too late, for the huge shadow rushed in and snatched Luc up and jerked him out the window, his sword spinning down toward the ground to land on the flagstones with a *clang!*

Even as she ran toward the gape, Liaze nocked an arrow to bowstring.

The shaft was already half drawn as Liaze reached the window. She stared into the night, and saw something small and dark shoot up from the distant trees, dragging the great shadow after, with Luc caught in its grasp. Up and across the sky they flew, and Liaze drew to the full and took aim at the blot resembling an arm and loosed her missile, the arrow to sail through the umbrous wrist and beyond to no effect whatsoever. And there came through the moonless dark a distant laughter of sinister glee as the shadow and Luc and something flying ahead of them disappeared into the night.

13

Desolation

Liaze collapsed to the floor, sobbing. She took up the silver horn and pressed it to her cheek. She did not note the ache in her left breast nor in her left forearm, the bowstring having struck both.

"Princess! Princess!" With a lantern in hand, Zoé came running in. "I heard the trump. What—?" Zoé dropped to her knees beside Liaze.

Liaze looked at the handmaiden through tear-laden eyes. "He's gone, Zoé, snatched away from me by a dreadful dark thing."

"Gone? Luc? Oh, Princess, I—"

The door slammed open. Zacharie and men of the houseguard came crashing in, weapons in hand. "Princess, are you—"

As men spread out and searched the chambers, Zoé leapt to her feet and ran to the bed to grab up a blanket.

"—hurt?" asked the steward, dropping down on one knee at Liaze's side and looking everywhere but directly at her naked form.

"He's gone, Zacharie," said Liaze, raising her face to him, indescribable pain in her eyes. "The shadow took him."

Zoé rushed back and enwrapped the princess in the cover.

"But you are safe? Nothing herein?" asked Zacharie, gesturing about.

"If there were," snapped Zoé, "don't you think she would be fighting them? And as far as being hurt, it is her heart and soul in pain, not her body." Exasperated, Zoé added, "Men!" She turned to Liaze and knelt down and embraced her and held her close.

Members of the houseguard came from the adjoining chambers. "Nothing, Zacharie," said one of them. "No Goblins anywhere."

Zacharie rose to his feet. "Two stand ward at the princess's door. The rest of you, help with the search of the manor."

Gaining control of her emotions, Liaze said, "I'm all right, Zoé," and the handmaiden released her embrace. Liaze then looked up at Zacharie. "Goblins?"

"Oui, Princess," said the steward, vaguely gesturing toward the open window. "Louis spitted with a crossbow bolt the only Goblin we saw as it climbed the wall toward your rooms."

Liaze set the silver horn aside and wiped an eye with her fist and said, "Why would a lone Goblin climb the wall?"

Zacharie shrugged.

Liaze frowned and then took in a breath. "Did it have a cudgel or other weapon?"

"Oui, Princess, a cudgel."

"It must have been sent to break the pane and let the shadow in, but Luc—" Liaze's voice choked, and she took a shuddering breath. "Luc opened the window himself, and—"

"Princess," called Rémy as he came striding in, an unsheathed falchion in his grip. "It was a witch."

"What?" asked Zacharie. "Did you say 'witch'?"

"Oui, Zacharie. Anton saw her silhouette against the stars as she flew up from the woods."

"*That's* what that was," said Liaze, more to herself than the others. She got to her feet and said, "A witch . . . and she dragged the shadow and Luc after, as she flew away."

"Four of you and four of them," said Zacherie, sighing. "Did I not say?"

"Rhensibé, Hradian, Iniquí, and Nefasí," agreed Rémy, nodding. "Since Rhensibé is dead, perhaps it is one of the three who are left."

"But why take Luc?" asked Liaze. "Why not me instead?"

Zacharie and Rémy looked at one another, and neither had an answer, but Zoé said, "Through Lady Michelle, Rhensibé struck at Borel."

"That's right," said Zacharie. "It was indirect revenge. Perhaps the same is at work here. Whichever witch it is, mayhap she simply wanted to reave true love from you."

Liaze stooped and took up her bow, her blanket gaping wide. "Which way did she fly, Rémy? I lost sight of her and the shadow and Luc in the darkness."

"So, too, did Anton," said Rémy, looking away.

Liaze sighed and shook her head. But then she looked at Zacharie. "Did we take any casualties?"

"Oui," said Zacharie. "Two members of the houseguard— Adrien and Paul—were crushed, as if by a giant hand."

Liaze's face fell. "The witch's dark clutch, the shadow," she said, now stepping toward the window. Rémy tried to get between her and the opening, but she waved him away. Liaze looked out upon the starlit lawn, the faint light now augmented by the lanterns of searching men. "It tried to rupture the manor with its terrible grip."

"I heard the timbers groan," said Zoé, her eyes flying wide.

"I will have the carpenters and masons and roofers inspect every inch," said Zacharie.

"My lady," said Rémy. "We can take part of the warband and go searching for Sieur Luc."

"Which way would you ride?" asked Liaze.

"I . . . I don't know," said Rémy.

"Precisely," said Liaze, tears welling unseen, for she stood at the window looking out.

"A seer might know," suggested Zoé. "We could ask Malgan. He lives in the Autumnwood."

An image of the seer sprang to Liaze's mind: a reed-thin, sallow-faced man with lank, straw-colored hair, his hands tucked across and within the sleeves of his buttoned red satin gown.

Rémy snorted. "This Malgan: he's the one who continually whispers to himself and looks about and flinches as if seeing invisible things. Princess, I think him perhaps untrustworthy, mad as he is."

"I would not disagree with you, Rémy," said Liaze. "Alain calls him a charlatan, and Camille says Lord Kelmot—the Lynx Rider—calls him a mountebank."

"But he's all we have," said Zoé.

"I would rather travel to the Summerwood and ask the Lady of the Mere, or on beyond to the Lady of the Bower," said Liaze.

Zoé nodded and said, "They helped Camille."

"Ere we make any rash decisions," said Zacharie, "let us see what the daylight brings. There might be something we find that points us the right way."

Liaze took a deep breath and slowly let it out. "You are right, Zacharie. Let us wait until daylight."

Zacharie bowed, as did Rémy, and they withdrew. Zoé lingered and asked, "Would you like me to stay with you, Princess?"

"Non, Zoé. I'd rather be alone."

"Then I'll just close this," said Zoé. She stepped to the window and latched the shutters, then drew up the sash and locked the frame into place. She pulled the drapes to, then curtseyed and said good-night and slipped from the room.

When she was gone, Liaze threw herself onto the bed and released her pent-up grief.

14

Riddles

Weeping off and on, Liaze did not sleep the remainder of that night, and just ere first light she arose and donned her leathers, wincing a bit from the darkening bruise on her breast. She strapped on a long-knife. She took up her bow and quiver of arrows and started for the door, but turned and stepped back and retrieved Luc's silver horn. Then she went into the hallway beyond.

"My lady," said Didier, one of the wards at the door. Patrice, the other guard, bobbed his head. "Zacharie says we are to accompany you, wherever you go."

"Non," said the princess. "I need to be alone to think."

"We can stand off a good distance," said Patrice.

Liaze sighed. "Very well, but at a good distance: I want no distractions."

"How far, my lady?" said Didier.

"A hundred paces or more."

"A hundred paces? But my lady—"

Liaze lifted the silver horn. "At need I will call."

The warders looked at one another, and reluctantly agreed, and Patrice said, "As you wish, Princess."

Down the stairs they went, and the manor was silent, and those whose duties began this early were creeping about, despair on their faces, as if they were in mourning. And as the princess went by, some opened their mouths as if to speak, but they knew not what to say, while others simply curtseyed and lowered their gazes and hurried away on their errands.

Out from the manor Liaze went with her two guards, and she strode across the lawn toward the willow grove, the early light of dawn just barely in the skies.

As they reached the golden leaves and drooping branches, Liaze said, "Wait here."

Didier raised his hands in protest. "But my lady, we will not be able to see—"

"I will be within a hundred paces, or thereabout, and I have the horn," said Liaze, cutting off his objection. "I need to be alone, and the pool with its welling water is soothing unto me."

Again the guards looked at one another, and Patrice said, "As you will, Princess."

"But please, my lady," said Didier, "keep the horn at hand, always within reach."

"I will," said Liaze, then she turned on her heel and walked in among the golden leaves, soon to be lost to sight.

With willow branches swaying behind her, Liaze came to the glade, and in the light of dawn she saw a crone at the water's edge, weeping.

A witch!

Liaze raised the horn, preparing to blow, but then she hesitated.

Wait! It is said witches are unable to weep ought but falsely, shedding no tears whatsoever.

She scanned the crone's face, and real tears flowed down.

Loosening the keeper on her long-knife and nocking an arrow to string, Liaze stepped toward the side of the pool across from the crone.

As she took station on the flat rock opposite, the hag looked up and uttered a wail. "My shoe, my shoe," she cried, and pointed at the wooden sabot floating in the welling water. "Will you fetch my shoe?" And she wailed and buried her face in her hands.

Liaze looked over her shoulder and listened for racing footsteps.

The guards. They'll come running at the crone's keening.

But they did not.

The ugly, withered old woman looked up and again wailed. "My shoe, my shoe; please, oh please, fetch it."

Liaze frowned. *A hag who has lost her shoe: where have I heard that be—? —Borel!*

Her heart pounding with hope, Liaze slipped the arrow back into the quiver and stepped 'round to the rill flowing outward and waited. Soon the shoe came drifting toward the outlet and into the stream. She stooped and took up the sabot, its straps tattered, and part of the wooden sole missing. With her long-knife yet unfettered—just in case—she stepped across the rill and walked about the remainder of the pool to the crone and held out the wooden shoe.

"Why, thank you my dear," said the hag, smiling a single-toothed grin. "Would you slip it on my foot? I am old, and bending to do it myself causes a pain in my weary bones."

Liaze set aside her bow and knelt and slid the shoe onto the crone's knobby, dirty, and hammertoed foot.

And in the pale dawn light shining silver above and down into the glade, the hag transformed into a slender and beautiful woman, her eyes argent as was her hair. And from somewhere nearby there came the sound of an unseen loom.

"Lady Skuld," cried Liaze, and she threw herself into the woman's arms and wept as if her heart would break.

"There, there," said Skuld, holding Liaze close, and rubbing her back, and rocking her ever so gently.

"Luc, he's gone, snatched away by a witch," sobbed Liaze.

"I know. I know," said Skuld. "And on the happiest night of your life, until she and her shadow came."

Snuffling, Liaze drew back and looked with amber eyes into those of silver. "You know?"

"Indeed, child, I know."

Liaze got control of her breathing and wiped her nose on a sleeve of her leathers. "Of course you know, Lady Wyrd. You are the weaver of the future. Oh, Lady Skuld, I have always believed that I was strong, but here I am"—Liaze wiped her cheeks with both hands—"weeping like a lost child."

Skuld nodded and said, "It is good for one to know there are times one can lose all strength. It signifies one is only Human . . . or Elf . . . or of another race. Yet, heed, the force of your will must surely return if you do not give in to despair."

Liaze disengaged and said, "Lady Skuld, I throw myself upon your mercy."

"You threw yourself upon Fate, as well," said Skuld, smoothing out her dress.

A wan smile flickered at the corners of Liaze's mouth but then vanished. And she said, "Oh, Lady Wyrd, will you help me?"

"Perhaps, for I am bound by the Law: it requires a favor from you—which you have done. Then there comes a riddle from me, a riddle to be answered by you. If you accomplish that, then, lastly, I am permitted to give you a bit of guidance, perhaps obscure to you, but quite clear to me. It is the Way of the Three Sisters."

"I know the Law," said Liaze. "You helped Camille and then Borel, and all I ask is that you help me."

"Very well," said Skuld. "This then I pose."

Before Skuld could speak her riddle, Liaze said, "My Lady Skuld, ere you ask, I must warn you I know of the riddles you and your sisters put to Camille, as well as those put to Borel. I also know the riddle of the Sphinx."

Skuld canted her head in assent and said, "Indeed you do, Liaze. Yet the one I will put to you is none of those."

Liaze nodded, and then she scrambled to her knees and braced herself as if for a physical challenge. "I am ready."

Skuld took a deep breath and said:

> *I cry in alarm,*
> *I cry in delight,*
> *I speak of many things.*
> *I cry for arms,*
> *In the midst of a fight,*
> *Or in joy for what the day brings.*

> *I cry at the grave*
> *While others weep,*
> *And I cry when day is done.*
> *I cry for the brave*
> *Their vows to keep.*
> *And I cry at the rise of the sun.*
> *Name me.*

At first Liaze's heart sank, but then her eyes opened in revelation. "You are a trumpet, a bugle, a clarion," she said, and she raised Luc's silver horn.

"Quite right," said Skuld, smiling.

"Then, Lady Wyrd, obscure or plain, I would have guidance, please, for I would find my heart mate."

Skuld nodded and said:

In the long search for your lost true love
You surely must ride with Fear,
With Dread, with Death, with many Torn Souls,
Yet ride with no one from here.

For should you take a few with you,
Most Fear would likely slay.
Instead ride with the howling one
To aid you on the way.

He you will find along your quest.
He is the one who loudly cried.
He will help you defeat dread Fear,
But will not face Fear at your side.

You must soothe as you would a babe,
And speak not a loud word;
Silence is golden in some high halls;
Tread softly to not be heard.

In the dark of the moon but two moons from now
A scheme will be complete,
For on a black mountain an ever-slowing heart
Will surely cease to beat.

"Oh," cried Liaze at this last verse as Lady Skuld fell silent. "The dark of the moon two moons from now is all the time I have?" Liaze's eyes filled with tears.

Skuld sighed, then added, "I now remind you of something you already know: you will meet both perils and help along your trek, but beware and make certain you know which is which.

"And this I will add as well: take Deadly Nightshade with you; a bird shall point the way."

In that very moment beyond the willow grove the rim of the sun rose above the edge of the world, and Lady Skuld vanished along with the sound of the loom, leaving behind the song of the brook singing in the glade.

15

Outset

Liaze stepped from the willow grove, emerging at the point where Didier and Patrice waited.

"My lady," said Patrice, bowing, "we heard you coming, and— Oh, my, have you been weeping? —Ow!" He leaned down and rubbed his leg where Didier had kicked him.

"Yes, Patrice," said Liaze, "I wept some, but I did not wail as loudly as did the crone."

"Crone?" said Didier, jerking about to stare at the grove while reaching for the hilt of his sword.

"Did you not hear her?" asked Liaze.

Both Didier and Patrice shook their heads, and Patrice said, "All was silent, my lady."

Liaze looked down at the trump hanging at her side, and she wondered if it, too, would not have been heard had she sounded it while Lady Skuld was present in the glade.

"About this crone . . ." said Didier.

"It was Lady Skuld in disguise," said Liaze, now starting for the manor.

"Lady Wyrd?" blurted Patrice alongside. "Oh, but I am glad I didn't see her, for I would rather not know my fate."

"Patrice, you fool," said Didier, "she only comes at great need and not for just any piddling thing."

"Wull, how do you know I am not in great need?"

"It takes more than personal tragedy," said Didier. "Something greater has to hang in the balance."

At these words, Liaze stopped in her tracks. Didier and Patrice stuttered on a number of steps before stopping as well. Then they turned and started back, just as the princess strode onward. Reversing course again, they marched at her side.

Liaze said, "Exactly right, Didier. She would not have come unless something greater hung in the balance. Losing Luc, though an extreme blow to me, is but a personal tragedy. There is more to this than we know. Something critical in the scheme of things."

She picked up the pace and headed toward the forecourt lawn where a large group of men were gathered. "Come, I have to confer with my armsmaster and steward."

As the princess drew nigh she could hear Rémy call out, "All right, men, pair up. And remember, the slightest thing, no matter how insignificant it might seem, if it has even a remote chance of pointing toward the witch or the Goblin or ought else, send for Claude, for he is our best tracker. He will look at what you espied, and say whether or no it was of unnatural origin."

The men nodded and selected partners, and stepped to Zacharie to get their sector assignments.

"Didier, Patrice, join them," said Liaze.

"But, Princess, Zacharie told us to—"

"Never mind that. There are no Goblins in the manor, and whatever houseguard remains within will be more than enough to protect me."

"As you wish, Princess," said Patrice, bowing. Didier bowed too, and then they went to Zacharie.

Liaze paused a moment at Rémy's side. "I need to speak with you and Zacharie. When you are free, come find me."

"Where, Princess?"

"I'll be in the kitchen with Cook for some moments, breaking my fast, after which I'll be in the armory."

As Liaze entered the manse, Zoé leapt up from a bench in the reception hall. "Oh, Princess, I couldn't find you, and none knew where you went, though some of the staff said you had gone to the willow grove."

"You needn't have worried," said Liaze, "for I was protected by Didier and Patrice."

"That's what Zacharie said, and Rémy had men standing by, just in case."

Liaze sighed. "Zoé, I would have you find Eugéne and tell him to come to me in the armory."

As Rémy and Zacharie entered the armory, the princess was selecting arrows and placing them in two quivers: one to carry across her back, the other to hang from a saddle.

"My lady," said Zacharie. Then he looked at what she was doing and lifted an eyebrow in query, but she did not respond.

Eugéne strode in, the stable master puffing a bit, as if he had run most of the way. "Princess, you wished to see me?"

"Oui, Eugéne." Her gaze swept across the three men. "I will be going on a long journey, and, Eugéne, I would have you make ready supplies for me and Pied Agile and Deadly Nightshade— grain for them, food for me, cooking and camping gear, and the like. I suspect I'll need three or four packhorses to bear it all."

"Mares or geldings," said Eugéne, "else the chevalier's horse is likely to run any pack animals off."

"My lady," said Zacharie, "where is it you plan to go? To a seer?"

"Non, Zacharie. I am going after Luc."

"Oh, Princess," protested Zacharie, but Rémy interrupted

and said, "When we find something to show the way, there'll be no need for you to ride after Luc, for my warband and I will—"

"Non, Rémy, Zacharie," said Liaze. "I must go alone."

"*Alone?*" burst out Rémy and Zacharie and Eugéne together, and all began raising objections, each trying to be heard above the others.

Liaze pushed out a hand for silence, and when it fell, she said, "Lady Skuld was at the willow pool at dawn, and this is what she said. . . ."

". . . And lastly, she told me a bird would point the way."

As she fell silent, Rémy ran a hand through his red hair. "I know not what Skuld meant when she said you must ride with fear and dread and death and torn souls, except, perhaps, she might be telling you to go with caution; nor do I know why fear would kill any who accompany you, for we are stalwart and true, and have faced Goblins and Trolls without blenching; nor do I know who this 'howling one' might be, other than some Wolf or Dog; I do understand about treading softly, for that's only prudence, but I know not where a black mountain lies; and as to a bird pointing the way, what bird? Princess, each of those things either I know or know not, yet of this I am certain: for you to go alone is folly, and my warband and I should ride with—"

"Do you argue with Lady Wyrd?" asked Liaze, looking first at Rémy, then Zacharie, and finally Eugéne.

Eugéne looked away, and Zacharie sighed, and Rémy, tears of frustration in his eyes, shook his head. And Zacharie said, "When do you plan on leaving?"

Liaze turned up her hands. "Soon, Zacharie, soon. Tomorrow or the next at the very latest, for the dark of the moon two moons from now rides a course that cannot be stayed."

Rémy frowned and said, "My lady, I now ask you a question you once asked me: since we know not whence the witch did fly, which way would you go?"

"I don't know, Armsmaster. I don't know. I simply must trust to Fate."

In that moment a footman entered—a young lad, Cook's son. He bowed and said, "My lady, the funeral pyres are set."

For a moment Liaze frowned in puzzlement, but then her visage cleared. *Ah, me, I had forgotten—Adrien and Paul—the two who were crushed by the witch's terrible shadow.*

"Thank you, Gaston," she said. "We will be there shortly."

As the lad bowed and left, Liaze turned to Zacharie. "After the funeral, have the entire staff—searchers included—gather in the welcoming hall. We shall see if any know of a black mountain, or the one who howls, or of ought else in Lady Skuld's rede."

Even as the pyres were burning and many wept in grief, Jean, the falconer, stepped to Liaze's side and said, "My lady, one of the peregrines comes . . . from the Summerwood by the course of his flight."

Liaze looked up in the direction Jean pointed, and the grey-and-white raptor came winging in swift and true.

Liaze sighed. *I had completely forgotten we flew them yestermorn, bearing news of my betrothal to Luc.* She turned to Jean and said, "Bring the message to the welcoming hall."

Jean nodded and set out for the falcon mews.

There was an uproar in the welcoming hall, shouts of protest and cries of alarm.

You can't go away alone, Princess!

Take the warband!

Oh, my lady, please stay.

'Tis much too perilous, Princess Liaze. . . .

Liaze let the clamor run its course, and then she raised her hands for silence. When it came, she quietly said, "It is the only way, for I would not go against Lady Skuld's words." She looked at Didier standing nearby and added, "As I was reminded, there is much more at stake than a personal tragedy, else Lady Wyrd would not have come. I *must* go."

A murmur swirled among the staff, some nodding, others wiping away tears, yet all seemed to agree that an appearance by Lady Skuld could not be ignored.

Liaze cleared her throat, and a hush fell once again. "Do any of you know of a black mountain, or of one who howls, or can any shed light upon any part of Skuld's rede? If so, speak now."

Men and women looked at one another and shrugged or shook their heads. Finally Liaze said, "If you think of ought, then find me."

After the members of the staff returned to their duties, and the searchers to their task, Liaze read the message from the Summerwood. Tears welled in the princess's eyes, for the tissue-thin note was full of joy, Alain and Camille congratulating Liaze and Luc on their betrothal.

"Zacharie."

"Yes, my lady?"

"Send messages to each of the manors and to my père and mère, and tell them what has passed."

"Yes, my lady."

Throughout the day, Eugéne, Zacharie, Rémy, and Liaze decided what to take on a long journey. They were interrupted several times by members of the staff, each one bringing some speculation or other to the princess's attention. But they shed no more light upon Skuld's words.

And as the sun slipped across the sky, messenger falcons arrived bearing congratulations: from Celeste in the Springwood; from Arnot, steward of the Winterwood; and from King Valeray and Queen Saissa. In addition to Valeray and Saissa's felicitations, they added that they knew nothing of a child abandoned in the woods, nor of a foundling raised by an armsmaster named Léon.

With each of these received messages, tears ran down Liaze's face, while those with her looked the other way and waited.

During the day as well, the manor remained silent, people yet creeping about, desolation on their faces, for two men were dead, and Luc was gone, and the princess was going away. Only Martine seemed unaffected by the loss of Luc, and she came unto Liaze and said, "We make our own fate, Princess—not some *Skuld* person. There is no need to leave the manor on a perilous quest simply because of the word of this—this Lady Wyrd. Besides, for you to go off alone to search for nought but a common hedge knight is foolish in the extreme."

Rage flared in Liaze's eyes and she snapped, "Tutrice, one more such statement and I will banish you forever from the Forests of the Seasons."

Martine quailed and fell to her knees. "Oh, my lady, forgive me. Forgive me."

Liaze stood rigid with anger, and Martine rose to her feet and dipped a humble curtsey and meekly crept away.

Dusk found Liaze and Zacharie and Rémy and Eugéne in the stable, having just finished the planning for her trek: Liaze would need four packhorses in addition to her own mount and Luc's. And as they looked over the animals, Didier came running in. "My lady," he called, and bobbed a short bow, and said, "in the search Patrice and I found a Goblin campsite, well used, though we could only see a single set of footprints, as if a lone Goblin occupied it. Patrice is yet there, warding the place. The campsite has a crow cote, we think for messenger crows, and but one is left. Shall we kill it?"

Even as Rémy started to nod, Liaze cried, "No!"

"No?" said Zacharie.

"No," affirmed Liaze. "A bird shall point the way."

"The riddle, the rede, Lady Skuld's words!" exclaimed Rémy.

"Indeed," said Liaze. "Surely the Goblin sent messages to the witch. He must have informed her that Luc had escaped the Troll and Goblin party, and this Goblin kept watch on him."

"Oh, my," said Eugéne, "perhaps it was that same Goblin that caused the horses, especially Nightshade, to raise a ruckus that first night Luc came." Eugéne looked at Zacharie. "You recall, Steward, it was just before we searched Luc's goods to see who he might be." Eugéne frowned and added, "And they were disturbed again last night, when the shadow came. Probably the Goblin again."

"Perhaps it was the same one we slew climbing the wall," said Zacharie.

Rémy turned to Didier. "Find Claude and see if he can tell if more than one Goblin occupied that camp you and Patrice found."

"Didier," said Liaze, "find Jean, too, and have him care for the crow and feed it well, for it will point the way to the witch's abode, and perhaps to Luc."

As Didier raced away, Eugéne growled, "Goblins."

Rémy looked at Liaze and said, "I told you there were more out there."

"Indeed you did," said Liaze. "Still, it will not stop me from hewing to Lady Skuld's words."

She paused a moment, then said, "Rémy, I would have you and your warband search throughout the entirety of the Autumnwood. Mayhap there are other Goblin dens in the demesne, Troll holes too."

"A difficult task, that, my lady," said Rémy, a pensive look on his face, "for the Autumnwood is wide, and Goblins could be anywhere within." He took a deep breath and let it out. "Nevertheless, where there is one Goblin, there is likely to be more. We will find a way."

Liaze wrinkled her brow in thought and then said, "The wee ones can aid you in this. Go to Lord Chaûn of the Lynx Riders.

Have him and his folk ask the Sprites and other Fey throughout the Wood to bring word of any Redcaps or Ogres or Trolls within the realm. Tell him it is my wish."

Rémy's face brightened. "Yes, my lady."

Liaze looked at Eugéne and said, "Tomorrow at dawn, saddle Nightshade and lade Luc's errantry gear thereon. Saddle Pied Agile as well, and lade on my gear. And fit the packhorses with the supplies we discussed. When all is ready, we will release the crow, and I will ride the direction it flies. —Oh, and Zacharie, make certain that the message capsule the crow bears is open and empty, as if whatever message it might have held has been lost."

"My lady?" said Zacharie.

"Zacharie, we do not want the witch to know that someone is on the way, perhaps following her crow. Instead let her believe that one of her minions elsewhere sent the bird, or that this one simply escaped."

"Princess," said Rémy, "how can you follow a messenger bird—crow or otherwise? I mean, once they take flight, they are gone, and no horse can keep pace with them."

"Lady Skuld only promised that a bird would point the way, Armsmaster. I merely intend to ride in the direction of its flight."

"You will not be able to hew to its exact course, my lady," said Zacharie.

"If I stray to one side or the other of its line, well, I can only trust in Lady Skuld's words and fare more or less on the bearing the bird takes."

"My lady," said Eugéne, "are you certain you want to do this thing—riding out alone on a quest and into the teeth of who knows what perils?"

"Eugéne, as I said before, I would not argue with Fate."

Rémy started to say something, then shut his mouth with a *click!* of teeth.

*　　*　　*

The next morning, just after dawn, Liaze sat upon Pied Agile, with Nightshade tethered behind, and four gelding packhorses tethered after. Most of the staff was on hand, and many wept, especially Zoé, and even Martine shed tears. Rémy and the warband stood at attention nearby, a pained look upon the armsmaster's face. And Zacharie and the houseguard stood in ranks opposite, the steward with tears in his eyes.

Liaze looked down at Jean; the crow from the lone Goblin's campsite sat hooded on the falconer's wrist, an upside-down uncapped message capsule upon the bird's left leg, as if a missive had been lost along with the absent cap.

"Remember, Jean, Zacharie," said Liaze, "let not the falcons fly until the crow is long gone."

"Oui, my lady," replied Jean.

The princess's gaze swept across the assembly, and with a confidence she did not feel, she said, "My friends, keep well and do not weep, for just as I place my trust in the words of Lady Skuld, so should you. Luc and I shall soon return."

A feeble cheer rose from the staff, yet not enough to override the weeping.

"Now, Jean," said Liaze, "release the bird."

Jean removed the hood from the crow, and the bird looked about and ruffled its feathers. Jean loosened his hold and cast the dark messenger into the air.

Up it flew and circled about as if taking a bearing, and then it shot off and over the trees, and Liaze watched the line of its flight through the chill autumn air for as long as it could be seen.

"Rémy, it looks to be heading along Luc's track when he rode knight-errantry into the Autumnwood, but going in the direction whence Luc came," Liaze said.

"Yes, Princess," the armsmaster replied. "But as we said last night, keeping on the exact course of a messenger bird cannot be done."

"Nevertheless, I go, and, should I come out somewhere else altogether, Lady Skuld said I would find help along the way."

Liaze took a deep breath and waved to those gathered on the lawn and called out *"Au revoir! For we shall meet again!"* She then heeled her horse in the flanks and rode across the lawn and into the woods, towing the other animals after.

Behind her the weeping intensified, though both the warband and the houseguard managed a respectable cheer. And as the princess vanished among the trees, Zoé turned to Rémy and said, "Oh, Rémy, where is she bound?"

"Sunwise, Zoé," said Rémy. "She rides for the sunwise marge of the Autumnwood, for that's the way the crow flew. Beyond that, only time and the Fates will tell."

16

Wing-to-Wing

Into the greens and reds and golds and umbers and russets and browns of the Autumnwood rode Liaze: into the embrace of yew and cedar and pine, and of oak and maple and elm, and of cherry and apple and other such trees, all of them readying themselves for a slumber that never comes; into the fragrance of fruits and grains and berries and other ripened harvest everlasting she went, as well as into the bouquet of autumnal blossoms abloom in the sweet loam. Liaze did not look back toward the manor at the members of the staff calling out their good-byes, for to do so would reveal her tears and belie the face of courage she wore. And so, towing a stallion and four gelding packhorses, on she rode, deeper into the woodland, until she could no longer hear the sounds of weeping and farewell.

At last Liaze wiped away the tears on her cheeks, and after a moment she found her voice and reached forward and patted her mount's neck. "Where will we end up, Pied Agile, eh? Somewhere on the far side of the daystar, I think. May our goal not be too distant, for time is short, and a black mountain I must find, or so Skuld's rede would have it be:

> *In the dark of the moon but two moons from now*
> *A scheme will be complete,*
> *For on a black mountain an ever-slowing heart*
> *Will surely cease to beat.*

"It must be Luc's heart she speaks of, or so it is I deem. . . .

"So it is I fear. . . .

"And we have but this day and fifty-six more ere the dark of the moon two moons from now falls due. Why is it time has so little meaning in Faery except when peril is involved?

"Oh, Agile, I feel the need to gallop! —But where? Along the course a crow did fly is the only thing I know. And even then, I cannot be certain I will hew to its line. And with the twilight boundaries being what they are, an error one way or the other could put me in a realm remote from where I should go."

As she rode onward, in the trees of the surround and down among the grasses and undergrowth, furtive movement and rustlings kept pace with her progress. And from the corners of her eyes, Liaze could now and then catch glimpses of wee folk trotting alongside or riding small animals or flitting among the branches of the leafy overhead.

Of a sudden, Liaze slapped a palm to her brow. "Ahhh! How stupid of me!" Yet faring at an amiable gait, she looked up into a tree, and called out, "Be there any Sprites among you?"

Moments later, one of the tiny, iridescent-winged creatures flew down and managed to stay hovering in front of Liaze, even though the princess was yet moving forward, the wee being drifting backwards to match her pace. Liaze could see the Sprite was a female, for, as with all of her Kind—male and female alike—she wore no garments whatsoever. Flaming red hair this tiny Sprite had, and she held a strung bow in hand, and a miniscule quiver of arrows was strapped to her thigh.

"Yes, Princess?"

"Ah, good," said Liaze. "You know me."

The Sprite cocked her head and asked, "Doesn't everyone?"

Liaze laughed and the Sprite giggled in return. "And your name, little one?" asked Liaze.

"Feuille, my lady."

"Ah me, Feuille, I was so stupid this morning—"

A look of shock briefly registered on the face of the hovering Sprite. "My lady, I know not what to say. How could you possibly be, um . . ."

"Stupid," said Liaze.

"Your word, not mine," said Feuille, even so, she grinned.

Liaze gestured to her forebow. "Alight, Feuille, and I'll tell you why I am so stupid."

The just-under-two-inch-tall Sprite settled on the very tip of the high-arched saddlebow, and Liaze said, "This morning I set loose a messenger bird, one I meant to follow: a crow."

"*A corvus?*" Feuille leapt into the air, her wings beating frantically. "That was *your* crow with the message capsule? Oh, Princess, why did you—?"

"Shush, tiny one, and settle down," said Liaze. "It was not *my* crow, but rather one that belongs to a witch, a witch, I add, who has done me great harm, and one who might do the world great harm as well."

Somewhat reluctantly, Feuille lit once more on the forebow. "Crows are our deadly enemies, Princess. Why, if they get a chance, they'll take Sprites right out of the air or from nests or perches and swallow them whole. Why do you think I have this bow, these arrows? Crows, that's why. The whole of Autumnwood Spritedom has been on alert these last several days, for there have been entirely too many of those black killers flying above your demesne."

"Ah, good!" exclaimed Liaze.

Again, Feuille's face registered shock. "Good? You think that's good?"

"Oh, not that crows fly over the Autumnwood, Feuille. Rather that the entirety of Spritedom is alert for them. You see, I need to follow the line of those messengers, and if the Sprites know the birds' course, that will be an immense help to me in running down their mistress."

"Oh, well, that's different, my lady," said Feuille, relaxing. "Why didn't you say so in the first place?"

"Well, that's why I was so stupid," said Liaze, "for, in hindsight, before releasing the witch's bird I should have thought to ask the Sprites of Autumnwood to follow the crow and let me know whence it flew."

"Hindsight you say, my lady? Well in hindsight many things are, um, er . . ."

"Stupid," said Liaze, smiling. "Still, I am so glad I met you, Feuille, for Lady Skuld said—"

"*Lady Skuld?*" blurted Feuille, nearly taking to flight. But at a small calming gesture from Liaze the Sprite took a deep breath for one of her size and let it out and managed to settle.

"You met Lady Wyrd herself?" Feuille took another deep breath. "Oh, my, something hazardous must be on the wing."

"Indeed, Feuille, though I know not what it might be. Regardless, she told me that I would meet both perils and help along my trek, but that I should beware and make certain I know which is which. And you, Feuille, and the rest of Spritedom, are surely an aid."

"You are our liege, Princess. Of course we will aid."

"Then about these crows . . ."

"My lady, most have been flying in the direction you follow. I will dart ahead and speak with other Sprites and determine the line and thereby I'll keep you on course."

"Oh, no, Feuille, for I cannot have you accompany me more than but a short way."

"Princess, why not? I am certain that I can be of help."

"Oh, you most assuredly could, yet let me tell you of Lady Skuld's rede. . . ."

"Hmm . . ." mused Feuille. And then she chanted:
For should you take a few with you,
Most Fear would likely slay.
Instead ride with the howling one
To aid you on the way.
Feuille frowned in puzzlement. "What does that mean?"

"I think I'll not know until I meet the so-called howling one," said Liaze.

"Well, I propose that I wing ahead and find the next Sprite who watched the flight of the crows, and then that one can fly onward to the next and so on, and altogether, we Sprites can, um . . ." Feuille cast about for the right word.

"Hand me from Sprite to Sprite along the line," suggested Liaze. "I believe it is called a relay."

"Ah, yes," said Feuille, "a relay. And that is exactly what we'll do: pass you from wing to wing to keep you on the course of the witch's messenger."

"Let us hope such a plan will keep you and the others out of Fear's way," said Liaze.

"I am not certain that Fear would do any of us in," said the Sprite. "Nevertheless, we will not go against Lady Wyrd's rede."

Feuille took to wing and hovered a moment in the air and said, "As you ride on, I will go ahead and locate the next Sprite who watched the crows over these past few days. Then we will find you farther along, Princess, and there I'll hand you off to whoever it is that will fly the next leg."

"This is Brindille," said Feuille. "She has sent her mate, Rameau, ahead to find the next guide. But she will keep you on the line until you meet up with him."

"*Merci*, Feuille," said Liaze, humbly.

"May your quest bear sweet nectar, my lady," said Feuille, and she flew up and darted back in the direction whence she had first come.

"Au revoir, Feuille, tiny guide," Liaze called after the winging Sprite, but she had disappeared among the foliage from which she had taken her name. Liaze then turned to Brindille, and that female Sprite said, "After me, my lady," and off she flew.

Throughout the morning a succession of Sprites led the way toward the sunwise border of the Autumnwood, and as Liaze rode, other wee ones followed along in the underbrush or scampered among the branches above.

Liaze stopped several times to let the horses take water at running streams, and she also fed them each a bit of grain from the goods stored in the packs.

And the sun rode up in the sky and across, and Liaze herself paused for a meal as the golden orb reached the zenith, the princess sharing her repast with Arbuste, who only took a few crumbs from one of her biscuits, though he did enjoy a spot of honey from the drop she dripped into the jar lid.

As the sun slid down the sky, onward she fared, now with Buton her guide, and then Pomme, and then others; and she crossed a long stretch of open land with Fleur, a Field Sprite, her escort.

Dusk found her in the forest again, where she made camp and unladed the packhorses and unsaddled Nightshade and Pied Agile and rubbed all six of the animals down, curried away the knots of hair, and fed and watered them. Liaze then took a short meal herself, and a long drink of water. She fell asleep the moment her head touched the bedroll beside the small fire.

The next day, the first escorting Sprite—Cerise—told her that waiting Sprites now went all the way to the twilight border of her realm, and tears welled in Liaze's eyes and she could not speak for a while. But at last she managed a whispered *"Merci beaucoup,* Cerise."

For two more days did Liaze ride along the line of the Sprites, once faring through a shallow fen, guided by a Marsh Sprite who kept her and the horses to solid land. It was at the edge of a birch thicket on the far shore of the bog that she met a Ghillie Dhu—Breoghan, his name—the small, knobby man dressed all in twigs and leaves such that he seemed part of the copse itself, and who traded mushrooms for a biscuit or two and had lunch with his sovereign. They spoke of a limited number of things, mostly that which the Ghillie Dhu encountered within his section of the woods: newts and beetles and the loam of the forest, and how the moles seemed to improve the soil, loosening it as they did, though at the temporary loss of rootstock as well as a diminishment of earthworms. Breoghan pointed out that even though some folk considered the moles to be miserable pests, these tunneling creatures—with the help of field voles—also ate a terrible kind of predatory flatworm, all to the good of the woodland.

Liaze rode on afterward, a succession of Sprites yet showing the way. And on the fourth morning after she had set out from Autumnwood Manor, the sole remaining guide, a Field Sprite named Pétale, finally brought her to the twilight border rearing up into the sky along the sunwise marge of the Autumnwood.

"My lady," he said, "this is the last we saw of the murdering crows. Their flight went straight on, through the border and toward the mountains beyond."

Liaze's eyes flew wide with hope. "Mountains? Is there a black one among them?"

"No, Princess, just— Here, let me show you."

Pétale flew into the crepuscular wall, Liaze riding after. Into shade she fared, the way getting dimmer with every step, and then lighter again, and when she emerged she came unto a wide and barren dark plain, and in the distance a somber gray wall of mountains reared up toward the sky.

A frigid wind blew thwartwise, and Liaze pulled her cloak tightly about and gazed afar at the distant grim chain. "Is there a way through that formidable barrier?" she asked.

"I-I d-don't know, m-my lady," said the tiny Sprite, his arms wrapped about himself as he shivered uncontrollably, his wings but a blur as he held his place in the blow. "I have n-never flown y-yon. But this ch-ch-chevalier you spoke of, if he came opposite the l-line of the crows then perhaps he r-rode across the r-range."

Liaze now looked at the Sprite and said, "Oh, Pétale, I am sorry. I didn't see you were suffering." She opened her cloak. "Come. Seek warmth out of this gale."

As Pétale took shelter within, he said, "Here a c-cold wind b-blows all the time. We Sprites shun this place. But farther away along your own sunwise border, my lady, there are much better realms."

"Yet this is the way the crows came?"

"Indeed," said the Sprite.

"Which way did they fly then?" asked Liaze.

"Well, I did not follow them through the border to see, but if the birds kept to the same line as is likely with such messengers— crows or not—I imagine that double-fanged peak yon was along the course."

"Then, Pétale, I thank you for your guidance."

"I would go with you, Princess."

Liaze shook her head. "Non, tiny one. I would not risk your life, for Lady Skuld said I must go alone, but for the howling one."

"I could howl," said the Sprite.

Liaze laughed but said, "I think that is not what Lady Wyrd meant."

Pétale gave a tiny sigh and said, "I suppose you are right, Princess. And so, I will not delay you longer, for your mission is urgent." He slipped out from Liaze's cloak and took to wing. "Safe journey, my lady, and may you find that which you seek."

"Au revoir, Pétale. And again convey my thanks to the Autumnwood Sprites, for without them I surely would have strayed off course, and even a few paces to the left or right might have put me in another realm altogether, rather than this bleak demesne."

His teeth chattering, his wings whirring to offset the gusting wind, still Pétale managed a laugh and said, "I would n-not have th-thought anyone would have b-been glad to come unto this p-place." Then, with a salute, he shot away, back into the twilight border, seeking the warmth of the Autumnwood beyond.

Liaze pulled her cloak tightly about against the harsh flow and heeled Pied Agile in the flanks, and, towing five horses after, into the dark plain she rode.

17

Pocks

Into bleakness fared Liaze, the princess aiming at the twin fangs in the mountain chain to the fore, for it was all she had as a goal, and even that was but a guess. Pétale the Sprite had said that if the messenger crows held to the same line of flight as they had in the Autumnwood, then these two jagged crests were along that route.

And the chill wind blew, buffeting Liaze and the horses, agitating them all. For the most part the animals plodded along with their heads low and their ears laid back, as if seeking somehow to get out of the wind but failing. And now and again Nightshade would snap at one of the geldings; and they would temporarily shy away, but then return to plod side by side with the stallion, as if all sought warmth from one another.

What a dreadful domain! Inhospitable dirt and sparse—rare I would say—patches of weed; and its growth is misshapen, warped as if the wind always blows. And so far, no streams, no pools, no water at all, just a bleak gray realm running up to the fangs of dark mountains. Oh, Mithras, of all the splendid lands along my sunwise border, why did the crows have to pick this one? 'Tis a place I've ne'er before seen, hence the way through the shadowlight border from my realm to this one must be somewhat narrow. 'Tis well I had the Sprites to lead the way, else I would likely have missed this land altogether—ha!—as if one could ever hope to enter such a drab demesne.

Throughout the day she rode, occasionally stopping in the lee of a hillock, or down in a dent in the land, where she would give the animals grain—food to help keep them warm. And when she did so, all the horses would huddle together, their tails to the wind, their heads low. And though Nightshade was a well-trained steed, still he was a stallion, and he took a nip at Liaze, and she slapped him on the nose and barked "No!"

She did not worry overmuch about the animals getting cold, for, living in the Autumnwood as they had, with its chill nights and cool days, they had a fair bit of shag, the start of a winter coat, though it would never become full-blown in that realm.

And as for water, fortunately Liaze that morning had filled all the skins to the stoppers, and she meted out shares to the steeds.

After these pauses, Liaze would ride onward, and she came to hate the ceaseless wind. And the mountains seemed no closer when day came toward the end.

She found shelter in the lee of a hill, and there she unladed the horses and tethered them to thin weeds—knowing they would not hold in the event of something unexpected. Then she fed them some grain and thoroughly rubbed them down and curried out the knots, and, even though the horses clustered together for warmth, as an extra precaution Liaze covered each with a blanket against the night chill.

She had no fire that eve, for there was nought to burn, and, after she ate a cold meal of hardtack and jerky, she rolled up in her own blanket and spent a miserable night, and was certain that she would never get to sleep.

Yet in the morning . . .

*　　*　　*

. . . she awakened with her cheek to the ground. Liaze groaned, for the wind yet blew, and she did not immediately rise. And as she lay, in the low-angled sunlight aglance across the land, she saw in the wintry soil—*What are these? They look like . . . hmm . . . pockmarks?*

With her blanket wrapped 'round her shoulders, Liaze rose and stepped to the first of the impressions, then lay down once more to see—*A line of them, along the lee edge of the hill. Just dimples, more or less, running toward the mountains, getting shallower and disappearing once they leave the windbreak.*

Liaze rolled over and looked the opposite way. *Hmm . . . They continue toward, or perhaps come from, the way I rode. Yet they were not made by me.*

Now the princess studied the mark nearest her. It was nought but a shallow depression. Liaze pressed her hand into the dent; the spread of her fingers did not quite cover the pock. She frowned. *Could this be a hoofprint? If so, it is quite eroded by the wind.* Once again she lay down and sighted along the line of the impressions; she rose up slightly and looked at the pattern. *It could be a horse at a trot.* Then Liaze's eyes widened in hope. *Oh, please, Mithras, let it be Luc's trail, for if the crows fly opposite the path he took when he rode from his woodcutter's cote and to the Autumnwood . . .*

Liaze did not finish that thought, for she leapt to her feet and rummaged through the supplies and fed the horses some grain and watered them. Then she ate a quick meal. After relieving herself, swiftly she stowed the blankets and laded the cargo on the packhorses and saddled Nightshade and Pied Agile.

Once more she lay down and looked along the line of marks. They headed in the general direction of the twin fangs.

She mounted her horse and rode toward the mountains, her eye upon the soil, and as she left the lee of the hill and fared into the buffeting flow, she could no longer see any dimples in the land.

If those pocks are the remains of hoofprints, and if the rider—oh, let it be Luc—rode as I do now, then he would have sought every windbreak he could find, and mayhap at those places there will be more marks I can use as a trail.

After a while Liaze saw in the distance ahead a dip in the land, and she angled Pied Agile toward it, for it would provide some proof against the constant blow.

At last she came to the dent, and she despaired, for it was too shallow to provide ought more than scant shelter. Nevertheless, she dismounted and stepped to the fore, then lay down and looked for a dimple. But the sunlight was no longer aglance upon the land, and if there were any depressions whatsoever, Liaze could find them not.

Sighing in disappointment, once again she mounted, and continued onward.

She rode some distance before veering rightward to come to the next windbreak—a sheltering knoll—where she found a very limited set of pockmarks, and they yet pointed toward the twin fangs.

Onward Liaze rode, and now and again in dips in the land and along the flanks of hills she managed to locate more marks, yet whether they were hoofprints or merely wind erosions of spinning air, she could not say. Even so, she continued on toward the twin pinnacles, presumably along the line of flight of the messenger crows, or so she sincerely did hope.

That night when she camped, the mountains seemed much closer. At this place she ran out of water, for she had to let the horses drink from the supply, and they drained it all. And in this land she had seen no streams nor pools, and—other than the scraggly weeds—no living things whatsoever: no birds, no beasts, nor any small creatures, and no insects, no reptiles . . . nothing.

And the wind yet blew and was like to drive the princess mad, and the animals were even more agitated, especially

Nightshade, who bit at the geldings more often, and tried several times to nip Liaze.

The princess spent another miserable, fireless, cold night.

In midafternoon of the next day, Liaze rode in among foothills, and—lo!—she came unto a stream. The horses eagerly pushed forward, yet Liaze held them back and dismounted and tethered them unto a twisted stalk. She stepped to the rill and stooped down and took up a handful of water and sniffed; it had a faint acrid smell. She cautiously tasted; it was slightly bitter.

'Tis nought worse than some other streams I've drunk from.

Nevertheless, she took a small swallow and waited. After a while, when nought untoward had disturbed her stomach, she knelt on hands and knees and quenched her thirst. Again she waited, and after another while, she led the horses to the water, and they drank deeply, while Liaze filled the waterskins to the stoppers.

Once more she looked for pockmarks, but she found none nearby. *If a rider and his steed took from this stream, it was elsewhere . . . or perhaps his marks have faded away.*

As Liaze fed the horses a bit of grain, she looked up at the mountains. The twin-spired peak lay straight ahead, yet there seemed no way through, certainly no way between them.

Taking her bow and quiver, and leaving the horses tethered and munching barley, Liaze trudged to the top of the hill at hand. She stood in the wind, her cloak pressed tightly against one side and flapping about on the other. She shaded her eyes and peered for a passable col. *Ah, that looks like a possibility.* She let her gaze slide along the range, where—*Oh, my, two of them: one to the left and one to the right, each with what seems a trail up and perhaps over, and yet in Faery taking the wrong one could lead to a place altogether elsewhere. One sinistral and one dextral; which, I wonder, is the correct choice?*

Her gaze followed the traces of the two paths down into the

foothills to the fore, where the knolls shielded the trailheads from her sight. *The ways seem to be coming together, mayhap even to join.*

Sighing, Liaze took a bearing on where she thought the routes might begin, and then she trudged back down to the horses below.

As dusk came upon this bleak land, Liaze made camp in a narrow canyon and well out of the wind. Just ahead, the canyon branched, one way leading up and to the right, the other unto the left.

That night she slept well, for only faint traces of the constant blow reached down into the rift.

The next morning, Liaze walked away from her campsite and took the cleft to the right. She searched for traces of what might have been a rider passing this way. The trail itself was fairly smooth, yet the well-packed pathway showed no sign of hoofprints: there were no dimples, no impressions, no pocks whatsoever.

Liaze returned to the split and walked the left-hand way. Here the trail was even more hard-packed, and stones littered the way, and Liaze despaired of finding—

Wait!

Liaze stooped and looked at one of the fist-sized rocks. Its color was darker than that of the stones nearby. She turned it over. *It's lighter on what was its down side.*

She turned over a nearby rock of nearly the same size. *And this one is darker on its bottom. Mayhap . . .*

Liaze continued onward, and she found several more stones that looked as if they had been turned over. *Perhaps the hooves of a horse kicked these loose as a rider rode this way.*

Liaze looked up the twisting path and beyond to the col on high and sighed. *Just my luck: he picked the harder way, and the sinister one at that.* Then she smiled. *Though if it were Luc on his way to the Autumnwood, going opposite would have been dextral for him.*

Liaze walked back to the animals and saddled Pied Agile and Deadly Nightshade and tied on their gear, and then she laded the packhorses with the goods. Mounting up, she said to the steeds, "Brace yourselves, *mes amis,* we've a long climb ahead."

Liaze heeled Pied Agile in the flanks, and up the canyon and into the left-hand slot she rode, the horses on tethers behind, all the animals calmer today—even the stallion—for they had spent a night out of the wind.

Up the twisting way they went, at times in the lee of the broad shoulders of the slopes, at other times exposed to the hurtling blow, which became fiercer the higher they went. And the climb was rugged and stony, the way quite difficult in places, especially at twisting turns, where the rocks seemed to have piled up in the corners.

At times, Liaze switched off from Pied Agile to Nightshade. At other times she walked and led the animals, the packhorses limiting the pace, for they were never relieved of their burdens, as were the stallion and mare.

Often, Liaze stopped to give them all a breather, and she watered them and fed them some grain—especially the pack animals—to keep up their flagging energy. And then she would continue.

As the sun neared the zenith, Liaze afoot entered a long slot leading to the crest of the col. "Ah, my friends, we are nearly over the top. But I think walking downslope will not be much easier, for making a long descent is almost as difficult as the opposite."

And out of the fierce wind, on upward toward the summit of the way they went. And just as they reached the crest—

The ground trembled, and there came a great loud grinding of stone on stone, and a massive slab slid out across the way, and rock clattered down the slope beyond, while at the same time, from arear there came another heavy grinding, and a rattle of stone cascading down the pathway behind.

Even as the horses skitted and shied, Liaze quickly set an arrow to string and looked about for the foe who had sprung this trap. Yet she saw none whatsoever, only two giant blocks barring the way, just as would immense stone gates. And then she gasped in surprise, for these weren't truly great rough slabs of granite, but had the look of giant hands.

And then to the right a huge stony eye opened in the massif, and, grating and rumbling like an enormous wedge of rock sliding on rock, a deep voice said, "Urrum, hmmm, another one disturbs." And a second eye opened in the mountainside.

18

Caillou

Her gaze scanning the precipitous rise, Liaze looked for the one who had spoken, yet the only things she saw were the two great stony eyes and, directly below them, a slender, deep crack running horizontally across the sheer rock for some six feet or so.

Even as she looked on, again came the grinding and gravelly voice, its words ponderous: "I have you now . . . and you will not pass as easily as the other one did."

Liaze's eyes narrowed, and she looked into the shadows of the cleft, for it seemed as if that were the place the voice had come from, yet she could see no one within—no tiny Sprite, no Twig Man, no one. *Is it possible that the mountain itself is—*

"What other one?" she asked.

There was a long pause, as if whoever the speaker was, he was mulling over his answer. At last came the reply: "The one with the stone."

Indeed, the voice is coming from that cleft.

Liaze relaxed her draw. "What stone?"

Another long pause, then, "The one he bore."

"Who is it you speak of?" asked Liaze.

There came a low grumble, like that of a distant slippage of heavy stones. It went on for a while, but finally, "I know not his name," came the slow reply, "but he had one of those things that you have six of. What do you call them?"

"Six things?" Liaze looked about.

The mountainside creaked, and a scatter of pebbles rattled down into the path. The great flinty eyes slowly turned somewhat leftward.

"There with you. About the size of minor boulders."

"Oh." Liaze waved at the animals. "The horses?

Another distant rumble sounded for a while. "That is as good name as any. He, too, had a black, um, horse . . . much like the one you have."

Liaze's heart jumped. "Did he wear a metal shirt and a metal cap and carry a metal horn like this one?" She held up Luc's silver trump.

Slowly, grinding, the eyes turned toward Liaze, the flinty gaze to at last come to rest upon her. "Yes. . . . It was but a short pebble cascade ago when he came across."

"Oh, Lord Montagne, it was my Luc," said Liaze. "It must have been when he was on his way to my realm . . . back whence I came. Did he recently return this way? Oh, I must find him, and I could use your help, Lord Montagne, if you have any to give."

As she waited for the answer, she returned her arrow to its quiver and her bow to its saddle sheath.

At length, the being said, "Many things spill out of you all at once, as if in avalanche. . . . Indeed. . . . Avalanche. . . ."

Liaze waited, and just as she feared there would be no answer to her questions, the stone being said, "Yes, he went down the way you came. . . . No, he has not yet come back this way."

At these words, Liaze's heart fell. Even so, she knew that only by wild chance would the witch in her flight have flown through this pass, dragging the shadowy hand after, Luc in its grip.

Again there came a rumble, and she realized that the mountain was yet responding to her questions. "Rrr . . . I have seen him but once, and though I tried, I could not stop him, for he bore the stone. . . . He passed through without giving me my due."

"He bore what stone?"

As if thought moved slowly through a being who seemed to be made of the mountain itself, again there was a long pause ere the creature answered. "A tiny bit of keystone." The eyes, grinding, slowly looked upward and then back down at Liaze. "It was the color of the sky."

Liaze frowned, then brightened and said, "The gem on a chain about his neck?"

"I asked if he was going to open the way, but he did not know what I was . . . speaking of, and I did not enlighten him."

"Open what way?" asked Liaze.

After long moments, the creature did not respond, and Liaze decided that he would not speak of it again, not tell her what he meant, just as he had not told Luc.

Finally she said, "I am Princess Liaze of the Autumnwood. Have you a name, Lord Montagne?"

Once more there was a long pause, but finally he responded: "I suppose you could call me . . . Caillou."

Liaze laughed, for in the old tongue, *caillou* meant *stone*. "Clever, Lord Montagne."

The gape on the cleft of a mouth widened, to the rattle of pebbles down into the path. As the last of these finally clattered away, "We are not dense, just solid," replied Caillou.

Again Liaze laughed, but then sobered. "Lord Caillou, I must needs move on, for I am on an urgent mission. Yet you have the way blocked. You speak of 'your due,' my lord. What bounty do you require to let me pass freely?"

Slowly the eyes closed and then opened again. "The thoughts

of my Kind are weighty . . . ponderous . . . deep . . . and they reach down to the very bottom of the foundation rock itself. . . . We like to assay burdensome problems . . . or mull over questions of considerable heft . . . things of sizeable gravity. . . . All I require is one of these . . . posers . . . issues . . . something I have not weighed before. . . . Propound to me one of those, and I will let you go."

Oh, my. Can I give him a deep enough riddle? An enigma to occupy him? One he has not considered? The riddle of the Sphinx? Surely he knows that one. Some of the riddles posed by the Fates? No, all of those were meant to be answered. Mayhap I can give him an unanswerable problem.

As she puzzled over what to try, she said, "What happened to the valley below?"

Caillou moaned from deep within, and the great stone eyes slowly ground leftward and down. As they came to look upon the plains, he said, "He destroyed it." A trickle of grit poured from the creature's eyes, and again he moaned, the sound so low as to be more felt than heard. And then Liaze realized he was weeping.

"Not the one with the metal shirt, surely," she said.

Now the eyes ground back toward her. "No . . . It was another one."

"How did he do it? Was it fire?"

Deeply he rumbled and then said, "Fire?"

"As from a firemountain, where red-hot, molten rock pours forth."

"Fire . . . Red tongues . . . Yes, I remember."

"Then it *was* fire."

The stone eyes slowly peered down at the path near where Liaze stood. "No . . . Not the red tongues . . . Instead it was him."

Liaze frowned and said, "Him?"

Another deep groan sounded, and what was perhaps Caillou's brow wrinkled, and stones clattered down. "He came with four others . . . all in black."

Liaze waited, and finally Caillou continued. "They . . . marked the path with soft blue stone—five mountains all joined at the roots—and he stood on a marked crest . . . and the others, each of them stood on separate crests as well. . . . Then he spoke in a language I do not know, and . . . the sky boiled with gray . . . and the wind blew and the gray swept down and covered the mountains and the valley . . . and all was gone . . . all plants . . . all animals . . . all birds. . . . Only stone and sand and barren dirt were left . . . and the wind has never stopped."

"Oh, my," said Liaze, horrified.

"The birds," groaned Caillou, "I miss their singing." Again grit tumbled from the great stone eyes.

Now tears spilled down Liaze's own cheeks, and she turned toward the barren plains below—barren but for sparse bushes of scrub here and there. *One and four others are responsible for the devastation. And all stood on the scribed peaks of five mountains joined at the base. Five—*

"Lord Caillou," blurted Liaze, "were four of these beings such as am I?"

Again a frown crossed Caillou's brow, and again a small shower of pebbles fell. "Such as you?"

"Yes, females like me."

The frown increased, and a tiny fracture split upward. "Females?"

"My Kind come in two types: male and female—*mâle et femelle; homme et femme.* Females have breasts for nursing their young." Liaze cupped her hands beneath her bosom. "Males do not have breasts, but they sometimes do have beards—hair growing on their faces, their chins." Liaze used her fingers, as if stroking a beard. "Were there four females who aided in this destruction of life, and was the fifth being a male?"

There came a deep rumble, and finally Calliou said, "Perhaps . . . Perhaps not . . . I do not know. . . ."

Liaze sighed and said, "Regardless, I think I know who did

this terrible thing: Hradian, Rhensibé, Iniquí, Nefasí, female witches all, and Orbane, a male wizard. Only he would be so wicked, and only they would aid him in this foul deed. They stood here on the points of a pentagram and took away all life from this realm."

"Um . . . not all life," said Caillou, "for I . . . yet live."

"Yes, you do, my friend. 'Tis good you're made of stone."

Caillou groaned and said, "They . . . need to be punished."

Liaze nodded. "Some have been," she said. "Rhensibé is dead, and Orbane is imprisoned beyond Faery. The others yet live freely, and I think that one of these sisters—Hradian, Iniquí, or Nefasí—is perhaps the witch who stole my Luc away. It is she whom I pursue, and her cote lies somewhere across this range."

"You . . . hunt one of the ones who . . . helped to slay the land?"

"If my suspicion is correct, then I do."

The ground trembled, and there came a great grinding of stone on stone, as Caillou withdrew his hands. Rocks clattered and rattled down the path to the fore and to the aft. "Then you may . . . pass, Princess Liaze."

"Thank you, Lord Montagne," said Liaze, as she stepped to the horses and settled them down, for they had skitted and shied when the path under their feet quivered a second time. "Even so, I will give you your due."

The stone above one eye lifted upward, and more rock tumbled down. "No need, Princess," said Caillou. "The fact that you pursue one of those who did such great harm is . . . enough."

"Nevertheless," said Liaze as she mounted Pied Agile, "here is a problem to ponder: how do you know that you are you? How do you know that you are not me, and I am simply dreaming of me being you and asking myself for a riddle to solve?"

The stone gap of a mouth turned up at the corners, and a rocky chuckle issued forth, sounding rather like a small avalanche. "A substantial puzzle and deep, concerning what is real and what is not, what is solid and what is not. . . . Merci, Liaze, for although my thoughts are . . . slow and dwelling, in the end I sometimes find gold in the ore. . . . And now you have given me a hefty problem to ponder. Voluminous it is, and I might be . . . eroded down to bedrock ere I can come to any bottom. 'Tis good, um, good. . . . I hope I can find the core. Now tumble off with you; gather no moss; be on your way; and may you succeed. As for me . . . thanks to you, I now have something to weigh. . . ."

"And my sincere thanks to you, Lord Montagne, for you have shown me that I am perhaps on the right track." Liaze grinned and gave Caillou a salute, and she heeled Pied Agile in the flanks, and down the far slope she started, while behind, amid a shower of pebbles, the great stone eyes and the horizontal rift of a mouth slowly ground shut, and, as he had said he would do, Caillou began to ponder.

19

Free Rein

Down the slant of the mountain rode Liaze. And as she did so, she looked about at the stone rises to the right and the steep drops to the fore and left.

Are these ramparts the flanks of Caillou? What kind of creature is he? Is he truly made of stone, as it seems? Surely he cannot be an entire living mountain . . . or can he? Think, Liaze, did you see where he might have left off and the mountain itself might have begun? No, you did not, and so the entire mass he might be. Liaze shook her head and laughed aloud and called out to the stark and windblown surround, "Ah, Faery, thanks to the gods that be, your wonders never cease."

And as she rode on down, she recalled an evening at Summerwood Manor, when she and Celeste and Camille had been preparing for Camille and Alain's wedding:

"When I was with Raseri—"

"Oh, Camille, that you survived that Drake is a wonder," said Celeste, catching her breath.

"I bore with me a good reference," replied Camille. "Besides, Raseri is quite the honorable being, in spite of his reputation."

"Do go on," said Celeste, her eyes wide in marvel.

"When I was with Raseri," said Camille, "it occurred to me that the Keltoi bards told such wonderful and gripping tales that the gods themselves became so intrigued they made Faery manifest. And all the wondrous people and places and creatures and things herein sprang from the stories spoken by those bards 'round campfires and in kingly halls and on the roads from here to there and in wayside inns, or wherever else they told such tales."

"Why would the gods do so?" asked Liaze. "—Make manifest the works of bards, I mean."

"For entertainment," said Celeste, smiling and nodding in agreement with Camille's posit. "The gods must revel in wonder and joy." Then she frowned and added, "But that would also mean Redcaps and Trolls and other such vile beings— mayhap even Orbane himself—came from the Keltoi tales, too." Celeste then looked from Camille to Liaze and said, "Why would the Keltoi tell of such terrible things, and then the gods bring them into existence?"

"You answered your own question, Celeste," said Liaze. "They did so for entertainment, for what is a story without challenge, without peril? Dull, I think."

Camille canted her head in assent. "I know that when I lived in the mortal world, Giles and I—and my sisters as well— would revel in the exciting tales told by my père, stories of deadly danger and grim events. Yet, now that I have actually lived through one, I see that what is exciting at a distance is quite dreadful up close."

The three sat in somber silence for a while, but then Liaze laughed, and when the others looked at her, she said, "I am put in mind of what Borel once said about adventures."

Camille raised a quizzical eyebrow, her question unspoken,

and Liaze said, "An adventure is someone else in dire straits a thousand leagues away."

And they all had laughed. . . .

As the princess rode down a mountain path with a stallion and four gelding packhorses in tow, she shook her head at the memory and heaved a great sigh. *Ah, me . . . now I am in an adventure of my own, and it is not a happy one. Oh, Mithras, let the goal be less than a thousand leagues away and the straits be not so dire.*

In the bleak distance far ahead, she could see a looming wall of twilight, the sunwise border of this barren demesne, perhaps a two-day journey from the foothills below. She stopped to feed the animals and to give them water, and as she took some jerky and hardtack, she looked for a landmark along the way upon which she could take a bearing to stay on what was presumably the course of the crows. But the way down had twisted and turned, and even when she sighted on the twin spires behind, she could not be certain of the exact line. Liaze sighed, for with but a slight angle away from the path, by the time she came to the twilight bound she could be leagues off track.

Her heart fell for she had no certain guide; and given the vagaries of the twilight borders, she could end up at some place altogether different from that o'er which the messenger birds had flown. *How can I possibly find the way the crows went? The only thing I know of their direction is that they seem to be flying back along the trace Luc rode when he came to the Autumnwood, for surely the witch had tracked him. Mayhap I can find some more pockmarks in the soil and follow those. If not, what then, Liaze?* She heaved a great sigh and shook her head and finally said to Pied Agile, "All we can do is trust to the Fates."

That eve, among the dwindling crags at the foot of the mountain and alongside a small runnel, she found meager shelter out of the constant chill wind, and there she made a fireless camp, for there was nought to burn, and just as she was going to sleep, she startled awake, knowing what she would do as a last resort if nought else presented itself.

After a restless night with little sleep, Liaze roused to a blowing, icy rain. Her groan matched the moan of the wind, and she got to her feet and fed and watered the animals, and then she saddled Pied Agile and Nightshade and laded the four pack-horses with the supplies. She covered the horses with their drenched blankets and tied them on, for they would give some protection from the driving rain. As she replenished the water-skins from the swift-flowing runnel, she looked out o'er the drab, grey plain, water pelting across the barren soil. *So much for seeking pockmarks, Liaze. Now we will have to trust to Nightshade, and if not to him, then to the Fates.*

Liaze tethered the geldings to her mare, and then the mare to the stallion. Mounting Nightshade, she said, "All right, my lad, they say every horse knows its own stall, so off with you, and please find the way." And, leaving the reins slack and riding without giving Nightshade any guidance whatsoever, she heeled the stallion in the flanks, and forward they went.

Through the icy blow they trotted, Liaze with her cloak tight around, her hood up, the tethered animals following, all of their breath steaming white in the cold rain.

All that miserable day they went thusly: Nightshade heading toward the distant shadowlight border, with Liaze stopping now and then to feed the animals some grain and to briefly take sustenance of her own. As for water, pools here and there sufficed, and so they were not without. And just ere the fall of night the rain slackened and then ceased altogether. Even so, the camp itself was sodden, and the blankets drenched, and the wind yet blew.

And there was no fire.

*   *   *

Aching and chilled to the bone and weary beyond telling, Liaze mounted Nightshade the next morn and once more she let the stallion choose the route, as out from the lee of the hill and back into the ceaseless blow they went.

"Nightshade, if for nought else but this maddening wind, Orbane deserves to die."

The stallion grunted.

Liaze laughed aloud and said, "Ah, me, my lad, this adventuring: some joy, eh?" Then she pulled her cloak closer in the damp, chill wind and hunkered down for the long ride.

It was midafternoon when they came unto a pitch of land falling away toward the twilight bound some three or so leagues hence. And Liaze gasped at the sight immediately below, for lying in the flat just beyond the foot of the long slope stood the ruin of a small hamlet.

She urged Nightshade down, the mare and geldings following. And as they came to the level and rode toward what had once been buildings, Liaze could see that something terrible had happened here: parts of stone walls yet stood, and stone chimneys, and rubble from collapse. Though thatch might have once covered the dwellings, of roofs there were none. Wood seemed absent, and here and there only foundations of houses remained. Grit sloped against the windward side of remnants of walls, and some were completely drifted over.

Nightshade, yet picking the route on his own, went down what must have been the main street of this village, and only sections of stark walls and tumbled wrack and windblown piles of bleak dirt watched their progress.

Oh, my, all things alive or once living are gone from this once fertile place. —Orbane! Bastard Orbane, this is your doing. You and your acolytes have much to answer for.

And Liaze rode on beyond the ruins and out into the barrens once more.

*   *   *

It was late in the day when they came unto the sunwise twilight marge, and Liaze reined Nightshade to a halt and looked at the looming wall of crepuscular glimmer. "I hope you have chosen aright, noble steed." Then she heeled the stallion, and forward they rode into the dimness, which turned darker the deeper they went and then lighter once more as they passed the ebon midpoint and began to emerge. And they came into low-angled afternoon sunlight and warmth and grass and trees, where but a slight waft of air softly caressed them all, and Liaze broke into tears.

That night, with the horses cropping sweet grass, Liaze slept in her only dry blanket on a bed of boughs beside a warm fire burning, with sodden cloak and clothing and the remaining blankets strung from ropes and drying in its radiance. Nearby a gentle brook flowed, its purl singing in the silvery light of a gibbous moon waxing against the stars above.

Nixies

Liaze awakened to the sound of distant shrieks. Feminine they seemed, as of demoiselles at play, or in peril. Liaze leapt to her feet and swiftly donned her undersilks and threw on her leathers. She pulled on her boots and strapped her long-knife to her thigh, and then strung her bow and slung a quiver of arrows across her back. She glanced at Luc's sword in its sheath, but shook her head, for she was not skilled in that blade. Briefly she thought of saddling Nightshade, but instead she nocked an arrow and set off afoot through the woodland, following the stream in the direction of the ongoing screams.

Scanning the surround as she went, but seeing nought of peril, Liaze slipped among the boles for a furlong or so, the shrieks growing louder with every step. And as she came within sight of the furor, the brook she followed joined a wide and deep flow, and where the tributary fed into the larger watercourse a broad pool slowly swirled 'neath ascending rock ledges against the far shore. And on the highest outcropping stood a slim, naked demoiselle, another one climbing up to reach her; and in the river nigh the foot of the drop swam several others. And with a shrill cry, the one on the ledge leapt outward, and, clutching her knees to her chest, she plunged down amidst the shrieking damsels below, a great gout of water exploding upward.

Liaze heaved a sigh of relief. *They are at play.* And she stepped out from the trees and onto the wide, grassy bank.

As the princess emerged from concealment, the climbing demoiselle's eyes widened in fright, and she screamed in dread and pointed across at Liaze, then dove for the pool, and *transformed!*

Even as the damsel clove the lucid water, and as the others spun 'round to see Liaze and flipped over and dove for the depths, the princess gasped in surprise: *Mithras! Did my eyes deceive me, or did she become part fish?*

Only swirls on the surface of the clear-running river answered her—a language she could not read.

Why did they flee?

Liaze frowned and looked down at herself, then laughed. *Ah, they think I am a warrior, coming armed as I did.* And she slipped the arrow into her quiver and slung her bow across her back. Then she stood on the shore and waited.

Long moments passed and long moments more, and finally a dark head briefly broke the surface and looked her way . . . then disappeared. Several heartbeats later another head bobbed up . . . and then down. Finally, one came to the surface and stayed long enough for Liaze to show open and empty hands.

The demoiselle's brow furrowed in puzzlement, and then she called out: "*Femme?*"

"*Oui!*" answered Liaze, and she sat down in the grass along the bank. *Mayhap they will think me less a threat this way.*

Briefly, the damsel submerged, and then reappeared with the others. Timidly they approached, and, as they did so, in the clear flow Liaze could see that each of these females had a diaphanous dorsal fin running down the length of her back and held erect by spines, and instead of legs each had a broad tail stroking; it was as if these people were half fish and half women. Yet one and then another of these beings transformed into two-legged demoiselles as they came to the shallows.

And the one who had called out stood and stepped to the bank and spoke in the old tongue: *"Qui êtes vous?"*

And Liaze smiled up at the dark-haired, small-breasted damsel and answered in kind: *"Liaze, Princesse de la Forêt d'Automne . . ."*

"Liaze, Princess of the Autumnwood. And you are . . . ?"

"Eausiné," answered the demoiselle. Then she added: "Are you one of the hunters who now and then come to spear our fish with their bows and swift arrows?"

"We went to warn them," said the second one as she came to shore, she with hair as golden as the heart of a water lily.

"Ah," said Liaze. "I see. You went to warn the fish. And no, I have not come to take them from you." Then the princess looked from one demoiselle to another, each of them slender and comely, with green eyes large and aslant, tilted up at the outer corners and set in narrow faces. They had long, flowing hair, and now and then movement revealed shell-like ears. Exotic were these damsels, as were those yet in the water, their graceful tails slowly fanning the flow. "But tell me," Liaze asked, *"what* are you?"

All looked at one another in puzzlement, for they didn't understand.

"I mean," added Liaze, "you look like demoiselles, but you can become half fish."

"Ah," said the yellow-haired one, sinking to the grass beside Liaze. "Nixies. We are Nixies."

"Oh, my," said Liaze. "I have heard of your Kind, but never before encountered any."

Yet standing, Eausiné glanced at Liaze's bow and arrows and

said, "We, on the other hand, have dealt with your Kind before. Are you certain you are not a hunter?"

"Oh, I am a hunter, all right," said Liaze, and collectively the Nixies gasped. "B-but of a different sort," the princess hurriedly assured them.

"There is only one kind of hunter," said the dark-haired demoiselle, at least for now the nominal leader of the Nixies. "The kind who seeks to kill."

"Oh, I would not kill the one I hunt, for he is my true love," replied Liaze.

True love? True love? A murmur ran among the Nixies.

"What is this true love?" one in the water asked.

How can they know not true love? Liaze sighed and said, "A true love is a person you would wish to have forever at your side. One who is a companion, a lover, a friend. Someone who gives you joy, makes you laugh, and who consoles you when you cry. Someone you need and someone who needs you. Someone with whom you can face the trials of life and share its delights as well. Someone who was meant to be . . ."

Liaze's words fell into hesitance, for the demoiselles yet looked at her with puzzlement in their eyes.

". . . a mate," finished Liaze, feeling as if she had ended lamely.

But the Nixies giggled, and one said, "Ah, mating we understand." And they broke into giggles once more.

"And who is this mate of yours?" asked Eausiné.

"A man, a knight: his name is Luc," said Liaze.

"Luc? Luc? You know Luc?" cried one.

"You have mated with him?" gasped another.

"Would that it were I," said a third.

"What?" cried Liaze. "You know of Luc?"

"Oh, yes," said Eausiné, plopping to the ground beside Liaze and then gesturing about. "He camped right here."

"My Luc? Metal shirt? Black horse? Silver horn?"

The dark-haired damsel nodded. "We swam in the moonlight with him," said one of the Nixies yet in the water, now transforming to come ashore.

Liaze said, "Did he . . . ? I mean, did you . . . did any of you, um, er . . . ?" But then she thrust out her hands and shook her head, saying, "—No, no! I don't want to know."

Eausiné looked at her in puzzlement.

Oh, Liaze, it's not as if you were without experience when you first made love to Luc. Nevertheless . . .

Of a sudden, Eausiné's eyes widened in understanding. "Oh, no, we did not mate with him, though it's not as if we did not try. It was clear he was ready"—Nixies giggled—"but he was too shy." Eausiné pointed at the golden-haired Nixie. "Jasiné was the first to see him cross the river on his great black horse."

"Yes," said Jasiné. "I called the others, and we watched, fearing that he was a hunter, too. But he merely made camp, and then, in the evening, he dove into our pool, and, of course, we went to meet him. When he discovered we were swimming with him, he cried out that he was *sans vêtements.*"

"As if that mattered," said one of the Nixies yet in the water.

"It was one of the things that attracted us to him," said another. "—Being without clothes, I mean."

"That among other attributes," said a third, giggling.

"Yes," said Eausiné, sighing in remembrance, "other attributes. But it was as I said: we wanted to mate with him—every one of us—but he was too shy. Not only that, but he said something about waiting—oh, now I remember—waiting for true love. I knew I had heard that somewhere before. I didn't understand it then either."

"We even sang to him," said one of the part-fish demoiselles, her dorsal fin now folded down against her spine, "but he resisted our songs."

Liaze momentarily glowed with satisfaction, for she had been his first love, his one and only, yet, even as it came on, the warm feeling was quenched under a pang of guilt, for, unlike Luc, she had not waited for true love. Liaze sighed. *Still, there is some consolation: because one of us had some experience, we avoided all of that awkward fumbling.* With this minor bit of self-justification, the guilt receded but did not vanish.

"We would have sung to him the next night and perhaps swayed him," said Eausiné, "but that very morn he said *adieu* and rode on into the woods."

"Whence came he?" asked Liaze. "—I am following his track opposite the path he rode."

"But why?" asked Eausiné. She pointed into the forest back in the direction of Liaze's camp. "That's the way he went."

"Yes, but you see," said Liaze, "someone—a witch, I believe—snatched him up and flew off with him. I despaired of ever finding him, but then we discovered the witch had left behind a messenger crow—"

"*Ssss . . .*" hissed several of the Nixies. "Crows," said Eausiné, "murderers of stranded minnows and larger fish when we do not get there in time."

"Have you seen crows flying above?" asked Liaze.

Nixies nodded, and the yellow-haired one pointed upstream. "Over the ford they sail, dipping low to see if any gasping fish has drowned in the sea of air. Pick at their flesh, they do, and then fly on."

"Ford?"

"Yes, a bit that way," said Jasiné, again pointing upstream. "It's where Luc crossed just before he made camp here."

"Then that's the way I intend to go, for I follow the crows, and if Lady Fortune smiles down on me, I will find Luc at the end of their flight."

"Oh, but that means you will pass through the Forest of Oaks," said Eausiné.

"Forest of Oaks? You make it sound somewhat dire."

"It is if the Fauns enspell you."

"Fauns? But I thought them quite benign."

"They are, my lady, but their pipes are enchanting, and they might enspell you as they do the Nymphs."

"Nymphs," said Liaze. "Still—"

"Oh, it's not the Nymphs nor the Fauns you need fear, but the Satyrs."

"Satyrs," said Liaze.

"The always-rutting Satyrs," said Jasiné. "When they hear the pipes, they come running, just on the chance that Nymphs are enspelled."

"And . . . ?" said Liaze.

"And," said Eausiné, "should you be entranced and a Satyr capture you, he will keep you for long whiles and pass you about to other Satyrs until all weary of you."

"Ugh," said Liaze. "Still, I must follow the line of flight of the crows, else I might never find Luc, certainly not in the time given."

"Time given?"

"I must find him before the dark of the moon—not the next, but the one after"—Liaze paused and counted on her fingers—"a moon and twenty days from now." Tears welled in Liaze's eyes. "If I fail, I believe he will die."

"Oh, no," gasped Jasiné, her face falling, "not Luc."

Eausiné said, "Then among the Fauns you must pass, but you must ward off the sound of their pipes and completely avoid hearing them. That is their enchantment, and the lure that brings the Satyrs."

"Yet if Luc rode through," said Liaze, "he must have heard them."

"He is male and you are not," said Jasiné, as if that explained all.

"You must not hear their pipes," stressed Eausiné.

Liaze frowned. *Then I need go deaf. But how—? Ah yes, there is honey among my goods.*

Liaze smiled and said, "Fear not for me, my friends. Yet tell me: where does this Forest of Oaks lie?"

"Beyond our realm," said Eausiné, "past the very next sun-wise twilight border."

Again Liaze smiled and her gaze swept o'er the Nixies all. "Lady Skuld told me I would find help along the way, and—"

The Nixies all drew in sharp breaths, and Jasiné said, "Lady Skuld? Oh, my, dire events must be aswim."

Liaze nodded and said, "Indeed, and so I must not tarry, for the moon itself tarries not." Liaze stood and looked upstream, but she could not see the ford.

The three Nixies stood ashore as well and stepped back into the water, and Eausiné said, "You must be careful, Princess Liaze."

"That I will be," replied Liaze. "And thank you for the warning as well as confirming to me that Luc did ride this way, and opposite flew the crows." She glanced once more upstream, and then with a farewell salute, she spun on her heel and strode into the forest.

A candlemark later, Liaze rode Nightshade across the ford, Pied Agile and the packhorses in tow, and downstream in waist-deep water stood the Nixies, all waving and calling out their *Au revoirs!* and *Bon voyages!*

Liaze held a hand, palm out, to them, and rode on across, and when she reached the other side of the wide ford, she turned to look one last time, but the Nixies were gone.

21

Croft

Up and out from the ford rode Liaze, Nightshade yet choosing the path. "Well, my good steed, it seems you truly do know the course, for Caillou and the Nixies both confirm Luc went opposite this way. But even more importantly, the crows flew this line bearing their messages to the witch, and so perhaps we can rescue Luc if the witch's dwelling lies between here and your stall. But if her place lies beyond your own home, then we'll need to seek more help. Regardless . . . fare on, black horse, fare on."

Nightshade made no comment, but continued his pace, the gait a trot for the nonce, the mare and four geldings coming after as the steed followed a trace of a trail among the trees and headed for the sunwise bound.

All day they followed the hint of a path, stopping now and then for the horses to take food or to drink from running streams, or for Liaze to take sustenance or relieve herself. At times the princess heeled Nightshade into a faster gait, or lightly pulled on the reins to change into one slower, Liaze varying the pace to preserve the endurance of the animals; at other times she dismounted and walked the horses and stretched her own legs. But always she let the black choose the way.

In midafternoon the sky overhead began to darken as brooding clouds crept thwartwise o'er the forest. "Well, my lad, it looks as if we're in for a storm, not now, but ere the night is done. We'll need to find shelter by the coming of dark."

Just before dusk drew down, and as the wind kicked up, she rode out from the forest and onto a fall-away slope overlooking a land of low, rolling hills. In the near distance to the fore she saw a farmstead, where a handful of workers in a field hurriedly laded forkfuls of cut hay into an ox-drawn wain. And down that way Nightshade went.

Even as Liaze neared the meadow, a few spatters of rain blew down, and one of the men afoot began driving the oxen toward a near byre, the others running ahead.

Liaze hailed the drover and he glanced back at her but kept moving forward. Moments later she rode alongside the wain and the man afoot, even as more rain came on the forerunning wind. "Have you shelter for me and my steeds?"

"Aye," replied the drover, a rather grizzled and sun-baked man, his faded blue eyes appraising her and the horses, especially eyeing Deadly Nightshade. His gaze dwelt a moment on the silver horn slung across Liaze's shoulder, but then he looked forward and lowed at the oxen, flicking a long flexible switch against their hindquarters, seemingly with no effect whatsoever.

"I am Liaze of the Autumnwood," said the princess.

"Matthieu," said the man. He gestured ahead, where the four other workers stood waiting just inside the doors of the now-open barn. "Vincent, Thierry, Noël, and Susanne," said Matthieu, his words laconic.

Into the byre rolled the wain, Liaze following. And as she passed the youths and the maid, they all looked up at her, their eyes filled with curiosity, especially those of the girl Susanne, a *fille* of no more than thirteen summers.

Outside, rain began pouring.

"We really needed the sun one more day," said Vincent, the young man the eldest of Matthieu and Madeleine's brood, raising his voice slightly to be heard above the water hammering against the shake-shingle roof of the modest house.

They all sat about a plank-board table and dined on a supper of fresh-baked bread and gravy and beans and rashers of bacon, and Liaze was reveling in the food, for it was the first hot meal she'd had in the seven days she'd been on the trail.

Vincent gestured toward the outside. "But the storm was coming and we could not leave this cutting lying afield to be ruined. Still, it is a bit green, yet we spread it out in the loft atop the other hay. Soon it will be dry enough."

"Well, my horses certainly appreciate the taste of it just the way it is," said Liaze, smiling.

"Your horses, you say?" said Matthieu.

"All but the black," replied Liaze. "It belongs to Luc, my betrothed."

"Your betrothed?" cried Susanne, her face falling.

But Matthieu and Madeleine looked at one another and nodded, as did the boys. And Matthieu said, "As we thought. —Oh, I mean about the black being Luc's horse."

"You knew it was his?" asked Liaze.

"He stayed with us two days," said Thierry, "then rode onward."

"Bon!" exclaimed Liaze.

"Bon?" asked Noël.

"It means I am yet on the right track," said Liaze.

"Right track?"

"Oui. You see, a witch has flown away with Luc, and I am out to find him."

The entire family gasped, and Susanne cried, *"Witch? Oh, my poor Luc!"*

"You must tell us of this witch," said Madeleine.

Liaze nodded and said, "I know not overmuch of her, but I can tell you of Luc's taking." Liaze paused and took a drink of water, and then spoke on: "It was some weeks past at Autumnwood Manor when I heard a silver horn sounding an alert, and—"

"Autumnwood Manor!" exclaimed Vincent. "Oh, we've heard of that. Tell me, is the princess as beautiful as they say?"

The corner of Liaze's mouth turned up slightly and she said, "I hardly think so."

"But they say she has auburn hair like yours and amber eyes and— Oh! *Oh!*" Vincent's eyes widened in revelation as did those of the other members of the family, and Madeleine said, "Oh, my lady, forgive me my humble fare, for we knew not who you truly were." She turned to Matthieu and said, "Quick, the wine. We must have wine."

As Matthieu leapt to his feet and headed for the back door, Liaze called, "Matthieu, you do not need to—" but the man was already out and into the storm. The princess turned to the mother. "Lady Madeleine, as to your so-called humble fare, it is as ambrosia to me, for I have been long on the ride."

Susanne sighed, her face glum, and she muttered, "A princess. A princess. I might have known."

Madeleine leaned over to Liaze and whispered, "She was enamored of Luc."

"Still is," said Thierry, overhearing.

Liaze reached out and laid a hand atop one of Suzanne's. "I don't fault you, my lady, for I, too, was instantly enamored of him, even as he fell off his horse."

Suzanne's eyes widened. "He fell?"

"Indeed."

"Was he hurt?"

"Let us wait for your père, and then I will tell all."

Even as she said this last, Matthieu came hurrying back in, dripping wet, with a jug of wine in hand. " 'Tis good I went to fetch this; the brook is running high; a bit more of this downpour, and it would have been swept away."

While Madeleine served wine 'round to all, Matthieu dried off and, still a bit damp, resumed his place at the table.

Suzanne said, "He fell from his horse, Papa."

As Matthieu frowned, Liaze said, " 'Twas Luc who fell, wounded as he was." All eyes widened, and Suzanne cried out, but Liaze went on: "You see, I was at a pool among some willows when I heard Luc's horn crying out the alarm, and . . ."

"But that will mean you need go through the Forest of Oaks," protested Madeleine.

"Full of Fauns, it is," said Matthieu, "and they bring the Satyrs."

"I have no choice," said Liaze.

"We can go with you and protect you," said Vincent, glancing at his father.

Liaze shook her head. "Nay. Recall: Lady Skuld said I must go alone, but for the howling one."

"I think it's a Wolf," said Thierry.

"Or someone quite mad," said Noël.

"Regardless of who or what it is," said Madeleine, "the pipes of the Fauns stand between you and your goal."

"Perhaps," said Liaze. "Perhaps not. For Nightshade might turn aside ere reaching the oaks. Besides, I am told I simply must avoid the sound of their music, and *that* I will do."

"Stuff your ears, I've heard say," said Matthieu, "though I know of no one who's done so."

"Then mayhap I will be the first one of your acquaintance to try it," said Liaze.

Matthieu nodded, an uncertain smile upon his face. "True."

*　　*　　*

With dinner done and the dishes washed, Liaze said to Madeleine, "Could I beg of you some hot water? I need a bath desperately, and all I've had were the cold streams along the way to—"

"Oh, yes, yes, my lady," said Madeleine.

Sometime later, as Susanne poured the contents of a steaming kettle into a round copper tub, she looked at Liaze and sighed and said, "If I had to lose Luc to anyone, I am glad it was you, Princess."

"Why, thank you, Susanne. I am sorry and yet not sorry I spoiled your dream."

"Perhaps I was foolish to ever dream it in the first place," said Suzanne.

"Oh, child, no dream is foolish, though some are not meant to be. A few dreams come true quite by accident, while others will happen only if you make them so and perhaps get help along the way. Hence, keep on dreaming your dreams, Suzanne, and work toward those ends, and one day, mayhap, some of those dreams will be realized."

The next morning dawned to a freshly washed world, and, after a hearty breakfast, Liaze mounted up on a fretting, sidlestepping Nightshade and said, "Merci, Matthieu, Madeleine. I am grateful for your hospitality. Even so, I wish you had slept in your own bed and left me to the barn."

Madeleine shook her head and said, " 'Twas only fitting."

As Liaze sighed, Vincent looked to the hills in the direction she was to ride, and then he stepped back and said, "The black seems anxious to go, my lady." He bowed, as did his brothers, and Noël added, "*Bonne chance,* Princess."

"Merci, Noël. I hope your good wishes for me come true. Oh, and Matthieu, I thank you for replenishing my supplies, for I know not what will be needed on the road ahead."

Matthieu bowed, and Madeleine curtseyed, and Susanne

curtseyed and then, her face twisted in anguish, said, "Oh, please save Luc, Princess. If you don't then I think I'll just die."

"So will I, Suzanne," said Liaze. "Indeed, so will I." Sighing, with a farewell wave she heeled Nightshade and gave the black his head, and off toward the sunwise bound he cantered, Pied Agile and the four geldings in tow.

"That horse must be enchanted," said Thierry.

"Just well trained," said Vincent, and he looked at his père.

Matthieu shrugged and said, "Enchanted or well trained, he seems to know the way." And the family stood and watched as Liaze rode up and over the next hill and then was lost to sight.

"Come, there is work to do," said Matthieu, and he and his sons headed for the barn, while mother and daughter turned and went inside, where Madeline's eyes widened in surprise, for in the mid of their plank-board table lay a gold piece.

For two more days did Liaze ride in this sparsely populated land, and on the eve of the third day she came to the sunwise twilight bound, where she reined Nightshade to a halt, and set about making camp.

On the morrow I will enter the Forest of the Oaks, but on this night I will sleep in peace.

22

Lure

In the dim light of the following dawn, Liaze fed the horses rations of oats that had come from Matthieu's croft. As the animals munched, the princess sliced off an end of the loaf of bread Madeleine had gifted her with, and opened the jar of honey and liberally slathered the piece with the sweetness and then ate. When that was gone, she besmeared another slice of bread, and enjoyed the taste of it as well. She washed all down with clear water, and then broke off a large corner of honeycomb and popped it in her mouth and gently chewed as she broke camp.

She laded her packhorses and saddled Nightshade and Pied Agile. She tethered the mare and geldings to the stallion, and mounted the black.

Nightshade started to move forward, but Liaze pulled the reins and stopped him. And as he looked back at her, she took the pliable wad from her mouth and divided it in two, and then plugged her ears with the softened beeswax.

She loosened her long-knife in its scabbard and then said to Nightshade, her voice somewhat muffled to herself, "Now, my lad, lead on." And she heeled the stallion in the flanks, and into the twilight marge they fared, even as the sun broke free of the horizon.

Through the shadowy wall they went, to emerge in a hoary old forest, the trees mostly oaks, though here and there stood elms and maples and green conifers. A low fog curled among the boles, and the forest itself appeared to spring from the mist, as if there were no ground beneath. But Nightshade, under his own guidance, trotted ahead, the stallion seemingly undaunted by the unseen footing, the mare and geldings trailing after. Onward they fared as the sun rode up into the sky, and by midmorn the fog was gone.

As she rode Liaze scanned the surround, for she could hear nought but her own breathing, for that came from within and not without. And she was disturbed by her deafness, and for the first time in her life she realized just how important hearing was, for she heard no birds, no chitterings of insects nor chatterings of tree runners, no rustle of leaves, no scurryings, no snap of twigs, no fall of foot or hoof, nor burble of water when they stopped at streams. *I thought the constant wind was bad as I crossed Caillou's realm, but this eternal silence is worse. Why, something could be galloping toward us, or creeping stealthily, and I would hear it not.*

"Keep a sharp ear," she said to the animals, "for you are the first line of defense."

And so, lacking hearing, she kept a sharp eye out, frequently gazing 'round, and now and again she saw animals and birds and crawling things, but she heard them not. Still, even though the silence was oppressive, she heard no pipes playing, and of that she was glad. Her sense of smell, however, seemed to intensify, for the scents of the grass and leaves, of the earth, and of the horses heightened. But it was her sight she most depended upon, and so she scanned this way and that, her gaze ever roving.

Thrice throughout the day she did see lone maidens, demoiselles much like the Nixies in look—exotic beauties—though these did not appear to transform into anything other than what they seemed. One was sitting among the broad limbs of a large oak and combing her russet hair. Another one, quite distant, seemed to be digging at the roots of an oak. And one just ahead and slightly off the line along which Nightshade fared looked at Liaze coming toward her, and then the demoiselle stepped directly into the solid trunk of her tree.

Liaze gasped in wonderment, yet it was as she had suspected: the maiden had been a Dryad, a Wood Nymph.

That night Liaze camped by a stream, her bow strung, arrows at hand, her long-knife at her side. And she burned no fires, for she would have no light to summon Satyrs or flames to upset the Dryads.

And she did not at all sleep well, waking often to peer about in the light of the full moon.

The next day was much like the previous, and the farther she rode, the more irritated Liaze became with the lack of hearing. But then she saw a storm-slain tree lying on the ground, and she recalled the old conundrum: should a tree fall in a forest with no one to hear, would it make a sound? Long she and her siblings had argued the question, first taking one side, and then perversely taking the other. She smiled in the memory, knowing that should a tree fall this day, it would make no sound as far as she was concerned. She would have to remember to tell her siblings this. But then a stricken look overcame her features. *Oh, my, was a Wood Nymph also slain when her tree died?*

On Nightshade trotted, a league and then two, mare and geldings coming after, and as they entered a wide glade, in the near distance in the center of the clearing Liaze espied a gathering on the banks of a small mere, with a large weeping willow o'erhanging, and a small grove of oaks nearby. Nightshade paid no heed, and as he fared nigh, Liaze could see demoiselles lolling on the sward at hand, and midst them stood a beautiful youth, a willow-root pipe at his lips, his fingers dancing upon holes along its length. In Liaze's self-imposed silence, she realized he was playing, but she could hear nothing of the tune. And then she could see the youth had the ears and hindquarters and tail of a deer.

Faun! Liaze scanned to fore and aft and aflank, yet she saw only the forest. *If the Nixies were right, surely Satyrs will come.*

Liaze haled on Nightshade's reins, halting the stallion. And she reached for her bow, as if to take it up. *Should I! No! 'Tis the Faun's nature to—*

Instead, Liaze gave a sharp whistle, but the Nymphs paid no heed, for they were entranced. Yet the Faun looked up and saw Liaze, and he took the pipe from his lips and smiled a glorious smile, and gestured for her to join his circle. But then his eyes widened in fright and his deerlike ears flared up, and he looked beyond Liaze.

She swung her gaze in that direction, and over a crest among the trees came five or six hairy and horned Satyrs running, their goatish legs driving cloven hooves, and, for all Liaze could hear, they ran in total silence. The Nymphs scattered, some to disappear into the trunks of oaks, others fleeing into rocks, and two diving into the mere.

"Hup, hup, hup!" called Liaze, alerting the string of horses; and their heads came up and their ears pricked forward. Then, *"Hiyah!"* she cried, and kicked Nightshade in the flanks, and the stallion sprang forward, the princess continuing to shout and goad him onward, the black galloping away from the pool, the mare and geldings running in his wake.

The Satyrs changed the angle of their run, rage on their faces, their mouths wide as if shouting, and they dashed toward fleeing Liaze. She whipped her strung bow out from the saddle scabbard and nocked an arrow and let fly, striking one of the Satyrs in the leg. He fell to the ground bleating loudly—though Liaze heard him not—and the ones with him sheered off, and Nightshade and the line of horses raced on into the forest, leaving the creatures behind.

Liaze did not stop to camp that night, but continued to fare onward instead, sometimes astride the stallion, sometimes walking, at other times riding the mare, though the black yet led the way.

As Liaze dozed off and on in the saddle, it was nigh noon of the following day while mounted on Nightshade that she came to the sunwise twilight bound. She clucked her tongue and urged the stallion forward, and in that moment, trailing, Pied Agile reared, and someone or something landed behind Liaze and grabbed her by the hair and jerked her hindward and threw an arm about her neck. Liaze managed to stay in the saddle, and she smelled a musky reek and glimpsed a goatlike leg alongside her own. *Satyr!* She kicked Nightshade in the flanks and wrenched her long-knife from the thigh scabbard even as the stallion sprang forward into the twilight, the other horses nearly stumbling, but following. But the Satyr yet had its fingers tangled in her hair, and with his bristly forearm he began choking her into submission. Reversing her grip and praying to not hit the black, Liaze blindly stabbed down at the leg of the being, and in the shadowlight she felt the blade strike home.

In the darkness of the border, the creature fell away, yet his fingers were still entangled in her tresses, and she was nearly dragged from the saddle, and she felt as if her hair was being yanked out by the roots. Of a sudden she was free, the Satyr gone, and Nightshade hammered on through the blackness and beyond, out into sunlight and an open field.

Panting, her heart racing, Liaze kept the stallion running, the mare and geldings galloping in tow. The princess looked behind, and nothing, no one, no Satyr, came charging after.

She was free of the Oak Forest and its perils, and she burst into tears and wept uncontrollably, to her own dismay.

23

Village

Liaze reined back on Nightshade and slowed him and the mare and geldings to a walk. She loosed the reins and gave the stallion his head and let him choose the trail.

As the black wended between sparse thickets and a few stands of timber, with low rolling hills to the fore, Liaze gained control of her emotions and berated herself for weeping like a silly goose. She cleaned her long-knife of Satyr blood and slid it into its sheath. She removed the beeswax from her ears and reveled in the trilling of birds, of the humming of insects, of the clop and breathing of her horses and the creak of leather, and the soft wafting song of the gentle breeze. As she listened to the surround, Nightshade came upon a trace of a road. Wagon ruts marked the way; it was a two-track farm lane used to reach the field they had left behind, though whatever crop it had held—most likely hay—had been harvested.

They followed this route and soon came in among other fields: grain mostly—rye, barley, wheat—though here and there grew turnips and squash and other vegetable crops. *By the reach of the fields, it has to be an extensive croft.* Soon Liaze's suspicions were confirmed, for she came unto a large farmhouse— *With numerous rooms, no doubt; a considerable family must live here; prosperous, too.* Behind the dwelling sat a great byre; abundant cords of firewood lay under a wide, sloped roof held up by tall poles; on beyond, several round grain storage sheds squatted next to a silo; a number of other croft structures were scattered here and there.

Liaze reined Nightshade into the yard, and a yellow-haired, matronly woman in a fine-woven linen dress the color of a clear sky at noon stepped onto the porch and shaded her eyes and watched as the princess rode nigh.

"Might I have some water for me and my horses?" Liaze asked.

"Indeed you might," said the woman, gesturing toward the side of the house. And as Liaze rode past: "Oh, my, you're a fille," declared the woman, stepping down from the porch and walking alongside. "I thought you a warrior, dressed as you are and riding that big black horse."

"Would that I were," said Liaze, glancing back in the direction she had come. "It would have made things easier."

"Oh, you didn't pass through the Forest of Oaks, now, did you?"

"Indeed I did," said Liaze.

The woman's brown, golden-hued eyes flew wide. "Oh, you poor child, did they keep you long?"

"They did not keep me at all," said Liaze, reining Nightshade to a halt at a watering trough, an axle-driven, bucket-chain pump at one end atop the stone rim of a well.

"Then you are certainly warrior enough, or very skillful, or extremely fortunate," said the woman.

"I think the Fates themselves were watching over me," said Liaze, dismounting, a faint smile on her face.

As Liaze turned the wheel-crank 'round and 'round to spill

water into the trough, the horses crowded forward, though on their long tethers the geldings gave Nightshade considerable leeway.

With the vessel three-quarters full, Liaze stopped turning the wheel and ducked her head under the surface next to Pied Agile and, after a moment, came up sputtering.

"Oh, dear," said the woman. "Let me get you a towel." She rushed to a side door and into the house and quickly returned with a soft cotton cloth.

Liaze patted her face dry and then briskly rubbed her hair, wincing occasionally, for her yanked-upon scalp was yet tender, especially where strands had been torn loose.

The woman said, "Would you like a cup of hot tea and perhaps a bite to eat?"

"Oh, I would treasure it," said Liaze.

The woman eyed the packhorse goods and said, "Well then, why don't you give your animals a bit of grain while I prepare, and then you can tell me what in Faery you were doing coming through that most dreadful Forest of the Oaks. —Oh, and I am Madame Divenard, but at times my sisters—one on each side— call me Midi, as can you."

"And I am Liaze of the Autumnwood," replied the princess.

"Well and good," said Midi, smiling. She turned and hastened toward the house, calling back over her shoulder, "Now hurry, for I shan't be long."

". . . And that's why I had to come through the oaks," said Liaze. She took the last bite of buttered and honeyed biscuit, and washed it down with bracing hot tea.

"Well, my dear, that's quite a tale. And, oh, from what you've told me, you've crossed the four twilight borders that your Sir Luc rode going the opposite way."

"Did Luc come past your croft?"

"If he did, Liaze, then it was when my sisters and I were busy elsewhere."

Liaze's face fell, and she sighed. "Always before, I had confirmation that Luc rode this way, what with Caillou and Matthieu's corroboration. But now it seems . . ." Liaze's words fell to silence.

Madame Divenard reached across the table and patted the princess on the hand. "Fear not, Liaze, from what you tell me, the black follows the way."

Heartened somewhat, Liaze asked, "Do you know of any witch living nearby, or of a woodcutter—an armsmaster—named Léon?"

"Non, but someone in the village might know," said Midi.

"Village?"

"Oui," said Midi, gesturing in the direction Liaze had been faring. "Ruisseau Miel is but an afternoon's ride hence. You go down my lane until you reach the main road, and then follow it onward till you come to the town. A sign will point the way."

Liaze stood. "Then I'll be going now, for if someone there might know of a witch or a woodcutter, I—"

"But Liaze," protested Midi, looking up at her, "you have had little rest and a terrible experience in the Forest of Oaks. Surely you can stay here one night and catch up on your missing sleep."

"Non, Madame Divenard. My horses and I can last long enough to reach this town you speak of; it is there we will rest."

Midi sighed and stood, and then brightened. "It has but one inn, L'Abeille Occupée, with quite a good stable. Its kitchens are, um . . . adequate, and the wine, eh . . . tolerable. L'Abeille is where the honey buyers stay when they come in the honey season."

"Then, merci, madame, I shall always be grateful for this respite you have given me."

Midi smiled and said, "And I shall be certain to tell my sisters of this venture of yours . . . as far as it goes, that is. And, oh, Liaze, may you find what you seek."

Liaze and Midi stepped from the farmhouse and to the horses, and Liaze removed the nosebags and packed them away, and let the horses have another small amount of water. Then she mounted up on Nightshade and bade Midi "Au revoir," Midi replying in kind. The princess wheeled the black about and rode to the lane and onward.

And when she had gone from sight, the lush farm fields and the large farmhouse faded away, and the matronly woman, smiling to herself, silently vanished as well.

Dusk was falling when Liaze reached the small village of Ruisseau Miel, and as she rode down the main street, she saw a signboard proclaiming a rather modest inn to be L'Abeille Ocupée—a depiction on the board of a honey bee at work echoed the name of the inn.

Liaze's eyes felt gritty from lack of sleep as she gave the horses over to the hostler. Wearily she trudged into the inn and engaged a room. Before going upstairs, she had a meal, and, given her rations over the past several days, the "adequate" food tasted rather scrumptious to her palate, as did the "tolerable" wine.

She barely got through her hot bath without falling asleep, and when she collapsed onto her bed, slumber came on instant feet.

It was nigh noon when next she awoke. She found her undersilk garments and leathers cleaned and ready to wear, and her boots polished and well aired. She washed and dried and took care of her feminine needs and got dressed.

Down to the common room she went, and though the hour was late, she broke her fast with delicious eggs and rashers and well-buttered toast and honey and tea, a splendid meal to her mind. Afterward, she looked about for the innkeeper, but he was nowhere to be seen, and so she walked out to the stables and spoke to the horses and stroked them.

The hostler told her to take care, for the black was untrust-worthy. "Why, he had a ruckus with another stallion, but when they were moved to stalls at opposite ends they both settled down. Even so, tried to nip me, he did," said the man. "I dodged just barely in time."

"I tap him on the nose when he gets feisty," said Liaze. "That puts him in his place. You should do the same."

"Oh, no, not me," said the stableman. "I just keep a sharp eye on them all . . . and never let down my guard."

Liaze laughed and then frowned and after a moment said, "As a hostler, you must know of all the comings and goings here-about."

The man lifted his chin in modest pride. "I suppose I do."

"Well, then, know you of a witch nearby?"

"*Witch?*" The hostler flinched back from Liaze and made a warding sign. Then he vehemently shook his head. "I don't have any doings with witches, mademoiselle, and don't ever plan to."

"Neither would I," said Liaze, "but I have a score to settle with one."

The man relaxed a bit, yet he looked at her warily, as if she were someone ready to nip him. Finally, he said, "Non, made-moiselle. I know of no witches nearby. None afar either."

"Whom would I talk to about such?" asked Liaze. "Someone who is familiar with the area."

The hostler's brow furrowed and then cleared. "Claude, I think."

"Claude?"

"The innkeeper. He speaks with folks from all over. Buyers who come for the honey in season. Oui, Claude is the one."

"Ah, I see. But he seems to be absent for the nonce," said Liaze.

"Goes fishing this time of day. Down to Honey Creek. Trying for the big trout that hangs out in the deep pool. Ha! As if any-one will ever catch that lunker. But he'll be back come midafter-noon. Till then you'll have to deal with Odette."

"Odette?"

"The serving maid, though I doubt she knows ought about witches."

"Merci, um . . ."

"Paul, my lady," said the hostler, touching the bill of his cap.

"Merci, Paul. I'll wait for Claude to return."

Liaze stepped away from the stalls and went outside, and she walked through the village streets, noting in passing a small café, and a dry-goods store with a milliner and tailor in residence. There was a barber who also seemed to be a chirurgeon, and across the street a—Liaze stopped in her tracks—a bookshop. *A bookstore in a hamlet this small? Luc told me there was one in the village he and León delivered cordwood to, an establishment that never seemed to do any business, but for Luc's own.*

Liaze stepped over to the store, and when she looked in, the place was empty, abandoned, though the sign above yet proclaimed it to be the COIN DU LIVRE—the Book Nook.

Next door was a shoemaker-and-leatherworker's shop. Liaze stepped in and a man with an awl and a length of belt in hand looked up from his bench. "May I help you, mademoiselle?"

"Oui. The bookstore next door: has it always been empty?"

"Non, my lady. Only recently did the owner—Jaquot—move away. I don't blame him. I mean, even though he appeared to be prosperous, it seemed he never had any customers, but for that Luc boy."

Liaze's heart leapt into her throat, and tears filled her eyes, and for a moment she could not speak. Finally she managed, "Luc? Luc was here?"

"Oui, demoiselle, but not for a while." The man lay down his awl and belt and stepped around the table. "Are you well?"

Liaze took a deep breath and said, "Oh, yes, monsieur."

"Here, mademoiselle," said the leatherworker, and he offered her a dipper of water.

"Merci, monsieur," said Liaze, sipping a bit from the hollowed-out gourd. Again she took a deep breath. "I am looking for Luc; a witch snatched him up and flew away."

The man made a warding sign and said, "A witch, you say? We know nothing of witches in this town, only that some are vile and others are not. Ah, mademoiselle, but if Luc has been taken, then Léon needs to be told this dire news."

"Léon, his foster sire, is he nearby?"

"Oui. A half-day walk down the road and off into the woods."

"Tell me how to get there."

Dusk was drawing down on the land, when, astride Nightshade and towing Pied Agile and the geldings, Liaze came into the clearing where stood a small, one-room cote, with a modest horse barn off to one side.

She rode to the cottage and dismounted and tied Nightshade's reins to the hitching post near the door. Then she stepped to the planked panel and knocked.

A tall, redheaded man bearing a lantern opened the door. He raised the light on high for a better look, and surprise filled his pale blue eyes. "Might I help you, mademoiselle?"

"Armsmaster Léon?"

He glanced at the silver horn at her side and looked at Nightshade nearby and frowned. Finally he answered, "Oui."

Liaze followed his gaze and said, "I have come about Luc."

"Luc? Has something happened to Luc?"

"Oui."

The armsmaster blanched and moved aside, and Liaze stepped in through the doorway.

24

Secrets

Clearly beset by anxiety, still Léon stepped to the hearth and swung a kettle over the flames. Then he took down two mugs from a cupboard and fetched a small jar of honey as well, and placed them on the table, where Liaze sat. He spooned tea leaves into a pot covered with a cozy and set it beside the cups. Liaze could see that with these small domesticities Léon was calming himself for whatever news was to come.

Finally, he sat across from Liaze and placed his hands on the table. Then he looked at her and nodded.

"Luc has been taken away by a witch," said Liaze

Léon clenched a fist, his knuckles white, but otherwise made no move. At last he said, "But why?"

"Perhaps you can better answer that than I," said Liaze.

Léon sighed and leaned back in his chair and looked at Liaze as if assessing her. "What is your interest in Luc?"

"He is my betrothed," said Liaze. "And I am out to find him."

Léon raised an eyebrow. "Your betrothed?"

"Oui."

"How came this to be? I mean, when did you meet him? And where? And under what circumstance?"

"I met him when he fell off his horse," said Liaze. "And as to where, it was in the Autumnwood. And the circumstances were that a raiding party of Redcap Goblins and Trolls were on my grounds and coming toward my *château.* Luc, though wounded in a running battle with them, sounded the warning, and we managed to repel the marauders."

"Have you any proof of what you say?"

"I have his horn and Deadly Nightshade and much of Luc's gear. I also know that you raised Luc, but you are not his true sire, but a foster sire instead. I know you disguise yourself as a simple woodcutter when you are anything but. Too, I know about Luc's tutors and his training in arms and armor and combat, and in etiquette, and dances, and other such courtly things."

"What does he wear about his neck?"

"A blue stone set in silver on a silver chain."

Léon nodded, and the kettle over the fire began to steam. He got to his feet and swung the bronze pot-arm from over the flames and took the kettle from it, and poured steaming water into the teapot. He replaced the kettle on the arm and sat down. As the tea steeped, again Léon nodded to himself as if coming to a decision.

"You are right, my lady, in that I might know why a witch has stolen Luc away from you. And if I am correct, it does not bode well for him."

"Tell me," said Liaze.

"First, my lady, you have the advantage of me: you know my name, but I—"

"Liaze of the Autumnwood."

"Liaze," repeated Léon, absently, as if his thoughts were not on her name. He took a deep breath and then slowly let it out. Again he nodded to himself. "Luc's real sire was *Comte Amaury*

du Château Bleu dans le Lac de la Rose et Gardien de la Clé.
But Amaury was slain in combat, yet he left behind *Comtesse*
Adèle and his newborn son: Luc.

"A year after Amaury's death, Adèle married Guillaume, a *vicomte* with ambitions of being a duke or a king, and, with hopes
of becoming a full comte, his marriage to Comtesse Adèle was
a step along that royal road.

"But Luc was and is the rightful heir, as evidenced by the
gemstone the boy wore about his neck, an amulet given to the
wee babe by Amaury just before he rode to battle."

Léon paused and poured tea through a strainer into the mugs,
and offered honey to Liaze. She spooned in a dollop and stirred
it, then gave over the jar and utensil to Léon, who did likewise.

Leaving his cup sitting idle, Léon continued: "Guillaume
would have none of that, for as long as Luc was alive, the vicomte could never become the comte of Château Bleu. Furthermore, his three-year-old brat of a son could not inherit the title
unless Luc were dead."

A dark look came over Léon's face, and he said, "In Guillaume's retinue was an unsavory man by the name of Franck,
and he wished to take my place as armsmaster of the hold. Guillaume and Franck always had their heads together whenever
Comtesse Adèle was seen cooing over Luc, and I knew then that
ill deeds were afoot, and I said so to the comtesse. Yet she did
not believe that Guillaume could harm such a sweet child, and
she nearly dismissed me. So I kept quiet and watched.

"One night to take air I came to the battlements and saw the
ward was absent, all men gone. I turned to go to the guard quarters, but then I saw someone galloping across the causeway, and
he had a bundle in his arms.

"I ran to the stables and took the courier horse, for it was always saddled, and over the downed drawbridge and across the
causeway I raced after. Ah, my lady, to make a long story short,
I came upon Franck in the woods just as he was preparing to slay

Luc, for that was the bundle Franck bore. Even as he drew his knife to kill the babe, I threw my dagger and saved the boy. Ere Franck died he cursed me, and said that there were more who were prepared to carry out Guillaume's wishes."

Léon drew a long shuddering breath and tried to master his relived rage, for as he had told the tale, Liaze could see he had experienced it again.

Léon stared into his cup of tea, yet lost in the memory, and he growled, "Guillaume."

Liaze nodded and said, "What a wicked stepfather he was."

"Indeed," said Léon, looking up from his cup and across at her. "Because of him, I knew the child would never be safe as long as Guillaume was in the castle, and so I rode away with the babe in my arms.

"And though I hid Franck's corpse in the bushes and under brush and leaves, I knew that it would be discovered by the trackers' dogs. But since they would not find Luc, I also knew that Guillaume would send killers after the child, at that time not quite a year and a half old. By devious ways, up streams and down and over stone, to throw trackers and dogs off the scent, with the lad I came here, where I took on the guise of a simple woodcutter in this place far from Luc's rightful home— the Blue Château on an isle in the middle of the Lake of the Rose.

"By happenstance, a trusted former soldier of mine—Jaquot, a courier—was living just up the road in the village of Honey Creek. Through him, I did send word to the comtesse that Luc was safe in my care. By this time, in the aftermath of the stolen child, she had discovered what Guillaume had done, for she heard him talking to one of his henchmen. Still she could do nothing to oppose him.

"Further, she told me that I had been blamed for the taking of the child, and that 'brave' Franck had gone after me, but that I, in a dastardly act of murder, had stabbed him the back. She said that Guillaume had placed a price on my head, and the man who killed me could claim the reward."

Léon gritted his teeth and said, "And so, I am a murderer and fugitive in my own realm."

The armsmaster fell silent and stared bitterly into his tea, but after a moment he sighed and said, "Regardless, I raised the lad as my own, making certain to teach him all I knew of arms and armor and combat and other such things. And the comtesse secretly sent funds for me to hire tutors, and to set up a bookstore in the village so that the child could broaden his knowledge. She wanted him raised as a proper gentleman, knowing all the noble arts of a man of his station, and I did my best. Why, I even hired etiquette advisors and dance instructors so that he would be completely at home in any court in Faery."

As Léon paused to take a long draught of tea, Liaze said, "You did very well, Sieur Léon. Luc is truly a noble gentleman."

Léon turned a hand, palm up, and a fleeting smile showed he was pleased by her remark. Even so, it was immediately replaced by a worried frown. After a moment he said, "Throughout the years, by Jacquot—who took on the guise of a bookstore owner in Honey Creek—I sent secret reports to the comtesse of Luc's progress."

"Ah," said Liaze, refreshing her own tea and Léon's.

Nodding his thanks, the armsmaster continued: "When Luc came into his majority, the comtesse sent Deadly Nightshade with arms and armor as a gift, for both she and I would have him become as was his true sire: a worthy chevalier and a comte, as Luc was meant to be.

"I sent him on errantry, to gain experience, for before he can face that man who would be a comte and more, Luc must needs win his spurs in single combat or in the battle of war and become a true knight, and then would I tell him of his rightful heritage."

Liaze raised a hand to stop his words and said, "But he is a true knight, Armsmaster Léon. He accounted for more than twenty Redcap Goblins in battle and slew a Troll as well, and he alerted my manor to the oncoming threat. I knighted him myself."

Léon frowned. "And just who are you to have done so?"

Her voice taking on imperious authority, Liaze declared, *"Je suis Princesse Liaze de la Forêt d'Automne, la fille du Roi Valeray et la Reine Saissa.* And in my demesne I am the sovereign, the absolute ruler, and knighting someone who has proved himself in battle is mine to do."

Léon rose from the table and went down on one knee. "Princess Liaze, I beg your—"

Seeing the man humble himself before her, of a sudden Liaze relented and softly said, "Kneel not to me, Armsmaster, for we are not in my court, but in yours instead."

Léon resumed his seat and took a long drink of tea. Then he looked at Liaze, his eyes glimmering with unshed tears, and he whispered, "My Luc, a knight."

Liaze smiled and nodded. "Indeed, he is. You trained him well, Armsmaster."

Léon shyly bobbed his head, and then took a long sip of his tea.

"My friend," said Liaze when he set his cup down, "you started this tale by saying you might know why a witch snatched up Luc and flew away with him."

" 'Tis a guess on my part, yet perhaps it is Guillaume who hired her to find the blue gem, and he chose a witch to seek it out, for Guillaume needs it to claim the rank of comte in that demesne."

"I see," said Liaze. "And when the witch scried out the jewel, she found Luc wearing it."

"Perhaps," said Léon. "Perhaps."

"It is a worthy guess, Armsmaster, one most likely to be. —Ah, then, that's why the Redcap Goblins and Trolls were after him. They were the witch's minions sent for the silver-set stone."

Léon faintly smiled. "Even should she recover it, little does

Guillaume know that only the true heir can wear the amulet. It will not benefit a usurper. Comte Amaury told me this in confidence, for there is some deadly secret concering the amulet that he would not reveal. —Once I tried to remove the talisman for safekeeping, and it nearly did me in."

Liaze nodded and said, "As we discovered in Autumnwood Manor when we were tending to Luc's wounds."

Léon got to his feet, the man seeming somehow relieved now that the secret he had kept so many years had finally been told. "Well, Princess, let me tend to the horses, and then we'll have a meal and talk about how Luc came to you, and why you are riding alone rather than in a retinue, and how you and I are going to rescue Luc."

"I'll help with the horses, Armsmaster," said Liaze, "and tell you what you want to know, as well as why you cannot go on with me, though you can help me plan what next to do."

". . . And so you see, I yet have trials ahead. And Lady Skuld said I must go alone, but for the howling one."

"But, Princess," said Léon, "perhaps you have already ridden with fear when you came through the Forest of the Oaks."

"Oui, I admit I was fearful in that place, yet I think had any been with me—a retinue of warriors—they would not have been slain by fear, as Lady Wyrd said would happen."

Léon sighed in agreement. "There is that. Men have nothing to fear in the Forest of Oaks. Only women."

Liaze nodded and neither one spoke for a while, and then the princess asked, "Have you seen any crows flying over?"

Léon shrugged. "If any did, I took no special note of them. —Still, if they were flying across sunwise borders, that's the way the Blue Château lies."

Liaze raised an eyebrow. "Ah, I see. Then perhaps that's the way the witch lies as well. As such, it gives a bit of credence to the idea that Guillaume is behind Luc's taking."

They sat quietly a bit longer, and only the crackle of the fire broke the silence. After a moment Liaze stood and took up her mug and tin plate and knife and spoon and looked about the single room. "Where do we—?"

"There is a spring nearby where I clean them," said Léon. "Runs all year, summer, winter, it matters not." He got to his feet and took up his own tableware and a modest stewpot and ladle, as well as the lantern, and together they walked to the rock face of an upjut of land. Water poured out from a cleft in the stone to run in a clear stream and away, and together they knelt thereat to wash the utensils.

As Léon scoured away at the pot, he said, "What do you plan to do?"

Liaze stopped her own scrubbing and sighed. "I think the only thing left to me is to ride to wherever lies this Blue Château of yours on an isle in the Lake of the Rose and take on a task of some sort in the hold and see what I can discover."

"Take on a task?"

"Oui, as a goose girl or some such."

Léon shook his head. "You cannot ride in on Deadly Nightshade, towing your mare and four packhorses and claim to be a goose girl. You will need to leave them somewhere safe and go in on foot. —Ah, and perhaps I have just the place. There is a widow I used to visit when I was armsmaster of that keep, and . . ."

Liaze stayed with Léon another day, but neither the princess nor the armsmaster could come up with a better plan. And so, the next morn, seventeen days after setting out from Autumwood Manor, eighteen days after Luc was taken, and forty-one days ere a heart would cease to beat in the dark of the moon, Liaze rode away from the woodcutter's cote, heading in the direction of the sunwise marge, for that's the way the Blue Château lay, though seven borders beyond. Liaze had in her possession a note written in code to deliver to the comtesse, in the hopes Lady Adèle could aid in the finding of Luc.

And so, astride Pied Agile and towing Nightshade and the four geldings after, Liaze fared into the woods.

Léon stood looking after her as she rode away, his hands clenching and unclenching, as if seeking weapons but finding none. And he despaired, for he would go at her side, yet he could find no way to get around Lady Wyrd's rede. And though he had said he would ride with the princess even if it meant yielding up his life, Liaze had refused to let him accompany her. "Trust to the Fates," she had said, and he had no recourse but to do so. And so he watched her ride away into the forest, and, when she was gone beyond sight, he turned and took up an axe and furiously began hewing cordwood.

Three days later, Léon saddled his grey and laded on supplies, and then dressed in his armor and took up his arms and rode away from the woodcutter's cote and toward the sunwise border.

25

Musings

As Liaze rode deeper into the woods she could hear the distant sound of Léon's axe hewing. *Ah, but I would have loved his company, just as I would have liked Rémy and his warband at my side. Yet Lady Skuld said, "For should you take a few with you, / Most Fear would likely slay." Ah, me, but I cannot have the blood of others on my hands can I help it. And if that means riding alone, then let it be so. Au revoir, Léon, mon ami, foster père of my Luc.*

On she fared, and the sound of hewing faded. Finally, she could hear the axe no more, and it was as if she had lost a friend.

All morning she rode, as the sun rose up the sky, and occasionally she stopped at rills and streams to give the horses a drink and to take water herself. And at the noontide she found a lea with red clover growing, and there she stopped and let the horses graze, while she ate a bit of jerky along with biscuits slathered with honey.

As she sat watching the animals crop sweet blossoms amid bees gathering nectar and pollen, she mused on what Léon had told her, and at one point she laughed. *Ah, my Luc, you are a comte. I cannot wait to see the look on Tutrice Martine's face when I tell her.* Hedge knight, *she called you, when you are anything but. Not that it matters one whit, for I love you for what you truly are and not for the title you bear. But Martine, now, she is caught up in status, for did she not say that instead of you, a mere chevalier, I should marry a duc or a comte at least? I am certain, though, she would prefer that I wed a prince or a king. Hedge knight, indeed. Ha! When I introduce you to her as Comte Luc du Château Blu dans le Lac de la Rose et Guardien de la Clé, ah, but she will be shocked.*

A snort from Nightshade brought Liaze out from her reflections, and she leapt to her feet and drew her long-knife and looked about. Yet she saw nought of a threat, and Nightshade and the other horses yet grazed placidly.

Again the black snorted, and Liaze laughed at the cause. "Eating bees, are we, my lad? Or did they sting your tender nose?" She stepped to the stallion and when he raised his head to her, she lifted his chin and looked at his muzzle. No bee stingers did she see embedded. "Ah, then, it was the *eating* of bees, eh? Regardless, 'tis time we were on our way."

Liaze rearranged the tethers for the mare to follow with the geldings in tow and for the stallion to lead, and she mounted Nightshade and rode away from the red-clover meadow.

Down sank the sun through the sky as Liaze continued riding in the direction Léon had said the Blue Château lay. Léon had fled far with the child, and seven shadowlight borders stood between her and that goal. She fretted that she might fail to see the landmarks the armsmaster had told her to follow, and if she drifted too far off line and simply rode ahead, then she might altogether miss the realm wherein she would find the Lake of the Rose. To avoid going elsewhere, when she reached each sunwise border, if she found herself off course, she planned to roam along the near side of the given twilight wall until she came upon the marker described by Léon denoting the place to cross.

As dusk drew its lavender cape o'er the land, with the black of night to follow swiftly after, Liaze made camp in a small hollow through which a stream ran. After taking care of the horses and laying a fire, she sat on her blankets and took a bite to eat. As she savored the last of the boiled eggs Léon had given her, she reflected on what the armsmaster had said. *Château Blu occupies the whole of a small isle in the center of the lake. There is a manmade causeway running from the shore to the manse. The manor itself is really a walled castle, and it is made of a grey-blue stone, hence the name "Blue Chateau." The Lake of the Rose is so named because of the reflections of the red-hued rock cliffs along one shore, giving the water a rosy appearance. Too, Luc's ancestors planted roses along the banks, and the briers spread, and some now follow the outlet stream that flowed forth from the sundown end of the lake. Together with the mirrored color of the cliffs and growth of the roses themselves, that's where the name came from, as well as the title of the comtes and comtesses who ruled there. And as soon as I find Luc and free him, he will take the title: Count Luc of the Blue Château in the Lake of the Rose and the Keeper of the Key.*

Liaze frowned. *Keeper of the Key? What key? Why is a key part of the title? What might that mean? And why should it be guarded? Oh, I should have asked Léon. Shall I ride back?* She sighed. *Non, that would just waste two days—one going and then one returning. No doubt I will find the meaning when I reach the château itself. Surely the Widow Dorothée will know. I wonder, were she and Léon lovers? There was a certain fondness in Léon's voice when he spoke of her as someone I could trust, as a person who would keep the horses while I go to the château as a goose girl and deliver his coded note to Comtesse Adèle.*

Even so, I would like to know what this "Guardian," this "Keeper of the Key" means in Comte Luc's full title.

Liaze spent a moment washing herself in the nearby stream, and she rubbed her teeth with a chew-stick and took a mint leaf and munched it to sweeten her breath, all the time wondering about the "Key."

The puzzle was yet flitting at the edge of her mind when she fell asleep.

Just ere dawn, Liaze startled awake. "Caillou!" she said aloud. By the light of the embers of the fire and of the waning gibbous moon, Pied Agile looked at her, and then about, as if seeking a threat. Nightshade remained adoze. Liaze got to her feet and stepped to the mare and stroked her muzzle and along her neck to calm her.

"Perhaps Caillou knew the answer," murmured Liaze to her horse. "But then again, perhaps not." And scratching Pied Agile's forehead, Liaze recalled that day on the stone creature's flank when he said he had seen a man with a black horse:

Liaze's heart jumped. "Did he wear a metal shirt and a metal cap and carry a metal horn like this one?" She held up Luc's silver trump.

Slowly, grinding, the eyes turned toward Liaze, the flinty gaze to at last come to rest upon her. "Yes . . . It was but a short pebble cascade ago when he came across."

"Oh, Lord Montagne, it was my Luc," said Liaze. "It must have been when he was on his way to my realm . . . back whence I came. Did he recently return this way? Oh, I must find him, and I could use your help, Lord Montagne, if you have any to give."

As she waited for the answer, she returned her arrow to its quiver and her bow to its saddle sheath.

At length, the being said, "Many things spill out of you all at once, as if in avalanche. . . . Indeed. . . . Avalanche. . . ."

Liaze waited, and just as she feared there would be no answer to her questions, the stone being said, "Yes, he went down the way you came. . . . No, he has not yet come back this way."

At these words, Liaze's heart fell. Even so, she knew only by wild chance would the witch in her flight have flown through this pass, dragging the shadowy hand after, Luc in its grip.

Again there came a rumble, and she realized that the mountain was yet responding to her questions. "Rrr . . . I have seen him but once, and though I tried, I could not stop him, for he bore the stone. . . . He passed through without giving me my due."

"He bore what stone?"

As if thought moved slowly through a being who seemed to be made of the mountain itself, again there was a long pause ere the creature answered. "A tiny bit of keystone." The eyes, grinding, slowly looked upward and then back down at Liaze. "It was the color of the sky."

Liaze frowned, then brightened and said, "The gem on a chain about his neck?"

"I asked if he was going to open the way, but he did not know what I was . . . speaking of, and I did not enlighten him."

"Open what way?" asked Liaze.

After long moments, the creature did not respond, and Liaze decided that he would not speak of it again, not tell her what he meant, just as he had not told Luc.

"Pied Agile," said Liaze, speaking softly to her horse, "Caillou said a piece of keystone was about Luc's neck; it was a gift given to him by his père, or so Léon said. Could this be the key of the comte's title? If so, what door does it open? —No, wait, perhaps it is not a door, for Caillou instead said it opened a 'way.' A way to where, I wonder? Or is it a way *from* somewhere instead?"

With Pied Agile now soothed, Liaze returned to her bedroll and lay down. Yet, unable to answer her own questions, she could not fall asleep. After a while she gave up her chase of elusive slumber and arose and started breaking camp—drenching the fire, feeding the animals, feeding herself and taking care of her needs. She led the horses to the stream and let them take water, and then she laded the geldings and saddled the stallion and mare. Dawn was just breaking on the sunup bound as she rode on toward her goal.

All day she fared toward the sunwise border, riding, walking, and riding again, pausing to feed the horses and herself, stopping for water, and then moving on. She passed by hunters' shacks and woodcutters' cotes and through hamlets and by farmsteads, and whenever she fared by or through those places some people would ask her for the news, but she had none to give, while others stood and watched in curious silence.

As the day sank into the sundown bound, Liaze came to a small town, where she engaged a room for one night at a tiny inn, with a village stable across the way.

"We don't get too many travelers along this road," said the proprietress. " 'Cept in the honey season, and then it's mostly buyers going up to Honey Creek, but surely you aren't one of them."

"Umn," said Liaze, shaking her head but offering nothing more.

"Regardless," said the innkeeper, "I've stew in the pot for tonight, and I'll cook you breakfast afore y'leave in the morn."

"Speaking of leaving, how far is the sunwise border from here?" asked Liaze.

"Oh, now, most of a day on a horse, if y're goin' direct sunwise."

"I am."

"Well, you take care, going that way, for I hear there's strange doings down t'th' ruins."

"Strange doings?"

The woman shrugged. "J'st a rumor, now. Som'thin' about ghastly goings-on."

"Ghastly?"

"Spirits, maybe, or ghosts. I couldn't say which. But—*pshh*—'tis j'st a rumor. Most likely some'n havin' their fun." The woman turned and started for the common room. "Come, mademoiselle, I'll fetch you your food."

As Liaze sat drinking weak ale and eating her stew—a hodgepodge of beef, tubers, and beans, all cooked together with a seasoning of salt and pepper and a bay leaf or two, along with other herbs—she pondered what the proprietress had said. *Can the ruins she speaks of be the same ones that Léon has said would be my first landmark? If so, what might be afoot in that place? Ah, Liaze, you will not know until you get there. And even if there are strange doings, still you have to pass nearby.*

The next morning after breaking her fast Liaze settled her bill and went across to the stables to retrieve her horses. She laded the geldings and stepped into Nightshade's stall to saddle him. "I hear there's something about the ruins along the sunwise border," she said to the stablehand.

" 'At's wot they say," replied the man, "though I don't know what it can be. Started about a moon ago. Haunting, I think some'n said. You plannin' on going there?"

"Nearby," said Liaze. "Down through a vale along the sunup side."

"Well, ain't no one lived there for uncounted seasons," said the man. "Not since they fled the place."

"Fled? Who?"

"Who fled? Them wot lived there, 'at's who, or so the tales tell. Seems a wizard or warlock cursed the place long past."

Orbane? "Did this wizard or warlock have a name?"

" 'F'he did, I know it not."

Liaze moved to Pied Agile's stall. "Is there ought I should know or be wary of?"

"Well, I'd steer clear o' that place, 'f'I were you, ma'am. It's got an evil reputation."

"Because of . . . ?"

"I dunno what it's because of, ma'am, j'st that it's not a place to visit."

Liaze led the mare from her stall and then tethered Night-shade after, and then the geldings to him. She paid the hostler and led all outside. As she mounted up, the inn proprietress stepped out onto her porch, and she and the hostler watched as Liaze rode away. As the princess came to the end of town, she angled the mare toward the sunwise border and kicked her into a trot.

In midafternoon Nightshade's ears pricked forward and he snorted. Liaze looked back at Pied Agile now in tow, and her ears as well as those of the geldings were pricked forward too. *What are they hearing?* she wondered, but then the sound came to Liaze:

It was a distant yelling, as of a single voice crying out.

On Liaze rode, and the shout became louder, and finally, as Nightshade broke out from the forest and into the open, the sound came clear.

A howling. Someone is howling in rage or fear or grief, or is it in agony instead? And whence comes it?

Straight ahead, the land fell away into a forested vale before her and toward a marge of twilight at the far end; a glittering stream tumbled o'er rocks at the bottom of the dell. Down in the notch a tangle of trees marched up the steep slopes to either side, but to the right and on the very brim of the vale and amid a twisted snarl of woods stood a vine-covered castle, or rather the remnants of one.

And it was from there the yowling came.

And the words of Lady Skuld echoed in Liaze's mind:

> *Instead ride with the howling one*
> *To aid you on the way.*
> *He you will find along your quest.*
> *He is the one who loudly cried.*
> *He will help you defeat dread Fear,*
> *But will not face Fear at your side.*

Liaze frowned. *Can this be the howling one? Someone within that wreck?* But then she recalled the hostler's warning. *"Well, I'd steer clear o' that place, 'f'I were you, ma'am. It's got an evil reputation."*

Liaze sighed and said to the black, "Evil or not, my lad, I cannot let this pass," and she reined Nightshade toward the ruins.

26

Castle

Circling 'round to come at the remains from a less tangled way, Liaze urged Nightshade forward. And as they approached the snarl of woods surrounding the ruins, louder came the yowling. The stallion seemed to take it in stride, but Pied Agile and the geldings snorted in apprehension and drew back on the tethers, dancing and sidle-stepping nervously. "All right, all right, I'll not force you to go," said Liaze, and she reined the black to a halt and dismounted. "Besides, I doubt you can work your way through the beringing clutch I see ahead." She tied the animals to a nearby tree, and strung her bow and took up her quiver, and loosed the safe-keeper from her long-knife in case the blade were needed.

"Ward the others, Nightshade," she said, patting the stallion along his neck, "while I find out just who or what is wailing like a grieving banshee."

She nocked an arrow to string, and then slipped this way and that past clawlike limbs reaching out to grasp.

Now and then beyond the branches and boles Liaze caught

glimpses of the castle: walls whose upper reaches were broken, rubble lying at the foot; turrets with missing shingles or holed roofs; thick wooden outer gates that gaped wide; and, on the upper levels, curtains, tattered and gray with age, stirred in the windows like uneasy wraiths.

Clearly, it's been abandoned a goodly while, for it seems more damaged from neglect than from ought else. And did the stableman not say whoever it was that had lived here had fled? Yes, I recall: "Who fled?" he repeated my question and then answered: "Them wot lived there, 'at's who, or so the tales tell. Seems a wizard or warlock cursed the place long past." Liaze caught another glimpse of the ruins and again the threadbare curtains wafted in and out. *Can it be ghosts or spirits possess the place? Is that what the wizard did—call up a haunting?*

Liaze pressed forward, her eyes her main defense against lurking foe; her ears were now useless, for the closer she had come, the louder the howling, and all other sounds were drowned under that wail.

Now she reached the outer wall, where vines grew upward thickly, their tendrils digging deep into the mortar, bringing slow ruin to the bastions. She made her way through the open and age-worn outer gate, and across a leaf-littered stone courtyard she stepped, and weedy grit and dirt ramped low against the walls of the main hall, blown there by winds long past. And here, too, the inexorable fingers of vines climbed upward and grasped at the stone to gradually erode away its strength.

Liaze paused for a moment and looked for the spoor of a beast or beasts, for, given the howling, this place might be the lair of one or more such creatures, but she found no tracks, and there was no odor of a den.

The castle door was open, its wood also badly weathered: all the softer parts were eroded away, leaving behind close-set, grainy ridges standing gray in relief; the studs and bands yet holding the stark, worn planks together were green with years of verdigris.

And still the castle shrilly wailed as of someone or something in unendurable torment.

As she stood before the portal, Liaze berated herself for not having brought wax to stopper up her hearing, for the anguished yawling was earsplitting, and it pierced her to the bone. She frowned and tried to locate the source, yet it seemed to come from the very stones themselves.

Gritting her teeth, she stepped o'er the threshold and into the hall beyond, but she took no more than a step or two before she was driven out by the agonized shriek, and she knew that not even beeswax could fend off such terrible grief.

Liaze backed away and stood a moment in painful indecision. *Ah, Mithras, this is more than I can bear.* And she turned and fled out through the gateway, and took refuge behind a bastion wall, where the howl was somewhat less piercing. She replaced the arrow in her quiver and shouldered her bow and slapped her hands over her ears to mute the sound even more, for she had to think.

Are the stones of the castle shrieking in pain? If so, how can I ride with the howling one? Lady Wyrd told me that I must take him with me, and a castle in the old tongue is a "he," a masculin term, but I cannot take an entire castle anywhere! —Wait, Liaze, and think! Did not Lady Skuld also say "He is the one who loudly cried"? Perhaps there is someone inside who started this howling. But how can I find him when I can't even get more than two paces inside the door?

Liaze sighed and shook her head and glanced back in the direction of the horses. *Surely there must be a way, else She Who Sees Through Time's Mist would not have said what she did.* Liaze's brow furrowed in thought. *If she did not steer me wrong, then there might be an answer in her words. What else did she say? Recall, Liaze, recall:*

You must soothe as you would a babe,
And speak not a loud word;
Silence is golden in some high halls;
Tread softly to not be heard.

Soothe as I would a babe! Soothe what! Soothe the castle it-
self! Again Liaze reviewed Lady Wyrd's rede, seeking a different
answer, but she could think of nought else to try. *Though it*
sounds completely foolish, mayhap that's the answer, or at
least I think it might be. Ah me, if this works—ha!—only in
Faery.

Liaze gritted her teeth and prepared to step into the full of the
yowling again, wishing that she had something, anything, to
lessen the wail somewhat.

Back through the gate she strode and to the very threshold,
for 'tis said that the doorstone, though not the heart of a home,
is the first test of approval, for it is there one might be welcomed
to step within.

Liaze knelt on the stone and stroked it, saying, "Shh, shh, my
sweet one." She began crooning a wordless song—*Soothe as you*
would a babe—and slowly the wailing diminished . . . and diminished . . . and diminished. And Liaze murmured, "Shh, shh,"
and the wailing fell to a weak cry, and that in turn was replaced
by a faint *shh . . .*

Liaze got to her feet and drew her long-knife and quietly
stepped into the manor and crept down the corridor beyond—
Silence is golden in some high halls / Tread softly to not be
heard—and doors were standing open all along the way.

She looked into the rooms and chambers and halls, dusty
with disuse, the furniture tatty, tables and chairs dilapidated,
books and pamphlets yellowed, all things within shabby beyond
redemption, and no person or persons did she see. As she quietly
moved throughout, all about her the stone walls and floors and
ceilings murmured *shh . . .*

She found no one on the ground floor nor the second or third ones. Up into the turrets she went, sections of the roofs open to rain, but, again, no one was there. She pondered a moment in the hush, and then nodded to herself. *There must be chambers below ground.* She found a lantern, its oil yet within. She knelt and huddled her cloak 'round in the hope of muffling sound, and she thumbed the striker. The lamp lit, and the soft *shh . . .* murmured by the stone of the castle changed into a faint *whssh . . .* of a burning wick.

Liaze took up her long-knife and the lantern and stood, and, with the blade in her right hand and the lamp in her left, she crept down to the first floor, where she found a way leading below, and at the bottom of the steps she came into the wine cellars 'neath. Therein were abandoned—perhaps useless— stores along with dusty bottles in racks, and large kegs along one wall. And she found an open door at one end of the cellars, with a stone stairwell leading down. Deeper she went, into dankness and darkness, her lantern illumining the way, heading for what she imagined might be and in truth were the dungeon rooms.

Past several barred lockups under the cellars and below the main hall she came to a large damp chamber, and water seeped across the floor, and a faint odor of excrement wafted on the air. Therein sat a bronze cage in the middle of the wet stone, a large padlock on the door, and within the pen lay a bundle of leaves amid a scatter of small bones and bits of fur and—*No, wait! Those are not leaves, but a little person or a child in rags instead.* Liaze raised the lantern for a better look. *'Tis a small man.* He lay on his side, his knees drawn up against his chest, and his hands were clapped over his ears. His face was twisted in agony, with his eyes squeezed shut and his lips tightly clamped. He shifted in the glow.

Liaze reached through the bars with her long-knife and tapped the flat of the blade against the being's arm.

His hands yet over his ears, the man jerked back and looked at her, his gaze flying wide, and then he squinted against the light, and flung up a hand to enshadow his eyes. It was then that a second look of startlement flooded his features, and up he sat and took his other hand away from his ear and cocked his head and listened; then his face collapsed in relief, and he quickly pressed a finger to his lips and gestured a *No, no* to Liaze, for he would have her make no sound.

Liaze nodded in understanding, and then she motioned at the lock.

The being—a wee brown man in brown tattered clothes and standing no more than three feet tall—quietly got to his feet and pointed at a far wall. And on a peg hung a ring with a single key dangling thereon. Liaze fetched the key and slipped it into the lock. *Snick!* the lock opened, and the stones of the castle clittered *Snick . . . snick . . . snick . . .* over and over.

Cautiously, Liaze edged the door open, and the hinges emitted a muted squeal, and the castle began quietly squealing in kind: *eee . . .*

Out slipped the wee man, and he and Liaze crept up the steps and into the wine cellar above, and then started for the following stairs. But the wee man turned and tiptoed to the wine racks and took up a dusty bottle and then another, and he eased back to Liaze and up they went, and all the while the castle softly squealed.

They quietly stepped along the central corridor to finally reach the outside, and dusk was on the land. In the twilight, past the outer gate they went and through the woods and to the horses.

There the little man set one wine bottle down, and against a rock he broke the neck off the other and took a long drink. He then offered the bottle to Liaze.

Liaze gestured *non* and said, "What is your name?"

The little man shook his head and pointed to an ear and

shrugged and in an overloud voice as of one who is hard of hearing, he said, "F'r the moment I canna ken y'r soft words, m'lady, f'r ma tortured ears yet ring wi' ma verra own howls." He glanced at the packhorses and said, "I see ye ha'e cookin gear. Could I borrow a stew pot? And ha'e ye anythin t'eat?"

Liaze laughed and stepped to one of the geldings and began unlading equipment and supplies, while behind her the little brown man took another long pull from the bottle, then reached under his shabby clothes and unbuckled and drew forth a many-pocketed belt.

27

Gwyd

As night drew down and Liaze unladed the animals and fed them each a ration of oats and then set them to graze, the wee brown man cleared a patch of ground and lay stones in a ring, and then he gathered a bit of dry grass and twigs and branches, and shortly he had a blaze going. Liaze handed him a small pot, and he asked for water, and soon steam rose in the air. He scrabbled through the pouches in his peculiar belt, and finally found what he was looking for. It appeared to Liaze to be nothing more than a few small dried leaves. The man crumbled two of them into the bubbling water, and added a pinch of sulphurous powder taken from another belt pouch.

"Is that tea?" asked Liaze, frowning, as she handed the man a biscuit of hardtack.

"I still canna ken y'r soft words, lady, but gi'e me a moment and I'll be as fit as new." He gobbled up the biscuit, washing the dry tack down with wine, all the while watching the bubbling pot, the liquid of which was turning a sickly yellowish green.

Finally he removed the vessel from the fire and after a moment, while it yet simmered, he drank it all, his face screwing into a knot of disgust.

"Hoo. *Brrr.* Nasty," he said, a shiver racking his spine. He took deep breaths and looked somewhat ill, and Liaze thought he would vomit. Yet he managed to keep the concoction down.

"Might I hae a second biscuit, please?" he said. "It'll help settle ma stomach." Liaze reached into the food sack and drew out another. This one he gobbled up as well. And when it was gone, he said, his voice softer, "All right, m'lady, ma hearin, it be comin back."

Liaze looked from the empty pot to the little man. "Good, for I have much to tell you. But first, are you a healer?"

"Nae. J'st a bit o' an herbalist."

"What did you drink?"

"Oh, that? A mere somethin t'get rid o' the ringin and bring back ma hearin. Now, what be it ye want t'tell me? Oh, and pardon ma manners, lady. Thank ye f'r savin ma sanity and gettin me out o' that horrible place. I be Gwyd, Manor Brunie, at y'r service."

"You are a Brownie? Oh, my. What with the tatters you wear looking much like grass and leaves, I thought you a Ghillie Dhu."

"Ghillie Dhu? Ghillie Dhu?" Incensed, Gwyd leapt to his feet and in the firelight he drew himself up to his full three-foot height. "Can ye nae see ma clothes? Brun they be. See ma skin, ma hair, ma eyes: brun they be! Brun! I'll hae ye ken I be a respectable Manor Brunie. Ghillie Dhu, pfaa!"

Liaze smiled and said, "I apologize, Gwyd, for thinking of you as something you are not. I am Liaze, Princess of the Autumnwood."

"Princess? Oh, my." Gwyd dropped to one knee and dipped his head. "I dinna mean t'rail at ye, m'lady, ye bein a princess no less, and what in Faery be ye doin out here, in the wilderness and all? Ah, but I suppose that'll be one o' the thin's y'll be tellin me. In the meanwhile, hae ye any more o' them fair biscuits, now?"

Liaze laughed and handed Gwyd another helping of hardtack, and he plopped down once more.

"Tell me Gwyd, how long were you imprisoned?"

"Nigh a whole moon by ma count, though I might hae lost track down in that dungeon deep, what wi' there bein no day and night t'tell by."

"A moon? A moon in that cage?"

Gwyd nodded.

"What have you been living on?"

"Raw rats mostly, and drinkin seep water, though now and again I took great pleasure in a beetle or a crawlin worm. Spiders, now, they're a bit bitter, but I ate them when I could."

As revulsion swept over Liaze's face, she realized whence came the small bones and bits of fur she had seen in the cage. And she shuddered at the thought of eating raw rats and spiders and worms and beetles.

Gwyd looked at her contorted visage and smiled and said, "The stayin alive was the easy part. 'Twas the noise that nearly drove me mad. And the terrible thin' was, it was ma verra own howls taken up by that cursed place. Why the rats nae did flee fra the howlin, I'll ne'er ken, but they nae left the castle at all." He took another slug of wine, emptying the bottle, then cocked his head and looked at her. "And speakin o' the howlin, j'st how did ye manage t'quieten it down?"

"I soothed as I would a babe," said Liaze, "and that's part of what I want to talk to you about."

"Soothed as ye would a babe? Now that be somethin that ne'er would o' entered ma own mind." Gwyd got up and stepped to the second bottle of wine. He broke off the neck against the same rock and then returned to the fire. Liaze shook her head when he offered her the first drink. Yet standing, Gwyd took a swift gulp and said, "Princess, before you begin on y'r story, would ye wait until I take me a bath? I smell something terrible t'ma own sel', and so it must be e'en worse f'r ye. And hae ye got something t'wrap masel' in, f'r ma clothes need washin too?"

Liaze smiled and fetched a cloth and pointed off toward the stream that flowed downslope and toward the vale.

By the time Gwyd returned, Liaze had brewed a pot of tea and offered him some, but the Brownie stuck to the wine.

Gwyd hung his wet garments on a nearby limb, and then settled down by the fire and looked at Liaze. "Weel then, m'lady, whater'er it be ye would tell me, say on."

Liaze nodded and said, "It concerns the quest I'm on, and it all started at a pool in a willow grove on my estate. Eve had fallen and I had just taken a swim when I heard a horn sounding an alert. Moments later a wounded chevalier on yon black horse you see agraze came crashing through the willow branches and . . ."

". . . And so you see, Gwyd, that's why I think you are the so-called howling one of the rede."

The waning gibbous moon had risen and the second bottle of wine was empty by the time Liaze finished her tale.

"Tell me this rede again, m'lady," said Gwyd, and he braced himself as if for an ordeal, for when she had first spoken Lady Wyrd's words he had cried out in alarm. She had asked him why, but he had put her off until the telling was done.

Liaze nodded and in a somber voice said:

> In the long search for your lost true love
> You surely must ride with Fear,
> With Dread, with Death, with many Torn Souls,
> Yet ride with no one from here.
>
> For should you take a few with you,
> Most Fear would likely slay.

Instead ride with the howling one
To aid you on the way.

He you will find along your quest.
He is the one who loudly cried.
He will help you defeat dread Fear,
But will not face Fear at your side.

You must soothe as you would a babe,
And speak not a loud word;
Silence is golden in some high halls;
Tread softly to not be heard.

In the dark of the moon but two moons from now
A scheme will be complete,
For on a black mountain an ever-slowing heart
Will surely cease to beat.

As Liaze fell silent, "Weel then," said Gwyd, "I ken nothin about a black mountain, but I do agree I be the howlin one, and since ye set me free, and because Lady Skuld said so, it seems I hae nae choice but t'accompany ye. Yet as the rede says, I'll not face Fear at y'r side, f'r he be a dreadful thin', he be."

"A dreadful thing? Know you what that part means, Gwyd?"

"Aye, I do." Gwyd looked about for more wine, yet only broken-necked bottles did he find. One after another he turned up both and caught a drop from each and then muttered, "I should hae brought more out wi' me."

"Gwyd, I ask: what does it mean I must ride with Fear?"

The Brownie sighed. "Let me tell ye ma own tale, startin wi' the most recent first. Then I'll get t'Lord Fear hisself."

"I was the Manor Brunie at Laird Duncan's mansion. But then Redcap Goblins and Trolls came and occupied the place, and ma laird and lady barely escaped alive. I stayed behind, tryin t'think o' a way t'oust the greedy poltroons.

"I slipped about unseen by the brutes—we Brunies can be verra sneaky—and I list t'their Goblin talk. It seems they were fleein a mighty warrior when they came upon ma laird's manor, and they thought it e'en better than the castle they fled when the mighty warrior got loose. Y'see, it seems this warrior had been gi'en t'them as their pris'ner, and he had slain two o' their Redcaps as he broke free. Then, as he was gettin away, he killed two o' their Trolls as he escaped on a raft, accompanied by a Sprite and a wee little bee. They recked he would nae doubt return wi a warband, and so they fled."

Liaze laughed and said, "Oh, Gwyd, 'tis my brother Borel whom they fear. And, indeed, he did slay Goblins and Trolls as he escaped their prison. They were Hradian's lackeys or minions or allies—I know not which."

Gwyd frowned. "Hradian?"

"A witch. One of Orbane's acolytes."

Gwyd made a warding sign at the mention of Orbane, but he motioned Liaze to go on. Liaze nodded and said, "Hradian: she is the one responsible for Borel being imprisoned in the first place. She cast a great spell that bore him away, and when he awoke, in the Troll prison he was, shackled to a wall. But as you know, he escaped, and slew some of his jailors in doing so."

"Weel," said Gwyd, "if he comes back and tracks them down, he won't slay these."

"Why not?"

"They have some o' ma elixir o' life-givin'."

"Life-giving?"

"Aye. It be made fra the golden apples in a faraway realm, fermented in ma laird's own special crystal decanters. Brandy it be, and wondrous, but only if given wi'in moments o' death, or j'st ere dyin."

"Oh, could we get the elixir, perhaps it will save Luc's life. Where lies this estate?"

Gwyd gestured at the moonlit twilight border looming in the near distance. "Yon way, I think, though I be not at all certain. Y'see, I was carried away in a sack and didn't see nought, but if I be right, it be not too far."

Liaze nodded and said, "Go on with your tale, for I would hear of this Lord Fear you named."

"Weelanow, Princess, I was caught by the Trolls while tryin t'steal that very life-givin brandy. I thought they were goin t'kill me, but instead they brought me here. It seems in their flight fra y'r brother, they had come upon this cursed place, and they knew how terrible it was. Jeerin and jibin, they bound me and gagged me and threw me in that sack I told ye about and haled me t'that cursed castle yon.

"I knew somethin was up when I heard a great deal o' snickerin and sneerin, but it was a bloody lot more than j'st two Trolls and a handful o' Redcaps could make. It was the castle o' course, echoin back their own cruel glee.

"They dumped me fra the sack and locked me in the cage where y'found me. And then they went away, leavin me bound and gagged, and leavin their derision behind.

"But among the snickerin and sneerin I could hear them takin bottles, and it had t'be wine they were after, f'r why else would they bring me all this way j'st t'throw me into a cage? Nae, 'twas the grape that brought them here, and they took me along f'r the jape o' it.

"When I got free o' ma bonds, and ripped the gag fra ma mouth, I called after them, shouted what a filthy lot they be, and so the castle yelled back at me as t'what a filthy lot I maself be.

"I tried everythin I could think of t'quieten the castle adown, but nothin seemed t'work. O' course, I didn't try soothin, like y'did. Anyway, I took it as long as I could, and finally I howled out louder than what I had yelled before, and that be the way it hae been f'r nearly a moon. Like t'drive me mad, it did, and I ween ye came j'st in time."

"In my case," said Liaze, "I nearly went mad from an ever-blowing wind and then, later on, from silence. I cannot imagine what it must have been like, living in a constant howl as you were, especially for an entire moon."

"What made it worse," said Gwyd, "was that it was ma own howl screamin in ma own ears."

Liaze nodded and reached out and patted Gwyd on the arm. "I am both sorry and not sorry that I found you thus, for I need you to go with me. —Now tell me of the one you call Lord Fear."

"Ah, him," said Gwyd, shuddering. "Weel, this be the way o' that. Y'see, Laird Duncan's manor was the second home I've lost, f'r I used t'be the Brunie o' a splendid inn. But then Lord Dread and his hideous band came, and everyone fled but me. They sat around drinkin a strange black ale, one I ne'er saw ere then. Me, I hid till Lord Fear got up and he and his followin were gone . . . but nae gone f'r good, f'r he and his riders continued thereafter t'stop at the end o' their day—or night, I should say, f'r 'twas always night when they came. I continued t'hide when Lord Death, Lord Dread, Lord Terror, Lord Fear stopped by, and I was ever glad when he and his ghastly bunch rode on toward their mountain fastness each day j'st ere dawn. But I was alone, and the inn fell into disuse, what wi' him and his band comin there every night. Finally, I could take it no longer, and I fled."

"When was this?"

"Long past."

"Is Lord Fear still stopping there at night?"

"I don't know."

"Well, I must ride with him."

"Oh, m'lady, no matter what the rede says, I think that would be t'y'r doom."

Liaze shook her head, and again she quoted lines from Lady Wyrd's rede:

> *In the long search for your lost true love*
> *You surely must ride with Fear,*
> *With Dread, with Death, with many Torn Souls . . .*

"Gwyd, know you what means the phrase 'with many Torn Souls'?"

"It be his ghastly band, m'lady. They be not men but the souls o' men instead."

Liaze gasped. "Can this be true?"

"Aye, f'r Lord Fear rides the Wild Hunt."

Liaze paled. "Oh, I see."

They sat in silence for a moment, and then Liaze took a deep breath and said, "Nevertheless, I must ride with him."

"There be only one way I ken how that be done," said Gwyd.

"Tell me."

"He must find ye in the open at night, on the moors or in the fields or along a lonely stretch o' road."

"Know you such a place, Gwyd?"

The Brownie frowned in thought, and then said, "As I was journeyin away fra the inn and—though I didna ken it at the time—toward Laird Duncan's manor, I crossed a bleak moor and j'st as I got t'the woods on the far side, Lord Death came ridin past. Mayhap it be a place he oft travels nigh. If that be so, we can wait there, and each night y'can stand on the moor until he comes."

"It does not seem like a certain plan," said Liaze.

"Nae, Princess, it does not, but hae ye a better one?"

"Can I not merely wait at the inn?"

"Then, m'lady, he would slay ye outright, f'r ye will not hae passed his test."

"His test?"

"Aye. Ye must suffer his dogs wi'out fleein or e'en flinchin, else they'll take y'r soul. Those that survive his test are then asked if they would ride wi' him. That be the only moment y'can politely turn him adown, or take him up on his offer. But those that do are doomed t'ride wi' him f'r e'er."

"Ah, there must be some way to ride with him and not suffer that doom."

"If so, I ken not what it be," said Gwyd.

"Well, on our way to Laird Duncan's manor and then to that bleak moor, we'll just have to think of one," said Liaze.

"Laird Duncan's manor? Y'plan on goin into what be now a Troll hole?"

"How else are we going to get the elixir of life-giving?" asked Liaze.

Gwyd laughed aloud and then sobered. "Ah, m'lady, 'twill be dangerous, but, oh my, what a splendid thin' t'do." Again he broke out in laughter, while Liaze nodded and smiled.

28

Troll Hole

Just after sunrise, Liaze awakened to the clink of glass as well as a voice from afar, and when she sat up Gwyd was removing wine bottles from a basket and wrapping them in cloth. At her wide-eyed look, Gwyd said, "Weel, Princess, I got t'thinkin I should go back and get some bottles o' refreshment f'r the trail ahead . . . as weel as somthin t'wrap them in t'keep them safe from the jostlin, and so I did."

Liaze smiled and shook her head. Then she turned toward the distant sound. "And that is . . . ?"

"Och, it be a message f'r any who might come by. Y'see, when I was leavin, j'st ere steppin out the door, I simply called out, 'Warnin: this castle be cursed. It be best t'stay away.' O' course that now be what the place itself be sayin, and it might keep folks fra the door. Besides, if I e'er come back this way, there might still be some o' this glorious and verra-weel-aged wine in the cellars f'r the takin."

Liaze laughed and said, "Clever of you, Gwyd." She got to her feet and kicked up the fire and set a pot of water on the flames for brewing tea. And while the liquid was heating, she took up a small pouch and went among the bushes to relieve herself and then down to the stream to wash and take care of her feminine needs. When she returned to the fire, the tea was steeping, for Gwyd—Brownie true—had taken care of the undone. Too, he had set out jerky and hardtack for their morning meal.

Liaze did not show gratitude to Gwyd, for as with all of his Kind, any offer of a reward or even a simple "merci" would drive a Brownie away. Just handing him the hardtack biscuits yestereve was coming close to breaking the Brownie proscription; but since they were not offered as a gift or a reward, but rather as something needed, Gwyd had accepted them and gladly.

"Would that I hae some eggs, Princess, then we would hae ourselves a feast."

Liaze smiled and said, "The first town we come across, we'll take a room at an inn, and, even if just for a day, we'll eat sumptuously and rest in comfort, and then be on our way."

Gwyd's face fell into a troubled frown, as if trying to determine whether or not this was a gift or an offer of recompense. Finally he shrugged, and his visage once more took on its normal good-natured grin.

They ate jerky and hardtack and drank strong tea, and finally they broke camp—Liaze lading and saddling the animals, Gwyd quenching the fire and rolling the blankets into bedrolls and tying them with leather thongs.

Liaze looked at the diminutive Brownie—three feet tall at most—and she knew there wasn't a way to shorten the stirrups enough on Pied Agile's saddle to fit his small stature. Instead, she fashioned a second set of stirrups from a length of rope strung high along the sides between the forebow and cantle.

"Y'dinna expect me t'steer that great big thin', now, do ye?" asked Gwyd.

"No, Gwyd. I'll tether her behind Nightshade and tow you along."

"Ah, weel and good. Me, I prefer a pony, and should we come across any—"

"Ah, Gwyd, there might come a time when we need to run at speed, and a pony would slow us down."

"Ah, woe," said the Brownie. "Then I be sentenced t'this great galootin beastie until our venture be done, eh?"

"It seems so," said Liaze. "Now here, let me give you a boost up."

Again Gwyd frowned, once more trying to determine if this were a gift of sorts.

" 'Tis necessary," said Liaze, as if reading his mind.

"Ah, weel then," said Gwyd, and he offered himself for a lift.

Once upon the mare, Gwyd let out a crow. "Ah, if ma adopted cousin, a Pixie named Twk, could only see me now. I mean, here I am on a great horse, while Twk himself rides a saddled rooster."

"A saddled rooster?"

"Aye. And Twk takes great glee in keepin the poor rooster awake and causin him t'crow at all hours o' the night and disturbin folks fra their sleep. Ha! Those so disturbed always say the rooster must be pixilated, but they nae hae any idea j'st how right they be. Ah, but I do miss wee Twk and his pranks."

Liaze laughed and said, "Mayhap we will meet him along the way, for it sounds as if he is a clever wit, and perhaps a wit such as his would come in handy, for we need a scheme to defeat Lord Fear after I have taken my ride."

Liaze mounted up on Nightshade, and she turned him toward the vale with its twilight border at the far end.

Downslope they rode, the mare with Gwyd astride, and the geldings following. And as they wended toward the dell, Gwyd fell silent, the Brownie immersed in deep thought.

Into the vale they went, and Liaze stopped and let the horses take draughts from the brook running along the bottom. And she filled the waterskins to the full. As she did so, Gwyd said not a word, rapt as he was in his own pondering.

On down the dell they went, and then through the twilight at the end, and they came out on the crest of a tall hill, the slope falling away into a land of rolling plains, and in the distance a river glittered in the morning sunlight. Farmsteads dotted the 'scape, and leftward afar a forest spread o'er long slopes.

"Well?" said Liaze.

Gwyd made no response.

Liaze turned in the saddle and said, "Gwyd?"

"Huh?" The Brownie was jerked from his thoughts. "What?"

"Is this the place? If not, we can ride back through the border and try somewhere else."

Gwyd looked about. "Ah, yes, Princess. Duncan's manor be in those distant woods."

"Hmm . . . Well then, we'll head that way, but once I reach the line of trees, you'll have to guide us toward the mansion."

"Aye," said Gwyd, and once again he fell to pondering.

It was nigh midday when they came to the forest. At Liaze's call, Gwyd surfaced from his thinking, and he said, "Tell me, Princess, can ye sing?"

Liaze looked at him and frowned. "What has this to do with stealing the elixir?"

"Nought," replied the Brownie. "Regardless, can ye sing?"

"I've been known to carol a *ballade* or two, not as well as Camille or Alain, but I'm a fair hand at it."

"Can ye play a harp?"

Liaze sighed. "Oui. My père and mère thought it proper that all of us—Borel, Alain, Celeste, and I—learn several instruments: harpsichord, flute, lute, harp, and drum. But what does—?"

"I might ken a way t'break Lord Fear's hold o'er ye, but y'll hae t'do y'r part while I do mine."

Liaze's eyes flew wide in surprise. "You do? You have a way?"

"I nae be certain, and I'll hae t'ponder on it some more, but I think it j'st might work, given the Fates be on our side."

"Oh, tell me, tell me," urged Liaze.

"Nae. Gi'e me more time t'think on it. But I'll tell ye this: we need t'steal not only the elixir and the crystal decanters fra the Trolls and Goblins, but also the silver harp I left behind—'twas ma own—and we'll need t'take one o' the laird's red scarves."

"You're not going to tell me, are you," said Liaze, her words not a question.

"Ah, Princess, I dinna want t'get y'r hopes up. Besides I need t'take consultation wi' them what might know. Then I'll tell ye what I hae in mind."

Liaze sighed in exasperation, but Gwyd said, "Go straight on f'r a ways. Up ahead we'll stop and get some good rest—e'en sleep if we can—while we wait f'r night, cause we'll nae be goin in t'the place until the wee marks. Then we need approach the manor fra the downwind side so as not t'be scented, especially the animals, f'r Trolls and Redcaps prize horse flesh above e'en that o' Humans, though I think they would find ye a tasty morsel."

Liaze shuddered to hear of the dietary habits of these Folk, and she said, "Then let us make certain that they do not sniff us out."

In the moonlight they quietly slipped from tree to bush to tree and then to the low stone wall surrounding the mansion, Gwyd leading the way, for he knew every nook and cranny and rock and plant on the laird's manor grounds. As they crouched by the wall, and as Gwyd peered through a slot where a brick was missing, Liaze softly said, "Tell me, Gwyd, with Trolls and Redcaps about, how think you the farmsteads nearby deal with such?"

Without taking his gaze away from the manor, Gwyd said, "I would think they ne'er go out alone at night—in fact put up barricades and stay wi'in—and they are nae doubt weel armed by now."

Liaze nodded and said, "My thoughts exactly. Yet, were these Trolls and Goblins in my demesne, I would take a warband and clean out this vipers' nest. Is there no one nearby to do the same?"

" 'Twould hae been the laird's t'do, f'r he was the first one raided and taken by surprise."

"Were there no guards posted?"

Gwyd shook his head. " 'Twasn't needed ere the Trolls came, and then it were too late. —And speakin o' guards, there do be a Redcap makin rounds."

Gwyd moved aside and let Liaze peer through the slot. In the moonlight a Goblin shuffled alongside the building.

Liaze and Gwyd waited and watched, and finally, after several rounds, they determined that this Redcap seemed to be the only sentry.

"We'll wait until he turns the corner on his next pass," said Gwyd, "then we'll make f'r the door t'the root cellar."

"The root cellar?"

"Aye, it connects t'the wine cellars, and they in turn lead up and in. And we can slip through the halls and t'the second floor and t'the laird's study, f'r that be where the elixir be kept as weel as the crystal decanters. Too, ma own quarters be in the cellars, and that's where ma harp lies, assumin o' course they have nae melted it adown f'r the silver it bears."

"And the red scarf?"

"Next t'the laird's study there be a dressin' room, and several should be inside."

"Ha, then, the most dangerous part is getting from the cellar to the study and back, eh?"

"Aye."

"Then let's have at it, my friend."

As they waited, Gwyd said, "It be nae meet t'blame the laird f'r nae bein ready. He took a bad wound in his escape, and where he went I know not. But I hae nae doubt as soon as he be mended, he'll be out raisin a warband. Yet all his weapons and armor and such lie in yon manor, and it'll take a bit o' time t'gather up the men and the gear he needs in order t'take this place back and t'slay all o' those what took it away in the first place."

Finally the sentry passed once more, and the moment he rounded the turn, across the lawn they zigzagged, keeping to shade and bush, Liaze with an arrow nocked and a rucksack at her side, Gwyd with Liaze's scabbard at his waist and her long-knife in hand, the blade a sword to one of his stature.

They came to a slanted cellar door, and, as Liaze stood watch, Gwyd haled on the handle, but it didn't budge. "Garn! It be barred fra inside."

Liaze glanced 'round and up. "We can climb to the balcony."

"Aye," said Gwyd, and he sheathed the long-knife and up a trellis he scrambled.

Liaze slipped her arrow back into the quiver, and slung her bow, and followed.

Just as she swung her leg across the balustrade, "Oi!" came a call from below. It was the Redcap guard. And he stood gaping up at them.

In the moonshadow, Liaze whipped her bow off her shoulder even as the sentry took a deep breath to shout.

"*Foe!*" he yelled. *SsssThock!* The arrow took him in the throat, and he fell clutching his neck, a bubbling gargle now his cry. Momentarily his feet drummed the sod, and then he fell still.

In the near distance sounded a door opening.

"Come, quickly," hissed Gwyd, and he stepped to the glass doors, but they were locked. Liaze jabbed a leather-clad elbow into a pane, and it shattered. Gwyd reached through and twisted the handle, and they slipped into the darkened room.

By moonlight they crossed the chamber, and Gwyd stood with his ear to the door, listening.

From outside the manor there came a deep call: 'twas the voice of a Troll.

Footsteps went running past in the hall just beyond the door. Silence followed.

Gwyd opened the panel a crack and peered outward. *"Now!"* he hissed, and he stepped into the corridor.

Down the passageway he ran, Liaze following, and he darted into a chamber. Liaze came after, and Gwyd stood, his fists clenched in rage, peering at a large desk. "Those bloody fools!"

In the moonlight on the desk Liaze saw a jumble of papers and a heap of coins—gold, silver, bronze—next to an empty crystal vessel lying on its side and another standing upright, with their stoppers and a crystal bar lying between. "What is it, Gwyd?"

"Knobbleheads! They've drunk all the elixir."

Liaze groaned.

"Stupidly thinkin, no doubt," said Gwyd, " 'twas nought but apple brandy."

"What can we do?"

"The decanters are here and unharmed"—he took up the crystal bar and examined it—"as well as the bridge, and can we get some more o' the golden apples, we'll be all right." Liaze drew squares of cloth from the rucksack at her side, and Gwyd capped and wrapped each decanter separately and then the bar and slipped them into the bag. Then he laded fistfuls of coins onto another square and tied it tightly so as not to jingle and slipped the improvised purse into the rucksack, saying, "We ne'er ken when treasure might be needed."

On the grounds outside there was a hue and cry and a thrashing about of bushes.

"The red scarf," said Liaze, and Gwyd stepped to a hidden door and within the chamber beyond, and a moment later he emerged with a scarlet length of winter neckwear. Into the rucksack it went.

"Now f'r ma harp."

In the yard a Troll roared and Goblins squealed, as the search for intruders went on.

Back into the corridor went Gwyd and Liaze, blade in hand and arrow nocked. Gwyd ran to a stairwell and listened, then darted downward, Liaze running quietly after.

Down they went to the first floor and along a short hallway there. And then down more steps they ran, and they came into the cellars. Gwyd hissed, "Wait," and after a moment and the sound of a striker, light seeped out through a crack of a hooded lantern. Broken wine bottles were strewn about the floor and sacks of supplies were torn open. Cursing at the mess, Gwyd quickly strode to a small door and opened it and stepped within, while Liaze again stood ward without. In moments Gwyd emerged with a small silver harp. It, too, went into the rucksack.

"Now t'escape," said Gwyd, and he led Liaze to another door.

They entered a root cellar, with tubers and leeks and beets and other such hanging from ceiling beams, and jars of preserves on shelves within. A short set of steps led up to a slanted door barred on the inside by a heavy beam. Together they slid the timber out from the brackets and set it aside.

"Wait," said Liaze, unlooping the heavily laden rucksack from over her shoulder and setting it down. "We need to draw them away from the grounds. Give me the lantern, and I'll take care of that."

"What be ye goin' t'do, Princess?"

"Start a fire on the first floor."

"In ma laird's manor?"

"Oui."

Gwyd groaned but handed Liaze the lantern.

Away she ran on light feet, and up the stairs to the first floor.

She stepped into a room—a dining hall—and went to a window facing the yard where the Redcap was slain. Flanking the window were ensconced lamps. Quickly she pulled one down and emptied its oil on the drapery. Then she took the other lantern and lit it and set the curtains aflame. *Whoosh!* Fire roared up the cloth, and Liaze hurled the second lantern crashing through the window and shouted, "Oi, uglies, I'm in here!"

Yells came from outside the manor, and Liaze grabbed up the shuttered lantern and bolted from the chamber and down the corridor and into the cellars below.

Swiftly she ran, and as she crossed the floor she heard footsteps pounding above. To the root cellar she fled, where Gwyd stood waiting.

"Now," said Liaze, closing down the lantern and shouldering the rucksack and then nocking an arrow, " 'tis time to fly."

In the dark, Gwyd opened the slanted door, and up and out and into the moonlight he stepped, right into the grasp of a great Troll.

"Rawww!" roared the twelve-foot-tall creature, snatching up the wee Brownie, the long-knife flying from Gwyd's hand.

But then the Troll gasped, and looked at his chest, where the arrow had pierced his heart.

Thock! And another shaft sprang forth from his left eye.

The Troll reeled and stumbled backward and thudded to the earth, the fiend dead even as it hit the ground, Gwyd yet clutched in its monstrous grip.

Liaze stepped out from the cellar, another arrow nocked, but it was not needed.

She helped pry the Troll's fingers loose, and groaning in pain, Gwyd said, "I think some o' ma ribs be broke."

"Nevertheless," said Liaze, taking up the long-knife and sheathing it in the scabbard at Gwyd's side, "we must flee before others come."

And so, across the lawn they ran, where Liaze helped Gwyd

over the wall. Into the forest beyond they fled, Gwyd gasping in agony, while behind flames roared out from the dining chamber window, the bellow of the fire counterpoint to the shouts and squalls of Redcaps and Trolls as they battled the blaze inside.

29

Moor

The sun had risen by the time they rode out from the woods, and Gwyd said, "Princess, head f'r the nearest burnie, I canna catch ma breath, and I need t'take a simple."

Liaze looked downslope to left and right and angled Nightshade a bit dextral, and they rode to a wee bourne running toward a farmstead below. She halted the horses and then helped Gwyd down from Pied Agile and said, "What can I do to aid?"

"I be needin a cup, if ye dinna mind, Princess."

As Liaze fetched a cup from the goods, the Brownie stepped to the rill and, groaning, eased down. He took a pinch of powder from one of his belt pockets, and when Liaze knelt beside him and handed him the cup, he dipped up some spring water and dropped the powder within. After swirling it 'round a bit, he gulped it down.

"We'll need t'sit awhile, m'lady," said Gwyd. "Soon I'll be ready t'ride, and ma ribs, they'll be mended in a day or two."

"A day or two? What did you drink, a magic potion?"

"Weel, I would nae call it magic, but merely quick healin.

Och, we Brunies seldom be injured in the daily course o' livin, but I would nae call gettin squeezed by a Troll as bein in the daily course. Nae, Princess, ma herbs nae be magic, but the laird's decanters do be."

"Ah, the decanters." Liaze stood and stepped to the horses to retrieve the rucksack.

"Och, m'lady, would y'fetch one o' them bottles o' wine while y'r at it? Ma ribs could use a bit o' soothin."

Liaze laughed and grabbed one of the cloth-wrapped bottles from the cargo, along with a corkscrew from the cooking gear.

She brought all back to Gwyd and sat down and popped the plug from the bottle and handed it to him. Gwyd offered her the first drink of the wine, but Liaze shook her head. Instead, she took the small harp from the bag and set it aside, and then one by one she took out the wrapped crystal goods and removed the cloth from each decanter and examined them: arcane runes were deeply carved into their sides.

She unwrapped the crystal bar. It, too, had runes carved into its sides, and along one side at each end there seemed to be a stopper. "You called this a 'bridge,' Gwyd. What is it for? And these runes: what are they?"

Gwyd took another long pull on the wine and wiped his mouth along his sleeve and said, "Wellanow, Princess—these runes?—they be what powers the magic. Them and the fact the decanters and bridge be carved fra the same single piece o' pure crystal. Y'see, when I came t'ma laird's place, he told me that the runes be used t'turn grape juice t'wine, and then the wine t'brandy. Here, let me show ye." Gwyd took up one of the decanters, uncapped it, and poured a cupful of wine in it, and then picked up the crystal bridge. "Though it now be wine therein, usually y'put ord'nary juice in this one and stopper it wi' the bridge, like so. Mind ye now, top j'st this vessel and nae the other. See this rune on the decanter—and this end o' the bridge wi' the matchin rune—that be the cap f'r this one." Gwyd popped the stopper on the side of one end of the bar onto the decanter, the bar itself now jutting out thwartwise. "Then ye wait f'r the juice t'ferment, which it does o'ernight. —And don't that be a wonder?" He paused in his explanation and took another slug of wine as Liaze examined the decanter and bar.

"Then what?" asked Liaze.

"Then, Princess, ye connect the other end o' the bridge t'the other decanter—see these runes on the bar and the matchin ones on the vessel?—so that it spans fra this one t'that one." Now the decanters stood side by side, with the crystal bridge spanning crosswise from the top of one to the top of the other. "This one, the first one, turns hot," said Gwyd, "and that one, the other, turns cold. Here, feel them."

Liaze reached out and placed a hand on each, her eyes widening in wonder. "Why, yes. Warm and chill. How splendid."

Gwyd took another gulp of wine and said, "As the heated vapors be driven fra the hot t'the cold, they drip out as brandy. And that do be a wonder in itself."

Liaze watched as the first drop fell into the cold side. "How long does that take altogether?"

"If the hot decanter be full when y'start, less than a candlemark, Princess. This one, wi' nought but a cup or so in it, well, it should be done right soon."

Liaze nodded and then shook her head in bemusement. "How marvelous these are. In the Autumnwood, we make brandy using copper vats and a coil of copper tubing."

"Aye, and that's the way I maself always did it, but when I heard my laird hae such wondrous thin's, I knew I could take ma golden-apple juice and turn it t'cider and then connect the bridge and distill the elixir o' life-givin all in a day or so. Och, wi' them, I could be done so much faster than I otherwise could."

Liaze nodded and watched as brandy was distilled from wine.

"Gwyd, what if we connected the bridge backwards? Would it make a death-dealing drink instead?"

"I nae ken, m'lady, f'r I hae ne'er tried it such. F'r all I ken, it j'st might explode."

They watched while more brandy dripped into the cold side, and finally Liaze said, "This life-giving elixir, how far must we go to fetch some golden apples?"

"Many a day, Princess. Many a day." Gwyd gestured toward the horses and said, "Though on Pied Agile and Nightshade, it'll be quicker than me afoot, as I hae always gone before. But, list: fetchin the apples be a dangerous thin', f'r the garden and the apples themselves be well warded."

"Garden?"

"Aye, a high-walled garden wi' but a single e'er-bearin tree."

"And this tree is well warded?"

"Aye, by a giant unsleepin serpent." Gwyd drank the last of the wine and Liaze got up and fetched another bottle.

"If it's warded by an unsleeping serpent, how did you get some of the apples in the first place?"

As Liaze sat down and opened the second bottle, "Ah, Princess," said Gwyd, "there be but one day a year when the serpent dozes f'r a moment—and a moment only—and that gi'es him all the rest he needs f'r another entire year. It be in that moment the tree itsel' be unwarded, and that be when I dart in, fetch a single apple and dart away fra the garden. I hae done it thrice altogether, and in the third instance I was nearly the snake's dinner. But I got o'er the wall j'st in time, and he missed his strike." Again Gwyd offered the princess first drink, and again Liaze shook her head.

"And when is this day he sleeps?"

"It be in the night o' the longest day o' the year."

Liaze's face fell. "Oh, Gwyd, the night of the longest day is three moons past and will not come again for nine or ten moons, and I now have but a moon and a sevenday ere a heart will cease to beat." Liaze sighed. "Mayhap we'll have to forgo the life-giving elixir."

They sat in glum silence for long moments, Liaze thinking, Gwyd sipping wine, while in the far distance downslope crofters worked in their fields.

"Ah," said Gwyd, "the brandy, it be done. Feel the decanters now, m'lady."

"Why, they're cool, Gwyd."

"Aye. The process be finished." He rinsed out the cup from which he had taken his powdered simple and handed it to her. "Here, Princess, gi'e it a taste."

Liaze removed the bridge and poured the distillate into the cup and took a sip. "Oh, my, it is quite good."

Gwyd rinsed out the decanters and the bridge, and set them in the sun to air-dry.

Together, Gwyd and Liaze sat awhile on the bank of the rill, she sipping brandy, he drinking wine.

Finally Liaze reached into the knapsack and pulled out the red scarf. "Why this, Gwyd? Why the red scarf?"

"Princess, let me speak t'some Pixies first. If I be right, then it be part o' the plan t'let ye ride wi' the Wild Hunt and yet escape Lord Death in the end."

Liaze gritted her teeth and said, "Gwyd, there is no reason for you not to tell me of this plan of yours. If it happens to be based on mistaken assumptions, well—"

"Ah, Princess, let me speak t'Pixies first, then I'll tell all."

Vexed, Liaze peevishly rewrapped the crystal decanters and the crystal bridge, and put them back in the rucksack, and tossed the scarf in after. "I don't know why I have to ride with the Wild Hunt in the first place, and your refusal merely adds to the frustration."

"Well, m'lady, I reck ye need t'ride wi' the Hunt simply t'find y'r Luc."

Liaze frowned. "Why, I would think he's at the Blue Château, or nearby. That's what Léon believes as well. Besides, that's the way the crows flew."

"Nae, Princess. 'Fit were that simple, why would Lady Skuld hae gi'en ye the rede in the first place?"

Liaze threw up her hands. "Who knows the ways of the Fates, Gwyd? Not I, and certainly not you."

"Nae, I dinna ken the Fates, and about that ye of certain be correct, yet here be the way I think on it: Lady Skuld says right in the beginnin o' her rede 'In y'r long search f'r y'r lost true love, ye must surely ride wi Fear.' T'me a key part o' the rede is 'long search,' which means y'r Luc will nae be easy t'find. Now this we do know: the Wild Hunt rides o'er many a realm, and if Luc be nae at the Blue Château or e'en nearby, then the only way ye might find him be if the Hunt passes o'er where he be ensconced, where he be imprisoned. If that be true, then the Wild Hunt be the only chance ye hae t'recover y'r Luc."

"Oh, Gwyd, think you that is true?"

"I dinna ken, m'lady," said the Brownie. "But Lady Skuld says it be a long search and that ye need ride wi' Fear, and that be Lord Dread and the Wild Hunt t'my way o thinkin."

Glumly, Liaze sighed and nodded.

"My ribs already be knittin," said Gwyd, getting to his feet. "I ween it be time t'be on our way, f'r the moor be some days afar, and, as ye hae said, the moon waits f'r no one."

The princess reladed the goods and then helped the Brownie onto Pied Agile. "Which way, Gwyd?"

"We'll hae t'go t'ward the inn where I once served as Brunie, f'r that be the way t'the moor. Besides, that also be the way t'the Pixies I ken, Twk among them, though the heath comes first."

Liaze stepped to Nightshade, and of a sudden Gwyd groaned. Liaze turned. "Are you in pain?"

"Och, nae, Princess, but I hae a revelation."

"A revelation?"

"Aye. A problem hae reared its head: a flaw in ma plan. Y'see, since the moor comes ere the realm o' the inn, and since in that realm be where the Pixies live, then if the Wild Hunt happens by ere I speak t'the Pixies, then you'll be aridin' ere we ken what I hae in mind will work or nae at all."

"Then, Gwyd, you had better tell me what my part in this plan is, for I will not forgo a chance to ride Nightshade with the Wild Hunt."

"Oh, m'lady, a normal horse canna run wi' the Hunt. Nae, ye must ride one o' Lord Fear's own steeds."

"If that's the way it must be, Gwyd, then our horses will be in your charge."

Gwyd sighed. "I'll hae t'lead them t'the Pixies, and fra there t'the woodland near the inn, where I'll wait f'r you t'gi' me the signal."

"The signal? What signal?"

"Aye, the signal that ye ken where y'r Luc be."

Liaze said, "Gwyd, you must tell me of this plan, for I must know what you have in mind if I am to do my part while you do yours. Heed me: whether or no it is deemed worthy by the Pixies, we must take the gamble, for I must ride with Lord Fear."

Gwyd groaned again and said, "Aye, Princess, ye be right."

Liaze mounted Nightshade and said, "You can tell me on the way, and we'll think of what might go wrong and what to do in case it does." And she heeled Nightshade in the flanks and down the slope they rode.

They turned on an angle between the sunwise bound and that of the sundown marge, and Liaze felt as if she were somehow betraying Luc by veering away from the path that would lead to the Lake of the Rose. Yet she knew she had to ride with Lord Fear, for to do otherwise would mean Luc's death, or so she now believed. And the only way to find Lord Fear was to be at a place he rode by, and the only one Gwyd or she knew of was on a distant bleak moor.

Down through farmland they rode, and they passed into forested country, and onward they came to more farms. Villages they rode through, and they spent two nights in inns, where they took warm baths and supped on roast beef and tubers and gravy sopped up with good bread, and they drank some of their "weel-aged wine." It was while Gwyd was deep in his cups that he began calling the princess "lass," and she smiled at the term, for it gave her pleasure.

In the mornings at the inns, eggs they had and buttered toast and jams and jellies.

And all was paid for with good copper coins taken from the Troll hoard, a hoard no doubt stolen from others.

At the end of the second day, Gwyd announced that his ribs were fully mended, and Liaze marveled at his recovery, due either to the medicinal he had taken or to a Brownie's natural healing.

And they rode onward.

And all along the way, they discussed and probed and examined every aspect they could think of concerning Gwyd's plan. Liaze practiced on the silver harp, a travelling bard's instrument, small and compact and more of a lyre than a full-fledged harp. And she sang love ballades and humorous ditties and songs of epic adventures, all to the delight of Gwyd, not only because of the content, but also because all of those things were part of his ploy for the princess to win free of Lord Fear. "Remember, lass, if we best him, he'll ne'er bother ye nor me ag'in, nor any o' those we treasure. And if ye ken what be his true name, ye can banish him altogether."

On the evening of the third day of travel they crossed a twilight marge to come into a mountainous realm, and it was land that Gwyd had trekked through on his way to Lord Duncan's.

The going was slow and tedious through this demesne, and they followed notches and deep vales and crossed several cols.

'Round the midday mark some four days after entering the

mountains they reached another looming wall of twilight, and they crossed that bound to come to a bleak highland moor, the land damp and chill, with scrub and peat and soggy bogs lying along the way. And a dank wind blew, and wraithlike mist fled across the scape.

"Ah, Gwyd, 'tis a terrible place, this moor."

"Indeed, m'lady. But it is here Lord Fear rode when I last came by. Up ahead we'll find a narrow stand of trees, the place I hid when he and his band passed nigh."

On they pressed, and soon they came to the strip of woods Gwyd mentioned. In they went among the trees, and, just ere emerging from the far side, they halted as planned.

Liaze set up camp and took a fortnight of supplies altogether, half of which she stowed in her rucksack, for as Gwyd had warned, "Take nae food nor wine nor any other drink fra Lord Fear, other than water that be, else ye'll be in his train f'r e'er."

Then Gwyd made ready to leave, and he hopped on a log and mounted Pied Agile, for during their time of travel—nine days all told—the Brownie, though only three feet tall, had learned how to care for the horses, and to guide Pied Agile. To deal with the animals, he needed a mounting block—not only to clamber upon the mare, but to manage the supplies and the saddles and the currying and other such tasks in the care and feeding of them. "You can use stumps and logs and rocks and boulders and slopes to give you the height you need," had said Liaze, and Gwyd had learned to do so. It was not as if Gwyd had had no experience with horses, for under Laird Duncan's tutelage, he had learned to deal with horse hooves, the cleaning and shoeing and other such; and during the journey to this place, one of the geldings had thrown a shoe, and, using the file and some nails and the hammer and one of the spare shoes in Liaze's gear, Gwyd had replaced it. "I be a fair hand at smithing as well, lass, though by no means an expert. Still and all, this fixin be good enough t'last till we can get t'a proper farrier."

But there in the woods on the moor, as Gwyd mounted, Liaze's heart beat rapidly now that it had come to this parting of the ways.

"Remember, Princess," said Gwyd from the back of the mare, "ye canna dismount wi'out Lord Fear's leave, else he'll strike ye dead; and durin the ridin stay tight in the saddle, f'r if ye fall off, ye'll die. And should ye die or be struck dead, ye'll be in his shadowy band f'r e'er. And when you see Luc you hae t'don the red scarf, and that way I'll ken ye've had success. Then, singin and playin ma harp, ye hae t'delay Lord Fear in the inn long enough f'r me t'do ma part. And though I think we hae but one chance and one chance only t'win ye free o' the Wild Hunt, if need be ye must wear the red scarf ev'ry niht thereafter, till I succeed doin what I must."

"I know," said Liaze, glancing at the rucksack, now containing just the harp and the scarf along with a sevenday of food and a small skin holding a day's worth of water. "We've gone over it time and again. Now off with you, and I'll see you at the inn after I've located Luc and you and I have bested Lord Fear."

"Oh, lass," said Gwyd, his voice choking, a tear sliding down his cheek. "Ye hae put this trust in me, and I dinna ken whether—"

"Go, Gwyd, go, else we'll both be weeping."

Wiping his nose across a sleeve, Gwyd turned Pied Agile and rode out onto the open moor, Nightshade and the geldings in tow. On he went and on, on into the mist, and slowly he faded into the gray swirl until he could no longer be seen.

Liaze took a deep breath and wiped away her own tears, and she took up a small trowel and stepped onto the heath and began digging peat for a fire.

That eve, wrapped in her cloak and with her bow across her back and the quiver at her hip and her long-knife strapped to her thigh and the rucksack over her shoulder, she stood out on the open moor and waited in the driven mist. It was the dark of the moon, and in but twenty-nine more darktides a heart would cease to beat if Liaze failed in her quest. And so she waited and prayed to Mithras, but Lord Fear did not come that night.

She stood on the moor on the next night and the next as well, and her heart fell with each passing mark, for time seeped by, and she felt as if her chances were vanishing.

On the following day, the moor cleared of its mist, and the sun fell down through a bright sky, the waxing crescent moon lagging behind and chasing the golden orb downward. But then in the sunup direction, wisps of tattered clouds came o'er the horizon, as if presaging a storm. And the sun set and dusk followed with dark night on its heels, and the moon, its horns pointing upward, sank toward the horizon as well.

And Liaze again stood in the open moor, her weaponry slung and the rucksack, with its harp and scarf and rations of water and food, hanging from a strap o'er her shoulder.

Again she fretted—*Will he come this night?*—and she wondered for the thousandth time if instead she should be at the Blue Château. *Have we completely missed the true meaning of Lady Wyrd's rede?*

A candlemark passed and then another, and the arc of the moon kissed the far earth. It was then that Liaze caught a distant baying sound, and she turned and looked behind.

At a shallow angle in the sky and among the ragged clouds they came running through the air, a vast boiling pack of ghostly dogs baying, two hundred, three hundred, four hundred or more, trailing long tendrils of shadow behind.

And beyond the pack came galloping horses, coils of darkness flying in their wake, black sparks showering from hard-driven hooves, though there was no stone for metal shoes to strike, high in the air as they were. And on the backs of the ghastly steeds were tenuous riders, twisting shadows streaming in their wake as well.

And in the fore rode the fell leader, his ebon cloak flying out after; and he lifted a black horn and pealed a long and dreadful call.

Lord Fear had come at last.

30

The Wild Hunt

As on the helldogs came, Liaze sucked in air through clenched teeth, and her heart hammered in her breast, and, in spite of the chill of the moor, perspiration coated her palms and her forehead and sweat ran down her face. She wiped her eyes on her sleeve and made certain her bow and quiver were well set across her back and her long-knife was secured in its scabbard.

Now spying their quarry, down came the hounds, baying their ghastly yawls, deadly jet fire gleaming in their eyes. And they rushed toward the standing maiden—five hundred savage, raven-dark hounds slavering blackness—Liaze remaining fast, though her heart cried out *Run!*

On came the hounds, leaping o'er one another to be the first to the kill, the vast pack a boiling inky mass, mad with the lust to rend the quarry asunder.

Yet Liaze did not move, and the howling swarm came on.

And the crescent moon looked across the moor in silence, indifferent to those in its light.

Dark fangs gleaming, onward they hurtled, tendrils of black

trailing away. And galloping after came the riders, streaming shadows vanishing behind.

But Liaze did not run.

One hundred, seventy, fifty-thirty-twenty feet vanished the gap and hurtled the hounds, black fire in their obsidian eyes. . . .

And then they hurled themselves at the lone femme . . .

. . . she to be lost in the boiling pack . . .

. . . the hounds . . .

. . . the dogs . . .

. . . the frightful dogs . . .

. . . brushing by, rushing past, their fangs bared but not striking.

And then the pack was away and gone. . . .

. . . but now came the riders.

Galloping, galloping toward the slip of a maiden, wraiths upon steeds streaming black.

All but the leader, who seemed substantial enough, ghastly though he was.

And he reined his steed to a halt at her side, the other riders stopping as well.

And from nowhere, somewhere, everywhere, there sounded groans of a thousand faint voices, like the wailing of the wind, yet the air itself did not stir a single reflection in the standing pools of the moor.

Dressed in ebon and wearing a dark crown, the leader on his huge black horse gazed down at the princess with his grim and cold eyes of jet.

And his voice came as an icy whisper, freezing the very marrow of bones. "Ye are brave," he hissed, "and I would have ye ride with me."

"Gladly, my lord," replied Liaze.

The rider turned and gestured hindward, and a wraithlike figure ahorse led a riderless mount to the fore, and it was gaunt and shadowy, as if it belonged to another realm altogether.

"My lord," said Laize, "have you one healthier?"

"This is your mount," came the bitter whisper.

"As thou wilt, my lord," replied Liaze. And she set her foot in the spectral stirrup and swung astride the ghastly steed.

Adjusting the bow on her back, she settled in for the ride, and then the dark lord raised his terrible horn to his lips and belled its dreadful call, and Liaze's heart quailed in fear at the sound of it, but she did not flinch, and all the horses sprang forward in pursuit of the forerunning hounds.

Liaze leaned into the saddle, urging her mount to haste as the wraithsteeds rose into the sky, writhing shadowstuff streaming behind and boiling off and away. And Liaze gasped in wonder and fright as the ground below receded, for she was up in the sky, in the sky, and if she fell, if she fell . . .

Durin the ridin stay tight in the saddle, echoed Gwyd's words, *f'r if ye fall off, ye'll die. And should ye die or be struck dead, ye'll be in his shadowy band f'r e'er.*

Liaze reached down and, first on one side and then on the other, she adjusted the stirrup straps to a length to her liking, setting herself more secure on the shadowy steed.

With ghastly riders all about and all of their cloaks flying out behind, the ghostly horses plunged through shredded clouds across a moonlit sky, while far ahead dark hounds bayed.

"My lord," called out Liaze, "what is it we do?"

"We chase the moon," came the icy answer, as they hammered onward, black sparks flying from strangely shod hooves. "That and we hunt cowards; not one such as you."

"And what of the cowards, my lord? What do you when we come across one or more?"

"Those I set my hounds upon, and they tear their craven souls apart. It is all they deserve."

Liaze gasped and looked at the other riders in Lord Dread's band—at the wraiths, the ghosts, the apparitions. "And these riders about us, Lord Fear: who are they?"

"The brave, my lady," whispered the answer. "They are those who did not run, but stood fast instead."

Liaze shuddered. *Will I become one such as they? Oh, Mithras, but I do not wish to be a ghostly figure riding forever through the night, hunting down any innocents who flee from this ghastly band, ripping their spirits to shreds.*

Oh, but I do pray Gwyd's plan works, for I cannot think of anything more dire than becoming a permanent member of this dreadful hunt.

And on they rode, chasing the moon, Lord Terror, Lord Fear, Lord Dread, Lord Grim riding at the fore, a ghastly band behind streaming bits of shadow swirling in their wake.

Oh, Luc, perhaps I am totally lost, totally and utterly lost.

And across the sky they plunged, trailing tendrils of black, dark sparks flying from under hoof. And twilight border after twilight border they crossed, as over the realms they rode, while Liaze scanned about for sign of Luc . . . or the black mountain, finding neither.

And of a sudden, the black horn sounded, and Liaze's heart jumped in fear, and, following the hounds, the horses spiraled down like ebon leaves on the wind. With her shadowy steed turning under her, Liaze remained secure. And down and down swirled the spectral horses, the dark hounds ahead and baying. And out before the hounds and across a plowed field ran a shrieking man, and then the pack caught him, and as each of the helldogs flashed by, one by one they slashed at the fleeing Human and then raced on beyond, black fangs not drawing blood but another essence instead.

One by one they slashed at him . . .

. . . and the man fell down, and still the dogs slashed and ran on . . .

. . . as one by one they tore at his soul . . .

. . . five hundred one-by-ones.

And now the horses thundered by, if a shade can be said to

thunder, and Liaze wept to see the slain man, his pale face white and staring, his dead eyes filled with fright.

And on through the night sky the Wild Hunt ran, ghastly hounds baying, ghostly horses racing, spectral riders astride . . . all but two: a Princess of the Autumnwood, and the Lord of the Hunt in the lead.

Though the horses ran swiftly after the crescent moon, it was swifter yet, and finally it set; but still horse and hound ran on, flying through a cloud-shredded sky.

But at last the dreadful horn sounded once again—Liaze's heart leaping in response—and down and down through the midnight sky swirled the deadly band, spiraling down as would black raven feathers fall. And they came to ground before a splendid inn, four storeys high in all, with peaked roof and weathercocks above, though it seemed quite dark.

And the lord of the Wild Hunt, a full goatskin in hand, came striding back to where Liaze yet sat ahorse.

"My lord," she said, bowing her head.

Hefting the skin, he coldly whispered, "Come inside and sip the dark ale."

Now having his permission, Liaze dismounted, her weaponry and the knapsack yet in her possession.

Across the sward and up the broad shallow steps paced Lord Fear, where the door swung open of its own volition, and they entered a great common room, and lanterns within sprang to light.

And Liaze and all of the riders followed.

The chamber itself held dark mahogany tables and chairs and a great long ashwood bar, and splendid tapestries decorated the walls—hunters ahorse with dogs—and scarlet velvet drapes hung with gold piping matched the scarlet and gold of the chairs.

From the black goatskin, Lord Fear poured himself a mug of frothy ale, a strange and darkling brew, and he offered Liaze some. She shook her head and partook not, but instead unslung the rucksack and sipped from her own waterskin.

Lord Dread then tossed the skin of brew to his shadowy riders, and they poured mugs of their own. They sipped the ebon ale, and somehow they seemed to grow a bit more substantial, though they remained wraithlike still.

Liaze withdrew the harp from the rucksack, and she set to a silvery tune and began to sing.

And she sang of life and living, and all the riders crowded 'round closely, as if by hearing the very words sung they could recapture the dear essence of that which they had lost.

All crowded 'round but Lord Terror, that is; he sat in a corner alone.

Now Liaze sang of children, and the shades of the riders groaned, sounding as would a cold winter wind swirling among bleak stones.

And Liaze sang of love, and spectral riders hid their faces in their hands.

And still Lord Fear sat unmoved and unmoving in his corner alone.

And Liaze sang of women and joy and of ships sailing on the sea, and of rivers and trees and of farming the land, and of buying horses and going to market, and of things and things more.

Her songs were happy and sad and short and long, ballads and ditties and lyric poems, and the riders wept dark shades of tears.

And then Lord Grim pushed away his mug and stood and whispered, " 'Tis time."

Liaze put the harp in the rucksack and shouldered the strap, and out they strode in the predawn night, where they mounted up and rode away.

Across the dark vault they hammered, black sparks flying, the hellpack baying out in the lead, while behind them the sky began to lighten. But ere the dawn came, toward a looming mountain they sped, and lo! a massive wall of gray stone split wide, and into the gap and darkness raced the Hunt—black hounds, spectral horses, wraith riders, Lord Fear, and the Princess Liaze—the mountain to boom shut behind.

Light bloomed in the stone cavern, and the horses trotted to a stable of sorts, and the hounds took to the kennels.

Lord Fear came and offered Liaze his arm, and he led her and the riders to a large banquet hall, where the table was laden with viands and roasts and goblets of black wine.

"My lady," whispered Lord Death, pulling out a chair on the right hand of his throne.

Liaze sat, and Lord Grim poured her a goblet of the black.

Yet Liaze neither ate nor drank, but merely asked for water instead.

The other riders dug in with gusto, though they remained wraithlike in aspect. How they could eat, Liaze did not know, yet eat and drink they did. *Perhaps the food is spectral, even though it looks very real.*

Liaze tried to engage Lord Grim in converse, mayhap in the hope he had seen Luc and would tell her where he was. But Lord Death only listened and did not speak, and he seemed fascinated by her vitality and by her auburn hair, so in contrast to the stark grays and blacks and whites of his halls within the cold depths of his mountain.

Finally the banquet came to an end, and once more Lord Fear offered his arm. He led Liaze to sumptuous quarters, though no colors graced the chambers other than black and white and gray.

He bowed to her and Liaze curtseyed in return, and then Lord Terror withdrew. And when he was gone, Liaze shuddered, and she sat on the edge of the black-curtained bed and wept. *Have I made a dreadful mistake? Oh, Luc, my Luc, mayhap I have lost you forever.*

Finally she dried her tears, and she opened the rucksack and took of biscuits and honey and drank water to wash it down, all the while thinking, *Mayhap morrow night I will see my Luc, or perhaps the black mountain of Lady Wyrd's rede.*

She found a bathing chamber, and there she undressed and saw to her needs. And then she took to her bed, and, exhausted, slept between black satin sheets.

A sonorous gong ringing somberly awakened Liaze from her rest. And she went about her toilet, and refilled her small waterskin. She dressed and took up her bow and arrows, her longknife, and her rucksack. And when she turned to step to the door, she gasped, for Lord Dread silently stood in her chamber and gazed at her with his cold, black eyes.

"My lord," she said, curtseying.

"My lady," returned his chill whisper, and again his sight came to rest on her flaming auburn hair.

"Sieur, I be hight Liaze, Princess of the Autumnwood; what be your name, if I might ask?"

"Name?" Lord Fear seemed to ponder the question, as if it were altogether an unfamiliar concept. "Ah, names," he whispered, his words like ice to the ear. "I am known by many names. To some I am Gwynn Ap Nunn, and to others Annwn, to still more I am at times called Odin, and to others still, I am Wotan. In some countries they think I am female and call me Perchta, and Holda, and the White Lady known as Gaude. These are a few of the names that have been attributed to me, yet they are all wrong—merely guesses—for I have only one name, my true name, which I will not reveal to any . . . not even to you, Princess Liaze. Nay, not even to one such as you."

Liaze felt a chill run through her heart at these last words: *Not even to one such as me! What does he think I am!*

"Come, Princess. Dusk has fallen, and we must ride."

"As you will, my lord."

Together they strode to the stables, where the wraithlike riders stood waiting, the ghastly steeds saddled and ready, and the

226 / D<small>ENNIS</small> L. M<small>c</small>K<small>IERNAN</small>

dreadful dark hounds excitedly leaping at the interior stone of the mountainside, the dogs keen to be loosed.

Lord Dread mounted his black steed, and all the ghostly men followed suit. And as Liaze clambered upon her shadowy horse she noted the dark-brew black goatskin depended from Lord Grim's saddle, yet the bag was flaccid, empty, and she wondered what brew the riders would drink this eve. Lord Terror blew a mighty blast on his horn of fear, and the mountainside opened to the night beyond, and out the dogs raced, baying their appalling howls, Lord Grim and the Wild Hunt speeding after as up into the sky they flew, Princess Liaze among them.

Once again they chased the crescent moon past many twilight borders, and they came upon a woman and child crossing a field, and when those two heard the helldogs baying, they fled toward a nearby cottage. Lord Fear sounded a dreadful cry upon his terrible black horn, and down swooped the monstrous pack, and mere paces away from the doorstone they embroiled the woman and child in an ebon cloud of snarling hounds racing by. With hideous fangs bared and slashing, yet leaving no marks behind, the helldogs rent their souls to shreds. And when the dark cloud was done, nought but death-white corpses lay asprawl in the wake of the beasts.

Liaze wept to see such appalling carnage, yet she hid her tears from Lord Dread. And on they rode, up into the sky, and across more twilight bounds.

They slew a drunkard along a road, and three fishermen on the shores of a tarn, for all of these made the mistake of fleeing before the terrible hounds. But three other people stood fast in the whirl of the dark pack—two men and one woman—and survived Lord Death's dreadful test, though he did not tarry to see if they would take passage upon his wraithlike steeds.

Several more victims fell to the horrid pack, but finally Lord Death blew on his ghastly horn, and once again they stopped at the magnificent inn, and lo! the skin was full. Liaze's heart sank, and she wept inside—*Oh, Mithras, they are drinking the souls of those who ran*—for now she knew whence came the dark brew. Yet by no outward sign did she permit Lord Terror to know she had guessed the appalling truth, but instead she followed him into the great common room. Once more Lord Fear sat alone, and he and the shadowy riders drank ebon ale, while Liaze played her harp and sang.

But ere dawn Lord Dread stood, and away they flew to the mountain and within. And as they did so, Liaze despaired, for though they had passed o'er many realms of Faery, still she had seen neither Luc nor the black mountain of Skuld's rede, and she was entrapped with a horrendous band, their leader most monstrous of all.

Even so, she drew upon the well of her courage and vowed to let nothing show her disgust, and at the banquet in Lord Grim's hall, Liaze asked, "Why do you do these things unto innocent souls?"

"Innocent?" came his icy whisper. "None are innocent, Princess Liaze. There are only the brave and those who are not, and the brave deserve to live, and the others to die."

"It is a grim philosophy you have, my lord," said Liaze.

Lord Death did not reply.

When the banquet ended, once again he escorted her to her stark quarters, and within her chambers his obsidian eyes glittered at her, and he reached out and touched her auburn hair. It was all Liaze could do to keep from shrinking away.

Then Lord Terror turned on his heel and stalked from the room, and Liaze fell upon her bed and wept.

The next night they rode through the skies, and folk did they find abroad, and so they reaped more souls that darktide, but Liaze did not see ought of Luc or a black mountain. Again, they stopped at the inn and Liaze played her harp and sang while Lord Dread and his men drank of the black ale. As before, ere dawn they rode on to Lord Fear's mountain, where they feasted as before.

During the banquet Lord Grim, cold as ever, whispered, "Princess, I would have you be my bride."

Liaze suppressed a gasp, and she felt as if she had been struck a terrible blow in the stomach. Still, she managed to say, "My lord, there are better mates for you."

"None so brave," he whispered, his words as of shards of ice falling. "Others have cried out in protest at my nightly deeds, but you have not."

"Even so, my lord, I yet say I am unworthy."

"I would have you in my bed, Princess Liaze."

Liaze inwardly shuddered and she remained mute, not trusting her voice to say ought.

"Think on it," whispered Lord Fear.

Liaze canted her head in assent.

That night she lay curled in a ball on her black-satin sheets and she slept only fitfully.

Again they rode the Wild Hunt, and again they reaped souls, and again they stopped at the inn where the princess played the harp and sang. Once more they feasted in Lord Dread's mountain hall, and this night in Liaze's chambers the icy lord said, "I am impatient, Princess. What is your answer?"

"My lord, I yet say, I am unworthy."

"*Pha*," whispered the dark lord, and he reached out and touched her hair, and she did not blench nor draw away. "None has stirred my heart as have you."

Can anyone stir a lump of ice?

Liaze merely smiled.

"Three nights from now, my lady," Lord Fear coldly said, "I will take you to my bed, whether your answer be yea or nay."

When he had gone, Liaze gave in to her tears, and she lay in bed and trembled, her knees drawn up to her chest, her arms wrapped 'round tightly.

Two more nights went past, and the Wild Hunt had ridden and had reaped souls, yet Liaze had seen nought of Luc nor of the black mountain. And each of these nights Lord Dread had pressed her for an answer, but had also coldly reminded her that, no matter, he would take her to his icy bed.

By this time Liaze had decided on a plan, and if that failed, then she would attempt to kill Lord Fear in spite of the legends that he was a deathless being. And she sharpened her long-knife and flexed her bow and examined her arrows and chose among them.

And on the third and last eve of his averral, when Lord Death came to her chambers to escort her to the ghastly horses to ride the Wild Hunt, Liaze said, "My lord, I have heard of two things I would see: one is a black mountain; the other is a blue château. Have you ridden o'er these in the past?"

Lord Grim looked at her, a glitter of curiosity hinted at in his jet-dark eyes. "Oui, I have," he whispered.

"Could our course this eve take us o'er these places?"

Lord Death pondered a moment.

"As a wedding present?" added Liaze, reaching out and taking the dreadful being's hand, gritting her teeth as she did so.

The dark lord looked down at his hand in hers and nodded, and on toward the horses they went.

If this does not work, Liaze, you will kill Lord Fear this night . . . or die in the attempt.

They mounted their wraithlike steeds, and Lord Grim blew the dreadful call on his dark horn. The mountainside opened; out flew the hounds; dark riders on dark steeds flying out after, black fire and shadows streaming in their wake. And in the lead rode Lord Death, Princess Liaze at his side.

Up they flew and away, up and into the night, a gibbous moon nearly full lighting the course among the ragged clouds.

O'er realms they sailed, Lord Terror passing over fleeing victims, ne'er sounding his demonhorn to signal the dogs to attack. For Lord Grim had a destination in mind, two destinations, in fact, and through shadowlight borders did he ride on his way to please his promised bride.

And over a blue manor in the center of a lake they flew, roses growing all 'round the shoreline. On the ramparts sentries stood, and knowing the fate of cowards they fled not as 'round the ramparts rode the Wild Hunt, hounds baying, shadows streaming, dark fire flying from hammering hooves.

Yet Liaze could see no sign of Luc, though he might well have been chained in the dungeons below.

Lord Death glanced at Princess Liaze and nodded, for he had delivered the first of the bridal gifts to her, and then he blew his horn and turned the Hunt onto another tack.

Through more shadowlight borders they ran, and still no victims did they take, for Lord Fear had other goals in mind this night.

And at last, in the distance ahead, Liaze could see a lone black mountain jutting up from a bleak plain, and the mountainsides glittered darkly in the moonlight, as if coated in obsidian. And the air above was cold, frigid, as if winter gripped the land, or as if the mountain itself was made of black ice.

And as they circled 'round the crest and 'round the crest once more, Liaze gasped and nearly cried out, for at the top, at the very top, under an open-sided pavilion, lay Luc, the knight asleep or deeply enchanted on a bed of black ice.

Lord Dread looked at Liaze and nodded, for the full of his bridal gift had been given.

"Straight to the inn, my lord," cried Liaze, "for I would celebrate this night."

Lord Death smiled a grim smile, and now he turned the Hunt, and away they flew.

As the dark horses ran through the air, Liaze took sight on guiding stars, for she planned on using them to follow on her return. And she fumbled into the rucksack at her side, and she withdrew the red scarf, her grip tight so as not to lose it. And she tied it 'round her neck, and it flew out behind in the wind of her passage. And she prayed to Mithras that Gwyd was in place and waiting, and that he would see the scarf, and that the plan he had hatched would work. *Oh, Mithras, please let it work.*

As they came to a twilight border, Liaze tried to espy a landmark at the point of their crossing, but on this side she saw nought to guide her; yet, as they passed out of the far side, she noted a twisted tree, its arms pointing toward the shadowlight they had just flown through.

On sped the Wild Hunt, and again they came to a crossing, and she noted a jumble of boulders on this side, and a wide pool on the other.

On they flew and Lord Fear sounded his dreadful horn, and there ahead lay the magnificent inn. Down swirled the dogs, down spun the horses, down went Lord Dread and Liaze. And nowhere did Liaze see any sign of Gwyd nearby; she could only pray that the Brownie was nigh and had seen the scarf and was ready.

Her wraithlike horse came to a stop, and when Lord Grim had given her his leave, Liaze dismounted and entered the inn at his side.

The ghastly spirits of the shadowy riders gathered at the bar, but they took up no mugs of dark brew, for they had taken no souls that nighttide. Lord Death then raised his empty mug in salute to Liaze and icily whispered, "This night to my bride."

The riders all hoisted their own empty glasses, and from many voices a ghostly echo wailed, whether in grief or joy Liaze could not determine, yet she smiled and took up her harp.

And once again she sang of life and living, and, as before, all the riders crowded 'round closely, trying to recapture the essence of that which they had once held dear.

And Liaze sang of children, and once more the shades of the riders groaned as would a chill wind swirl among icy crags.

And Liaze sang of love, and spectral riders wept ghostly wails at what they had lost.

And still Lord Fear sat unmoved and unmoving in his corner alone.

And Liaze sang of life and women and the joy of ordinary living: of fishing and hunting and the reaping of grain, of boats on a river and of sails on the sea, of farming and herding and planting trees, and of horses and cattle and going to market, and of things such as these and things more.

Her songs were filled with joy, and filled with tears, and filled with love. She sang ballads and ditties and long lyric poems, and the riders laughed ghostly laughs or wept spectral shades of tears.

And just as Lord Dread pushed away from his table, Liaze called out, "The Wild Hunt."

She struck a chord and began a chant, and Lord Grim settled back to hear:

> *The sky was dark,*
> *The storm clouds blew,*
> *A chill was on the land,*
> *Yet, Molly dear,*
> *The message read,*
> *I need your healing hand.*
>
> *Across the moor*
> *She started out*
> *To reach her father dear.*
> *For he was ill,*
> *And she would aid,*
> *Yet Lord Death she did fear. . . .*

Liaze sang as she had never sung, her words telling of the Wild Hunt and of its reaping of cowardly souls, as well as the doom of heroes. And she sang that these fatalities and dooms mattered not to Lord Dread, Lord Fear, Lord Grim, Lord Terror, Lord Death, for the leader of the Hunt was cold and forbidding. And as Liaze sang she moved among the shades, and they sobbed as would a frail wind, and still Liaze sang and sang, verse after verse pouring golden words from her throat. And the silver harp seemed enchanted, the notes pure and clear, the concordant strings voicing precious harmony.

Yet at last she saw through the narrow gap in the drapery a tiny glimmer; 'twas the sign she and Gwyd had said would signal either her rescue or her ruin, and in that moment the song, the very song, came to an end.

And as Liaze's voice and the silver strings finally fell silent, a quietness settled over all . . . only to be broken by a nearby cock's crow.

Liaze threw back a drape, allowing in light from the rising rim of the sun just now broaching the edge of the world.

And ghostly wails went up from the shadowy riders, and they shrieked and screamed, and as if something had reached up from the ground below, they were jerked down through the floor, down into the earth, down out of sight.

In the shadows yet mustered 'round his corner, Lord Terror stood and glared at Liaze, his face distorted with insurmountable rage; palm up, he reached out toward her, and slowly his fingers curled into a clawlike clench, as if he were trying to crush her heart; but nothing whatsoever happened, for the cock's crow and the light of the sun had rent his power from him.

And Liaze said, "Lord Death, though you aided me to find that which I seek, still, for the terror you bring to others and for rending from them their very essence, you deserve to be cast out of Faery. Hence, I call you by what I think Mithras Himself would say is your true name: *Voleur d'Âme*—Soul Thief."

On hearing this last, Lord Fear's gaze flew wide with fright of his own. He reached out to Liaze in a pleading gesture, but she said, "Voleur d'Âme, I banish you, I banish you, I banish you."

His eyes wide with dread, his face twisted in horror, Lord Terror hoarsely cried out "No! No!" but shrilling and screaming he, too, was jerked down and down, down into the darkness below.

The princess gazed now at the empty chamber, empty of all but her. "Thank you, Lord Mithras," she whispered.

And the air seemed to waver for a moment, and the fine inn, the splendid inn, became nought but a ramshackle ruin.

With tears in her eyes, Liaze packed the harp away, and Gwyd came running in and cried, "Ah, Princess, thank the Fates, ye still be here." And he broke out weeping with joy.

Liaze smiled through the tears running down her own face and she knelt and hugged the wee Brownie. "Oh, Gwyd, Gwyd, I cannot—"

"Princess, Princess, hush, now, hush, for I would nae hae ye be blurtin out somthin we would both regret. Y'see, I would stay wi' ye until this venture comes to an end, and f'r me t'be able t'do that, ye canna thank me, else I'd hae t'leave ye."

Liaze squeezed the Brownie tighter, and they both wept in relief, and finally Gwyd said, "Och, lass, come out and see the glorious new day. Besides, there be someone I would hae ye meet."

31

Rede

As they started for the door, Liaze said, "Are you certain, Gwyd, that Lord Fear will not retaliate?"

"Nothin be certain, m'lady. Yet if the legend be true, then he will nae bother ye nor those ye cherish, f'r ye've passed his test o' bravery, and ye hae ridden wi' him, and, lastly, ye hae outwitted him . . . or rather, t'gether we hae done so, f'r ye kept him entranced until the sun came and the cock crew and he and his deadly Hunt vanished in the light o' day."

"Ah, Gwyd, that isn't exactly what happened. You see, although the daylight caused him to lose his riders, he was yet present, though confined to the shadows in the inn. And so, there at the end, when the cock's crow and the sunlight reft him of his power, I banished him."

Gwyd's mouth dropped open in astonishment. "Ye did what?"

"Banished him. You told me that if I knew his true name, I could banish him. I guessed what his true name might be, and it seems it was so. Either that, or Mithras Himself decided I was right in that Lord Fear deserved to be cast out of Faery."

"Oh, nae, Princess. If ye banished him, he nae be cast out o' Faery; instead, he be trapped in that mountain o' his unless and until ye and your bloodline be nae more."

"Until I and my bloodline are dead?"

Gwyd nodded.

"Does that mean I myself *must* stay alive, else the Wild Hunt will return?"

"Och, aye. You or your get, that is; or your get's get, and their get's get, and so on down through the days o' Faery."

"Oh, my. What a terrible burden. If I die ere I have children, or if my line dies out, then—"

"Then Lord Fear and the Wild Hunt will ride again."

Liaze sighed, but said nought.

"Anyway, Princess, had ye not banished him, weel, the cock's crow would hae sent him away the moment daylight touched him."

As they stepped through the door, Liaze laughed and said, "And just where did you get the cock?"

Gwyd gestured outward. "Why, m'lady, it be the very bird of Twk's."

In that moment, a red-feathered rooster sprang onto the porch of the inn, and a diminutive Pixie dressed in green with a green feather in his cap sat in a tiny saddle astride the bird and held onto reins.

"Princess Liaze, this wee cock-a-whoop here be ma adopted cousin Twk. Twk, this be Princess Liaze o' the Autumnwood. And Twk, hear me: she *banished* Lord Fear."

Twk's eyes widened in surprise, and he leapt from the back of the chicken and swept off his green hat and bowed and declared, "At your service, Princess."

Liaze laughed and curtseyed in return, and then smiled at the tiny being, no more than eight or nine inches tall.

"And this cock-o'-the-walk," said Twk, motioning at the red rooster, "is Jester, my faithful steed and harbinger of the sun."

"Well met," said Liaze, and she canted her head toward the

proud chicken; the bird paid the princess no heed, for he was strutting about and peering into cracks in the weathered boards, looking for insects to eat.

Gwyd said, "Princess, I ken ye hae a need t'thank someone; weel then, let it be Twk here, f'r he was the one what got his rooster t'crow right at the dawnin."

"Pishposh," said Twk, waving a negligent hand, " 'twas no great feat. You see, I think Jester believes if he does not crow, the sun will not come."

Liaze laughed, but Gwyd looked at her and said, "Regardless, there be nothin better t'send Lord Fear and his grisly riders packin, or so Twk and his band o' Pixies say."

Liaze knelt and said, "Twk, I most deeply thank you and your Jester."

Twk shrugged a shoulder and said, "My lady, when Gwyd told me of your circumstance, well, it was the least we could do. Anyway, 'twas nothing."

Liaze shook her head. "Oh, no, Twk, I wouldn't call it nothing, for you and Jester and Gwyd saved me from a dreadful fate."

"Dreadful fate?" asked Gwyd.

"Oui," said Liaze. "The bed of Lord Fear."

"Oh, my," said Twk, nonplussed, "I have never heard of Lord Dread wanting to bed *any* female." He glanced at Gwyd.

"Och," said Gwyd, "look at the Princess, laddie. I canna blame Lord Fear f'r wantin what he did." Of a sudden, Gwyd clapped a hand over his mouth, and he flushed.

In that moment the rooster crowed loudly, and Twk said, "It seems Jester agrees with you, Gwyd." Then he burst out laughing, as did Liaze, and Gwyd only turned a deeper red.

"Come," said Liaze, once again kneeling and hugging the Brownie, "if you have the horses nearby, let us break our fast and celebrate the coming of day."

"They be next t'a burnie in yon thicket," mumbled Gwyd, yet mortified.

As Liaze and Gwyd walked across the overgrown field, Twk rode Jester at their side, the rooster veering this way and that through the weeds.

"Oh, and Gwyd, I have seen Luc and I know where he is—atop the black mountain of the rede. It is not too far from here and I know the way."

"Aye, lass, I recked it was so," said Gwyd, pulled from his embarrassment, "ye wearin the red scarf and all. Och, and that be good news! I ween we'll be ridin out t'day, though I think ye and I both need a wee bit o' rest ere we start, what wi' us stayin awake through the nights as we hae been doin."

Liaze frowned and said, "I want to be on the road at least by midday, for I think Luc is somehow enchanted, and we need to rescue him soon. After all, there are only eighteen more eves ere the night of the dark of the moon."

"How far be this black mountain?"

"Across two twilight borders; perhaps a sevenday, all told."

"Weel then, we hae plenty o' time, and so a bit o' rest should stand us in good stead."

"I agree," said Liaze, and on toward the thicket they strode.

Just before they stepped within the saplings, Gwyd paused and looked back at the inn where he'd once served as the house Brownie and said, "Och, ma inn, ma beautiful inn: it hae done fallen t'ruination."

They stood a moment to gaze at the ramshackle structure, the once-grand edifice no longer imposing, the building nought more than a weather-beaten hulk.

"Lord Fear must have cast a glamour over it," said Liaze. "It was quite striking those nights spent inside."

"Oui," said Twk. "Gwyd and I sat guard through these past several nights, and it indeed was majestic."

"We watched ye and the Wild Hunt ride in f'r a sennight in all, and we thought ye'd ne'er don that red scarf. But ye did at last, and ma heart leapt f'r joy."

"Mine, too," said Liaze, smiling at the Brownie.

"Well, the glamour is gone along with Lord Fear," said Twk.

"And it left ma inn a ruin," said Gwyd.

"Well, Gwyd," said Liaze, "now that Lord Fear is banished to his mountain, he and the Wild Hunt will not be stopping there at night, hence when this venture is over, you can come back and make it as it was of old."

"Aye, lass, that I could do, but Brunies nae be the proprietors o' public houses and such. 'Twould take someone else t'run the inn ere a Brunie'd take up residence. Anyway, most o' the folks hereabout hae done fled the region, what wi' Lord Death and the Wild Hunt flyin o'er ev'ry night; and so buildin up a clientele would be a mite hard what wi' nae one livin about. Besides, when Laird Duncan recaptures his manor, then I be goin back t'that household. E'en so, I hate t'see what happened t'ma inn."

With a sigh, Gwyd turned and entered the thicket, Liaze and Twk and Jester following. As they made their way toward the spring, Princess Liaze said, "What about you, Twk? Where go you from here?"

"Well, Princess, if you don't mind, I think Jester and I would like to stay with you and Gwyd and see this quest to a suitable end."

"Oh, Twk, I am not certain that we can take you along," said Liaze. "You see, there is a rede from Lady Wyrd telling me that I should take no one else with me but the howling one—Gwyd. I cannot put you in danger."

"But the way Gwyd told it," said Twk, "that only applied as long as Lord Fear was a threat."

"Aye, Princess," chimed in the Brownie, "that I did say, but I couldna remember all o' the words o' the rede, though I remembered the o'erall gist o' it."

"Be that as it may," said Twk, "now that Lord Fear has been banished for good—and if not for good, then at least for a very long while—you should be able to take more companions with you. I am certain Jester and I can be of aid."

"Oh, of that I have little doubt, Twk," said Liaze. "You already have been of more help than ever I could ask. When we get to the camp, let me tell you the rede, and then we'll decide."

They reached the site, and Nightshade and Pied Agile and the geldings were especially grateful to see the princess, the animals crowding in and nuzzling and begging to be scratched and petted. Liaze laughed and accommodated each, and then fed them some grain, and gave some to Jester as well, and then she and Gwyd spread out blankets and the princess and the Brownie and the Pixie took a meal of their own, Gwyd breaking out the last bottle of wine in celebration, the others having been drunk in the interim, Gwyd saying, " 'Twas thirsty work findin the Pixies and Twk and all."

Liaze laughed and Gwyd grinned and Twk merely shook his head.

They settled down to a meal of jerky and honey-slathered biscuits, and as they ate and sipped wine, Liaze said, "Twk, these are the words of Lady Wyrd's rede. . . ."

". . . and so you see, Twk, she only told me to ride with the howling one to aid me on the way, and she said nought about any others. She did, however, tell me that I would meet both perils and help along my trek, and you and Jester have certainly been part of the help of which she spoke. Nevertheless, she did not say that I should take any of this help with me."

Twk fell glum and then brightened. "But she didn't tell you to *not* take the help you found along your trek."

Liaze sighed. "But I would not put you and Jester in harm's way, for surely more peril lies along my journey, and Skuld only spoke of Gwyd in her rede."

Again Twk fell glum.

"Let me think on it," said Liaze, yawning and stretching. "But for now, Gwyd is right: we need rest ere setting out."

*　　*　　*

As the leading limb of the sun entered the mark of the zenith, Twk awakened both Liaze and Gwyd, and the princess got to her feet and moved off into the brush to relieve herself.

As she stepped back into the campsite, a familiar figure came through the woods opposite.

"Madame Divenard," called Liaze even as she loosed the keeper on her long-knife, for she knew not what might be afoot, "what are you doing here?" In spite of being wary, the princess scooped up a cup of water from the rill and held it out to the matronly woman as she reached Liaze's side.

"Thank you for the favor," said Madame Divenard, taking the drink from Liaze, yet tasting it not.

"Need you aid?" asked Liaze.

The yellow-haired matron looked at Gwyd and then at Twk and finally at the rooster and horses. "No, child, I have not come to fetch aid but to give it instead."

The princess frowned, for she heard the sound of looms coming from somewhere, nowhere, everywhere, and her heart leapt in her breast.

"But first you must answer a riddle, Liaze," said Madame Divenard.

Liaze took a deep breath and said, "Say away."

> *My name as you know it now*
> *Is scrambled in a manner somehow,*
> *But within that scramble all the same*
> *Is my one and only very true name.*

"Oh, oh," said Twk, hopping from one foot to another. "I know, I know!"

Madame Divenard then fixed the Pixie with a gimlet eye and said, "She alone must answer it."

"Oh, my," said Liaze, "I am to unscramble your name and

make another. 'Tis a riddle worthy of the— Hmm . . . Divenard: D-I-V-E-N-A-R-D: two *d*s, one *v*, one *e*, one *n*, one *i*, and one *r*."

In the background yet came the sound of looms weaving.

Twk continued to hop from foot to foot with one hand clapped over his mouth to keep words from popping out, but puzzlement yet filled Gwyd's gaze; even so, Madame Divenard fixed the Brownie with a gimlet eye as well. Then she turned to Liaze.

Liaze smiled and then curtseyed. "Madame Divenard"— Liaze glanced at the sun at zenith—"you are known as *Midi* by your older and younger sisters, one of whom I have already met, and whom I am guessing among you three are known as *Aurore* and *Crépuscule*—respectively, Dawn and Dusk. But you are *Midi*—Noon—and, along with your sisters, Skuld and Urd, you are one of the three Fates: Wyrd, Lot, and Doom. But you, being Midi, are the one known as She Who Fixes the Present and Seals Men's Fate. You are Lady Lot. And the name Divenard when unscrambled becomes your true name: Verdandi."

Verdandi smiled, and her eyes turned golden, and her hair became sunlight yellow.

"Lady Lot?" blurted Gwyd. "Oh, my." He bowed deeply.

Twk stopped hopping and bowed as well.

"Hae ye come wi' a message?" asked Gwyd.

"Of course she has, you ninny," said Twk. He turned to Verdandi. "Oh, tell us, tell us, Lady Lot . . . and if you please, might I join the princess on her quest?"

Verdandi broke out in laughter, and said, "Pixies."

"Even so, Lady Lot," said Liaze, "I would know why you met me just this side of the marge of the Forest of Oaks, and I would also know why you have come now."

Verdandi sighed and said, "At our first meeting, even though I had watched and woven in the Tapestry of Time the course of your journey through that Forest of the Oaks, I merely wished to see if you were well. Some things do not show in the skeins my sisters and I weave, and I wanted to gauge your spirit . . . which, by the bye, I found quite fit."

"And the reason you come now?" asked Liaze.

"Your companions are correct: I have come to give you a message."

Twk turned to Gwyd and said, "See, I told you so."

Verdandi smiled and glanced at the two of them. Then she said to Liaze, "By the rules my sisters and I must follow, I cannot answer straight out, but instead I must couch any aid I give you in the form of a riddle or rede."

Liaze sighed and said, "I know. But, please, whatever aid you can give me, I would have."

Verdandi smiled and then said:

> *Upon a bed 'neath ebon sky,*
> *One plans for one to slowly die.*
> *But if ye three are truly brave,*
> *A golden draught will surely save.*
> *Hence, ground your lyre and ground it well*
> *For you to cast the needed spell.*
> *Sleep must come, if it comes at all,*
> *For one to thrive beyond the wall.*
> *Take only one else one will die,*
> *As will the one 'neath ebon sky.*

Verdandi then turned to Twk and said, "Oui, my friend, you *must* go with Liaze and Gwyd, for you and yours will be needed at a critical time."

"Oh, thank you, Lady Lot," said Twk, clapping his hands.

In that moment the trailing limb of the sun left the mark of the zenith, and Lady Lot vanished along with the sound of the looms.

After a moment, Liaze fetched the food bag and settled to the blanket and took out jerky and biscuits and laid them out for a meal. Then she looked at her companions and said, "We must unravel the full meaning of Lady Verdandi's rede."

Gwyd nodded and his face drained of blood. "Aye, Princess, we must, and I ken part o' it, and a perilous thin' it be. But the most terrible thin' is, I dinna believe there be enough time t'do what must be done."

32

Vital Trek

Liaze looked at the Brownie. "What do you mean, Gwyd, that there isn't enough time?"

"J'st this, Princess: the rede says a golden draught will surely save, and t'me that means some o' the life-givin brandy made fra the golden apples, and—"

"Golden apples?" said Twk. "Do you mean Mithras' apples?"

"Aye, Twk: Mithras' apples. Anyway, Princess, the garden where they grow is far fra here, and, as I hae told ye before, it be warded by an unsleepin serpent . . . and that be why I say it be perilous, f'r the snake only sleeps f'r a moment on the night o' the longest day o' the year, and that day will nae come until it be too late. J'st how we might get one o' the apples when he be awake, well, that I nae hae any idea."

"Just how big is this serpent?" asked Twk.

"Och, mayhap fifteen, twenty o' ma paces," said Gwyd.

"Mithras!" exclaimed Liaze. "That makes him, what, some twenty-five, thirty feet long?"

"I told ye it were perilous," said Gwyd. "He be a great beastie."

"Why does he stay in the garden?" asked Twk. "I mean, that big, why not slither over the wall and away?"

"I nae ken," said Gwyd. "Mayhap he be cursed t'guard the tree and its fruit."

"What does he live on?" asked Twk.

"That, too, laddie, be a mystery. Mayhap the apples themselves. Mayhap those what come t'steal them."

"You mean he might eat us?" asked Twk, shivering.

"Mayhap," said Gwyd, looking at the princess.

"How far is it from here? —The garden, I mean," asked Liaze.

Gwyd paused and, frowning in concentration, he counted on his fingers. "Weel, fra the inn, when I hae gone before, it hae been a moon and a fortnight t'there. But, if I didna dawdle, I reck I could get t'the garden in but a single moon."

Liaze's face fell in despair. "A moon? Just to get there? And another one to return? That's two moons in all, and there are only eighteen nights till the coming dark of the moon falls due."

"I canna help it, Princess, that be the truth o' it." Gwyd glanced at the horses. "O' course, Princess, I was afoot, and not ridin any beastie."

Liaze shook her head. "Oh, surely, given the vagaries of the borders of Faery, there must be a swifter way."

"Lass, lass," said Gwyd, "ye might be right, yet I hae looked f'r a shorter way and ne'er found one."

"Princess," said Twk, "would Lady Lot have said we need the golden draught if there were no hope?"

"No she wouldn't, Twk. No she wouldn't. Hence, there must be hope." Liaze leapt to her feet. "Hurry and break camp; there's not a moment to waste."

As Liaze began lading the packhorses, Gwyd quickly rolled blankets and quenched the small fire, while Twk hefted jerky and biscuits and trotted them back into the food bag. Jester merely continued to scratch at the ground and peck at unseen things.

Ere the sun had travelled a quarter candlemark across the sky, they were en route: Liaze riding Nightshade, Gwyd in tow on Pied Agile, for although the Brownie could ride, he would rather simply be hauled behind. Twk and Jester rode atop the packs of the lead gelding, both seeming perfectly happy to perch on the cargo once more, as they had when Gwyd had brought the Pixie and the rooster from their secluded hollow to the inn.

"Which way now, Gwyd?" asked Liaze as they emerged from the thicket and into the overgrown field.

"Toward the sunup bound," said Gwyd.

Liaze turned leftward and kicked Nightshade into a trot.

"How far the border?" asked Liaze.

"On foot, four days, if I hied," said Gwyd, "but ahorse, I canna say."

Throughout the day, to preserve the endurance of the animals, Liaze varied the gait of the horses, going from a trot to a canter to a walk to a gallop. Occasionally, Liaze walked alongside the horses, as did Gwyd, and Twk would ride Jester. At these times they discussed the rede, trying to puzzle out its meaning.

"What I don't understand," said Twk, during one of these walks, "is she told me that I could accompany you, Princess, for I would be needed at a critical time. However, she also said 'Take only one else one will die,' yet here you have both Gwyd and me. That's taking two of us, not one."

Liaze nodded and said, "Oui, but she also told me that I would have to cast a needed spell, yet I am no witch, mage, wizard, no spellcaster whatsoever."

Twk nodded and said, "And how are we going to make a golden draught? That takes special gear. I mean, the juice will have to ferment, and that needs time, and then we have to heat it to drive off the vapors, and then condense and collect those vapors, and—"

"Och, Twk," said Gwyd. "Indeed, all that need be done, yet list, thanks to the lass here, we hae the gear wi' us t'do so."

Liaze frowned. "Gwyd, how many apples does it take to— Oh, wait, I recall you saying that each time you went to the garden, you had but moments to get just one and then flee. Is a single apple sufficient to make a golden draught?"

"That be the wonder o' Mithras' fruit," said Gwyd. "Though an ordinary apple by itself would only make a wee dram o' brandy, one o' the golden ones seems to entirely turn into brandy in the end—juice, peel, pulp, and all. Only the stem and pips and the very tip end at the bottom o' the apple remain un- affected."

"Pips?" asked Twk. "Why, if you have seeds, Gwyd, can't you simply plant them and raise your own crop of Mithras' fruit?"

"Ah, laddie, believe me, I hae tried that, but they dinna grow anywhere but in the soil o' the garden where we go."

Liaze shook her head and said, "Be that as it may, we at least understand the first four lines of Lady Lot's rede."

"We do?" asked Twk.

"Yes," said Liaze. And she chanted:

> Upon a bed 'neath ebon sky,
> One plans for one to slowly die.
> But if ye three are truly brave,
> A golden draught will surely save.

"The 'bed 'neath ebon sky' of Verdandi's rede is on the black mountain spoken of in her sister's rede."

"Her sister Skuld, you mean?" asked Twk.

"Oui, in Skuld's rede," said Liaze, "and I know where that cold mountain lies."

"Aye, lass, go on," said Gwyd.

"Then there is this," said Liaze. "When Verdandi said, 'One plans for one to slowly die,' I believe she means that the witch who stole Luc away is the one who plans for him to die. Hark back to Skuld's rede, where she said that one would die in the dark of the moon two moons from now, and that surely is the slow death of Verdandi's rede."

"Aye," said Gwyd, "I see where ye are takin this, lass, f'r the third and fourth lines o' her rede tell us we must be brave t'get the apple t'make the life-givin' elixir."

Liaze nodded. "That's what I think as well, for she did say 'if ye three are truly brave / A golden draught will surely save.' "

"Aye, and—whoosh now—we'll hae t'be truly brave t'face the unsleepin serpent."

Twk shrugged and said, "I do not question the bravery of the princess, for did she not face Lord Fear himself and triumph? As for you and me, Gwyd, perhaps we'll manage in spite of the serpent. Regardless, even though it seems we have ciphered the meaning of the first four lines of Verdandi's rede, what of the last six lines?"

They strode in silence a few more steps, but then Liaze said, "We've walked far enough; 'tis time to ride. Think on the rede as we press onward, and pray to Mithras that we resolve the quandary ere we reach the garden of the serpent. We cannot afford to yet be puzzling when we get there, for the dark of the moon comes toward us at a steady pace, and time dwindles even as we talk. Let us ride."

Liaze quickly shifted the tethers about so that Pied Agile would take the lead. She lifted Twk and Jester back onto one of the geldings and boosted Gwyd into Nightshade's saddle, and then mounted Pied Agile and led the train onward at a trot.

★ ★ ★

Walking, trotting, cantering, galloping, stopping at streams to take water, pausing to feed the horses and Jester grain and to take a meal themselves, onward they fared throughout the remainder of that day, passing through hamlets and across farmland and through forests.

They pressed on well into the evening, using the bright gibbous moon to light the way, ere at last making camp.

The next day, as the sun passed the zenith, they came unto the twilight wall, and Liaze said, "Gwyd, it has taken us one day, from noon to noon, to reach the place it would take you four days in all at a swift pace afoot. Hence, if the remainder of the trip continues in this fashion, what would take you a moon to reach the garden, we should be able to accomplish in a sevenday, but only if the horses hold out. Oh, Gwyd, it is but a desperate hope that we can reach the garden and get an apple and then return and push on to the black mountain ere the coming dark of the moon."

"Aye," replied Gwyd, "desperate indeed."

And on they rode to enter a realm of high moors, and Gwyd had them angle a bit leftward, though they kept riding in the general direction of the sunup bound.

Under Gwyd's guidance, the following day they crossed the next twilight border to come into rolling prairie. In the distance a great blot of darkness covered the land, and it slowly moved across the hillsides.

"What might that be, Gwyd?" asked Liaze, shading her eyes and peering intently, puzzlement in her gaze.

"That be a great herd o' shaggy beasties," said the Brownie. "There be nae reason to worry, lass, f'r they be gentle, though I dona think we should pass among them, f'r they hae young'ns and might get riled."

Swinging wide, they passed around the herd whose numbers seemed countless, and on they pressed. Within that day, they came to the following border and entered hill country, where rain swept across the land in blowing sheets. Gwyd and Liaze pulled cloaks tightly 'round and cast their hoods over their heads, and Liaze spread a weatherproof cloth o'er Twk and Jester; in the dimness under, the rooster went to sleep.

That eve they stopped when daylight was gone, for, under the dark overcast, the moon shone not.

Two days later, in unremitting rain, they came unto the third border and crossed over into a mountainous region of high peaks and low valleys.

"Princess," said Twk, "because of the rain, we've lost some time. Can we make it up?"

"Twk, we are among mountains," said Liaze, "but if the terrain is gentle in the valleys, perhaps we can do so."

"The terrain nae be gentle," said Gwyd, "f'r in a day or two we need climb to one o' the cols above."

Liaze groaned in despair, but on they pushed.

Another two days passed, and walking the horses to give them relief, they climbed the col and reached a high plateau; and in midafternoon they came to a sheer precipice. Mayhap a thousand feet below, a wide vale stretched out, and a river snaked its way toward a looming wall of twilight in the near distance.

"Beyond that bound lies the garden," said Gwyd. Then he pointed sinistral. "The way down the face o' the cliff be yon."

Leftward they turned to come to the path downward. "Oh, no," said Liaze, her face falling. "It is too narrow for the horses. Is there no other way?"

Gwyd slapped himself in the forehead. "Och, Princess, it

ne'er occurred t'me that the size o' the beasties would make a difference. I hae always come afoot."

"How far the garden?" asked Twk. "If it's close enough, perhaps we can leave the steeds here."

"Four days f'r me afoot," said Gwyd. "A day or so ahorse."

Liaze looked at the three-foot-tall Brownie and the tiny Pixie and his rooster. She shook her head, saying, "Even running, we can't go afoot, else we'll not make it to the garden and back in time; we must find another way."

"I ne'er looked f'r one," said Gwyd, "but ye be right, lass. Untether me, and I'll take the dextral."

"I'll go sinistral," said Liaze, dismounting and loosing the lines. "Twk, you and the geldings will come with me."

As the princess retied the packhorses to the stallion, she said, "Remember, Gwyd, it need be wide enough all the way down for Nightshade."

"What about the packhorses?" asked Gwyd. "They be wider wi' their gear."

"If necessary, we can leave the geldings and goods here," said Liaze.

"Och, aye," said Gwyd, and he turned Pied Agile and trotted away along the plateau to the right.

Liaze called out after him, "I'll sound the horn should I find a way."

Without turning, Gwyd waved, showing that he had heard her.

Liaze mounted the black, and she and Twk and the geldings went leftward.

Along the precipice they rode, seeking another way to the valley below, and at two places they stopped and looked at promising paths, but one became entirely too narrow within a short span, and the other one did not go all the way down.

The third path seemed wide enough, but it twisted away under an overhang, and Liaze could not see where it went.

"I'll go," said Twk, and he leapt into Jester's saddle and

goaded the bird into fluttering to the ground. Down the path the rooster darted and soon the two were out of sight.

Liaze sat upon Nightshade and gazed out across the vista and to the twilight border, so close and yet so far. And as she peered toward the shadowlight, of a sudden she knew the answers to Verdandi's rede.

33

Inference

With her heart racing in excitement, for she had solutions to Verdandi's rede, Liaze looked back along the precipice for Gwyd. But ere she could spot him, she heard the far-off crowing of a rooster. Frowning, Liaze dismounted, and she stepped to the brim of the cliff and peered downward. Again and again the rooster crowed, and at last the princess spotted a reddish dot in the valley at the foot of the sheer drop. *Is that Jester? Surely it must be. If so, then why would—? Ah, Twk must think the path is passable by horse.* Liaze turned and lifted the silver clarion and blew a call to Gwyd; it was the Autumnwood signal to return, and though he might not know its precise meaning, still it should bring him to her.

Shortly thereafter, Gwyd came riding Pied Agile up and over a slope on the plateau. *Ah, that's why I didn't see him.*

As the Brownie reached Liaze, he asked, "Ye hae found a way adown?"

"Twk and Jester did," said Liaze, switching the packhorse tethers to Pied Agile. She took the food sack and one of the water bags from a gelding and lashed them to Nightshade's saddle, saying, "We'll need these if the packhorses can't come down laden." She mounted and looked at Gwyd. "I'll ride down first, and if I deem the geldings can get through, I'll blow three short calls on Luc's horn, and then you follow. If I blow many long calls, it will mean I think the path too narrow for the horses and their packs; in that case, unlade the geldings—all but the remaining water bags and the crystal decanters and bridge; those we must have."

"Aye," said Gwyd. "If need be, I'll drop the rest o' the gear here. Now be off wi' ye, f'r the moon yet be sailin apace through the skies and gettin darker by the day."

Liaze wheeled the stallion, and down the path she went. Soon she was lost to Gwyd's sight as she passed under the overhang.

The path broadened, yet to the fore loomed a dark hole in an outjutting projection in the stone flank of the precipice, and into the gape the path plunged. *What's this? A tunnel?*

She reached the opening and dismounted, for the way was quite low. *I will have to pull Nightshade's head down to enter.* "Steady, my lad," she murmured to the stallion, praying to Mithras that he would not balk, and into the opening she stepped.

Nightshade followed without shying.

"Whoever trained you, boy, he had to be a horseman *extraordinaire.*"

On they passed, the light fading as they went, Liaze cautiously in the lead, making certain the footing was sure.

Around a gentle curve they paced, and ahead Liaze could see light, and soon they were again in the open, a looming cliff face to the left, a sheer drop to the right. Yet the way was wide, and Liaze mounted once more and on down they fared.

It took most of a candlemark for them to reach the bottom, and Twk on Jester called out, "Welcome, Princess. Where's Gwyd?"

"Waiting for my signal," said Liaze. "I had to make certain the laden packhorses could walk the entire route."

Twk clutched at his heart in mock distress and cried out, "You doubted?" And then the Pixie broke into giggles.

Liaze laughed and dismounted and raised Luc's horn toward the precipice above and blew three short calls. High up and leftward she saw Gwyd wave, and then the Brownie stepped back out of sight.

Shortly, they saw the horses and Gwyd begin the descent, and Liaze murmured to Twk, "I just hope he can figure out how to get the horses through the tunnel."

"Why is that?" asked the Pixie.

"The ceiling is quite low," said Liaze.

"Not for me and Jester," said Twk, and he broke into giggles again. But then he sobered and said, "I recked you would find a way, Princess."

Now Gwyd came to the passageway entrance. Liaze watched as he dismounted Pied Agile. The Brownie stood looking at the opening and scratching his head.

Liaze took Nightshade's reins in hand and turned the horse sideways to the cliff, and then she knelt and pulled the stallion's head down.

After a moment, Gwyd took Pied Agile's reins and pulled her head down and led her within the opening. The following gelding balked.

Gwyd reappeared and pulled that horse's head down and started inward, but the packhorse would not go. Gwyd turned to the horse, and a moment later he led the gelding within.

"What did he do?" asked Twk.

"He either sweet-talked the animal, or he slapped it in the jaw," said Liaze.

Once more Gwyd reappeared, and he led the second packhorse into the gap, this one without any trouble whatsoever. Then he led the third and the fourth ones through.

The sun had set and twilight had fallen when the Brownie finally reached the foot of the cliff.

They rode on a bit till full night came, and they paused to give the animals a drink from the river, and they fed them some grain. Then they waited for the moon, four days past full, to rise and light their way. Onward they fared, yet finally they stopped for the night. As they set camp, Liaze said, "I think I know the answers to Verdandi's rede."

"You do?" asked Twk, his eyes flying wide in amaze.

"What be they, lass?" asked Gwyd, looking up from the fire he was laying.

"Well, part of it we already know," said Liaze, dropping the gear from the second packhorse to the ground and turning to unlade the others.

"But not all," said Twk, darting into the food sack and fumbling about, then rushing back out bearing jerky.

As Liaze curried the animals, she said, "Remember the rede:

> *Upon a bed 'neath ebon sky,*
> *One plans for one to slowly die.*
> *But if ye three are truly brave,*
> *A golden draught will surely save.*
> *Hence, ground your lyre and ground it well*
> *For you to cast the needed spell.*
> *Sleep must come, if it comes at all,*
> *For one to thrive beyond the wall.*
> *Take only one else one will die,*
> *As will the one 'neath ebon sky.*

"The first four lines we think we know—"

"Yes, yes," said Twk. "But what about the last six lines?"

"Well, back atop the precipice, as I looked at the twilight boundary ahead, I thought of what we know of serpents, and then I knew the answers to Verdandi's rede."

"What be it we ken o' snakes?" asked Gwyd.

"They have no ears," said Liaze.

"No ears?" blurted Twk. "What does that have to do with anything?"

"Their hearing is poor, and though they can detect airborne sound—some say through their jawbone—they hear mainly through their skin," said Liaze.

Twk sighed in exasperation. "Yes, yes, but—"

"Twk, Twk, ma laddie," said Gwyd, striking flint to steel and setting the tinder to light and putting it in among the dried grass, "j'st let the princess finish." The Brownie began gently blowing upon the glowing ember.

"This means serpents can feel vibrations in the ground; it's one way they track prey and avoid predators."

Twk started to say something, but a glare from Gwyd silenced him before he could speak.

"Oui, Twk, I think I know what you were going to add: that they can also see and taste and some think they can sense the body warmth of their game. Yet, heed: Verdandi said, 'Ground your lyre and ground it well / For you to cast the needed spell.' But I am no spellcaster, so what might that mean? I think she is telling us that music will put the serpent asleep."

"Will? Or might?" said Gwyd, looking up from the flames now consuming the dry grass of his campfire. "Remember, lass, Verdandi said, 'Sleep must come, if it comes at all,' and t'me that means she's not certain."

"Be still, Gwyd, and let the princess finish," said Twk.

Gwyd smiled and began feeding twigs to the blaze.

"I think if I set the base of the harp well into the ground," said Liaze, "perhaps even dig a small hole and tamp soil about the base, and if I pluck the strings hard—hard enough for the serpent to feel the vibrations through the earth—and play a soothing air, then the creature might fall into slumber."

"I see," said Twk, breaking his own admonition. "Sleep must come, if it comes at all, / For one to thrive beyond the wall."

"Oui," said Liaze, smiling at the wee Pixie. "And that one who will thrive beyond the wall is Gwyd as he goes after one of Mithras' apples."

"Why can't it be me who goes after the apple?" asked Twk.

Gwyd roared in laughter. "What? Ye? Why, the apple might fall on ye and crush ye flat."

"Then I'll take Jester," said Twk.

"No," said Liaze. "Recall, the rede says for *one* to thrive beyond the wall, and you and Jester make two."

"Aye," said Gwyd, "The princess be right, laddie buck. It hae t'be me."

Twk sighed and nodded glumly, then said, "What about the last two lines?"

" 'Take only one else one will die, / As will the one 'neath ebon sky,' " quoted Liaze. "That means for us to take only one apple, for were we to try to take two of them, I deem the serpent will awaken, and Gwyd will not be able to escape; and if he does not get away with an apple, then Luc will also die there on the black mountain, for we will have no golden draught."

"Aye, Princess," said Gwyd. "When I delayed e'en a scant moment on ma most recent apple-takin, the serpent almost made the last o' me."

Tears welled in Liaze's eyes, and she paused in her currying. "Oh, Gwyd, 'tis a perilous thing you do, and I—"

"Hush now, Princess," said Gwyd, "f'r this be the way o' it: 'tis ye who must play the well-grounded harp, and I who must retrieve the apple. We'll fare all right, I ween."

"But what about me and Jester?" asked Twk. "What are we to do?"

"Nought that I can see at the moment," said Liaze.

"Bu-but Verdandi said that I and mine—Jester, I think— would be needed at a critical time," said Twk.

"Then, Twk," said Gwyd, now feeding larger branches to the fire, "this be not the time."

As he had done every day, Jester announced the coming of dawn, and shortly thereafter the trio was on the way. Down through the rest of the wide vale they rode, and in midmorn they passed through the twilight marge to come into an arid plain.

"Oh, Gwyd, have we missed the right point to go through the bound?"

"Nae, Princess," said Gwyd. "This do be the land o' the garden."

"But it is so sere," said Twk. "How can a garden grow in such a place as this?"

"There be a bit o' water, Twk, where the garden lies," said Gwyd. Then he turned to Liaze. "Princess, head f'r that darkness low on the horizon; they be mountains adistant."

And so, across the dry plain they ran, and dust flew up from galloping hooves. In sparse clumps here and there only thorny weeds grew, and the horses passed among them.

Galloping, walking, trotting, cantering, all day they fared toward the mountains afar, and Liaze wondered if the horses were making any progress at all. Often Liaze stopped to water the steeds, after which she fed them grain as they walked.

"You are certain there is water where we go?" asked Liaze, adding, "We will be bone-dry when we get there."

"Aye, Princess, a small stream meanders down fra the mountains and into the garden. Snowmelt, I ween, f'r it takes y'r breath away wi' its chill."

"Ah," said Twk, "that's what feeds the apple tree among all this dust."

"Indeed," said Gwyd, and on they rode. "But who would hae thought t'plant it here t'begin wi'?"

"Mithras," said Twk with finality.

On they pressed as the sun sailed up and across the sky and then fell toward the horizon. And then it set, and Jester fell asleep. They moved more slowly until the gibbous moon rose five days past full to shine brightly down upon them, and Liaze picked up the pace again.

But at last, ahead in the near distance a wall of stones loomed. "There, Princess," said Gwyd, "there be the garden."

"I see it," said Liaze.

"Weel," said Gwyd, "I think ye need t'leave the horses here, else they'll be affrighted by the smell o' the snake."

Liaze haled the horses to a halt and dismounted. Gwyd jumped down and stepped back to Twk, and the wee Pixie dropped to the Brownie's shoulder, leaving Jester asleep behind. Then Liaze and Gwyd with Twk aboard strode toward the rock enclosure, and as they neared, within the walls beyond they could hear the rustling of the great serpent, sleepless and standing ward.

34

Garden

Liaze eyed the rough stone wall, some twelve feet high and perhaps forty paces in length from corner to corner, or so it was on this bound of the garden. "Are the other sides as this one?"

"Aye, lass," said Gwyd. "It be square, though 'round the corner"—Gwyd gestured to the left—"there be a gate."

"A gate?"

"Aye. Ye can look through and see the tree and beastie, though the bars are set too close f'r me t'squeeze through."

"Could I get through?" asked Twk.

"Aye," said Gwyd, turning leftward, "ye could. Howe'er, the snake'd snap ye up like ye was nought but a morsel."

With the Pixie on his shoulder, the Brownie led the princess to a great bronze gate set midway along the stretch of the wall. Past narrow-set, heavy bars laden with filigree, in the moonlight Liaze could see in the center of the stone-walled garden a tall, yellow-leafed tree burdened with golden apples agleam in the argent glow. "Oh, Gwyd, how beautif—" Of a sudden, Liaze gasped, for coiled 'round the base of the tree lay a huge, great-girthed snake, its scales blotches of brown and tan held in a gold-laced pattern. And it raised its head and its long forked tongue flicked in and out as it *tasted* the spoor of these interlopers standing just beyond the portal.

"Oh, my," said Liaze.

Twk edged a bit behind Gwyd's collar. "Are you certain it won't come over the wall, Gwyd?"

"Nothin be certain, Twk," said Gwyd, "yet it ne'er did so in the past when I escaped wi' the fruit."

Liaze took a deep breath and said, "Well, I suppose there's nothing for it but that we fetch the harp and see if we can put this monster to sleep."

They turned and started back toward the horses. "Where lies the stream, Gwyd?"

"On the far side, Princess."

"Since there is no wind, I would ride the horses 'round and tether them fast, if there are trees."

"There be no trees, lass, but brush instead."

"That will do. Besides, I would gather some of that brush for a fire."

"A fire, Princess?" asked Twk.

"Yes, for though I can play the harp in total blackness, this night I would see the strings as I do so. Besides, I plan on having my bow strung and an arrow ready, and I would not wish to fumble about in the dark in the event they are needed."

Gwyd shook his head. "Did I mention, lass, that the snake be unkillable?"

"What?"

"Aye, I think he be protected by Mithras himself so that j'st anyone canna steal the apples."

Liaze sighed. "Nevertheless, Gwyd, I'll have an arrow ready."

They reached the horses, and Gwyd lifted Twk onto the gelding where Jester slept, and Liaze boosted Gwyd to Nightshade's saddle, and mounted Pied Agile and rode wide 'round the garden to the stream, well away from the wall. And there, as Gwyd gathered brush for a fire, Liaze watered the animals and fed them some grain, and refilled the waterskins and took a deep draught herself.

Twk wakened Jester, the rooster somewhat grumpy at being roused in the night, though it did take grain along with the horses.

Liaze strung her bow and shouldered her quiver and fetched the harp from the rucksack and her trowel from the gear.

And as they readied themselves for the ordeal—for none of them could think of it in any other terms—Liaze said, "Where do you enter, Gwyd?"

"J'st t'the right o' the gate, Princess, f'r there the stones be best f'r climbin' out, though not f'r climbin' in. I walked atop and studied all o' the wall carefully ere ma first foray. I think most o' the victims o' the serpent didna do so, and they took the easy way in, but it be the worst way out."

"Canny," said Liaze, smiling at the Brownie. Then she frowned and asked, "How will we know the serpent is asleep?"

"Ah, lass," said Gwyd, "that be the hard part, f'r snakes hae nae eyelids."

"No eyelids?" said Twk. "Then how do they blink away dust and such?"

"Och, Twk, ye ne'er looked?"

"Gwyd, Gwyd"—the Pixie spread his arms wide—"I'm nine inches tall. If you were me, would you walk up and look a snake in the eye?"

Gwyd laughed and said, "Nae, Twk, I wouldna. Anyway, snakes hae a clear scale o'er each eye. Like glass it be, and it protects them."

Liaze nodded. "Yes, but that still doesn't answer my question: how will we know when the serpent is asleep?"

"Weel," said Gwyd, "on the night o' the longest day o' the

year, I wait until he stops tastin the air wi' his forked tongue. Then I hie f'r the tree."

"Is there no better way?" asked Liaze.

"Lass, it'll hae t'do," said Gwyd.

Liaze sighed in resignation, and, along with her bow and arrows and the harp and trowel, she and Gwyd took up the brush and bore it 'round to the gate, Twk on Jester trotting along at their side, the Pixie with an armload of dry grass to use as tinder.

They set all down in front of the gate, and as Gwyd started a small fire on the dusty ground, Liaze used her trowel to gouge out a shallow hole in the hard soil, sized a wee bit smaller than the foot of the harp. When it was deep enough, she angled the base into the gap and wrenched the harp back and forth to auger the foot down into the hole to tightly wedge it in. Soon she had the instrument well grounded, the foot lodged in hardpan. She packed more dirt into the hole atop the foot and tamped it down. Finally, she glanced at the serpent yet coiled about the trunk of the tree, and she took a deep breath and looked at the Brownie and said, "Oh, Gwyd, I'm not certain that—"

"Princess, there be nae other way. Besides, we must trust t'the Fates." Gwyd squared his shoulders and turned and strode to another place along the wall.

Liaze watched as the Brownie walked away and began to climb, and she murmured, "But we don't know whether it will work."

"We can only try, my lady," said Twk. "Besides, I've been thinking about why the serpent sleeps on the longest night of the year. You see, it's that night that the music of the spheres is the loudest, or so I believe, hence that's when the snake can be lulled by the movements of the heavens."

"Ah, but Twk, I cannot match the magic of the spheres."

"Mayhap not, Princess, yet you are closer than any of the lights in the firmament, and so your soothing music might be enough."

"Indeed, Twk, 'might.' "

Gwyd had come along the top of the garden wall back to the right side of the gate.

"Ready?" asked Liaze, her voice quavering, and she did not trust it to say more.

"Ready," said Gwyd, his own voice tremulous.

Liaze glanced at her strung bow and the arrow at hand and then at the serpent. She took a deep breath and let it out and began forcefully strumming the harp in a lullaby, and she crooned along with the melody:

> *Hush, my child, and go to sleep,*
> *The moon sails through the sky.*
> *You, my babe, I safe will keep,*
> *Our day has said goodbye.*
>
> *Sleep, sleep, my darling,*
> *Sleep, oh sleep, I sigh,*
> *Sleep, sleep, my youngling,*
> *Hush now, don't you cry.*

Verse after verse did Liaze sing and play, and chorus after chorus, and the dust just in front of the harp danced in synchronism with the vibration of the hard-plucked strings. Slowly, ever so slowly, the serpent's coils relaxed and its head began to droop, and its forked tongue gradually tasted the air less and less.

Liaze sang and fiercely strummed, and the dust danced nigh the harp.

The moon sailed onward through a starlit sky, not heeding the desperate gamble below, as Liaze crooned and played, and Gwyd sat waiting atop the wall, and Twk stood by Jester and fretted.

Still the song and plucked notes graced the air, and still the ground ever so lightly shivered, and still the serpent tasted, but slowly less and less, and gradually it loosened its coils and drooped . . . until finally the serpent's head dipped to the ground, and it no longer sampled the air.

Gwyd slipped down the inside of the wall, while Liaze continued to play and sing, though her voice tightened with stress.

> *Oh, my sweet, sleep this darktide,*
> *Oh, my sweet, sleep this eve;*
> *I am here by your sweet side*
> *As sweet, sweet dreams you weave.*

> *Sleep, sleep, my darling,*
> *Sleep, oh sleep, I sigh,*
> *Sleep, sleep, my youngling,*
> *Hush now, don't you cry.*

Across the intervening space crept Gwyd, and the serpent shifted slightly. Sweating, Gwyd froze in place and waited, and Liaze, her voice trembling in dread, sang on:

> *Your papa's gone ahunting,*
> *And maman makes the bed,*
> *And lie you in your bunting,*
> *Nought but dreams in your head.*

> *Sleep, sleep, my darling,*
> *Sleep, oh sleep I sigh,*
> *Sleep, sleep, my youngling,*
> *Hush now, don't you cry.*

The serpent made no further movement, and Gwyd crept onward. Finally he reached the monstrous snake, and cautiously he stepped over coil after coil to come to the trunk of the golden apple tree.

Liaze could hardly bear to look, but look she did, as she played and sang:

> *The stars begin to glimmer*
> *And look upon your face,*
> *While in your dreams you murmur*
> *A song of sleeping grace.*
>
> *Sleep, sleep, my darling,*
> *Sleep, oh sleep, I sigh,*
> *Sleep, sleep, my youngling,*
> *Hush now, don't you cry.*

Up Gwyd shinnied to the first limb, where he pulled himself higher.

Liaze nearly choked in fear, and her fingers seemed stiff with anxiety. But she continued to play and sing:

> *Sleep, my child, and dream your dreams,*
> *The moon sails through the night,*
> *Bathing you in silver beams,*
> *And rinsing you with light.*
>
> *Sleep, sleep, my darling,*
> *Sleep, oh sleep, I sigh,*
> *Sleep, sleep, my youngling,*
> *Hush now, don't you cry.*

Now Gwyd reached out, and cautiously, silently, with two hands—one to hold the branch and one to grasp the fruit—he plucked a golden apple from the golden tree and slipped it into one of the many pockets of his raggedy clothes.

The snake stirred not . . .

. . . and Liaze, the tips of her fingers now bleeding, scarlet running down the strings, continued to pluck and sing:

> *Gentle quiet lies o'er the house.*
> *A distant owl hoots long.*
> *Somewhere squeaks a little mouse.*
> *A cricket chirps its song.*
>
> *Sleep, sleep, my darling,*
> *Sleep, oh sleep, I sigh,*
> *Sleep, sleep, my youngling,*
> *Hush now, don't you cry.*

Now Gwyd eased back down the tree, and once again the snake shifted, and once again Gwyd froze in place.

> *Day will surely come, my child,*
> *The sun will rise again.*
> *You will play in days so mild,*
> *And sing a sweet refrain.*
>
> *Sleep, sleep, my darling,*
> *Sleep, oh sleep, I sigh,*
> *Sleep, sleep, my youngling,*
> *Hush now, don't you cry.*

Again Gwyd eased down the tree and down the trunk, to come to the ground, and once more he stepped across the great coils, as Liaze watched, her heart in her throat.

> *My baby's gone afishing*
> *Among her pleasant dreams.*
> *And I sit here awishing*
> *She'll catch silver moonbeams.*

*   *   *

Sleep, sleep, my darling,
Sleep, oh sleep, I sigh,
Sleep, sleep, my youngling,
Hush now, don't you cry.

And as Gwyd stepped over the last coil, the snake twitched, and the tip of its tail slapped into the Brownie's leg.

Up snapped the serpent's head, and out flashed its tongue, and Gwyd fled.

Liaze screamed and leapt to her feet, and the serpent, mouth wide and gaping, fangs dripping, reared up and struck at the Brownie. But it was yet coiled about the tree and was jerked to a stop, its strike falling a scant inch short.

Twk shrieked, "Run! Run! Oh, Mithras, run!"

And Gwyd, his face twisted in terror, ran—

—but the huge serpent hurled itself after, its coils rapidly unwinding from the tree, and then, loose, it was swifter, much swifter than fleeing Gwyd—

—Liaze started to reach for her bow, but instead—

—"Oh, Mithras, run!" screamed Twk—

—Gwyd flew toward the wall—

—the massive snake overtook the Brownie and reared up to slay—

—Liaze snatched a burning branch from the fire and hurled it over the gate, praying to Mithras that—

—the flaming limb sailed between the striking serpent and the fleeing Brownie, and—

—the monstrous snake's strike veered and hammered into the blazing brand—

—Gwyd scrambled up the stones—

—"Oh, Mithras! Oh Mithras!" cried Twk—

—and again the serpent drew back and struck—

—just as Gwyd tumbled o'er the top of the wall and fell to the ground—

—and the serpent's strike slashed through nought but empty air.

Weeping, Liaze rushed to Gwyd's side, wee Twk running after.

Gwyd lay on the ground moaning, for he had fallen twelve feet.

"Gwyd, Gwyd, oh Gwyd," cried Liaze, tears running down her face as she dropped to her knees beside him, wanting to take him up, wanting to embrace him, but she knew not the extent of his injuries.

And just as Twk reached the Brownie, Gwyd opened his eyes and groaned and said, "I think some o' ma ribs be broke ag'in."

35

Desperate Journey

Liaze helped Gwyd sit up, the Brownie groaning. "I dona want t'get t'ma feet right now, but—" Of a sudden Gwyd began to chuckle, and, even as he clutched his ribs, he pointed.

Liaze and Twk both turned and looked, and now Twk started twittering. "What, Gwyd, what?" asked Liaze.

"Jester," said Twk, breaking into full-fledged giggles.

Its head under one wing, the rooster had gone back to sleep.

"Wi' desperation all about," said Gwyd, now cackling and groaning at the same time while pressing a hand to his chest, "and wi' life and death in the balance, it mattered not one whit t'the bird that I were about t'be done in." He paused and moaned and tried to catch his breath, but broke into guffaws, and held his ribs and gasped, "Oh, oh, but it hurts t'laugh."

"Well, at least one of us remained calm in the face of dire peril," said Twk, his gleeful laughter rising, "even if it was my chicken."

In relief and in the release of tension, the trio sat and guffawed at Jester, the bird paying no heed whatsoever, and that made them laugh all the harder.

Finally, Liaze said, "Gwyd, let us get you back to our camp and use some of that rib-mending simple of yours."

"Aye, Princess, if ye'll help me t'ma feet."

As Liaze eased Gwyd up, he gasped and said, "Y'r fingers, Princess, they be bloody."

"The harp," said Liaze, by way of explanation.

"Ah," said Gwyd, "y'did play long, aye, a lot longer than ye played of recent, longer e'en than ye played f'r Lord Fear, and ye plucked hard so the snake would feel it. Weel, I hae somethin t'fix y'up." Gwyd gestured at his pockets.

They stepped back to the harp with its now-scarlet strings, and Twk wakened Jester, the bird ruffling his feathers at being so rudely interrupted in whatever chicken dream he had been having.

Liaze knelt and wrenched the silver instrument back and forth to free the foot, and took it up, along with her bow and quiver, and then lent a steadying hand to the Brownie.

"What about the fire?" asked Twk.

"There's nought out here but dust," said Gwyd. "Leave it be. It'll soon burn itself out."

As they turned to start away, Liaze took one last look at the golden apple tree, where, once again coiled about the trunk, the monstrous snake coldly stared back at her.

Slowly they made their way 'round the wall and to the stream and horses.

The princess fetched a cup as Gwyd gently lowered himself down beside the rill and fished about in his belt pockets. Liaze dipped the cup in the stream, and, as he had done before, Gwyd dropped in a pinch of powder and swirled it about, and then drank it all.

"Now, Princess, f'r you." The Brownie replenished the water and dropped another powder within, and bade Liaze to soak her fingers. After a while, he bandaged each one, and when that was done he said, "Now, let us hae a fire, f'r I dona want t'make a mistake."

With Liaze collecting brushwood, and Twk fetching dry grass, soon, in spite of her bandages, the princess had a campfire ablaze.

"Now, lass, the decanters and bridge."

Liaze fetched the carven crystals and handed them to Gwyd, and in the moonlight and by firelight, the Brownie examined the runes and selected a decanter and handed it to her. "This be the one."

Liaze peered at the deep-set runes and nodded in agreement, and showed the carvings to Twk as well.

"And you say this powers the magic?" asked the Pixie.

"That's what I am told," said Liaze.

Gwyd rummaged through his pockets and withdrew the golden apple and handed it to Liaze. "Carve this up and drop it into the crystal, if ye please."

"All of it? Stem, pips, and bottom tip, too?"

"Aye, lass. Cut the whole o' it into chunks; the size doesna matter, j'st as long as ye can slip them into the neck."

Liaze withdrew her long-knife and, somewhat clumsily, carved the apple into pieces and dropped each one in. When the full of the apple was inside, Gwyd examined the runes on the bridge, and pointed at one end and said, "This be the cap f'r that decanter."

Once again, Liaze examined the runes and nodded in agreement, and she showed them to Twk.

"Hmm . . ." mused the Pixie. "Just how oddly shaped signs carved into crystal can do miraculous things, I'll never understand."

"Nor will I," said Liaze, as she capped the decanter with the rune-matched end of the bridge.

They sat and peered at the pieces of apple within, but nothing seemed to be happening. Liaze smiled. "A watched pot doesn't boil."

"Weel," said Gwyd, "I wouldna say that, m'lady. But as to

this decanter turning the apple t'cider, recall it takes a day all t'gether, a full twenty-four candlemarks."

Even with this admonition, they continued to stare at the contents. Finally Gwyd said, "How did I manage t'escape? What happened that the snake missed me?"

"The princess saved you," said Twk.

Gwyd looked at Liaze. "Did ye, now? Wi' one o' y'r arrows?"

Liaze shook her head. "No, Gwyd. You see, I remembered that serpents sense the body heat of their victims, and I flung a torch between you and him just as he was to strike, and the snake went after the burning brand. It seems it was barely enough of a delay to give you time to get over the wall."

"Mithras, but it was a close thing," said the Pixie. "I thought you a deader for sure."

"So did I, Twk," said the Brownie. "So did I."

Liaze glanced at the waning gibbous moon nearing the zenith and stood and stepped to the horses. "Let us set camp and get some rest, for dawn will soon come."

Jester's crowing announced the arrival of the sun, and Liaze groaned awake. *Too little rest and much to do, and but ten more nights till the dark of the moon. Oh, Mithras, but we have a long way to go and not enough time to get there.*

She sat up and looked at the capped decanter, now some quarter full with a yellowish slush.

To one side, Gwyd roused, and he, too, glanced at the decanter. "It be workin, Princess," he muttered.

From his perch on a bush, again Jester crowed; the chicken sat alongside Twk, the Pixie in a nestlike bower in the bush. Yawning and stretching, Twk said, "Come on, red rooster, let's get you fed and saddled."

"Good advice," said Liaze, and she got to her feet and, after taking care of her immediate needs, she laded the geldings and saddled the stallion and the mare.

She fed them some grain, and fed Jester too, and then broke her own fast along with Gwyd and Twk.

"Princess, it be seven days back t'the inn, and another seven t'the black mountain by y'r reckonin," said Gwyd. "That be fourteen days in all, and there be but ten left till the moon be dark. How can we possibly get there in time?"

"We'll just have to press hard," said Liaze, "and pray to Mithras the horses can hold up. We have this going for us, though: the farther we travel, the lighter the lade of the geldings."

"Och, aye," said Gwyd. "The grain be the heaviest o' their burden, and the horses . . . they be eatin it up on the way."

"They need it," said Liaze, "for we drive them to their limits."

"Perhaps," said Twk, "in some of the towns we go through, we can get fresh mounts."

Liaze shook her head. "I think we cannot afford the time it would take to bargain for such. Besides, I know these horses, for five of them are from my own estates, and I would never yield up Nightshade. Non, these are all worthy steeds, capable of long travel. I would rather have them than some unknown animal."

"Still," said Gwyd, "we took plenty o' coinage fra the Trolls, and so, should it come t'it, there be nae need t'bargain; we'll j'st board our own and take fresh mounts and pay whate'er be wanted."

Liaze sighed and nodded.

By pressing the horses a bit harder, they arrived at the twilight border and crossed over into the wide river valley at sundown. They paused for rest by the flow and replenished their water and waited for the moon to rise to light the way up the path along the sheer cliff.

Liaze and Gwyd walked the steeds along the narrow way and through the tunnel, and they camped that night on the plateau above.

That night as well, they unpacked the decanter, and they

found the apple had completely turned to cider, all but the pips and stem and floretlike very bottom of the fruit, now stirring in the yellow liquid. Gwyd then spanned the bridge to the other decanter, and they bedded down for the night.

The next morning, at Jester's alert, they wakened to find the distilled golden elixir in the brandy side, with the pips and stem and floret lying on the bottom of the cider side. Gwyd pulled the bridge and capped the decanters and wrapped all in cloth.

This morning as well, Liaze's fingers were healed and she left off her bandages.

The next two days they spent wending through the mountains, and in early afternoon of the third day they crossed into hill country, and rain fell from the sky.

"Mithras, it rained all throughout the time when we crossed this realm before," said Twk. "Is it going to do so again?"

"It hae been this way ev'ry time I hae come through," said Gwyd.

Liaze groaned and pulled her cloak tight around and cast her hood over her head, and, as she had done before, she covered the Pixie and chicken with the weatherproof cloth.

On they pressed, and even though they had no light in the overcast nights, still they rode onward, going slowly much of the eve, but eventually stopping to set a sodden camp.

Two nights they spent in that drenched land, splashing across streams, fording rivers, riding through dripping woodlands, but in the late morning of the third day, again they crossed a twilight marge to come into sunlight gracing wide, rolling plains.

On they pressed, and they reveled in the warmth of the day, and in the distance they saw one of the great herds of the shaggy beasts, but this day they did not have to pass around the animals, for the dark grazers were well off their path.

Cantering, galloping, trotting, they came to the next twilight border late in the night and crossed into high moorland.

The next day at noon they passed at last into the realm where lay the inn Gwyd had once served, and they stopped in a town and had a warm meal, the first one in a fortnight.

But soon they pushed on, for they could not afford to tarry.

The next day, at noon, they reached the ramshackle inn.

"We cannot rest," said Liaze, she and her companions weary beyond compare, "for the black mountain is far, and in four nights comes the dark of the moon."

And so on they pressed, anxiety gnawing at Liaze.

Following the track of the landmarks she had committed to memory, toward that distant dark peak she aimed, while the sun sank through the sky, night to fall at last.

There was no moon and wouldn't be until the wee hours, but, guided by the stars, still Liaze drove onward, the animals feeling the strain.

The next day at the remembered lake they crossed a border to come in among a jumble of boulders.

"Are we on track?" called Twk.

"Oui," said Liaze, and grimly they pushed on.

Two days after, late in the eve and some four leagues beyond a modest town, they came unto the shadowlight border across which lay the bleak plain wherein the black mountain stood, that dark pinnacle more than a full day's ride. It was at this border that one of the geldings, though now lightly loaded, went lame.

"Oh, no," said Twk, as the packhorse stumbled to a halt beneath him and his rooster.

After a swift inspection, "I hae some lameweed wi' me," said Gwyd, fumbling at a pocket in his belt, "but it will take three days f'r the animal t'be sound ag'in."

"We cannot spare the time to take him back to the town," said Liaze. She peered about. "There is grazing here and water nearby." She sighed and said, "Treat him; I will set him free."

As Gwyd stirred a powder into a cup, and then poured the solution into a feedbag with a small bit of oats, Liaze transferred Twk and Jester to another pack animal, and then unladed the lame horse and examined the goods, and set most of it beneath a nearby tree, and placed the rest upon the sound geldings.

Gwyd, who had not been watching, said, "Ye kept the hammer and nails and shoes, eh, Princess? We might need them should a beastie throw one."

"Yes, Gwyd."

"Good," said the Brownie, and, while Liaze rearranged the tethers, he fastened the feedbag over the nose of the animal. "He'll be done in a nonce, then we can push on."

Moments later, Gwyd removed the bag from the lame horse, and set it with the abandoned cargo.

Liaze boosted the Brownie into the saddle of Pied Agile, and she mounted Nightshade, and through the border she rode, the mare and three geldings in tow.

Into this cold, bleak, dark land they moved at a swift trot, for the mountain lay nearly two days distant, yet this was the last night before the night of the dark of the moon.

Darkness fell, and, once again setting her course by the stars, on Liaze rode through the chill. Just after mid of night they stopped for a rest, for the horses were weary, as were the riders thereon. Liaze rubbed the animals down, for she would not have their lathered sweat turn to ice against their hides.

Yet some two hours later, they pushed on through the dark, starlight alone illumining the way. And Liaze prayed that none of the horses would go lame or throw a shoe or step into a hole and break a leg or founder.

Daylight saw them still moving forward, though now at a walk, Liaze and Gwyd pacing alongside Pied Agile, the mare now in the lead, Twk on Jester trotting at hand.

"This is the final day, Gwyd," said Liaze. "Tonight is the dark of the moon."

"Till what candlemark do we have, my lady?" asked Twk.

"I do not know, but mid of night it reaches full depth."

"Aye," said Gwyd.

"How much farther?" asked Twk.

Liaze shook her head. "I am not certain. Riding high in the sky with Lord Fear as I was, I found it rather difficult to judge ground distances from the back of a spectral steed."

"Would that we had one o' those spectral steeds now," said Gwyd.

Liaze nodded. "It would have made short work of our journey."

"If we had Asphodel, the Fairy King's horse, that, too, would make the journey short," said Twk.

"My brother Borel rode that steed," said Liaze.

"He did?" asked Twk.

"Oui. He won the ride when he defeated the Fairy King in a game of échecs."

"Oh, my," said Twk. "Then your brother must be a wonderful player indeed, for I hear the Fairy King cannot be bested in that game."

"In this instance he was, and my brother managed to ride the steed and find his ladylove," said Liaze.

"Weel," said Gwyd, "let us hope that ye can find y'r own true love wi'out needin the Fairy steed."

Grimly, Liaze nodded and said, "Time to ride."

Soon they were agallop across the icy-cold plain, and as of yet the black mountain was not in sight.

It was in the noontide that Liaze espied the truncated tip of the dark peak, and on they rode, the mountain slowly coming up o'er the horizon ahead.

Even so, it seemed to Liaze that they would not reach the mountain in time, yet she could not press the flagging steeds any faster, and on they rode.

It was as the sun set and twilight came creeping o'er this

bleak and forbidding realm that Liaze saw up ahead a small girl sitting on a rock and weeping.

She drew Nightshade to a halt beside the fille, and she and Gwyd leapt down, Twk on Jester following.

"Child, what are you doing out here all alone?" asked Liaze, kneeling and embracing the girl, who was no more than seven or eight summers old. The thin youngling shivered uncontrollably. "Oh, child, you are freezing," said Liaze, and she whipped off her cloak and wrapped it about the little girl.

Snubbing and snukking, the girl looked through nearly black, tear-filled eyes at Liaze and said, "Thank you for the cloak, madame, but I am crying for I know not the answer to a riddle."

"A riddle?" said Liaze.

The child pulled Liaze's head close and murmured in her ear: "Feed me and I live; give me a drink and I die."

"Are you hungry?" asked Liaze.

The girl looked at Gwyd and then at Twk on Jester, and she managed a smile. "Non, madame," she whispered. "That is the riddle, you see."

"Ah," said Liaze. She frowned in thought for a moment, and then brightened and said, "The answer to that riddle is 'Fire.' "

Of a sudden a darkness enveloped the child, and the girl grew, and Gwyd gasped and Twk cried out in surprise, while Liaze stepped hindward and drew her long-knife.

And the darkness vanished, and now before the trio stood a toothless crone with black eyes. She wore a dark, shapeless robe, and she cackled in glee.

And there came to Liaze's ears the sound of looms weaving.

Liaze sheathed her blade and bowed and said, "Lady Doom."

"Doom?" squeaked Twk. "Lady Doom?"

"Urd," said Gwyd, bowing.

"Heh! Fooled you, did I?" The crone gaped a gummy grin.

Liaze nodded and said, "As did your sisters, Lady Urd."

"Well, ye have given me your cloak, but I return it," said Urd, holding out the garment to Liaze.

As Liaze donned the cloak, Urd said, "I have come to give you a message."

Liaze nodded. "I would have whatever aid you can give."

"Heh, it's in the form of a rede," said Urd.

Twk groaned, and Gwyd sighed mournfully, but Liaze nodded.

Urd shook a knobby finger at the Brownie and the Pixie on Jester and said, "If you three keep your wits about you, you can aid."

"Three?" said Twk. "Jester, too?"

Urd cackled and glanced at the dimming twilight, then turned to Liaze and, as the sound of weaving looms grew louder, said:

> *Precious steps will get ye there,*
> *As up black glass ye steeply fare,*
> *Do not dismount as ye try,*
> *Else by fire ye will surely die.*
> *On the flat ye can set foot,*
> *But nowhere else do place y'r boot.*
> *Remember war; loose the cry,*
> *So ye and y'r love will not die.*

Urd then cackled and turned to Gwyd and Twk and Jester. "I hear you have treasure."

"A-aye, Lady Urd," said Gwyd. "Would ye hae some o' the coin we took fra the Trolls and Goblins?"

"Pah, what good is gold or silver to me?" the crone asked. She turned to Twk and said, "And I hear that you and your rooster disturb folks at night. Heh!"

"Oui, Lady Doom. W-would you have me stop?"

"Heh! No. It's a fine thing that you have done in training y'r chicken to crow on command in the dark." Again Lady Urd cackled in glee, and then she glanced once more at the vanishing dusk, and the sound of looms swelled and Lady Doom disappeared, leaving only the sigh of chill wind behind as full night fell o'er the land.

"Are the Fates somehow entwined with your family, Princess?" asked Twk.

Liaze took in a deep breath and let it out. "It would seem so."

"J'st as are entwined these witches ye told me about," said Gwyd.

Liaze nodded. "Hradian, Rhensibé, Iniquí, and Nefasí."

"Rhensibé is the dead one, oui?" asked Twk.

"Oui," replied Liaze. "And I wish they were all very much dead. —Come, let us ride."

"What about the rede we just heard?" asked Twk.

"We'll deal with that as we go, for there is no time to lose."

On toward the mountain they fared, puzzling over Lady Doom's rede, yet they only knew that it had to do with getting to the top of the black mountain to reach Luc, and little else. Oh, they did understand that none of them were to set foot on the dark slopes, for should they do so, then somehow, according to Lady Urd, they would die by fire.

As they rode onward, the sky clouded over; there would be no stars this night. Liaze lit a lantern, and on they fared.

By dead reckoning, they reached the base of the black mountain with but a candlemark or so to spare, and Liaze wept in relief as she looked at the conical slopes leading up to a flat-topped crest.

"Ah, lass, ye weep out o' gladness that we made it," said Gwyd, "but now ye hae t'get t'the top."

"I'll ride Nightshade up," said Liaze.

"Och, Princess," said the Brownie, "that be no easy task."

"Your meaning?"

"See how the sides o' the mountain gleam in the lantern light? Now we ken why Lady Doom said, 'Precious steps will get ye there, / As up black glass ye steeply fare.' Princess, this be obsidian; it be up a glass mountain ye would ride."

36

Black Mountain

Liaze dismounted from Pied Agile, and Gwyd jumped to the ground from Nightshade. Twk wakened Jester and mounted the wee saddle, and the rooster fluttered to the ground. Untying the tethers, Liaze said, "Glass mountain or no, we cannot delay. I will ride to the top and awaken Luc."

"What if you cannot rouse him?" asked Twk.

Liaze looked at Gwyd. "If I cannot awaken him, will the life-giving elixir aid?"

"Aye, it should, but if he be in an enchanted sleep, ye'll hae t'go slow, else he'll strangle."

"How much should I give him?"

"A sip should do," replied Gwyd, "a spoonful or so."

Liaze slipped the decanter of elixir into the stallion's saddle-bags.

"Oh, Princess," said Twk, "will you be safe?"

"As long as I do not step on the slopes, or so Urd implied."

"And what about Nightshade?" asked the Pixie. "He will be setting foot upon the mountain; will he be safe?"

"Remember the rede, Twk. Urd said 'Do not dismount as ye try,' " said Gwyd, now lighting a second lantern.

"Ah, I see," said Twk. "The princess has to ride to the top, else Lady Doom would not have told her to not dismount. Horse steps: those are the 'precious steps' of her rede."

At these words, Gwyd fell into reflection, as if trying to catch an elusive thought.

Liaze checked her bow and quiver, and she took up her lantern and mounted Nightshade and set off up the slope of the obsidian mountain, glass chips flying in his wake. And even as the stallion clattered up the slant, now and again a hoof slipped, but the steed fared on.

Up he went and up, his breath blowing white in the air upon the frigid black mountain, Liaze urging the stallion higher, and still his shod hooves skittered now and again.

On the ground below, by the lamp Liaze bore, the Brownie and Pixie watched, and they sucked in air at every slip and slide. Of a sudden, Gwyd said, "Precious steps! Lady Doom said 'precious steps'! Oh, Twk, now I ken what those words mean."

Gwyd raced to the packhorse, and, struggling, he unladed the gelding. By lantern light he fetched the shoeing hammer and nails from the gear, and he threw the rucksack on the ground and took out silver coins.

"Nightshade has stopped about a third of the way up," cried Twk, then, "Oh no! He's sliding backwards."

Gwyd only spared a quick glance at what was happening above as he stepped to Pied Agile. The Brownie lifted a forefoot and cleaned away the dirt and mud and then began driving new nails through pure silver coins and into the hoof, affixing the soft metal in place upon the bronze shoe.

"Gwyd, Gwyd, we've lost," cried Twk. "The princess has turned about and is riding down. You were right: it is a glass mountain and entirely too slick for a horse to reach the top."

Gwyd moved to the opposite forefoot, where once again he

drove nails through silver coins and into Pied Agile's hoof. "Be nae certain about that, Twk," he said. "I ken what Lady Doom meant when she said 'precious steps.' And wouldna ye ken, she as much as told me what she meant by those words when she mentioned t'me that I bore treasure—the coins fra the Goblins and Trolls."

"I don't understand," said Twk. "How are coins going to help?"

"Well, laddie buck, I hear silver be a counter f'r some forms o' magic, and I ween this mountain hae a charm o'er it."

"A charm?"

"Aye, how else can somethin this cold cause one t'die by fire?"

"But why Pied Agile?" asked Twk. "Why not put the silver on Nightshade's hooves? I mean, he's bigger and stronger."

"Aye, but we canna waste the time. Anyway, Pied Agile's name in the old tongue means Nimble Foot in the new. She'll reach th'top, I ween."

Liaze, tears of frustration on her face, came riding back to the Brownie and Pixie. "I can't make it up," she said.

"Dona be certain, lass," said Gwyd, finishing the last of Nimble Foot's hooves. "Y'see, I ken what the words 'precious steps' mean in Lady Doom's rede. I ween ye'll get up this glass mountain yet. Pied Agile now be shod in silver, a metal more precious than shoes o' bronze."

Moments later and full of new hope, Liaze mounted Pied Agile, the elixir in the mare's saddlebags. Off she set, Pied Agile at a trot, and onto the obsidian slopes.

But even as she did so, Gwyd was nailing gold coins to Nightshade's hooves. "Gold be e'en a softer metal than bronze or silver. Mayhap it will cling t'the glass better should the princess need another try."

Up the glass mountain fared Liaze on Nimble Foot, black glass chips scattering in the mare's wake, and soon she passed the mark set by the stallion.

"Oh, Mithras," cried Twk, "I believe she's going to make it."

Still Gwyd hammered hard bronze nails through malleable gold and into Nightshade's hooves.

"She's nearly two thirds of the way there," cried Twk. "And still she— Oh, no! No! Oh, Mithras, no! Gwyd, Gwyd, she's stopped, and Pied Agile is sliding hindward."

Gwyd finished with Nightshade's last hoof. "Well, Twk, the black now be ready for another go. Bronze we tried, and silver— the moon metal—and now we try wi' e'en more precious gold— the metal o' the sun. If this doesna work, I ween we be defeated. Pray t'Mithras that the third time be the charm."

Liaze managed to turn Pied Agile, and back down the glass mountain she rode.

"Nightshade be shod wi' gold, Princess," cried Gwyd when she rode into earshot.

Frustrated once more, "What makes you think it will be any better than silver?" asked Liaze.

"It be a softer metal, and Nightshade be a heavier horse than Pied Agile. I ween wi' his weight and the softness o' the coinage, it'll cling better than both bronze and silver."

"Mithras, let it be so, for there is scant time left ere the full dark of the moon," said Liaze, dismounting and transferring the elixir to Nightshade and swinging up into the saddle.

Once again the princess rode onto the slopes, while Gwyd and Twk watched, their hearts pounding in anxiety, their breaths bated in fear. And they gasped at every perceived slip, whether or not Nightshade had done so.

Up rode the princess, now on precious steps of gold, the metal conforming to the arced ripples of obsidian, the shiny surface like glass.

Up she rode and up, up past the place where Nightshade had faltered before, up past the place where Pied Agile had slipped, and on up.

And Liaze's heart soared as Nightshade's steps of gold fared onward.

Yet just ere the white-blowing stallion reached the truncated top of the glass mountain, there came a steepening of the slant: no more than twenty feet all told.

"Hai!" cried the princess, kicking Nightshade in the flanks and leaning into the saddle, and the stallion leapt forward, and though his hooves were slipping the final few steps, up and onto the flat he clattered.

Liaze's eyes brimmed with the release of tension, and she wiped away the tears and sprang to the hard glass surface.

And by her lantern she could see her Luc lying motionless upon an icy bed 'neath the open-sided pavilion.

Oh, Luc, please, my love, be alive.

Liaze snatched the elixir from the saddlebag, and she stepped to the black slab and knelt beside Luc.

Mithras, he is not breathing.

She placed her ear against his chest and listened for his heartbeat. *Nought!*

Quickly, she stood and uncapped the decanter and opened Luc's lips, and slowly, drop by drop—*Oh, please, please, Mithras, let Lady Verdandi be right when she said a golden draught will surely save*—Liaze dripped the elixir into his mouth.

Drop by drop.

But nought seemed to be occurring.

Drop by drop.

Tears welled in Liaze's eyes. *Oh, Mithras, am I am too late in this dark of the moon? Is he dead? Oh, my love, my love.*

Drop by drop.

But he lay cold and unmoving.

Liaze wiped her free hand across her eyes and looked at the rune-marked crystal. Fully a quarter of the elixir was gone, and still he lay unmoving.

Oh, please, my love, let this not be.

Liaze burst into tears and leaned over and kissed Luc's cold lips—*Please, my love, oh please*—and, distraught, she sank down beside him and lay her head on his chest . . . in that moment he drew in a long, shuddering breath.

"Oh, Luc, Luc," Liaze cried, leaping to her feet. And she spun about, her arms spread wide, her face raised to the heavens, and she called out, "Oh, thank you, Mithras, thank you!"

—But her joyful cry was lost 'neath a shrill scream, and of a sudden, Liaze could not move. And down and down and riding a besom spiraled a woman in black.

It was a witch, and fury filled her face.

37

Iniquí

Gwyd and Twk, at the foot of the mountain, heard a distant shriek, and, by the dim light cast upward by the lantern Liaze had carried above, they saw something or someone spiral down out of the ebon sky.

"Oh, Gwyd, what might it be?" cried Twk.

Gwyd moaned and said, "Ah, laddie, I think it must be the witch what carried Luc away. She's come at the dark o' the moon t'see the result o' her evil handiwork."

"Oh, Gwyd, Gwyd, what can we do?"

"Nought, Twk, nought, f'r the mountain be enchanted, and we canna set foot thereon, else we'd die by fire, and that would be nae good t'anyone, much less the princess. We canna go up the mountain."

"But there must be something we can do," cried Twk.

"What, Twk, what? And e'en if there were, we canna defeat a witch."

"Well I— Oh, Gwyd, I don't know, I don't know." Twk was nearly in tears. "But we can't just stand here and do nothing."

Of a sudden the Pixie's eyes flew wide in revelation. "Gwyd, listen, listen, here's what we can do. . . ."

Down spiraled the witch on her besom, rage consuming her features. "Fool, you fool!" she shrieked, her fury directed at Liaze. "You have ruined everything! Now I will have to start over."

Liaze could not move, but for her eyes, nor could she speak.

Alighting upon the glassy flat, the witch stalked toward Liaze, the fury replaced with cold rage. Stopping before the princess, the witch glanced at Luc, the knight's shallow breath wafting white in the icy air. Once again the features of the witch twisted in rage, and she turned to Liaze and raised a black-nailed hand as if to strike. But then a look of recognition replaced the one of fury, and she laughed in triumph.

"You are Liaze, one of Foul Valeray's get, daughter of he who is most responsible for imprisoning my master." Again the witch laughed. "Oh, my, but this is too sweet, and almost makes up for setting back my plans by two more darks of the moon."

She strutted before Liaze, the hem of her long-sleeved black dress flowing behind. She was tall and imperious, and her black hair matched her eyes, and then she turned to Liaze and said, "You don't know me, do you." It was not a question.

"I am Iniquí, sister of Hradian and Nefasí, and of Rhensibé, whom your vile brother slew. Oh, this revenge will be most enjoyable well beyond your death, for Foul Valeray and his whore Saissa and their get will grieve long when word comes that the elder daughter has been slain by *my* hand. Oh, yes, sweet revenge.

"Ha! They say that revenge is a dish best served cold, and here we are on an icy mountain . . . cold indeed, how fitting."

Iniquí put a hand behind one ear in a pretense of listening. "What's that you ask? Why did I steal your lover and put him here to die? Ha! Little did I know it would come to this.

"Hear me: Vicomte Guillaume, he who would be a full comte, asked me to find the rightful heir—Luc his name—and slay him and recover the trinket about his neck. Yet when I saw Luc in my black mirror and realized what this so-called trinket was, I knew that fool of a vicomte had no idea of its true worth nor what it was for. What's that you ask? What is the trinket? Fool, it is a key forged in the hidden fires of this very spellcast mountain, a key struck by the enemies of my master to open one of their other creations—the Castle of Shadows beyond the Black Wall of the World."

Iniquí laughed and said, "Ah, by the look of horror in your eyes, I see now you understand, for with that key I will free my master."

The name *Orbane* hissed through Liaze's thoughts, and she would have groaned had she the power to speak. Yet she did not.

"Oh, now your gaze turns desperate," said Iniquí, gloating. "You would slay me if you could, but you cannot, for I am a sorceress dire. And, oui, it is Orbane whom I will free."

Iniquí glanced at Luc, his faint breath puffing white in the frigid air. Then she turned to Liaze and snarled, "But you, you fool, you have set me back, and I will have to start all over, for the stone cannot be taken by force; it either must be freely given or released by the natural death of the wearer"—Iniquí laughed—"and what better way to die a natural death than by very slow exposure, and what better place than this?"

Iniquí gestured about. "Indeed, this is the only place where he must die, here on this mountain, else the amulet will not be empowered for one who is not a natural heir or one to whom the amulet is freely given, for, as I said, here it was forged in the hidden fires."

There came to Liaze's ears a barely audible clicking and a fluttering of air. Yet Iniquí did not seem to notice, wrapped up as she was in her triumphant monologue.

"But you, Princess, I can slay out of hand, for you and your family have been thorns in the sides of my master and my sisters and me; and your brother killed my sweet Rhensibé, and so it is only fitting that I, Iniquí, return the favor."

The witch stepped back, and she began chanting, the words arcane and somehow causing the very air to tingle. Yet, underneath the intonations, Liaze could still hear a faint clicking and fluttering.

Of a sudden a great crevasse split open in the mountain between the sorceress and the princess, and fire roared up from the depths below, lighting the ebon sky above a deep crimson, as of a spill of old blood. On the far side of the split, Nightshade snorted and backed away.

Across the crevasse from Liaze, Iniquí laughed, and over the roar she gleefully said, "Incredible, isn't it, that a mountain can be so cold, and yet have unquenchable fires raging within, eh?"

Iniquí reached a clawed hand out toward Liaze and sneered, "I will beckon you into the fire, sister of my sister's killer, and there is nought you can do to stop me."

She made a single gesture . . .

. . . and Liaze jerked a single step forward.

Iniquí laughed in scorn and made another gesture . . .

. . . and Liaze wrenched forward another step.

Iniquí made a third gesture . . .

. . . and Liaze jerked ahead again . . .

. . . and now she stood poised on the very brink of the crevasse, and, as if sensing a victim, searing fires roared up from the depths.

And, as Iniquí flexed her black-nailed fingers for the final beckoning—

—Twk on Jester, the bird madly flapping, leapt up the final few feet of the slope and onto the flat. And at a single word from the Pixie, the rooster crowed.

Even as Iniquí hissed in surprise and twisted a gesture toward the Pixie and the bird, the enthrallment upon Liaze lessened, and a moan escaped her lips, and she realized that she could speak. It was then that the words of Lady Doom echoed in her mind:

> *Remember war; loose the cry,*
> *So ye and y'r love will not die.*

And suddenly the meaning came clear, and though she could not move, still she could shout a command, and she cried out, *"Night, attaques!"*

Iniquí glanced at Luc yet lying unconscious upon the black slab, and she laughed and said, "Fool, your knight is entirely too weak to—"

—in that moment, a golden-shod forehoof of Deadly Night-shade crashed into the back of Iniquí's skull—the stallion rearing and lashing out upon Liaze's command—and, shrieking, Iniquí pitched forward into the raging crevasse. Yet she somehow managed to catch hold of a ledge, but from below the roaring blaze engulfed her, and she screamed and screamed as her dress and hair caught fire. Terror filled her gaze, and she shrilled in agony, and then her body itself burst into flames, and the flesh of her fingers charred and sloughed away. She could no longer hold on, and, howling in dread, into the fiery depths she plunged.

The fires died down, and with a jolt the crevasse slammed shut, Liaze falling backwards upon the cold glass surface. But Iniquí's spell had died with her death, and the princess's enthrallment vanished.

38

Recovery

"I didn't know whether it would work, Princess," cried Twk. "I didn't know whether it would work," the Pixie both weeping and laughing at one and the same time.

Liaze scrambled to her knees and looked at Twk. "Oh, Twk, you and Jester saved us, for I could not speak until the rooster crowed."

And then Liaze's eyes widened, for gold coins had been tied to each of the chicken's clawed toes.

Liaze began laughing wildly even as tears ran down her face.

Twk joined her, the Pixie also weeping in joy and relief.

Jester ruffled his feathers and crowed once again.

To one side Luc groaned. Liaze, suddenly sober, spun 'round and scrambled to Luc's side. His eyes fluttered and Liaze grasped his hand. "Oh, my love, waken. Please waken."

Luc mumbled something in his semiconscious state.

Liaze said to Twk, "He is so cold, so very cold; we've got to get him down from this mountain. A fire, we'll need a fire."

"There is scrub below," said Twk, "but little else."

"It will have to do," said Liaze, and struggling, she managed to get Luc to his feet, the chevalier barely of aid.

Liaze called Nightshade to her, and the black came trotting. Groaning, lifting, heaving, and shouting at Luc to help, and finally calling for Nightshade to kneel, Liaze at last got Luc across the saddle, bellydown.

"Princess," said Twk, "would you mind carrying me and Jester back with you? I think my rooster is completely tuckered out."

Liaze lifted the gold-shod chicken and Twk to Nightshade's back, and then she packed away the decanter and took up the lantern and mounted behind the saddle and held on to Luc, and said, "All right, my boy, take us down," and she turned the stallion toward the way below and gently heeled him in the flanks.

Liaze gave the black his head, and to the edge of the flat and onto the slopes of the glass mountain they fared, Nightshade sliding the first twenty or so feet where the glass was steepest, but thereafter his footing was sound, for on precious steps of gold he went.

And as they went down, Twk said, "It was a wild idea, my riding Jester up, for, even though they say a cock's crow reaves power from witches and such, I thought it only true at dawn, as it was with Lord Fear. I didn't know whether it would work at night. I didn't know what was happening between you and the witch atop this mountain, but I thought if I could help, it might give you a chance to spit her with your long-knife, or to put an arrow through her heart."

"Jester's crow was just barely enough to let me speak," said Liaze.

"I am glad you did, Princess, for that motion the witch made at me and Jester, well, I was beginning to feel numb all over."

"No doubt 'twas sorcery," said Liaze.

"Oh, my," said Twk, "I've never been enspelled before, and I hope to never be again. Thank Mithras, you called Nightshade to attack."

"I wouldn't have been able if not for you and Jester," said Liaze. "Yet how did you know to come?"

"Well, Gwyd and I saw the witch fly down on her besom, and Verdandi said I would be needed at a critical time, and this seemed a critical time to me. And Verdandi's sister Urd said that it was a fine thing I had done to train Jester to crow on command; I think she was telling me then and there that a cock's crow would do the trick."

"It did, Twk, it did. But the gold on Jester's feet, how did—?"

"Oh, Princess, back when Urd spoke her rede, I thought it only applied to you, but then I realized it could include me as well. 'Precious steps will get ye there, / As up black glass ye steeply fare, / Do not dismount as ye try, / Else by fire ye will surely die.' That's what Urd said, and I was standing there when she said it, and I had Jester as my mount. Gwyd tied on the gold coins, and up my rooster and I started on our precious steps. Yet it was too slick, and I almost quit, but then Jester started flapping, and he flapped and flapped and flapped, and between precious steps and flailing wings finally we made it, almost too late it seems."

"I heard you coming," said Liaze, "but I didn't know what I was hearing. Your arrival was a complete surprise to me."

"A surprise to the witch, too," said Twk, laughing. "Who was she?"

"Iniquí," said Liaze. "One of Orbane's four acolytes, though now but two remain."

"Hmm . . ." mused Twk. "It seems those four are banes to you and your brothers and sister."

Liaze nodded. "That's exactly what Zacharie said."

"Zacharie?"

"My steward of the Autumnwood."

"Ah."

Both Liaze and Twk fell silent, and Jester had tucked his head under one wing and was asleep, as on down the mountain they rode.

At last they came to the bottom, and Gwyd had a fire going and hot tea steeping.

The Brownie and the princess managed to get Luc down from the horse, and they placed him on warm blankets next to the fire and covered him with more.

Liaze accepted a cup of tea from the Brownie, and she slumped down next to Luc and said, "Oh, Gwyd, I am so weary my very *teeth* hurt."

"Then sleep, Princess," replied Gwyd. "I'll make certain something warm gets in t'your Luc. You, m'lady, need sleep."

The next morning Liaze was wakened by a gentle kiss, and she opened her amber eyes to look into eyes of indigo. "Oh, Luc," she murmured, and reached up and embraced him and held him tightly and wept.

"Chérie," said Luc, reaching for another biscuit, "when I awakened at the foot of this dark mountain, I knew not how I had gotten here, for the last I remember was being snatched out through the window, there at Autumnwood Manor. Yet Gwyd and Twk have told me some of the story, but neither one knows the full of it, and they said to wait for you to recount all."

Along with Gwyd and Twk, they sat by the fire breaking fast; Luc was on his fourth helping of biscuits and honey and jerky and hot tea.

"It is a long tale, Luc, but first I must tell you this: I met your foster sire Léon, and he told me who your true parents are."

Luc's eyes widened in surprise, but he said nought.

"Luc, you are Comte Luc du Château Bleu dans le Lac de la Rose et Gardien de la Clé."

Luc choked on his sip of tea, and after he had gotten control of his breathing: *"What?"*

"I said, you are Comte Luc du Château Bleu dans le Lac de la

Rose et Gardien de la Clé. Léon was going to tell you just as soon as you had won your spurs," said Liaze.

"My spurs," said Luc. It was a statement and not a question.

"Yes, your knighthood, and I told him that you had more than won them in combat with the Trolls and Goblins in my demesne."

"Ah, I see."

"Your true père was Comte Amaury, and your mère is Comtesse Adèle. Your père was slain in a skirmish when you were but a newborn. A year later, your mère wedded Guillaume, a vicomte with ambitions. He also had a three-year-old son whom Guillaume wanted to be heir to the title of comte after Guillaume had obtained it for himself. Guillaume had a hench-man in his retinue—one Franck—and in the night Franck stole you away and took you to the woods to slay you."

"Oh, my," said Twk, "what a wicked stepfather."

Liaze nodded. "That's exactly what I said to Léon, Twk."

"Go on, Princess," said Gwyd. "What happened next?"

"Fortunately, Armsmaster Léon saw Franck riding away with Luc, and he followed on the would-be assassin's heels into the nearby forest." Liaze turned to Luc. "Just as Franck raised his blade to kill you, Léon spitted him with a dagger, and before Franck died he told Léon of Guillaume's guilt, and that there were more men ready to carry out Guillaume's order to kill the rightful heir.

"Léon knew that you would never be safe with the vicomte at the Blue Château, and so he fled away with you, Luc, far away, where he took on the guise of a woodcutter."

"What of my mère?" asked Luc.

"Léon sent word to her by a former armsmate—a trusted courier—but by that time Adèle on her own had discovered Guillaume's perfidy, but she had no direct proof, and he had put his own men in key positions. Hence, she could do nought to bring him to justice.

"However, she is the one who—via the same trusted courier—provided the funds for your complete education. Oh, Luc, she wanted you to be raised to become a comte, and the teachers Léon hired have well seen to that."

Luc frowned and gestured at Deadly Nightshade, and then at his arms and armor. "Is she the one who—?"

"Oui, Luc," said Liaze. "She sent the horse and accoutrements for you on the day of your majority."

Luc nodded and said, "And I am to become a comte."

"You are already one," said Liaze. "It is your birthright."

Luc nodded and said, "Then it only remains for me to claim it."

"Won't that lead t'fightin?" asked Gwyd, "even t'war?"

"Not necessarily to war," said Luc. "If Guillaume disputes me, I can challenge him to trial by combat."

"What of his son?" asked Twk.

"Him, too," said Luc, shrugging. Luc then turned to Liaze and asked, "Is Guillaume yet alive?"

"Oui," she said, "or at least he was two moons ago, for he is the one who asked Iniquí to locate you."

"Iniquí?"

"Oui. She is the witch who bore you away, and—" Of a sudden, Liaze's eyes widened in revelation. "Oh, now I understand."

"Understand what?" asked Gwyd.

"The meaning of Luc's title," said Liaze. "Luc, not only are you a comte, you are le Gardien de la Clé—the Keeper of the Key."

"Key? What key?"

"You wear it about your neck, Luc. It is the key to the Castle of Shadows beyond the Black Wall of the World. That is what Iniquí was after, for with it she would set free her master Orbane."

Gwyd sucked air in between clenched teeth, and Twk cried out in alarm. "She would loose that monster upon Faery again, lass?" asked Gwyd.

Liaze nodded. "She was one of his acolytes."

"Dead and gone," said Twk, glancing at Jester, the rooster scratching away at the cold soil. "Two are left."

Luc sighed. "You need tell me the whole of this tale. But first I would ask this: where lies this blue château, this lake of the rose?"

"Ah, that," said Liaze. "I know the way there from here, for I rode o'er it with Lord Fear and the Wild Hunt on the way to this black mountain. I marked it well, the way between, and I will take you there. But, heed me, Luc, you are yet weakened by your ordeal, and until you are fully recovered I would not have you face the one who seeks your death." Liaze pointed back in the direction she had ridden to get to the mountain and said, "There is a town across the border yon, and there we will stay until you once more have your strength and are ready to face this usurper."

Luc smiled and said, "As you will, my princess. As you will."

Two evenings later they rode into the town, Liaze on Pied Agile, Luc on Nightshade, and Gwyd and Twk on two of the four geldings, for they had found the one that had been lamed—now fully recovered—placidly grazing on the shores of the lake near where they had left him.

They took two rooms at Le Renard Noir—the Black Fox—the single inn in town: Gwyd and Twk and Jester in one; Liaze and Luc in the other. They took warm baths, and Luc shaved, for he now had two days' growth of beard; while he was enspelled on the black mountain, his whiskers had grown not at all. Afterward, they ate a sumptuous meal, and Gwyd and Twk both imbibed heavily of wine—Gwyd three bottles and Twk several thimblefuls—and they had to be borne to bed.

That night as well, though Luc yet felt the ordeal of his ensorcellment, he and Liaze made sweet and gentle love. " 'Tis a bewitchment of a different kind," said Luc.

*　　*　　*

They stayed at the Black Fox for an entire fortnight, and every day Luc took to the yard behind the inn and drilled with his sword—his movements like those of a dancer, or of a feral cat, graceful and powerful, whether measured or rapid, whether slow or swift.

And many of the townsfolk came to watch, for they had never beheld a true knight ere then, and they *ooh*ed and *ahh*ed to see him at swords and long-knives.

Some tried their hand at staves and quarterstaffs with the chevalier, but always they ended up in the tavern, holding aching hands and arms, ribs and heads, and drinking to his health and his prowess.

And for the full of the fortnight, they ate well, and drank good wine, and rested and recovered, though Gwyd was more likely to need his recovering every morning after an evening of imbibing.

On these eves as well, Liaze played Gwyd's silver harp in the common room, and she sang the songs she had sung to the specters of the men of the Wild Hunt, and townsfolk came to hear those songs as well.

Gwyd, too, played his harp, and his nimble fingers made lively songs all the livelier, and townsfolk called for more, and some even thought to pay him, but he would accept nought, for such came perilously close to an expression of thanks, and he did not wish to leave the comforts of the inn. Instead, acting upon Liaze's advice, the citizens would buy themselves a drink, and just happen to set it near the Brownie and then promptly forget about it, and not know whose drink it was when the Brownie asked.

And every night of the full of the two weeks, Liaze slept in Luc's arms.

But at last Luc said, "Let us be on our way to Château Blu, for I am fully recovered."

They tried to pay their bill, but the innkeeper would take nought, saying, "The extra trade while you were here more than made up for your keep."

And so, on the dawn two days after the full of the moon, they set out for Luc's demesne.

Some twelve days after, they rode to the outskirts of the village of Fleur Rouge, there on the Lake of the Rose, and Liaze led them to the Widow Dorothée's cottage, for Léon had told the princess where it lay. As Liaze dismounted she said, "Let us see if she will take us in until we can execute our plan."

A woman with dark copper-blond hair answered their knock, and her eyes flew wide at the sight of them, especially of the Brownie and a Pixie riding a rooster. Once they had introduced themselves, she smiled as if she held a secret and said her own name was Dorothée, and she welcomed them in, Jester included. Even as they stepped into the front door, and the widow bustled off to make tea, they heard a back door bang shut, and a heavily bearded man strode into the parlor, a load of wood in his arms. And it clattered to the floor in his surprise, and he exclaimed, "Luc!"

It was Léon.

"Armsmaster," cried Liaze, just as surprised as he, "what are you doing here?"

"Waiting for you, Princess. Waiting for you to bring Luc."

Château

The next morning, Liaze rode Pied Agile along the briar-covered, rose-bearing lakeshore and toward the causeway leading over the water to the Blue Château. Gwyd and Twk and Jester, all three on one of the geldings, rode at her side. Liaze had in her possession a letter of credence bearing King Valeray's signature and seal; she had as well a letter penned by Léon and a note penned by Luc.

Arcing about the opposite shore of the lake, rouge cliffs loomed upward a hundred feet or more, their color reflected in the lucid water. And in the middle of the lake blue stone ramparts stood in contrast, the château a walled fortress, the battlements crenellated, with towers at each corner.

"It must have been built during dire times," said Liaze.

"What, m'lady?" asked Gwyd.

Liaze gestured at the château. " 'Tis more of a bastion than a comte's manor, hence it must have been erected in perilous times."

"Or built by someone quite fearful," said Twk.

On they fared, and they came to the causeway and turned onto it. A pair of drawbridge towers stood halfway along the raised road across the lake, the bridge itself down. Two warders, playing at cards at one of the towers, looked up as the horses came onto the stone pave. They set aside their diversion and stood as Liaze neared, and when the horses clopped across the bascule, one warder held up a hand to stop them. Liaze drew Pied Agile to a halt before them, Gwyd halting the gelding as well. The two guards looked on curiously, especially at Gwyd and Twk and Jester.

"What be your business, my lady?" asked one of the guards, presumably the senior of the two.

"I am Princess Liaze of the Autumnwood, and I have come to call upon Comtesse Adèle."

Both warders bowed, and the junior guard asked, "My lady, is this your entire retinue?"

"Indeed it is, for I need none other than my mage to protect me."

Somewhat apprehensively, the guards took a step backwards and glanced at Gwyd and Twk, no doubt wondering which one might be the spellcaster.

"Pass, my lady," said the senior warder, and he and his companion stepped aside.

On beyond the two towers with their great counterweights rode the princess and her attendants: a Brownie, a Pixie, and a chicken.

They came to the main gate, where once again Liaze explained just who she was, and she and Gwyd and Twk and Jester fared into the passage under the walls and through the twisting way, machicolations overhead from which burning oil would flow down upon invaders, should they breach the outer gate.

They rode into a blue-grey flagstone courtyard, and attendants took their horses, the lads' eyes flying wide in amaze at the sight of the Brownie and the Pixie, Twk now astride Jester.

Liaze handed her letter of credence to the majordomo, and his gaze widened to see King Valeray's signature and seal, a signature and seal crafted that very morning by Gwyd, the letter of credence itself written by Liaze.

The steward bowed obsequiously. "Princess."

Liaze canted her head slightly in acknowledgment, and, with a faint imperious tone in her voice, she said, "Would you convey my greetings to the comtesse, and tell her that her distant cousin has come calling." It was not a question.

The steward's eyes widened slightly, almost as if in furtive avarice. "Indeed, my lady," he said, and he snapped his fingers, and a moment later an attendant appeared. The majordomo penned a note and, together with the letter of credence, he gave them to the lad and sent him running to the comtesse's quarters.

The steward then stepped aside and made an "after you" gesture and said, "If you would, my lady, the hunt room is open."

He led the princess and the Brownie, and the Pixie on the rooster, to a chamber off the great foyer. It was an intimate room, with dark red velvet-clad furniture set close for conversation 'round a fireplace. A wide tapestry hung along one wall, showing a running stag and hounds baying, with horses bearing men with bows and spears racing after. It reminded Liaze of the tapestry in the glamoured inn of the Wild Hunt.

The steward tugged a bell cord, and when an attendant appeared, he said, "Tea and biscuits and clotted cream for the comtesse and her guests."

After the attendant had gone, he turned to the princess and bowed and withdrew.

A time passed, and then a lavender-gowned lady came into the chamber, followed by a maid bearing a tray with a tea set and scones and milk and honey and clotted cream thereon. Both of the women momentarily paused just inside the doorway, each startled upon seeing a Pixie riding a rooster, and a tatterdemalion Brownie. But then they came on inward.

As the maid set the service down, the lady said, "That will be all, Charlotte."

"Yes, Comtesse."

As the maid stepped from the room, the lady, puzzlement in her indigo gaze, turned to Liaze.

"Cousin Adèle," said Liaze, stepping forward and embracing the comtesse and kissing her on the cheek. And then she whispered in Adèle's ear, "You have the same eyes as Luc, and he is not far."

Adèle drew in a sharp breath, but then she frowned and slightly shook her head and glanced toward one wall. Then she in turn whispered, "They can hear but not see."

They stepped away from one another, and Adèle asked, "Tea, Cousin?"

"Please," replied Liaze, resuming her seat. "For my attendants, too."

"And a few crumbs for Jester, if you will," said Twk, dismounting.

"What brings you to the Blue Château?" asked Adèle, as she poured and served.

"I thought to catch up on old times," said Liaze, looking at Gwyd and then Twk and frowning and touching a finger to her lips then glancing toward the same wall the comtesse had indicated.

"And how is your père?" asked Adèle.

"He is well," said Liaze. "Queen Saissa, also. They send their greetings."

Of a sudden the door opened, and a tall man with dark hair and dark eyes entered the chamber. Adèle stood and said, "Liaze, this is my husband Guillaume. Guillaume, Princess Liaze."

Liaze held out a hand, and Guillaume took it and bent over and kissed her fingers. "Ah, Adèle, you did not tell me you had so lovely a cousin, a princess, no less, a daughter of King Valeray."

"Oh, didn't I?" asked Adèle innocently.

"Non," said Guillaume, a bit sharply. He turned to Liaze, a predatory smile on his features. "Perhaps, my lady, one day you will introduce me to your sire. I am certain that he and I have much in common."

Not likely.

Liaze smiled and said, "One day I hope to introduce you to him I hold most dear."

Guillaume smiled and nodded and said, "We must speak of this at dinner. But for now, I have pressing matters, and you and Adèle must have much catching up to do. If you will excuse me?"

Liaze nodded in acquiescence, and the vicomte stepped away.

When the door shut behind Guillaume, Liaze handed Adèle the letter from Léon and the note from Luc. And the princess kept up a running patter of inconsequential things, as Adèle read Léon's words and then Luc's. The comtesse pressed the note from Luc to her heart, and, tears in her eyes, looked at Liaze. And she carefully folded the note and letter and slipped them into her gown, and then became engaged in the chitchat for a candlemark or so, she and Liaze making up a history as they went. Gwyd and Twk merely listened, the Pixie drinking tea from a thimble, and Jester continuing to peck at crumbs tossed to him by the comtesse.

Finally Adèle said, "Would you like to see my gardens? The flowers are lovely at this time of the season, especially the roses."

"Oh, please, let's do," said Liaze.

They stood and Twk hopped aboard Jester, and together they went from the chamber and down several halls to come to an outside door, where they stepped into a sunlit garden, flowers abloom. A small flagstone area lay in the middle of the plot, with a fountain centered and a bench at hand for resting. And as they moved toward the bench, "Eyes are watching," said Adèle, "but they cannot hear."

"Come, we will take our rest, and I'll have Twk and Jester put on a show," said Liaze.

"Right," said the Pixie. "Jester has always wanted to fly, we'll give it a go."

Liaze and Adèle took seat on the bench, and Gwyd lifted Jester and Twk to the rim of the fountain.

Twk glanced at Liaze and nodded, and he whispered a word to Jester, and the rooster crowed and then took off flapping madly, Twk yet aboard the now-squawking bird.

And as the chicken fluttered and yawped, Liaze and Adèle looked on and laughed, but their converse was anything but humorous.

Liaze said, "Luc has come to claim his birthright."

"He is near, you say?" asked Adèle.

"Both Luc and Léon. They are with the Widow Dorothée."

"If he's come to claim his demesne, Guillaume will not go willingly," said Adèle.

"Then Luc will challenge him to trial by combat."

"Oh, no," gasped Adèle. "Guillaume is a mighty fighter."

"You have not seen Luc," said Liaze. "He is perhaps the finest champion in all of Faery."

"Oh, Liaze, I would give almost anything to be rid of Guillaume, but not my son."

"You cannot flee?" asked Liaze, pointing as Twk and Jester ran across the garden, the chicken yet squawking, Gwyd hooting behind.

"I am a prisoner in my own house," said the comtesse. "And, and . . ." Her words fell silent.

"And what?" asked Liaze.

"And he forces himself upon me," said Adèle, her eyes brimming.

Even though Liaze gritted her teeth she reached out and took Adèle's hand. After a moment she said, "As Léon asked in his letter, are there yet men in the manor whom you can trust?"

Adèle took a deep breath. "Some."

"Can you put them on the gate and the walls tomorrow morning?"

"Tomorrow morning?"

"Oui, for that's when Luc will come."

"I, I—" Adèle took a deep breath and squared her shoulders. "Oui, I will have them in place as the morning guard."

"Bon!" said Liaze.

That evening Liaze, in a borrowed gown, took dinner with Guillaume and Adèle and Gustave, Guillaume's son, a beefy man, shorter than his sire and heftier. Gustave sat across from Liaze, a barely concealed leer upon his lips. And it was apparent Guillaume intended to make a match of these two: after all, having a princess as a daughter-in-law would certainly boost his career toward the dukedom he so desired.

But Liaze deftly deflected every attempt, and finally Guillaume asked, "Are you betrothed, my lady?"

"Oui, I am," said Liaze. She looked across at Guillaume's son. "You are what, Gustave, two or three summers past your majority?"

Gustave, ire on his face, jerked a nod her way.

"Well, the splendid man I am betrothed to just came into his majority a few moons ago."

Adèle's eyes widened at this revelation, but she said nought.

"And who is he?" asked Guillaume.

"A comte," said Liaze.

"A comte?" said Guillaume. "Who?"

"Oh, Vicount Guillaume, the banns are not yet posted, for I would first have my sire give his approval, and so I will not yet tell my truelove's name."

"Ah, then," said Guillaume, casting a significant glance at Gustave, "you are not yet formally betrothed, for a king must be notified and the banns nailed up before it is official."

"Oui," said Liaze. "Still, my heart belongs to my lover."

"Your lover?" said Gustave.

"Oui, my lover."

The rest of the dinner went poorly, with Gustave slamming down his tableware and storming out, leaving Guillaume enraged by his son's actions, and Adèle and Liaze smiling behind their napkins.

That moonless darktide, in the candlemarks ere mid of night, from the parapets of the Blue Château, a rooster crowed. Odd, this was, or so thought the inhabitants of the manor, for it was not to announce the coming of dawn, nor was it within the daylight marks; instead, the call came in the mid of darkness when only the stars shone down, and that was odd indeed. And the cock's crow echoed from the rouge cliffs and resounded o'er the crystal waters of the Lake of the Rose, and on a distant shore, Léon turned to Luc and said, "All is ready, my comte."

"As am I, Armsmaster," said Luc, his hand on the hilt of his sword. "As am I."

40

Birthright

Liaze did not sleep well that night, for she wanted nothing more than to be held in Luc's arms, or to be holding him in hers. And it did not help that sometime after mid of night footsteps came stumbling down the hallway outside her door, their owner to stop and pause and pound on the panel and demand entrance.

"Let me in, wench!"

Gustave!

Liaze drew her long-knife from its sheath.

"I said let me in!"

The latch rattled, but the door was securely locked, with a chair jammed under the handle as well.

Liaze stood and padded to the door and stood to one side and waited, her blade ready.

Bam! . . . Bam! . . . Bam! Gustave again hammered on the door.

Of a sudden, Liaze heard a loud retching, as of someone—Gustave—vomiting, a faint splashing against the floor.

Yet retching, he stumbled away.

Liaze returned to her bed.

She did not sheathe her knife the rest of that eve.

The next morning, the princess in her leathers and the comtesse in a gown took a constitutional walk on the battlements, the comtesse nodding to each of the men as she passed by, they touching the brims of their helms in return.

And then across the causeway came riding two clean-shaven men, a youth and a veteran, the youth on a black horse, the veteran on a grey. Adèle caught her breath and said, "How like his sire looks my son."

The youth and the veteran paused at the towers, yet what they said neither Liaze nor Adèle could hear. But when they came to the main gate there was no question as to their words, for when they were asked their business, the youth's voice rang out: "I am Comte Luc du Château Bleu dans le Lac de la Rose et Gardien de la Clé, and I have come to claim my heritage."

Into the courtyard they rode, the comte and his armsmaster, and members of the household gathered even as someone ran to alert Guillaume.

When informed of this claimant, Vicomte Guillaume came to the steps of the château and said, "Bah! Anyone can call himself Luc, yet I would have proof."

A rustle went through the assembly.

"I vouch for him," cried Léon, his voice ringing to the battlements.

"Another pretender, I say," shouted Guillaume to those same battlements.

"Non!" called Adèle, now standing on the steps as well, Liaze at her side. "This man I know, as do some of you: he is Armsmaster Léon, ever loyal to Château Bleu."

Again a murmur rustled through the gathering.

"Léon is a murderer," cried Guillaume, "for he slew Franck and fled for his own life."

"Liar, assassin-sender," gritted Léon, "you dispatched Franck to kill the babe who stood in your way. But I slew Franck ere he could carry out your vile plan, Guillaume, and I saved the lad for the day when he would reach his majority and the day he would win his spurs. And this I say: he has reached his majority and has won his spurs, and now he has come to cast you down, usurper, and take his rightful place."

A swell of noise muttered through the crowd, and Luc threw up a hand to quell it. When silence fell, he said, "You want proof?" Luc reached under his collar and drew forth the amulet, the metal gleaming argent in the sun, the gemstone sparkling blue. "Here is the sigil of Château Blu, the amulet of the rightful comte. Here is the token my father bestowed on me the day he rode to war, only to return on his own shield." Guillaume's eyes widened at the sight of the token, but Luc spoke on: "You were there on the battlefield, Vicomte Guillaume, and my arms-master tells me you fought by my père's side, but I think more likely, given the man you are, 'twas you who dealt my sire the fatal blow."

Guillaume's face flashed with guilt and then rage, "Why you little—"

"Vicomte Guillaume, since you dispute my claim, I challenge you to a trial of arms."

Ooo . . . breathed the gathering, for this rash youth had flung his gauntlet down before one of the most feared fighters in the realm.

"Ha!" cried Guillaume. "You are a fool, *boy.*"

In moments, Guillaume's arms and armor were delivered to him, and he spoke to Gustave and a handful of men, his words too quiet for Liaze to hear.

She turned to slip away, only to find Gwyd standing on the landing behind, her bow and quiver and long-knife in hand.

"Shush!" snapped Gwyd. "Thank me not, Princess, f'r I wouldna like t'leave y'r service f'r the nonce, though I will one day, when this be over, go back t'my Laird Duncan."

Quickly, Liaze strung her bow, and she strapped on her long-knife, then she turned her attention to the forecourt once more.

Luc had dismounted.

And, sword drawn, he faced Guillaume, the vicomte's sword in hand as well.

And the crowd had moved back to form a great circle.

Léon stood off to one side, his bow in hand, an arrow in his grasp, though it was not nocked.

Gustave came to stand on the steps, two or three down from Liaze and Adèle.

A quiet fell.

"To first blood?" asked Luc.

"Ha! First blood? Non. We fight to the death, *boy*, for you have called me a murderer."

Léon cried out, "And I called you a liar and a usurper and a sender of assassins."

"Pah! I will deal with you after I have taken care of this fool," said Guillaume—

—And without warning he attacked.

Shang! Blades met, bronze on bronze, and Luc was driven back before the assault, and Adèle cried out in fear.

Ching! . . . Shang! . . . Guillaume pressed the fight, ever driving Luc hindward, the youth blocking and parrying and slipping the vicomte's blade down and away as the circle yielded before them.

On the steps, Gustave laughed in glee, for certainly his own sire would take the measure of this boy who would think to sit on the throne instead of Gustave himself when his father became a marquis or duke or even higher.

And down in the courtyard, Guillaume attacked, battering at Luc's blade, and the vicomte laughed and cried out, "You're losing, *boy!*"

Luc smiled grimly and said, "I think I've learned enough of your manner of swordplay," and in a wink of an eye, Luc riposted, and a gash opened on Guillaume's wrist, there between gauntlet and chain, blood to flow freely.

Rage flashed across Guillaume's face, but now it was Luc who pressed the attack, his blade a blur, for he was quicker than Guillaume, though the vicomte was marginally stronger.

Clang! . . . *Dring!* . . . Luc drove Guillaume back and back, and another gash opened, this one across Guillaume's right cheek, deep and gushing, teeth showing through.

Guillaume's eyes flew wide in fear. He tried to disengage, but could not. He circled about and risked a glance at the ramparts. "Vincent!" he cried.

An arrow flashed through the air, and a man on the walls, nocked bow in hand, tumbled down to the flagstones below, slain by Léon's shaft.

On the steps Gustave reached for his dagger, but of a sudden, from behind, someone grabbed his hair and jerked his head back, and a long-knife was at his throat, and Liaze hissed, "Draw it and you die."

Elsewhere, throughout the courtyard, other men held knives and daggers upon Guillaume's henchmen.

And in the center of the circle, Luc spitted Guillaume, the lad's thrust so hard the blade pierced all the way through chain and gut and spine.

Guillaume looked down in disbelief.

"To the death, you demanded," said Luc, "and to the death it is," and he wrenched his sword free.

And Guillaume fell dead to the stone.

In that moment a rooster crowed, and Twk, upon the ramparts led the gathering in a cheer, joy filling the courtyard for all but Guillaume's own men.

Liaze turned Gustave over to Léon, and then she went flying down the steps and into Luc's arms. Soundly she kissed him, and then she disengaged and turned to the woman standing nigh. "Comte Luc, I present to you your mother Adèle. Adèle, this is your son."

Within the candlemark, Gustave and his retinue—henchmen, staff, armsmen, stripped of all their weapons but daggers—rode away from Château Blu, Luc granting them safe passage for a day but no more. And they took the corpse of Guillaume with them.

That evening, there was a banquet of celebration, and all the staff of the manor were invited—serving by turns so that all could partake. The Widow Dorothée was in attendance as well. There was gaiety and cheer, and good food and wine, and many a speech was given, for all were glad to see Guillaume and his ilk gone and the rightful heir in place.

Finally, Liaze stood and called for quiet, and when the banquet hall became still, she said, "Some believe that the dark of the moon brings ill things, and at times it is true, and at other times it is not. Yet heed: it was the dark of the moon when Luc was stolen and the dark of the moon when he was saved, and on this night once again it is the dark of the moon. And so unto you I say this: think not the dark of the moon only an ill omen, for on this eve—the dark of the moon—your comte is returned to you." She raised her glass in salute to Luc, and said: "To my beloved and your comte: Luc du Château Bleu dans le Lac de la Rose et Gardien de la Clé."

A great cheer went up, and all in the assembly stood and hoisted their glasses. Long did the clamor last, but then Luc stood and held up his hands, and, when quiet fell, he turned to Adèle and said, "Mother, long was the road to Château Bleu, but I would not be here were it not for my comrades: my foster père Armsmaster Léon, my truelove Princess Liaze, my companions Brownie Gwyd and Pixie Twk and a red rooster named Jester. I raise my glass to each of you and cry out for all to hear, 'Hail, hail, hail!' "

As one the crowd shouted, *Hail, hail, hail!*

And when at last silence fell, Jester decided to crow, and laughter burst forth from the assembly and rang the very walls. Gwyd though, deep in his cups, sat with a puzzled frown on his face, the Brownie trying to cipher out whether or not he had been thanked and therefore would have to leave. Finally, he shrugged and called for another goblet of wine.

And joy flowed throughout Château Blu that most splendid of eves.

41

Homeward

The next three weeks were a whirl of activity: Luc led an armed force out from Château Blu to harry Vicomte Gustave and his men from Luc's demesne; upon their return from harassing the vicomte, Luc and Léon spent time recruiting and training armsmen, including sharpening the skills of the veterans, instruction having been woefully lacking during Guillaume's reign.

Liaze and Adèle, on the other hand, spent long hours speaking of offspring and titles and who would live where, for Adèle would have Luc stay at Château Blu, and Liaze would prefer Autumnwood Manor; in the end they compromised, deciding that Luc and she would spend summers at the Lake of the Rose, and the remainder of the year in the Autumnwood; however, as soon as a second child was born to Liaze and Luc, upon reaching majority she or he would take over the reins of governance at the Blue Château. Until then, Adèle, with Léon as her war leader and advisor, would govern while Luc was away. It was also during this time that Léon and Dorothée wedded, and she was a widow no more.

Gwyd and Twk spent their days exploring the château, and they found the secret alcove behind the wall where spies listened to conversations within the hunt room. The very next day Adèle had the alcove bricked up.

Gwyd also often fished in the lake, sometimes from the walls of the château, at other times from a cockleshell. Twk accompanied Gwyd when the Brownie fished from the walls, but he refused to get in the small boat with Gwyd. "If it tips over, then I'm a goner," said the Pixie. "A pike or trout would make short work of me."

Twk and Gwyd also spent time in the château's cellars, sampling, for Château Blu had a splendid selection of wines. "We be tryin t'find the best o' the lot," said Gwyd, "and so far each selection seems better than the last." Gwyd and Twk also spent many mornings regretting this pastime, but the Brownie's many-pocketed belt provided needed relief.

From the top of the battlements, Jester announced the coming of dawn every morning, and in a fenced area at the back of the château he found a small flock of egg-laying hens to keep him occupied. "His flying has improved," said Twk, "what with his getting up and over and out of the chicken yard every day to announce the dawn, and then flying back in to see to his harem."

Thus did three weeks vanish, but at the end of that time Luc and Liaze began preparing for the journey back to the Autumnwood, for King Valeray and Queen Saissa would be coming to Autumnwood Manor on their annual rade, and both the princess and the comte would have Liaze's père and mère bless their union, after which they would post the banns and begin planning their wedding.

And so it was an eightday later Luc, Liaze, Gwyd, Twk, Jester, and a retinue of nine set out from Château Blu for Autumnwood Manor, leaving Adèle in charge of the demesne with Léon at her side.

The dark of the moon fell on that eve.

*   *   *

Starwise they went, on a bearing that some in the mortal world would call north, but in Faery it seems directions aren't always what they appear to be. And so, Luc and Liaze and their retinue set their backs to the sunwise border and headed starwise, for Armsmaster Léon had fled that way with Luc as a babe, and starwise would take them back to his woodcutter's cottage; he gave them a list of detailed instructions as to where to cross the seven twilight bounds so that they would not stray from the line.

In a leisurely fashion they rode starwise, and Liaze said, "This is certainly a much slower pace from that which I rode away from my manor on your trail, love."

"Shall we go swifter?" asked Luc.

"Non!" exclaimed Liaze. "Please, beloved, non. I've had my fill of desperate journeys."

Luc laughed and said, "As you will, chérie."

And so on they fared, and they stopped in villages and inns and took meals and drank wine, and in the inns in the eves Liaze sang while Gwyd accompanied her on his silver harp.

After a moon and some of travel and after passing through six twilight borders—having fared across a realm of rivers wherein manned flatboats bearing cargo drifted in the flow; and having crossed a demesne of shallow lakes, their shorelines whispering with the rustle of reeds; and having ridden through a land of tall grass, where swift-running animals fled before them, white and tan animals much like deer, but blunt-horned, and with the tan limned in black; and having traveled through deep, quiet valleys of a snowcapped mountainous realm, where the wind sighed in loneliness; and having spent days coursing along the sands of a dune-laden seashore, where gulls wheeled and sandpipers ran and terns dived, the birds mewing and pipping and crying, and the blue ocean waves ever rolling—at last they came to the demesne wherein lay Laird Duncan's manor.

Gwyd made enquiries, and then led the retinue to a village, where they found Laird Duncan readying a warband to retake his manse from the Goblins and Trolls. Gwyd told the laird what he and the princess had done, and he returned the decanters to Duncan. Luc pledged his men and himself to help Laird Duncan to recover his home, and the laird accepted gladly. But when the combined warband reached the mansion, they found nought but ruins, for it had burned to the ground.

Liaze gasped and said, "Ah, me, Gwyd, it seems the Goblins and Trolls were not accomplished firefighters."

Twk upon Jester fluttered to the ground, and he and the chicken searched through the cold ruins, while the men spread out and scanned the surround.

Of the former occupants, no sign whatsoever did they find.

Laird Duncan looked at Liaze and Gwyd and he burst out laughing. "Ah, lass and laddie, it seems y'r method o' getting rid o' the Goblins and Trolls worked well, but I wish ye hadna gotten rid o' my house, too." And again he broke forth in gales.

"My lord," said Liaze, "I will send aid to help you rebuild."

"Ah, lass, f'rget it," said Duncan, widely grinning. "I wanted a change in floor plans anyway."

"Well," said Twk, he and Jester black-smudged from their explorations, "can you dig all of the fallen-in burnt timbers from the cellars, you'll have a good foundation as a start."

As if in agreement, Jester took that moment to crow, and Laird Duncan laughed long and loud, the others joining in.

The next morning, with tearful good-byes, Luc and Liaze and their retinue set out starwise once more, Gwyd and Twk and Jester remaining behind to aid the laird in the construction of the manor.

"May ye twain e'er be happy," had said Gwyd, snuffling back tears.

"Invite us to the wedding," had added Twk.

Liaze had embraced her "howling one," her own tears flowing freely, and Luc had saluted the two. And then they had mounted up and had ridden away.

On through the next shadowlight border they went, where they passed by the cursed castle, the stones yet speaking their Gwyd-set warning for folk to stay away. Two days later they reached Léon's woodcutter's cote, and Luc paused in memories awhile. Then on they fared to stop in the village of Ruisseau Miel, where they stayed at the inn.

The people of Honey Creek were glad to see Luc again, for he was well liked, and they were amazed that he was Comte Luc—a noble—for they had only known him as a woodcutter's son. And would you believe it? he was betrothed to a princess, no less.

On rode Liaze and Luc and the men, and they passed through the Forest of Oaks. There Liaze saw Satyrs, but they kept their distance, for armed men fared with this maiden. Too, Liaze stopped to listen to a Faun play his willow-root pipe, and Liaze was bespelled, rapt, her mind completely entranced, though Luc and the men found it a beautiful tune and no more. However, the men of the retinue did appreciate the air, for it brought a gathering of Nymphs to listen, and many a man's loins ran hot with blood.

Beyond the following twilight border they came to the farmstead of Matthieu and Madeleine, and their sons Vincent, Thierry, and Noël, and the daughter Susanne. Susanne was overjoyed to see Luc, but though she sighed and her eyes were lost in what-might-have-been-if-only, she managed to smile at Liaze and not fall into fits of weeping.

They stayed at the croft that eve, and in spite of Matthieu and Madeleine's protests Liaze and Luc and the retinue slept in the byre on sweet-smelling hay, but after a hearty breakfast, they bid au revoir and set out once more.

They forded a wide-running stream and passed by the Nixie pool, but none of the Water Nymphs did they see, though as they rode past a great swirl of water spun, as if something or someone swam below.

Days later they crossed another twilight border, to fare across a bleak land up the slopes of a mountain. At the crest of the col, a stone creature opened his eyes and said, his words ponderous, "Rrr . . . I see you have found the one you sought, Princess."

The men of the retinue gasped in surprise, but Liaze said, "Indeed, Caillou, I did."

"And the witch?" asked Caillou.

"Properly punished," said Liaze. "She is quite dead."

"Um . . . fitting."

Liaze sat silent for long moments, waiting, and at last Caillou said, "I . . . yet ponder your puzzle . . . urm . . . Princess. No answer seems to . . . um . . . present itself."

"I think it has none," said Liaze.

More moments passed. "Good," said Caillou, "for then I can . . . urm . . . long contemplate."

Liaze glanced at Luc and then said to Caillou, "Au revoir, my friend."

Small pebbles cascaded down from the mountainside as Caillou's stony brow wrinkled. "Au revoir? That . . . rrr . . . means I will see you again?"

"Indeed."

The crevice that served as Caillou's mouth broadened, the rock splitting, more pebbles falling. "Then . . . hmm . . . au revoir."

The stone eyes closed, and Liaze and Luc and the retinue rode down the far side, leaving Caillou to dwell upon the enigma posed moons past by Liaze.

Another day went by, but late in the eve they crossed the eleventh twilight border since setting out from Château Blu, to ride into the Autumnwood at last.

Liaze spoke to the Ghillie Dhu, and Sprites winged 'round and asked about the witch and the crows, and they cheered the news of Iniquí's demise. And they flew ahead to alert the staff of

Autumnwood Manor that the princess had returned, and she had her truelove at her side, along with a retinue of men.

And onward through the scarlet and gold and russet woodland rode Liaze and Luc and the escort, wee folk darting alongside, tree runners overhead, unseen things scurrying in the underbrush, all accompanying their liege. And the men of the retinue looked about in wonder at these happy and grinning fey folk, and smiled great smiles in return.

The entire household of the mansion stood on the lawn waiting for Liaze and Luc and their escort to come riding out from the brightly hued forest. There as well stood King Valeray and Queen Saissa, for they had come the previous day on their annual rade. Too, Borel and Michelle and a pack of Wolves waited, for they had returned from Roulan Vale and had stopped at the manor on their way to the Winterwood.

And a great shout of *Hoorah* greeted the princess and the men as they emerged at last from the trees. And, unable to contain themselves, the gathering rushed forward to greet Liaze and Luc and the others, Zoé squealing in delight and leading the charge, with her dress hiked up to run, Rémy and Zacharie more dignified, yet not far behind. And the household surrounded the princess and her truelove, and they called out questions, voices babbling over one another.

Finally, Liaze, yet mounted upon Pied Agile, raised her hands and quiet fell. And she smiled down at her sire and dam and said, "King Valeray, Queen Saissa, I present my betrothed"—Liaze turned and smiled at her beloved—"Comte Luc du Château Bleu dans le Lac de la Rose et Gardien de la Clé."

Among the crowd, Tutrice Martine gasped and fainted dead away.

That evening there was a grand ball, attended by a king and a queen, a prince and a princess, a comte and the daughter of a duke, as well as the staff entire of the Autumnwood, serving by turns as was the custom at such gatherings.

During a lull in the dancing, Valeray said to Luc, "I knew Amaury, your sire, Luc. He was a fine man, and he aided in the imprisonment of Orbane. He was also a splendid warrior, and a fitting man to be the Keeper of the Key. Guard it well, Luc, for if it comes to either Hradian or Nefasí gaining hold of it, then all of Faery will lie in peril."

"You know of the key, Father?" asked Liaze.

"Indeed," said Valeray.

"Hmm . . . would that I had known," said Liaze. "Mayhap I would have been better prepared for what was to come, mayhap even prepared for Iniquí."

"I am so glad she is dead," said Saissa, glancing at Borel and Michelle across the ballroom, talking to the musicians. "It leaves but two of that dreadful sisterhood, two of Orbane's acolytes, sorcerous witches who would do harm to my brood."

"Speaking of the brood, Mother," said Liaze, "where are Celeste and Alain and his Camille?"

"Oh, perhaps wishing they were here," said Saissa, laughing.

Liaze smiled, and at that moment the music struck up again, and she was whirled out onto the dance floor by the handsome and dashing Luc.

A short while later, under a glitter of stars shimmering against a black night sky, on a balcony outside the chamber Liaze reached up and took Luc's face in her hands. "Kiss me, beloved, and I will kiss thee."

And so they embraced and kissed most deeply, their passion flaring as bright as the wheeling skies above, there in the night, the star-spangled night, under the dark of the moon.

Epilogue
Afterthoughts

And thus ends this part of the tale that began eight moons and a fortnight and a sevenday past, when, upon an autumn eve, Princess Liaze of the Autumnwood went for a moonlight swim, and a wounded knight came crashing into her quiet willow grove.

Or perhaps this tale really began some years ere that, when a babe was born to a comtesse, and a twelvemonth after a vicomte decided to do away with the child.

Or perhaps this story began when a dreadful mage was locked in a dark castle from which there seemed to be no escape but by means of a special key.

Or perhaps this story began even farther back when a Keltoi bard spun a tale so enthralling that the gods decided to make it manifest.

Regardless as to when this story began, at heart it is a romance, wherein we find a lonely princess, a noble knight with a wicked stepfather, Goblins and Trolls and a dreadful witch, three Fates, a howling castle, a Brownie, a terrible Wild Hunt, a Pixie with a crowing rooster, and a black glass mountain, and much more, indeed much more, including Sprites and a Ghillie Dhu and Nixies and Satyrs and a Faun and Nymphs and mysterious twilight borders and things unseen and unnamed, some perilous, others not.

That might seem an overabundance of wonder, but that is the way of fairy tales, and the way of Faery as well.

—Oh, and as to the answer to Liaze's last question, the one where she asked the whereabouts of Celeste and Alain and his Camille, the one where Saissa answered that they were probably wishing they were at the ball, well, Alain and Camille were reading poetry to one another in the great library of Summerwood Manor, but as to Celeste—the Princess of the Springwood—oh, my, she was . . . But wait, that is a different tale.

I thought you but a dream

Afterword

You might think I've woven several fairy tales together to form this single story, but to my mind they truly belong in a single tale. Perhaps the original bard who told the tale stepped through a twilight bound, and after he was gone, various parts of the single story were split away to become individual tales. Thank heavens, they are now back together again.

It is true, however that there is a story that has many of the same elements of my Faery tale: *The Glass Mountain*. In that fairy tale a boy helps a trapped, somewhat Gnome-like being, setting him free from his cage; in my Faery tale a princess sets free a trapped Brownie from his cage. In the fairy tale, a princess is trapped atop a glass mountain and a knight rides to the rescue; in my Faery tale it is a knight who is trapped and a princess who comes to save him. In the fairy tale, aided by the Gnome, the grown-up boy, who is now a knight, rides a third of the way up the glass mountain on a copper-shod horse, and then two-thirds of the way up on a silver-shod one, and to the very top on a gold-shod horse to come to where the princess is; in my Faery tale, it is the princess who rides up the mountain on bronze (akin to copper), then silver, and finally gold. Of course, *Once Upon an Autumn Eve* only faintly echoes *The Glass Mountain*, yet there are parallels. But my tale has witches and Fates and Trolls and Goblins and a wicked stepfather and Pixies and Nixies and other such throughout.

I have cast the story with a French flavor, for, in addition to a magical adventure, this tale is a romance at heart, and French is to my mind perhaps the most romantic language of all.

One other note: throughout this tale, I have relied upon the phases of the moon. I used the earth's own moon cycles to do so, and I hope they correspond to those in that magical place. But perhaps I am quite mistaken in my assumptions . . . who knows? For, once you cross the twilight borders and enter Faery, strange and wonderful are the ways therein.

Lastly, I enjoyed "restoring" this fairy tale to its proper length by putting back together the separated parts of the much longer story, as well as adding back those things I think should have been there in the first place, but which may have been omitted bit by bit down through the ages. I hope you enjoyed reading it.

Dennis L. McKiernan
Tucson, Arizona, 2004

About the Author

Born April 4, 1932, I have spent a great deal of my life looking through twilights and dawns seeking—what? Ah yes, I remember—seeking signs of wonder, searching for pixies and fairies and other such, looking in tree hollows and under snow-laden bushes and behind waterfalls and across wooded, moonlit dells. I did not outgrow that curiosity, that search for the edge of Faery, when I outgrew childhood—not when I was in the U.S. Air Force during the Korean War, nor in college, nor in graduate school, nor in the thirty-one years I spent in Research and Development at Bell Telephone Laboratories as an engineer and manager on ballistic-missile defense systems and then telephone systems and in think-tank activities. In fact I am still at it, still searching for glimmers and glimpses of wonder in the twilights and the dawns. I am abetted in this curious behavior by Martha Lee, my helpmate, lover, and, as of this publication, my wife of nearly forty-nine years.